The LAST TRAIN HOME

BLAYNE COOPER

Spinsters Ink
2008

Spinsters Ink
P.O. Box 242
Midway, FL 32343

First published by BookEnds Press
Published by Intaglio Publications - 2005

Printed in the United States of America on acid-free paper
First Spinsters Ink Edition - 2008

Cover designer: L. Callaghan

ISBN 13: 978-1-883523-61-9

Dedicated to my siblings, Bobby and Mandy, who, from cradle to grave, own a very special corner of my heart.

I love you.

—*Blayne Cooper*

To Alison Carpenter, Barbara Davies, Nancy J. Ashmore and Judith Kuwatch, your assistance was invaluable.

Kay Porter, this is a better story because of your efforts.

A big thank you is also extended to Susan for her sound advice.

Bob, your encouragement and love help me in all things.

—*Blayne Cooper*

Chapter One

December 31, 1889

It began to snow, tiny flakes shimmering in the lamplight until they collided with Virginia's worn, woolen scarf, and stuck, creating a thin layer of silvery crystals on the black fabric. The scarf covered her head, and she absently reached up to make certain its ends were tucked securely into her coat. She left her hand there as she walked, holding together the scratchy, woolen lapels of the coat with chilled fingers.

At the corner of Essex and Delancey streets, she stopped at the curb to allow a slow-moving wagon to pass in front her.

"Whoa." The burly driver reined in the single brown nag that was pulling his wagon. The back of the wagon was full of beer barrels. "Needing a ride, miss?" He stripped off his small, round hat and squinted as he looked into the night's sky, irritated when small flakes dotted the lenses of his spectacles. "Winter is finally here on this New Year's Eve," he pronounced, stuffing his hat back atop a mass of unruly dark hair and wiping his glasses.

Virginia smiled and shook her head. Six months ago, she wouldn't have understood a word he'd said. Then, the varied accents of Manhattan's Lower East Side immigrants had caused her to blink stupidly at nearly anyone who spoke to her. On this night, however, she understood the man perfectly and thanked him for his kind offer before continuing her trek to Orchard Street and home, which consisted of a tiny apartment on the sixth floor of a brown brick tenement house.

A laughing couple staggered past her, shouting their wishes for a happy New Year and addressing her by name. She dredged up another smile and waved her goodbyes as she continued to walk, her mind occupied more with getting off her aching feet than imbibing along with the rest of New York.

She had worked late tonight, along with two dozen other men, women, and children, stripping the feathers from stinking chicken carcasses, all for the promise of an extra dollar on top of her usual four-dollars-a-week wage. Despite the holiday, it was an offer Virginia Chisholm could ill afford to refuse.

Passing through a cloud of foul-smelling steam rising from the sewer vent, she opened the door to her building and was instantly greeted by several more partying tenants. She lowered her scarf and shook it out, sending a scattering of icy crystals to the wooden floor and revealing a head of red hair with golden highlights, now in complete disarray.

A pock-faced man poked his head out of his apartment door, and Virginia could hear the jaunty chords of an out-of-tune piano and a burst of laughter from behind him. "Evening, Ginny!" he slurred.

"Happy New Year, Mr. Belawitz," she dutifully answered, secretly hoping that he wouldn't want to chat. But he quickly ducked back inside his apartment, much to Ginny's relief.

A chorus of "Happy New Year, Ginny!" rang out through the narrow hallway as Ginny climbed the steep steps. She laughed, happy to see her usually grumpy neighbors enjoying the season.

It was already past ten, and her family's apartment was quiet and dark except for a single candle that sat on a small table near the stove, illuminating the bone-tired faces of Ginny's mother and sister. She sat down alongside her mother with a weary thump.

Ginny's older sister, Alice, rose to hang up Ginny's wet coat, and her mother reached over to the stove for a pot that still held hot tea.

"I was beginning to get worried, child." She hated it when Ginny walked the ten blocks from her work to home in the dark alone.

Ginny tucked chilled, red fingers under her arms for warmth. "I'm sorry, Mama, I had to work late." Then she smiled, remembering why she'd missed supper. "There's an extra dollar in my pocket this week because of it."

Both Alice and her mother's faces brightened.

"I can get it for you. I—"

"No need." Her mother waved her off, filling a chipped cup with steaming tea and sending the scent of mint wafting between them. "You can give it to me tomorrow when I go to the market. It'll be nice to have some meat for dinner." She looked gratefully at both her daughters and rose to her feet. As she stood, she brushed her lips against the top of her Ginny's cold head. "Happy New Year, babies. I hope it's the best one ever," she said softly. "For both of you."

"Same to you, Mama," the young women answered in concert, as their mother disappeared into one of the apartment's two small bedrooms. They smiled at the sound of their stepfather's deep snores, which faded when their mother closed the bedroom door.

When the apartment was silent once again, Alice scooted her chair next to her sister's and they began to chatter quietly about the day's events. Before long, Ginny's eyelids were drooping and Alice chuckled. Ginny was too tired. They were all too tired.

Her sister's heart-shaped face had begun to take on the lines and planes of adulthood, though in fairness, the skin around her eyes had always crinkled when she smiled, belying her true age. Right now, however, those same eyes were fluttering closed at irregular intervals as Ginny fought uselessly against an overwhelming wave of fatigue.

"C'mon, luscious," Alice teased. "Let me help you into bed." She pushed off from the table; then carefully set Ginny's empty cup in a washbasin.

"Hush," Ginny shot back testily, more than a little sensitive about her curvaceous figure. She was of average height, but only in the past year, since she'd turned seventeen, had her hips widened and her breasts taken on a full roundness not shared by either her mother or older sibling.

"Oh, all right." Alice laughed, guiding her sister toward their darkened room. Once inside they both carefully checked to make certain the blankets were tightly tucked around their young twin brothers, James and Lewis. Next they checked on the baby, Helen, and three-year-old Jane, who slept together in a crib at the foot of the girls' bed. Satisfied that everyone was warm, Alice climbed into bed.

Ginny stripped down to her underclothes and, as quickly as she could, snuggled under the covers of the twin bed she shared with her sister. Her contented sigh at the wonderful feeling of their collective body heat was lost amidst the loud creaking of the bedsprings.

"This is the year, Alice," Ginny whispered fervently after a long moment. She pulled the quilt up to her chin. "Eighteen-eighty-nine was the last year I'm spending in this place. I know Mama needs our help, but—"

"Me too, Ginny." A pause. "Hershel came calling for me earlier tonight." Ginny could hear the smile in her sister's voice.

"About time. You two have been mooning over each other for months. And sparking for almost that long," she added mischievously, knowing that Alice wasn't aware she'd inadvertently caught the pair kissing more than once. She squirmed out of the way of pinching fingers, causing Lewis to stir in the bed only two feet away.

"Quiet, Ginny."

"Sorry." But she wasn't really. She'd been waiting weeks for the perfect opportunity to torture Alice about that.

"Now, about tonight," Alice continued undaunted, "Arthur told him to come back next week after his visit had been properly announced."

Unseen in the darkness, both sisters rolled their eyes at their stepfather's old-fashioned notions.

"But Hershel said he'd be back. He doesn't want to work at the necktie factory forever. He wants to move out West next summer, you know. His uncle is a casket-maker in Tennessee."

"Oh, Al." Ginny's voice was soft and wistful. She'd seen photographs of rolling hills and imagined miles and miles of fresh, green grass. "That's wonderful." She squeezed her sister's hand, trying to ignore the pang in her chest that the news brought. She would miss her fiercely, but refused to begrudge Alice an opportunity for a better life. After all, she intended on having one herself. *There has to be more than this place. Endless work. The stink. The crime. There just has to.*

"He has a brother, Ginny. If you can get past those mutton chops and that long mustache, he's not such a bad looking fellow."

Ginny snorted. "No thanks." She absently glanced out the window, her eyes following the constant stream of glittering snow. "I'll get out of here without having to resort to him, thank you very much."

And Alice believed her willful younger sister. If anyone could do it, it was Ginny.

"Sweet dreams, Al."

"Happy New Year, Ginny."

Then only the muffled sounds of snoring filled the tiny apartment on Orchard Street.

"So long, String Bean." With a single shove between her narrow shoulder blades, Lindsay Killian went flying out of the slow-moving boxcar and into the night. She hit the ground cursing as she slid down an embankment made up of rocks and chunks of coal covered by a thin layer of snow. She winced as she felt her trousers and then the skin of her knees and hands tear. It was eerily silent out, except for the fading chugging of the freight train.

"Bastard," she spat, seeing her hat fly out of the boxcar, which was already several hundred feet down the track in front of her. She swore she could still hear his self-satisfied laughter. It was, in Lindsay's mind, the ultimate humiliation.

"Rolled by someone I know." She snorted derisively. "What next? My own father coming back from the grave to slap me in the face?"

With a shake of the head, she pushed wearily to her knees and wobbled there for several seconds before falling bonelessly backward. She sighed, sending a puff of hot breath into the cold air, and gazed up into the sky, its blackness overtaken by the muted glow of lights and smoke from the nearby city. Snowflakes rained down on her, and she wished briefly that she could see the stars instead of the endless sea of dingy gray-gold above. Like New York City, the stars made her feel small and insignificant—dwarfed. But unlike this place, they also made Lindsay feel free, as if the universe were stretched out invitingly before her and anything was possible.

With another dramatic sigh, she rolled over onto her side and paused to remove a small rock that had embedded itself in her hand. She winced and rose to her feet, brushing off her shabby coat. Despite her sudden fit of melancholy and her outright embarrassment over being robbed of her flint, pocketknife, and life savings, which consisted of a total of eighty-seven cents, she decided she could do better than freezing to death in the ditch. The city might be a cesspool, but there were plenty of pockets to pick, charity shelters that offered hot, if watery, soup, and places where she could go and warm her hands by a fire.

Her eyes narrowed. After she found some food, she would head down to Rat Face's favorite railway station and reclaim her stolen property, along with her pride. Lindsay's booted feet made a crunching noise as she walked.

"String Bean, my dear," she muttered to herself, as she bent to retrieve her battered hat, "how about a different resolution this New Year? Instead of getting rich, why not settle on keeping better company?" She tucked her shoulder-length hair deep into her coat and out of sight. *Yeah.* She nodded a little, satisfied with her decision. *Better company, it is.*

She climbed back up the embankment. "But that better company's gonna have to come after I find Rat Face and kick his arse!"

Feeling much better, she tucked her hands into her sleeves and whistled a happy tune as she began a solitary walk down the wooden tracks toward New York City.

"Ginny. Wake up. Please."

The words tugged at the edge of her consciousness, but they weren't enough to completely rouse her.

"Ginny."

She felt a small hand shaking her shoulder. "What is it, Lewis?" she mumbled, keeping her eyes firmly closed. *I just laid down. Tell me it's not time to wake up yet.*

"C'mon, Ginny!"

This time her brother's high-pitched voice was filled with panic, and her eyes fluttered open to find their room filled with… she blinked… *smoke?*

"Oh, my God." Alice sat up and pushed her hair from her face. "Oh, God. Oh, God. Something's burning," she said needlessly. "There's a fire."

Ginny threw off their covers and scrambled out of bed, not noticing that the floor beneath her bare feet was unusually warm. "I'll get Mama." She looked at Alice for confirmation, pushing down a wave of fear and dread.

"Go! I'll get the kids dressed." Alice was already hastily wiggling on Lewis's shoes.

Ginny nodded quickly and covered her mouth with her hand. Now that she was on her feet, the acrid smell and taste made the back of her throat burn and her head was well into the hazy layer of smoke that covered the top half of the room. "I'll be right back to help, Alice." She spared a glance into the crib, then stopped dead in her tracks. "Helen?" Her eyes darted around wildly. "Helen?" Ginny's normally rich voice cracked on the last word as she looked at Jane who was alone in the crib.

The toddler began to whimper as she awoke.

The sound of wagons, nervous horses, and raised, panicky voices floated up from the street.

Alice grabbed Lewis's coat from the closet and began to wake James, who was still oblivious in his peaceful sleep. "Mama took Helen out of the crib about an hour ago. She never brought her back." She didn't have to look up to know that Ginny hadn't moved. "Hurry, Ginny. Go!"

Ginny snapped out of her shock and jerked open their bedroom door. For the first time in her life she ran into her parents' room without knocking.

"Mama! Arthur, wake up. There's a fire."

"What? Oh, no." Her mother shot out of bed, her eyes wide with disbelief, all traces of sleep gone in an instant. She had Helen in her arms and awkwardly shifted her nightgown so that her breast would no longer be exposed.

The baby let out a loud unhappy shriek as her comforting suckling was abruptly ended.

Ginny looked away embarrassed.

Arthur Robson, Ginny's stepfather, lay stock-still except for the even rise and fall of his chest. Ginny shook his shoulder vigorously, but he only slapped her hand away and mumbled something unintelligible.

She turned questioning eyes on her mother, who was rummaging through her dresser for something more suitable than a nightgown and trying to calm Helen's cries. "What's wrong with him, Mama?"

"He drank too much celebrating the New Year is all. He'll be fine. I… I can wake him. Go help your sister with the other children." She fanned her hand in front of her in a useless attempt to clear away the smoke. "You need to get out now, Ginny, all of you." She stifled a cough. "Put on your shoes and coat." The older woman wrapped a blanket around Helen and sat her back on the bed as she dressed. "We'll meet you in front of the building."

Ginny's mother suddenly stopped talking and cocked her head toward the window. Short, quick steps took her across the small room and she grunted with effort as she threw open the window. A blast of cold air and the sound of distant screams filled the room. Despite the January air, sweat began to bead on Mrs. Robson's upper lip. Peering out, she could see flames shooting from the window of the apartment directly below theirs and a gathering of men, women, children, and a fire brigade on the street below. "Sweet Jesus." Wild brown eyes snapped sideways pinning Ginny, but she spoke with remarkable calmness. "Go and don't stop, Ginny. Get your brothers and sisters and run."

Ginny hesitated for only a second, but seeing that Arthur was beginning to wake up on his own, she reluctantly made her way back to her room. The entire apartment was filled with smoke now, and the short distance between the two doors somehow seemed longer in the pungent haze. "Ouch." She stubbed her toe on the edge of a small table.

Lewis and James were standing nervously at the door in their nightshirts, coats, hats, and shoes. Both eight-year-old boys wrapped themselves around Ginny as soon as she entered the room.

"Awww, it's gonna be okay, boys." But the smoke was making it hard to see and harder to breathe. "You'll see." She cupped both their chins and gently lifted them. "Are you ready?"

Two red heads nodded quickly.

Ginny gave them her best reassuring smile, and the boys visibly calmed.

"Good."

Alice was busy wrapping a blanket around Jane with one hand while she buttoned her coat with the other. She glanced up at Ginny, and their eyes locked.

Ginny swallowed hard, and her heart began to pound, realizing for the first time that this was more than a merely dangerous situation. It was deadly.

Alice opened her mouth to speak but could only cough. "Where…" she finally choked out, shaking her head as if to clear her throat. "Where are they?" Smoke filled the entire room now, and the boys began to gasp and cough as well.

Ginny spoke without taking a breath so she could get the words out all at once. "They're not ready, Al. Arthur drank too much. Mama's trying to get him up." She squeezed her watery, stinging eyes shut as the room began to blur.

Alice nodded and handed Jane to Ginny, who instantly wrapped the squirming toddler in a comforting embrace. Another second and Alice was on her knees fitting Ginny's feet into her shoes. "Get them out"—a cough—"of here." She began to cough again, and this time she couldn't stop for several long seconds.

When Ginny's shoes were securely in place, Alice grasped her sister's biceps and pulled Ginny and Jane tightly against her in a hug so tight it was painful. She pressed her lips directly to Ginny's ear. "Mama can't get Arthur and the baby alone. I'll help." She extended her arms and held her sister's gaze once again. "Never leave them, Ginny. They need you. Promise?"

"Pr… promise." Ginny drew in an uneven breath, and her eyes filled with tears of a different kind.

"Shh…" Alice quickly but gently wiped her cheeks, knowing her own were just as wet. "I'll meet you outside, luscious. Go," she whispered a split second before bolting toward her parents' room, drawing her fingers lightly across the top of her brothers' heads on her way out.

Ginny didn't bother sniffing or wiping her eyes. She let the tears come, allowing them to momentarily clear her vision and burn a path down her already flushed cheeks. Then she reached down and took one of James's small hands, instructing him to hold onto Lewis's. "Let's go."

Several blind paces later they were at the apartment's front door, where Ginny awkwardly shrugged into her coat. She repositioned Jane against her shoulder and reached for the knob, only to yank her hand back and scream when her skin stuck to the searing metal. She stumbled backward, only just maintaining her hold on her sister.

Lewis began to cry in earnest, and James abandoned his normal approach of telling his brother he was acting like a sissy when he wanted him to be brave. Instead he remained mute, glancing around the room with round frightened eyes.

Ginny's mind raced. If the metal was that hot, surely the fire was in the hallway. The window? No. They were on the sixth floor. She drew in a ragged breath. They had no choice. "Hold on, Jane." She screwed her blue eyes tightly shut and kicked the door.

Once. Twice.

On the third kick, much to Ginny's surprise, the rickety door flew open and a wave of hot air slammed against them all, forcing them to take a step backward and gasp in shock. Momentarily, the smoke seemed to clear and Ginny could see that flames had engulfed the apartments farthest from the stairs. The fire was working its way toward the other end of the hall, its deadly tendrils already licking at her apartment door. She glanced over her shoulder, desperately hoping to see the rest of her family, but the view was once again obscured by smoke.

"Run!" Gripping Lewis's sweaty hand, she ignored the pain in her own, as they burst through the flames that shot across their doorway. They began a dead run down the narrow hallway. Ginny tried to call out to her neighbors, on the chance that they were still sleeping unaware in their beds, but most of her yells were swallowed up by the coughing she could no longer hold at bay and the roar of the fire, which seemed to grow with every passing second.

Screams and the sound of breaking wood and glass echoed up from the floors below her and several of the apartments around her, the sounds nearly enough to drive all rational thought from her mind. The flames painted eerie, hateful shadows on the walls around them as they stepped over several pieces of smoldering paneling that had peeled away because of the blazing heat.

Just as they were about to reach the stairs, Mr. Gelfand, the tenant from the apartment directly behind them, burst out of his front door and ran past them in his bare feet. Smoke was coming from the tails of his nightshirt, but he didn't seem to notice them as he barreled over James on his way down the steps.

At the top step, Ginny looked back at their apartment door, which was nothing more than a blossoming ball of red-and-gold flames. *I can't leave them!* her mind screamed, even though she knew she had to get her brothers and Jane out of the building. She screwed her eyes tightly shut and added to the chaos by screaming, "Damn!" It was the first time in her life she'd sworn, and James looked up at her in shock from his position on the floor.

"Get—" A coughing fit interrupted her. "Get up, James!" Ginny cried, frustrated that she didn't have a free hand to yank him up with. "Go! Run!" She gestured down the stairs with her chin, deciding at the last second to let go of Lewis's hand and go back for the rest of her family. She had to. She couldn't leave them. The boys could run like the wind. They'd be fine. Unconsciously, she tightened her grip on Jane, who had stopped crying and was now burrowed against Ginny's shoulder, her head tucked under the blanket she was wrapped in. Responding to his sister's urgent command, James flew down the steps, his arms pumping wildly, his little legs a blur as he ran.

Terrified, Lewis refused to budge and clung to his sister's skirt. Ginny looked down at him and tried to pull away. "Lewis—"

"No, Ginny! You promised!"

Ginny froze, and the silence between them stretched out for what seemed like an eternity, though it was no more than a handful of seconds. Her heart in her throat, she nodded, and they began making their way down the stairs, hurrying to catch up to James. The steps creaked under her weight, and she watched in amazement as several stairs near the bottom buckled from heat or pressure, she didn't know which. But she could feel the heat radiating from them, seeping through the soles of her worn shoes.

Behind her there was more crashing and screaming, but she ruthlessly ignored it, telling herself that it couldn't be her family.

The fifth floor was a raging inferno.

Jagged flames shot up the walls and streaked across the ceiling, the blazing heat making every breath painful, the stench of burning wood, paper, and hair making her nose wrinkle. Ginny reached up with her burned hand to adjust Jane's blanket, and when she let go, dark splotches of crimson in the broken shape of a hand stained the cloth.

"Take off…" Ginny swallowed painfully. "Take off your hats, and press… press them against—like this." She snatched off Lewis's hat and pressed it to his face, forcing him to breathe through it. James immediately mimicked his brother's actions and began breathing through his own hat.

Behind her, the wallpaper on both sides of the staircase had caught fire, making the route to the sixth floor a tunnel of flames.

Ginny looked back again and squinted. There was… something… someone at the top of the stairs. She could only just make out the outline of a woman with something in her arms. The woman took one step then retreated. *Oh, God, is she on fire?* "Alice? Ma... Mama!" she screamed desperately. But there was no answer to her cries, and the figure moved away from the steps at the precise second a loud boom shook the entire building.

Ginny and Lewis fell, but were quickly on their feet again.

"Ginny?" Lewis's face was frozen in terror.

God forgive me, I can't help you. I'm so sorry, Mama and Arthur. Oh, Alice.

"Ginny?" This time Lewis and James were both tugging on her coat.

Ginny wasn't sure she could take another step without throwing up, but she moved anyway, turning to the top of the fifth-floor staircase. They traveled faster now, moving blindly through the smoke, kicking debris from their path. There was no turning back now, and there was no one behind them on the way down the steps.

The wall to the left of them was on fire, and Ginny turned away from the flames as she moved, feeling a painful stinging on the back of her neck. Then, with a sudden "poof," Lewis's coat caught fire, and he began to scream, breaking into a run down the steps.

"No! Lewis!"

James took off after his brother, tackling him a few steps up from the third-floor landing. They landed in a tangled heap of arms and legs, and Ginny took several steps at a time through the thick smoke until she caught sight of Lewis's feet. She grabbed James by the collar and pushed Jane into his arms. "Take her!" The toddler was far too heavy for him, and the girl's dangling legs reached well past his knees. He nearly crumpled under her weight, but fought valiantly to stay upright, bracing his back against the stair railing until he thought his spine would snap.

Ginny dropped to her knees and roughly yanked Lewis's burning coat from his body as he screamed, trying to roll away from her. She felt the skin of both hands searing, and she bared her teeth as she fought with her panicked brother.

"Stay still. Stop it! I have to—Ugh!" The old coat ripped at the seams, and the scratchy material stuck to her palm and fingers like glue. In a frenzy, she ripped it from her damaged skin.

Her hands felt like they were on fire, and she had to look at them for a second to assure herself that they weren't. The skin was angry and blistered raw, but Lewis was all right. The fire hadn't burned through to his skin.

"Ginny, I can't—"

The young woman stumbled to her feet and took Jane from James, just before the slender boy buckled.

"We're almost down, boys." Perspiration streaked her face and neck, and she could feel it trickling down her spine and between her breasts. "C'mon."

James helped Lewis to his feet, tears carving narrow trails down both boys' soot-covered faces as they moved in front of their sister.

The smoke on the second floor wasn't as thick as on the other floors, and Ginny drew in a deep breath, still gagging when her lungs rejected the foul air. Whereas the rest of the building appeared deserted, this floor was a study in chaos. Members of the fire brigade were breaking in doors as they searched for tenants. It was a cacophony of babies crying and screams of panic and pain and anguish. People in all states of dress, yelling in various languages, were running through the hall as their lives and futures went up in flames.

"Help!" Ginny coughed weakly. "We need help here." Her voice had dropped to a whisper, but a man standing nearby began moving toward her. He was wearing a uniform. “People are upstairs. They’re still upstairs!”

“All right.” He tried to calm her. “We’re getting there, miss. You and your children need to get outside.” He pointed down the final set of stairs, then had to move out of the way as several men rushed past him.

Ginny blinked. He wasn’t moving up the stairs. “But my sister and mother and step—”

“You can’t wait here, miss!” he barked back impatiently. “Go.”

“But—”

“Look—” he paused and consciously softened his tone as he stared into Ginny’s glistening, pale eyes, illuminated by the flames from the stairwell and accentuated by her ash-darkened face. “My men are going there now. They’ll do the best they can, but now you’re in their way.”

Ginny sniffed and nodded, and with one arm she herded her brothers down the final set of stairs and outside into the night. Their shoes hissed loudly when they stepped onto the snow-covered street, and tiny wisps of steam escaped from the smoldering soles.

Snowflakes were still falling, and it hurt to breathe. She couldn’t think straight, and her throat felt thick and her chest heavy, as if someone were standing on it. Men were rushing past her, too fast to stop or question, and she stepped around a wagon, leading the boys across the street.

They stepped up the curb and onto the sidewalk, where all turned around to see where they’d just come from, what they’d just survived. With her heart in her throat, Ginny’s gaze drifted upward.

And her mouth dropped open at the sight.

Everything above the fourth floor was burning. Flames shot from the windows, and great plumes of black smoke spiraled up into the night, disappearing into the hazy sky. In a small, rational corner of her mind, she realized that the fire had probably started on the fifth floor and spread from there. Her eyes fixed on her bedroom window, then her parents’ bedroom window. She saw nothing but flames shooting from them, lashing against the building’s dirty brown surface.

The pressure on Ginny’s chest increased, and a wave of nausea swept over her, threatening to send her to her knees. She bent at the waist and swallowed convulsively, the action causing the blanket to slip from Jane’s head.

Jane poked her head out from the rumpled cloth. Her fair, sweaty hair was plastered to her head, and rings of black soot circled her dripping nostrils. She was facing away from the building, and her arm snuck up between her and Ginny as she held out a delicate, open hand.

"Snow!" she cried, in a voice so delighted Ginny burst into tears.

"Yes, baby, it's snow." She straightened, her back and neck already growing stiff. So fast she wasn't prepared for it, her teeth began to chatter. "Are… are you cold?"

"Not cold," Jane answered confidently, trying her level best to catch a snowflake.

Ginny hugged the girl tightly. Her hands were numb, and she fumbled with the blanket, ignoring the blood stains before turning her attention to her brothers, who were standing a few feet away, their eyes glued to the burning building. Refusing to look up again, she took a step toward her brothers and spoke as calmly as she could. "Are you boys hurt?"

Lewis had his arms wrapped around himself in mute comfort. The snow was beginning to accumulate on his hat. He shook his head at his sister's question, and James didn't bother to answer at all. But neither boy tore his eyes from the flames to focus on Ginny.

Lewis began to shake. "Mama and Da—"

"No," Ginny interrupted him. "We just have to wait. Another fire brigade is here now. See?" She pointed a shaking finger toward the steam-powered engines with their local brigade's emblem emblazoned proudly on the side. The large machines were pulled by a team of three enormous, snorting horses.

"They're dead," James mumbled, his voice dull and flat. "It's all burning. Every bit of it."

Despite herself, Ginny looked up again. The horrific scene twisted her stomach, and she couldn't find it in herself to disagree with her brother.

"But we can still hope, right, Ginny?" Lewis's lower lip quivered as he spoke, and Ginny wrapped her arms around his small shoulders as she hugged him and Jane.

Not wanting to be left out, James joined in, slipping his arms as far around Ginny and Jane as they would go.

More people shouldered past, and curious onlookers began to jam the street. Another wagon stopped right in front of them to join in the effort to keep the fire from spreading to the neighboring buildings.

Volunteers jumped out onto the street, their hands full of axes and empty buckets.

Ginny pressed her cheek against the top of Jane's head and gazed up into the dusky sky. Snowflakes collected on red lashes. "Yeah." Her throat worked for several seconds before she whispered, "We can still hope."

Chapter Two

Lindsay moved quietly in the pre-dawn hours, inching her way in and out of the shadows as she tucked her collar up to ward off the icy breeze. Her legs ached from hours of walking, but finally, she had been able to hitch a ride on a boxcar heading in the right direction. She winced a little at the tightness in her calves. This Street-Arab-turned-young-woman was used to riding, not walking. And while she could run a fifty-yard dash with the best of them, when it came to endurance she found herself seriously lacking. And she didn't like it.

Lindsay made a note to do something about that. *Reminder to self: Avoid long, dreary walks in the snow at all costs.* She paused mentally. *Exception to reminder: Ignore the first reminder when you've got to find the peckerwood that stole your stuff.*

The sound of muffled cheers and cursing drew her attention from her woes. She continued a few feet farther, then planted her palms firmly on the cement deck of the railway platform and jumped up, still managing to remain completely silent.

The station was deserted at this time of night, but several hundred feet beyond the end of the platform, underneath a bridge over another set of tracks, she could see a few men gathered in a circle. She peered through the darkness at them, unconsciously holding her breath. To the left of the men was a large steel drum, and occasionally one of them would step away from the circle and warm his hands over the fire burning brightly inside it.

Lindsay moved closer and closer, alert eyes no more than slits, as she tried to determine the men's identities. A short, stout man lumbered over to the drum. *Ahh... there you are, Rat Face. Did you really think I wouldn't come and find you?*

Her mind suddenly put names to the two unidentified figures, and she raised an eyebrow as she considered Rat Face's companions. Not good. These men were cousins, or so they claimed, and were among a small minority of vile rail riders who preyed on their own kind. They were rough and ruthless—Lindsay swallowed—and very large. But they wouldn't matter at all if she could get Rat Face alone. Which was exactly what she intended to do. After that—well, she could take care of herself.

And this time she wouldn't be sucker-punched, or pushed, as the case had been. It never even entered Lindsay's mind to cut her losses and stay away from trouble. If it got around the tracks that she'd been robbed easily, any sense of safety or measure of respect she'd earned over the years would evaporate as easily as the morning fog. In her mind, she simply had no choice.

It wasn't until she was about thirty feet away, her presence hidden, that she ventured a guess at what the men were hooting and hollering about. They were standing around several crates and staring down at the ground. *Shooting craps?* But another two paces and she could tell the stacks of wooden crates had been placed in a rough circle. Her face twisted in disgust when she heard the low panting, then growling, of a dog.

They were ratting. And where there were rats there was sure to be "Rat Face." God, but she hated rats.

"Two bits says the mutt kills ten in under thirty seconds," Albert barked out.

"Forget it," Jean, the tallest of the three men shot back. "Do I look stupid, you loser Wop?"

"Yes. And by the way… go to hell, *Frenchie*." Rat Face, otherwise known as Albert Mineo, though only to his grandmother, and only before he'd turned seven and the old woman gave up the fight and called him Rat Face like everyone else, turned to the third man. "What about you, shit for brains? That's ten rats." Jacque grabbed his crotch and gave it a jiggle, indicating his displeasure at Albert's offered bet.

Albert sneered, showing off stained teeth as he stared at the man's groin.

"You wish, pee wee."

The barrel-chested man lifted his chin. "Like hell I do."

Bored with their banter, Albert sighed and turned his mind back to the game. More action was what he wanted. And he had a pocket full of someone else's change. Life, he decided, was very good. "All right then…" he paused as he considered the dog's sorry state.

The beast was part French bulldog, part hellhound. While only half the size of his English cousins, his thirty-pound body was rock solid and his teeth razor sharp. His nose was swollen and bleeding, as were his pointy ears and dirty paws, though how much was his blood and how much was rat blood, Albert couldn't be sure. His thick throat was rubbed raw from the rusty chain that prevented his escape from the circle of crates, and he was covered in a fine layer of snow. A rat that had latched onto the dog's haunches with its razor teeth swung lifelessly from the mutt's body, refusing, even in death, to let go. The dog shifted sideways as Albert stared. His glistening black eyes were wild and reflected the light of the fire as he stared at Albert with the icy gaze of madness.

Albert shivered, then with fingertips that poked out of the holes in his gloves, he scratched his short beard speculatively. "Ten seconds, ten rats."

"Done!" both men shouted, throwing their change onto the ground just outside the circle of crates. Their coins made tiny indentations in the snow.

"But I count!" Albert clarified.

The next sound Lindsay heard was the growling and snarling of the dog, followed rapidly by the hooting and cheering of the men. She picked up a broken bottle from the ground and carefully got a firm grip on the neck, its icy surface stinging the nicks in her palm. "Time to go, boys," she whispered. "Now all I need is a little luck." With that, she drew a deep breath and concentrated on lowering the pitch of her voice. At the last second, she threw in a thick Irish brogue for a touch of authenticity. "This is the police! Stay where ye' are!"

The three men's heads snapped sideways toward her, but she was pressed up against the fence and safely out of view. Before they could react, Lindsay launched the bottle into the darkness, over their heads and the bridge, sending it crashing against the side of a building.

"Cops!" Jean pushed Jacque with fumbling hands. "Run!" The cousins spun around in circles, bumping into each other for a few seconds as they decided which way to run. They chose to head back toward the station, and the young woman's eyes widened as they approached her with surprising speed.

She pressed herself as tightly against the fence as she could, her face smashing into the cold metal as she held her breath and prayed.

The men sped past her, so close she could feel the cold whoosh of air against her back as they flew by. They climbed onto the platform and ran through the station, their shoes clomping loudly in the quiet night.

Albert, who had stayed behind to scoop the coins out of the snow, cursed roundly as a nickel slipped between his pudgy fingers. "Cops.

Cops. Shit." Finally giving up on the nickel, he began lumbering toward Lindsay. But just as the woman was ready to jump him from the shadows, he changed his mind and turned back toward the crates and the steel drum.

"Oh, crap." Lindsay bolted from her hiding place and caught up to Albert when he was even with the barrel. She dove forward and clipped his heels with her hands, sending him crashing to the ground and sliding through the snow.

"Don't," she panted, "even think about getting away from me."

Albert rolled onto his back, automatically kicking out with a booted foot and connecting with the top of Lindsay's head. "What the—?"

"Ugh." Lindsay felt the blow all the way down her back but managed to twist sideways and avoid Albert's other foot. For a second she was dazed, seeing tiny stars instead of Albert as she tried to force her eyes to refocus.

Albert's jaw sagged. "String Bean? Is that you, you stupid bitch?"

"Shut up!" Lindsay shouted, launching herself at the man once more. "I want my," she drew back her fist and punched Albert squarely in the jaw, wincing when she heard a sickening crunch in her own hand, "stuff."

Albert squealed in pain as his skin split and blood began dripping down his neck. "I'm gonna," they began to wrestle, "kill you, bitch."

They rolled over several times, until Lindsay ended up beneath Albert and they crashed into the crates that were stacked two high and formed the edge of the rat pit. Lindsay's elbow went right through one of the crates, and the cracking sound sent the remaining caged rats and the dog into a squealing and barking frenzy.

"Gimme my money and my knife and flint!" She brought her knee up into Albert's groin. Hard.

He tumbled off her, gasping. His hands flew to his crotch, and his wild flailing toppled one of the crates onto Lindsay, scattering mutilated rat carcasses all over her. "Ahh! Jesus!" She knocked the crate from her chest and frantically began yanking the smelly, bloody bodies off her face and chest.

"Bitch," the man howled, spittle dotting the corners of his thick lips. Lindsay's stomach roiled, but she managed to get to her feet, a little dizzy from all that spinning and the blow to her head. "Yeah, well, I never said I wasn't a bitch." She kicked the prone man in the guts as he tried to get up. He went sprawling. "My money and my knife, Rat Face. Right now, God dammit, you fat bunghole! Before I feed you to that dog! Though I'm sure your greasy blubber will taste worse than those sewer rats."

"Okay, okay," he grumbled. "Hang on. Stupid"—a cough—"Rotten"— another cough. "It wasn't even a dollar and the knife's dull besides." He wiped his dirty, bleeding cheek with the back of his hand, then pushed to his knees. He sighed and shoved aside the tail of his tattered coat so he could dig into his trouser pocket.

Lindsay took a step closer and glared down at him warily. She was breathing heavily, and the sound of the barking dog was frightening her, though she didn't want him to know it. She glanced sideways at the dog and swallowed hard.

"Hurry up, idiot."

"Here, String Bean." Albert offered her a closed fist; his other hand threw a large clump of snow at her face.

"Uh." The snow felt like grains of sand stinging her eyes and cheeks, and Lindsay stumbled backward.

Albert made the most of her temporary blindness and pounced. He toppled her with a blow to her ribs, then kneeled on her heaving chest, his weight pressing her hard into the cold ground. "Well… well." He leaned forward and pinned both her arms with his meaty hands.

Lindsay looked up at Albert with frightened brown eyes.

"Not so talkative now, are ya bitch?" Lindsay lifted her head and spat in his face.

Albert growled and backhanded her viciously, then did it again for good measure. "Uppity for a street gypsy, ain't ya? Didn't anybody ever teach you not to mess with somebody bigger than you? That's the law of the jungle, String Bean. I'm a lion, and you're a… well, you're a… a smaller lion."

She coughed as blood filled her mouth and slid down her windpipe. "I… I must have missed that lesson when I wasn't in school."

He cracked a tiny smile and roughly pulled her to her feet by the front of her coat. Albert could tell she was barely capable of standing on her own, and he quickly rifled her pockets. Finding them empty, he decided he had better things to do, like trying to sell the dog he'd swiped from another ratter. Brutal beauties like him didn't come cheap, and he could buy two lesser dogs to use quickly and discard. "Now get the hell out of here, String Bean, before…"

"What do we have here?"

The disembodied voice came from behind Albert, and Lindsay closed her eyes when its owner registered. *Oh, shit. This is bad. Bad. So bad.*

Jacque, then his cousin Jean, came into view.

Albert cruelly shoved Lindsay up against one of the bridge's wooden support posts hard enough to send a shower of powdery snow down on them. Her head cracked against the frozen surface, and once again she saw stars.

Rat Face's voice sounded very far away as he kept her from crumbling to the ground with his firm grip. "Don't you recognize String Bean?" he grumbled as he decided what to do next. He'd been content with smacking her around and letting her go… it wasn't like she had any more money to steal. But he didn't want to look soft in front of Jacque and Jean. They were fairly new to the tracks, and Albert was sure they would be important people to know. Besides, he had a reputation to uphold. "What are you guys doing back here?"

Jacque brushed a thin layer of snow off his sleeves and tapped the brim of his hat to dislodge even more. "We didn't see no cops, and we figured this was just some scheme of yours so that you could steal our bets."

"No," Albert protested indignantly. "I would never do a thing like that." Though he was already wishing he'd thought of it.

Jean looked down at Lindsay. Then he grabbed the hat off her head and exchanged it with his own, carelessly tossing his old hat into the steel drum's dancing flames.

"Aww… my hat," Lindsay protested weakly. *Shit. I loved that hat.*

"Hey!" Jacque, who had been staring at Lindsay's face, suddenly grabbed the front of her much abused coat and wrenched her away from Albert.

"Fine," Albert groused. "You hang onto String Bean then. See if I care." She began to struggle as she was dragged closer to the steel drum.

"He's a girl." Jacque's surprise showed in his voice. "A woman," he clarified as he looked a little harder. He smiled.

"So?" Albert shot back a little confused. "Everybody knows String Bean's a girl, don't they? She's a bitch," he added for clarity's sake. His jaw was starting to hurt even more, and he wondered briefly if she'd cracked the bone.

Jacque's smile twisted into a leer, and Lindsay could feel her heart beating out of her chest. She'd seen that look a dozen times before, even had to jump off moving trains if it was coming from somebody especially dangerous. This man, she felt deep in her bones, was *very* dangerous.

"Don't know any woman who'd hang around on the tracks 'cept for a few whores me and Jean know from Queens. They sometimes get real hard up and have to go lookin' for customers. You a whore?" His eyes glittered with the promise of danger, and he darkly intoned, "Not like I'd have to pay."

"Do I look like a whore?" Lindsay asked through gritted teeth as her mind scrambled for a way out.

"No," Jacque allowed, shaking his head slowly. "Not like no whore I ever met. On the other—"

"She's not a whore," Albert interrupted, impatiently. There was a perfectly good dog and at least a half a crate of rats waiting for them, and they were wasting their time on String Bean? "She's an annoying bitch rail-rider just like the rest of us."

"I ain't no bitch!" Jean smacked Albert upside the head.

"Ow!" Grimacing, Albert rubbed the back of his head. "That's not what I meant, and you know it." He spun around and glared at Jean. "Are all whoring Frenchies as stupid as you?"

Jean's hands curled into fists. "Why you—"

"Stop it!" Jacque roared. "I don't want to watch you two losers fight." He jerked his chin toward Lindsay. "I wanna know what we're going to do with her."

Unaccountably, Lindsay smiled at Jacque. "Know what I'd like to do?" she purred.

The seductive quality of Lindsay's voice snared Jacque's attention and he leaned in closer to her, pressing his body against hers and gulping when Lindsay licked her lips with excruciating slowness. He gulped again, his eyes riveted on those pink lips. "What, baby?"

"This." With all the force she could muster, Lindsay slammed her forehead into the bridge of Jacque's prominent nose.

Albert winced. Head butts were the worst.

Jacque screamed and covered his face with his hands as hot blood pooled in his palms and light wisps of steam rose from the thick liquid and vanished into the night sky.

Lindsay made a break for it, but in three strides she felt herself hitting the ground. Her chin struck snow-covered rocks hard, leaving a dark trail on them when she moved her head. Jean was on her back, pummeling her with large fists. His third strike was to her left kidney, and she shrieked in pain, her body jerking away from the violent blow.

Then Jacque took over for his cousin and pulled her to her feet.

"Rat Face is right. You are a bitch," he hissed.

Albert shrugged. "Toldja."

Jacque dragged a stumbling Lindsay back toward the rat pit and kicked several of the crates out of his way. The dog began to bark again, pulling on the chain and baring bloodstained teeth in anticipation of another fight. "String Bean, that's your name, right?"

Lindsay didn't acknowledge the question. She couldn't even hear it over the ringing in her ears. Jacque shook her to gather her attention, and a searing pain shot through her side, making it hard to breathe, much less think.

"Hey." Albert's heavy brow furrowed as his gaze traveled first to the dog, then to Lindsay. "What are you gonna do?"

Jacque looked at Albert as though he were an imbecile, which of course he was.

"He's gonna feed her to the dog, moron," Jean advised Albert coldly. He tucked his chilled hands under his armpits.

Albert looked around nervously. "What about the cops?"

"There are no cops!" Jacque yelled, punching Lindsay in the stomach. Next, he punched her in the nose, smiling at the satisfying crunch of cartilage and the stream of hot blood that went pouring down her chin and splattering onto the ground. Steam rose from it.

Lindsay felt like her entire head had exploded in pain, and she doubled over, feeling sick and dizzy all at once. For an instant, she wished she'd hurry up and pass out, but her heart was still pounding furiously, sending a surge of adrenaline singing through her blood. She swung an ineffective fist at Jacque, who merely laughed and slapped it away.

Jean moved over to help Jacque hold her upright as he continued to rain blows down on her. "Do you see any cops?" Jacque asked Albert condescendingly.

Albert glanced around again. "Guess not." A look of uncertainty chased across his face. "But still…"

Jacque didn't wait for Albert's next words. He lifted Lindsay off her feet and tossed her, back first, into the rat pit.

She landed on a pile of rat bodies, and the force of her fall squashed them beneath her. The air was forced out of her lungs, but before she could manage to draw in another breath, Jacque casually reached over and picked up the rat crate. He tore the lid off, and without so much as blinking, dumped the dozen or so remaining rodents directly onto Lindsay's screaming, writhing body. He turned to Albert and Jean and in an eerily calm voice said, "One woman, one minute, one dollar?"

With deadly intent, the snarling dog surged forward toward the rats and Lindsay's pale, exposed throat. She could smell his foul breath the instant before he was upon her, and his filthy teeth began tearing into her flesh, sending white-hot bolts of agony through her already damaged frame. "Noooo!" she howled, clawing wildly at the insane dog's face and eyes.

Albert looked on in horror as Jean cried, "Done!" and threw his bet onto the snow at his cousin's feet.

Lindsay's ear-splitting screams could be heard for blocks as the New Year's sun started to rise over Queens.

It was nearly time for the first morning train to arrive at the station, and the locomotive's whistle wailed as it sped toward its destination. Because of the holiday, only a few passengers waited impatiently for their morning commute. They stood shifting from one foot to the other, hands stuffed in pockets, scarves tucked neatly around their throats to ward off the chill, as they read their newspapers and glanced worriedly at their pocket watches. Their bosses never seemed to understand that sometimes the train was just late.

A thick layer of snow-laden clouds hid the newly risen sun, and so, despite the hour, the city was still cast in an ethereal silvery glow and its shadows still held the secrets of the night. Out of one of those shadows emerged a slowly traveling figure that stopped and covertly watched as Albert unhooked a bloodstained dog and turned him loose. Albert was scared witless by what had just happened and couldn't bear remaining for even another second with the beast he was sure would now haunt his dreams.

The dog snapped at Albert's hand, and then tiredly limped away. In a matter of seconds, the mutt found a hole in the fence that lined the tracks and disappeared into an alleyway.

Jacque and Jean kicked at the rough circle of crates, scattering the evidence of their game before heading toward the railway station and the two plates of steaming eggs and hot coffee they intended to purchase with their winnings.

Albert had been elected to do "something" with Lindsay, and he had grabbed her limp body by the arms and dragged it well out of view of anyone who might happen by. Carelessly, he kicked snow over her and laid a few sheets of old, torn newsprint across her face.

He let Jean and Jacque get well ahead of him before he pulled his cap farther down onto his head and scratched at his chin. He knew a soup kitchen about three blocks from here where the line for lunch didn't really queue up until around nine a.m. Maybe he could find someplace to curl up and go to sleep for a few hours. After that he could snatch a purse or two, and then track down Jean and Jacque. They seemed like the sort who would always be up for some sort of betting game.

Albert kicked several rat carcasses out of his way as he stepped onto the tracks and followed Jean and Jacque's footprints in the snow.

As soon as the coast was clear, a figure bolted from the shadows and frantically began brushing the newspapers and clumps of snow from Lindsay's face and body.

The young woman was a ghostly white, splashed liberally with red. She looked dead.

Shaky fingers checked for a pulse and found a faint but steady beat.

There was a thankful sigh as the fingertips stilled for a split second then moved from Lindsay's neck to her battered face, where they tenderly traced her cheekbones.

"Still alive. But gotta hurry"—a shifting of weight—"God, you're heavy. I don't think—I can—yeah. Okay. Maybe—Yeah, okay." Lindsay was settled over a strong shoulder, and she let out something between a wheeze and gasp of pain as her world turned upside down. One eye opened and stared out at the fuzzy world before rolling back. She gratefully sank into the safe haven of oblivion.

"It'll be all right." A hand grasped one of Lindsay's dangling ones and squeezed gently. "Whoa!" A misstep nearly had them both tumbling to the ground.

Lindsay cried out softly, though she remained unconscious.

"I'm sorry. I'll be"—a step over a pile of broken bottles—"more careful." Lines formed on Lindsay's normally smooth forehead. She began to whimper every time she was jostled, which turned out to be nearly every step, and a steady stream of blood dripped from her face, soaking through the black coat beneath her cheek.

"Sorry. I couldn't help it. Shortcut… up ahead. Damn. This is… hard." Breathing that had started out slow and deep was now labored. "I have to take… the tracks though. If you just hang on." Their pace increased. "Just hang on."

A cold wind whistled through the station just as the chugging train came to a halt. Not a single passenger debarked, and the few men and women who were waiting to board settled into their seats in a matter of seconds. A skinny Negro footman exited the lead car and ran along the length the train, slamming shut each door with a practiced hand. The train's shrill whistle sounded three times in quick succession before there was a loud hiss and a black, noxious cloud exploded upwards from the smoke stack.

Lindsay couldn't hear the sound of panting or the rapid footsteps that pounded along the tracks beneath her.

"Not… far…"—the words were interrupted by several ragged breaths— "now."

The rails on either side of them began to vibrate, and worried eyes glanced backward toward the station, then widened. "Shit."

The train lurched forward and began to gain speed quickly. Soon, the massive machine was eating up twenty feet of ground for every one of theirs. The whistle blared again, warning anyone foolish enough to be on the tracks, especially in the wan light of early morning, to move or be run down.

Faster and faster he ran. The sound of leather boots furiously striking wooden tracks with greater force than before and the loud panting of Lindsay's rescuer was nearly enough to drown out the deafening monster on their heels. But they couldn't move off the tracks. This particular stretch of rail was lined not only by a rickety fence but also by buildings set so close to the tracks that even a worn out, rat-killing dog had to squirm to fit between them and the fence to enter the alleyway. They *had* to keep going.

"Please. Pleeease. Almoooost!"

Heat poured off the gasping body in waves, and sweat flew from a flushed face.

The train's shadow loomed over them, and the roar grew louder and louder as the tracks shook.

"Ahh! Almost there!" Then the tracks—"God!" —widened—…"Yesssss."—and forked.

The train whizzed past them on its way to the next station.

A ferry worked sluggishly across the East River from Manhattan to Blackwell's Island. A mile and three-quarters in length and just under two hundred-square acres, the narrow strip of land was located directly in the middle of the East River, which separated Queens and Manhattan. A layer of clean snow covered the flat terrain in a blanket of pristine white, and the ice-laden tree branches swayed in the frigid wind, causing intermittent cracking sounds as wood struck wood. But for many of the island's inhabitants, the simple beauty of a frosty January day was lost.

Blackwell's was home to the solid stone, four-story, seven-hundred-fifty-cell New York State Penitentiary that held both male and female prisoners, its gloomy walls looking out over the murky waters of the East River. To the north of the prison stood two foreboding, side-by-side stone buildings that housed over fourteen hundred hapless souls who had been sent to the Work House as punishment for their misdeeds, typically public drunkenness. A brick Lunatic Asylum established in eighteen thirty-nine, together with a School of Nursing established in eighteen seventy-five, resided on Blackwell's Island, serving as models of modern architecture and civic-mindedness.

Virginia Chisholm, however, was on her way to the island's Charity Hospital, a proud granite structure surrounded by several majestic oak trees and well-maintained shrubbery. Inmates and patients from the island's other facilities cared for the grounds. The waters of the East River were choppy and dark, and as the ferry holding the limp body of Virginia Chisholm moved closer to its destination, Ginny began to dream.

It seemed as though she and her siblings had been sitting out in the snow on Orchard Street for days, though it had only been several hours. Her hands were numb, but her lungs, stomach, and throat felt as though she were continually being force-fed searing-hot coals. Every breath required more effort than the last as the band around her chest continued to tighten.

Jane lay sleeping on Ginny's shoulder, her fair hair mixing with Ginny's darker locks with every gust of wind. The excitement of the night had finally proved too much for the three-year-old to withstand, though it had still taken three renditions of her favorite lullaby to coax her into a fitful sleep.

Lewis's eyes were riveted to every fireman who entered or exited the smoking building. A harried fireman had thrown them a spare jacket for the coatless boy, and the charcoal-colored woolen covering dwarfed him, making him look like one of New York's thousands of street urchins.

His brother James stared straight ahead with unseeing eyes, knowing he should be sad. Instead, he just felt tired and empty and craved a bed where he could pull a blanket over his head and shut out the world completely.

"Look, Ginny," Lewis said glumly as he pointed to the doorway of the tenement building. Two pairs of firemen carried two full litters draped with dull gray cloths and placed them at the end of a line that had grown steadily longer through the early and mid-morning hours.

Ginny's stomach churned, and she coughed weakly. "No more, please," she mumbled, not realizing that her brothers could hear her, that they were hanging on her every word, every gesture. She'd already fought her way across the crowded street three times to identify the bodies that lay under the cloths next to the hospital wagon.

Ginny had seen Sophie, the bright-eyed girl whose mother worked in a quilting factory as Alice did. The Frederick family who'd only arrived from Hamburg two months before. All six of them lay cold and lifeless, growing stiff as the snow accumulated atop them. Vincent and Joan from the fifth floor, who had sung Happy Birthday to James and Lewis just last month when they'd passed the boys in the hallway, were gone too. Vincent had been so badly burned that Ginny had calmly replaced the cloth that had covered him and turned her head to throw up. If she lived to be a hundred, the young redhead was sure she'd never forget the smell.

But every time she lifted a cloth and didn't find her mother, or one of her sisters, or stepfather, she thanked God. And she felt bad about that too, knowing that the people she was seeing were kin to someone. Someone just like her, only they didn't know the horrible news. Not yet.

"Lew—" Ginny swallowed painfully; her voice was nearly gone. Something was terribly wrong, but she couldn't worry about that now. "Lewis, can… can you hold Jane?"

The little boy nodded and unbuttoned his coat. He opened his arms to his chubby baby sister, and she snuggled happily into his warm embrace, falling back asleep before she even realized she'd woken up.

"I'll go, Ginny," James offered manfully as he began to push to his feet. His expression was grim, but resolved, and wholly unbefitting a boy of his age.

"No, honey." Ginny moved in front of him to stop him.

"But, Ginny—"

"No."

"But—"

"I said no!" she snapped, instantly regretting it when a look of hurt flashed across her brother's face. "Oh, James, I'm sorry," she whispered, her voice cracking. She gave the boy a watery but heartfelt smile of apology. "I didn't mean to do that, James."

James trained his eyes on his legs and picked at a loose thread on the seam of the bulky coat. He and Lewis were the men of the family now. And they should be strong. Men didn't cry like sniveling babies, no matter what. A single tear snaked down his flushed cheek, and he angrily wiped it away with dirty fingers. "S'okay."

"No." Ginny shook her head. She wanted to tell him that it wasn't okay, that she shouldn't have been so harsh, and that she loved him… and so much more than that. But she felt as though a heavy weight was pressing against her breastbone, and it just wouldn't stop and let her catch her breath. She would, she decided, see to her own injuries later. After she'd crossed the street and found the rest of her family one way or the other. I need to get the kids someplace warm and dry. And they'll need to eat and use an outhouse. *She shivered as goosebumps erupted on her arms, missing her coat for the first time.*

"Ginny." Lewis's voice was suddenly panicky, and Ginny followed his wide-eyed gaze. Men in dark pants and white coats were loading the stretchers that had just come from inside the building onto a wagon.

"I'll be back," Ginny called scratchily over her shoulder, making her way through the throngs of emergency workers and neighborhood residents. She was panting now and felt a little faint.

Her mind raced. What now? Where do we go if I find them? No. I can't think like that. Not while there's still a chance. *But no matter how Ginny tried, she couldn't make herself believe it. Not a living occupant of 88 Orchard Street had emerged from the building after she and her siblings had escaped. Not one.* God. *She closed her eyes at the feeling of her heart tearing in two.* How do you give up on your family? How will I tell the boys… and Jane?

Halfway to her destination, she had the sudden urge to stop. So she did, turning back to see what she knew deep in her soul were her only remaining living relatives. They were sitting patiently on the curb, waiting for her return. She lifted her hand to wave, and both boys waved back, causing a tiny, affectionate smile to twitch at her lips despite the situation. "I love you. Be good," she mouthed silently.

Lewis mouthed back, "I will," and James just rolled his eyes, pulling his cap down over his face.

When Ginny turned back to the fire, she felt dizzy and she grasped onto the side of one of the fire wagons to keep her balance, but for some reason her fingers wouldn't work and she slid to the ground. The sounds of the people rushing around her, the spraying of fire hoses, and the crackling of burning wood all seemed to fade as tiny dots danced before her eyes. She caught a glimpse of the wagon carrying the stretchers starting to move a split second before her world went black.

The ferry butted gently against the dock, and several bulky men from the New York Penitentiary, clad in striped prison attire, plain brown caps, and shabby coats, loaded the injured and ill from the boat onto wagons. A nurse quickly picked through the coughing, crying, or unconscious bodies, separating the critical patients from the rest and loading them onto a blue wagon that would be allowed to leave for the hospital first.

Ginny's stretcher was placed alongside an elderly vagrant who'd been stabbed in a robbery the night before and who'd waited in the receiving area of Manhattan's finest hospital as the hospital administrators argued over where he should receive treatment. Ginny had been much more fortunate and was routed directly to the docks where the Charity Hospital Ferry was just about to cast off.

With a quick snap of the driver's reins, the blue wagon began to move, and Ginny gazed up into the winter sky. She was confused, and she blinked several times trying to gather her scattered thoughts. *Am I dead?* she wondered dazedly. *Where are the boys and Alice? Why can't I breathe?*

She rolled her eyes sideways in time to see a nurse, who was riding in the wagon along with her patients, scowl as she checked an old man's pulse. Ginny closed her eyes again, welcoming the darkness. She didn't want to see the blanket that was covering him pulled over his head. *No more,* she told herself. *No more death today.*

On the other side of Blackwell's Island, a second ferry carrying patients bound for the Charity Hospital docked with a muted thud, sending a small wave of dark, dirty water sloshing over the wooden landing. This transport was nearly empty and its few injured passengers were unloaded quickly. A single stretcher holding Lindsay Killian was placed in a blue wagon and rushed toward the hospital emergency room.

On this day, the fates of two young women were about to collide, and each would be changed forever.

Chapter Three

It was full dark before Lindsay was moved from the surgery to a bed at the east end of the women's third floor. Two prisoners lifted her from the stretcher she was on and gently placed her on a bed. It was clad only in dingy white sheets and topped by a thin pillow inside a pale pink pillowcase.

Her head sank onto the pillow, and the sheet was draped over her. Lindsay let out a little moan and licked her dry lips as the orderlies disappeared. She cracked open one eye, and the room spun a little as she tried to gain her bearings. She had awakened to a world of hurt that reeked of bleach mixed with the metallic scent of blood. *Where am I?*

Most of the ward's lights had been turned off, casting the unfamiliar institutional setting in haunting shadows. Gone were the bridge and the railroad tracks, which were the last places Lindsay could clearly remember being, though she had a vague recollection of being carried down the tracks, of the cavernous but warm interior of a church, and a frantic wagon ride.

She blinked with exaggerated slowness, realizing that she was seeing out of only one eye. Her entire body ached and felt impossibly heavy, and the room appeared to be draped in a dense haze.

Lindsay tried to open her other eye. When she couldn't open it at all, a surge of panic tore through her. What if she'd lost it in the fight? Her heart began to pound. *What if the dog…? God.* The room swam as she tried to sit up. "Damn," she cried out brokenly, as a bolt of searing pain halted her movement instantly. Her abdomen felt as though someone was twisting a knife in it, and her head throbbed. Where the dog had torn into her shoulder, she could feel the tight, burning sensation of new stitches holding together tender skin.

"Now then." A nurse, whose accent clearly indicated she was from Queens, startled Lindsay. But despite the woman's somewhat grating tone, Lindsay was relieved to hear a voice, any voice, being directed at her. *That means I'm not dead, doesn't it?*

"You shouldn't move," the nurse chastised mildly. The woman was middle-aged and plump, her dress protected by a white apron that stretched to the floor. A crisp white hat sat atop her head of dull brown hair.

Cool air tickled Lindsay's legs as her sheet was pulled back. She fought the urge to cover herself. "Clothes?"

"Those rags are long gone. But your soiled coat and shoes are under your bed." The nurse made a face. "I'll see if we can't clean up the coat tomorrow so they won't be forced to give you a new one."

"They?" Lindsay's voice was weak. She thought she remembered several nuns hovering over her. *Or was that years ago?* "The church?"

"Hardly," the nurse snorted. "I mean the State of New York." She tapped a syringe in her hand, removing the air bubbles. "No one's told you anything, have they?"

Lindsay's silence was her answer.

"You're in the hospital on Blackwell's Island."

"Jail?" Lindsay squealed, again trying to sit up.

"No." The nurse gently coaxed her back down with a practiced hand. "The hospital isn't part of the prison… or the lunatic asylum," she assured before Lindsay could ask. Then her voice took on a slightly impatient edge. "Now hold still."

Lindsay felt a prick on her thigh as a needle pierced her skin, then a stronger, burning sensation as a liberal dose of medicine, whose primary ingredient was morphine, was administered.

"What's your name?" The nurse lifted the chart from its holder at the end of Lindsay's bed and noted the time and dosage of the medication. "This says 'unknown.'" She quirked a grin. "You'd be surprised how many women in the State of New York decided to name their babies that. I swear sometimes it seems as though we're overrun with them. But somehow I doubt that's your real name."

A deep crease appeared on Lindsay's forehead as she thought. *I know this… I think…* "I…I…"

The young woman's fear must have shown on her face, because the nurse laid a comforting hand on her leg.

Lindsay tried not to jerk away from the unexpected contact, but her reaction was instinctive. She didn't like people touching her. That was dangerous.

"It's all right," the nurse said calmly. She lifted her hand from Lindsay's calf, then continued to thumb through the chart. "Ahh. That explains it. You have a concussion among other things. I'm sure that tomorrow things will seem much clearer." She replaced the chart and tucked her pencil behind her ear.

"Okay. But—"

"You need to rest now. You've only recently come out of surgery." The older woman tugged Lindsay's sheet up to her chin and tucked its sides tightly into the thin metal bed frame. Then she pulled a threadbare blanket from the cart she'd left parked in the aisle and laid it over her patient. "Hush now, or you'll wake up the others. Someone will be back around to check on you later. My shift is finally over." The "thank God" was left implied.

Surgery? Damn. I don't have the faintest idea of how I got here. I can't think about that now. They cut me open? Lindsay licked her lips to speak and caught a glimpse of a moving shadow. "Wait," she rasped. *So thirsty.* "My eye?"

But the nurse was already gone.

She whimpered a little, wondering how long it would be until the drugs would take effect. Unwilling to follow orders without question, Lindsay refused to try to sleep. Instead, she took in her surroundings as well as she could, trying her best to ignore the pain.

To one side of her bed was a plain white wall. *At least that's all I see… I hope that's all that's really there.* She was, she finally discerned, at the very end of a long, dark ward filled with single beds. She couldn't muster the strength to turn completely over, but she could shift just enough to see that in the bed next to hers, so close that she could reach out and touch her if she wanted to, was a fitfully sleeping woman. Lindsay took a moment to study her neighbor to determine whether her coat and shoes would be safe under the bed or if she'd have to sleep with them.

Moonlight spilled over the stranger's drawn face, highlighting her slightly upturned nose and small, delicate mouth, and making her appear a ghoulish gray. Her breathing was harsh and thick, and Lindsay wondered what tragedy had befallen her, causing her to end up here, so isolated from the outside world. *She's younger than me, I think, but with the same piss-poor luck or she wouldn't be here at all.*

The passing interest faded as the drug began to seep into Lindsay's bloodstream. Her chest and neck began to itch, and she lifted a shaky hand to try to scratch them. Her brow furrowed when she fuzzily realized that her hand was wrapped in a thick bandage and her fingers splinted. *How did that happen?* Then she moved her hand upward to her face, still worried about her eye, which she could feel was swollen completely shut. She poked the tender flesh gently until she was more or less convinced that her eyeball itself was still there. Higher still, and she could feel that her head was wrapped in gauze.

The constant thudding in her temples and the sharper pain below her breast were beginning to fade, and her eyelid began to grow heavy. But she continued, her fingertips tracing her nose, which was splinted and bandaged. Now *that* she wasn't surprised about. In a blinding flash, she could see Jacque's heavy fist coming straight at her and hear the sickening crunch of cartilage all over again. An unexpected wave of nausea swept over her, and she swallowed hard against it. She grimaced, causing her to feel the sting of two deep scratches that ran from just below her eye to her chin.

A soft groan drew Lindsay's attention sideways to the next bed. The woman had turned from her back onto her side and was now facing Lindsay. String Bean frowned at the sound of the redhead's shallow gurgles. The breaths were wet and weak, something that Lindsay could easily place now that her mind wasn't so preoccupied by her own misery. She'd heard it many times before, especially in the winter. *Pneumonia. But then why are her hands bandaged?* She blearily noted the covered appendages that were now sticking out from under the sheet.

Finding it hard to concentrate as the sense of dislocation grew within her body, Lindsay felt sleep's irresistible tug. She was about to give in to it when she caught a glimpse of moonlight shimmering off the eyes of the woman who had been sleeping. She blinked in surprise but held the stranger's pale, frightened gaze for several seconds before the woman's eyes helplessly fluttered shut once more.

Lindsay had a sinking suspicion that when she woke up, the bed next to her would be empty. *Maybe I should call for a nurse. But wasn't a nurse just here?*

Everyone can't be saved, String Bean; the grim thought came unbidden, and she resolutely turned her mind elsewhere. Which wasn't hard, considering she now felt as though she was floating atop a wispy cloud, high above the earth and all its petty troubles.

"String Bean," she blurted out suddenly. A soft giggle bubbled up inside her. *That's my name.* She smiled to herself as the last bit of discomfort she'd been feeling floated away as if on a gentle breeze. *Drugs,* Lindsay decided as the mental fog she was drowning in finally reached out and claimed her, *could be a very good thing.*

Sunshine streamed through the windows of the women's east wing of the third floor at Charity Hospital. Lindsay awoke to the sound of a commotion coming from the bed next to her. Before she even opened her eyes, she knew what it was. *The girl who couldn't breathe is dead.* There was no particular emotion tied to the thought. Save for the fact that Lindsay thought it was a waste and felt sorry for the soul who died all alone. *Like I will someday. Like we all do.* But then she heard a raspy, strained voice above what she assumed was the clamoring of medical staff. *She made it. Whaddya know.*

"You don't… you don't understand." Virginia Chisholm's normally warm, somewhat husky voice was barely audible. "I can't stay. My parents, the kids… they—"

"Listen, young lady." The nurse straightened her back and crossed her arms over her chest, as two other nurses threw their hands in the air and stalked away.

"You're still running a high fever and we almost lost you twice last night." She lifted an eyebrow. "Aren't you glad the doctor said you could have a small sip of water?"

Her patient nodded quickly.

Lindsay rolled her eyes at the nurse's condescending tone. Apparently she'd missed a lot during her drug-induced stupor. *Good.* Her eye drifted to the clock above the door, which she could barely make out. It read four o'clock. *Did I sleep an entire day?*

"If we hadn't given you enough painkillers to fell a horse not an hour ago, I don't think you'd be so sassy now," the nurse informed Ginny tartly. "Don't move, and be quiet. Girl, you are staying here until a doctor says you're not."

"My name is Virginia… Ginny." A weak cough, "Not girl."

A grin twitched at Lindsay's lips, and she turned her head to see who was giving the nurse such a hard time. She couldn't quite swallow the groan of pain the movement caused. "Oh, nuuuuuuurse? I'd appreciate enough painkillers to fell a horse right about now," Lindsay called out. It came out more smart-ass than she intended, but it was the God's truth.

The nurse spun around. It was the same heavy-set woman who'd given Lindsay a shot the night before. "You're awake. Good. Now it'll be easier to change your bedpan."

Lindsay frowned.

"And annotate your chart and figure out if you have any family—"

"Who can pay for my stay here at this bang-up hotel," Lindsay finished wryly, groaning a little as her body shook with silent laughter. *What did they do to my side? And my ribs?* "Ugh."

"I don't understand what's funny about that," the nurse said crisply.

"Medical treatment is not free, you know." The nurse narrowed her eyes. "You and Miss Chisholm here are going to be nothing but trouble. I can see that. Now," she lifted an expectant eyebrow at Lindsay, "family?"

"Nope. No family." Lindsay ground her jaw together to keep from cursing as a fresh wave of pain washed over her. "My head is killing me, and it's just little ole me in the great big wicked city."

"Am I supposed to write that here?" The nurse tapped Lindsay's chart, which was still in its holder at the foot of Lindsay's bed, with her pencil.

"'Little ole me?' I'll tell you my name if you like?" She hesitated, as though she was waiting for an answer, so Lindsay nodded. "I'm Miriam Goletz, but you can call me Nurse Goletz." She smiled. "See how easy that was? Now it's your turn."

"If it will help me to get my drugs faster, I'll be anyone you like. President Cleveland even. But I really need something." Lindsay's voice dropped to a rarely used pleading tone.

The nurse's lips thinned as she continued to wait.

Oops. "Umm… I mean… my name is String Bean." Lindsay smiled triumphantly then quickly added as an afterthought, "ma'am." *Amazing how quickly pain has turned me into a boot-licker.* She hadn't even considered giving her birth name. It had been so long since she'd heard it spoken, it didn't even seem like hers anymore. *Has it really been so long? Six, nearly seven years?*

The older woman shot Lindsay a self-satisfied smile before turning back to Ginny. It wasn't an actual name, but it was better than President Cleveland. Ginny had quieted during the nurse's brief exchange with String Bean, which worried the hefty woman, especially considering how the girl had been kicking up a fuss about her family and a fire ever since she'd awakened. "I'm going to ask the doctor if there's anything we can do about your fever, Ginny." The nurse laid a cool palm on Ginny's forehead, then shook her own head ruefully. "Mmm… still too high."

Ginny nodded as her eyes began to fill. She didn't feel hot; she was shivering. *I'll bet the kids are cold– and scared.* "Hurry, please? I need to leave. I… my family."

"Honey." The nurse gave Ginny a sad, sympathetic smile, and her voice took on a kindly edge, despite her earlier gruffness. "Your hands… they—"

Ginny lifted her hands and studied the white bandages with an almost disinterested air. "Were burned," she finished simply. They didn't hurt really. There was only a little discomfort between her heavily wrapped fingers, and she wondered briefly if the lack of serious pain was because of the drugs or the nature of the injury itself. *The drugs,* she figured. Her burns hadn't been that bad, had they? But then again, she couldn't be sure of anything at the moment. Everything felt fuzzy.

Ginny thought hard, forcing herself to concentrate. *There was a fire… And I tore Lewis's coat… The baby was with Mama. Oh, Mama. Why didn't you come downstairs? And who is that annoying woman in the next bed who doesn't even know Cleveland isn't President anymore? What did she say her name was?* She snorted to herself as her mind flittered out of her control. *A vegetable, she said. Beetroot? Lima Bean? That can't be right. God, I'm so confused. I need to get out of here. I'll bet no one knows I'm here at all. Alice would be here if she knew.*

"Yes," the nurse confirmed, breaking into Ginny's mental ramblings, "your hands were burned and the inside of your throat. The back of your neck is blistered too. I'm afraid we had to cut your hair. You won't be going anyplace for quite some time. Your injuries need to heal."

Ginny reached for her hair, but couldn't grasp it with her bandaged hands. She scowled.

Lindsay winced, imagining how it would feel to burn your hands and throat. *Even worse than having the shit beaten out of you and being attacked by a rat dog,* she guessed. "Oh, nurse?"

The older woman whirled around again and shot Lindsay a disapproving look. "Can't you see that I'm dealing with another patient?"

Lindsay was glad she hadn't said "helping" another patient. She might have had to take exception to that, since as close as she could tell, the nurse was merely nagging the sick girl. "Someone said surgery?" *At least I think they did.* Her headache was back with a vengeance and so was the splitting pain in her side. "What happened to me?"

"What didn't happen to you is a better question. You have animal bites and scratches on your neck and shoulder. And I'm afraid a chunk of your ear is missing."

"What?" Lindsay screeched.

The nurse turned back and started to take Ginny's pulse. She spoke to Lindsay without turning around. "Your doctor will be around shortly to explain your condition."

"There's more? Oh, Christ!"

"There'll be no blasphemy in this hospital, young lady," the nurse scolded before marching away.

Ginny coughed. "Did you—" her throat worked a few times before she could continue, "Did you have to say that?"

Lindsay awkwardly rolled over until she was at least partially facing Ginny.

"Ugh. That hurts." She jerked a thumb toward her own chest. "Are you talking to me?" She knew, of course, that Ginny was, but she didn't want to appear interested in talking to a stranger. Even though, given the circumstances, she didn't really mind now.

Ginny's pale, still disoriented eyes flashed with sudden anger. "Yes," she ground out harshly. "If the nurse is… if she's mad at me, she won't help me get out of this place so I can find the kids."

"What did I do?" Lindsay queried honestly, sorry she'd even bothered to acknowledge the girl in the first place. "I just want some goddamned medicine, that's all," she lashed back.

"Don't curse at me!"

"I wasn't!" But Lindsay's voice was contrite. *Maybe I've been in the company of assholes for so long that I don't remember how to talk to a regular person anymore, especially a woman.* Females were something that String Bean rarely encountered on the rails, and the few she had met had been just as vulgar and twice as mean as the men.

"Okay, then." Ginny's brow furrowed, and she all but growled in frustration. "I don't know what you did," she admitted frankly. "I can't remember anymore." Her eyes fluttered shut. "I'm all messed up. But I know it was something, Cabbage Head," she whispered as the sounds of the rolling hospital carts, squeaky beds, and muffled voices all faded away into nothing.

"Cabbage Head? Who would have a stupid name like that?" String Bean exhaled long and slow, mentally willing the nurse to return with a shot— painkiller or whiskey, at the moment she didn't care which. She stared at the ceiling, knowing that Ginny wouldn't hear her answer. "Considering I *always* seem to be in some sort of trouble, I must be doing something wrong."

It was three a.m., and the ward was dark the next time Lindsay awoke. The sound of a different nurse's voice came from the narrow space between her bed and Ginny's. This time when Lindsay tried, both eyes opened, though the vision in her right one was still a little fuzzy.

The nurse was in a pale blue dress and a crisp, white apron. She appeared to be barely out of her teens, and her starched hat sat slightly askew on her head. Even with her damaged nose, Lindsay could smell the scent of medicine wafting from the nurse's apron. The woman dipped a small washcloth in a basin of cool water and draped the dripping rag across Ginny's forehead. Carefully, she lifted one of Ginny's hands and pressed it lightly against the cloth, holding it in place.

The nurse told Ginny, "I'm sorry, I can't stay." The distress in her voice was palpable. "A building collapsed on Mulberry Bend Street, and nearly a hundred emergency patients are on their way here now," a frustrated sigh. "Can you hold this?"

Ginny gasped as the cool water soaked through her bandage and hit her raw fingertips. *I least I can feel something*, she thought grimly. Her eyes were closed, and she was trembling, but at her insistence they'd changed her medication to a lighter dosage painkiller and something for the fever. Nothing more. She could focus now, and Ginny wasn't sure whether that was a good thing or not.

Lindsay sat up a little, biting her lip as the stitches on her side were pulled taut. "What's wrong?" she whispered.

"Oh, good. Can you move?" The nurse searched Lindsay's eyes, and Lindsay licked her lips nervously, sensing something was seriously wrong.

"Yes." She took a brief inventory of her body. Her head no longer felt as though it were going to explode, and even sitting down, she could tell that most of her sense of balance had been restored. She still hurt, but not as badly as she had earlier that day.

"All right." The nurse nodded firmly. "Hang on." She quickly moved around to the other side of Lindsay's bed and pushed it up against Ginny's.

"What… what are you doing?" Lindsay's apprehensive gaze flicked to the nurse.

"Miss Chisholm's fever is worse. Someone needs to cool her down with this cloth, and I can't stay. No prisoners are allowed in the women's wards after dark, or I'd use one here." She gestured toward Ginny. "If her fever doesn't break soon, we'll have to resort to an ice bath for her. After all she's been through, I hate—"

"No," Lindsay heard herself say. "I'll do it. I'll help." *I will?*

The nurse quickly passed Lindsay the basin of water and a towel in case she spilled any. "Dab her forehead and neck. Like this." She demonstrated.

Ginny shook her head "no" but didn't open her eyes. *Now the vegetable woman is going to play nursemaid to me? She's hurt, too. She can barely move.* "She doesn't need to," Ginny whispered hoarsely. "I can—"

"Fine," Lindsay snapped abruptly. She pushed the basin away, sloshing a small amount of water onto the towel that lay next to it. "Do it yourself." She turned away from Ginny. "I'm still tired anyway. You—"

"No," the nurse interrupted Lindsay firmly. "She can't do it herself. I don't know what I was thinking, but her bandages need to stay dry. You can use your good hand, and you'll be fine." She didn't wait for Ginny to argue with her. She simply pinned Lindsay with a withering glare. "I can count on you, right?"

Do they learn that stare in nursing school? "Well… she doesn't want…"

"Right?" the nurse repeated a little more forcefully. She didn't have time for this.

Lindsay stuck out her jaw, preparing to refuse, when out of the corner of her eye, she saw Ginny shiver. Her heart clenched at the sight, and she found herself wanting to help, despite Ginny's apparent rejection. *Stubborn girl needs somebody.*

"You can count on me."

"Good. I knew when I heard you two were troublemakers it was probably an exaggeration." The nurse told Lindsay, "If her fever gets any higher, you yell. There's a nurse on the other end of the bay with a woman who is critical. She'll hear you if you call loudly enough." With that, she lifted her skirts and hurried to the exit.

"I'm *not* trouble," Ginny insisted quietly, gulping back tears. *God, what is wrong with me? I need to get hold of myself and stop blubbering.*

"Well, don't tell it to me. I never said you were trouble." Lindsay dunked the washcloth and squeezed out the excess water. "I know you don't want my help." She paused with her hand hovering over Ginny's face. "I won't touch you if it really bothers you." *I don't give a shit what I told the nurse. I won't force my help on you.*

"No. I need to get well. Please."

After a moment's hesitation, Lindsay wiped the cool cloth gently across Ginny's forehead.

Ginny sighed at the contact, but her shivers increased. *Time to apologize. She probably thinks…* "Thank… thank you." She felt the cloth trail down her sweaty neck.

"It's all right." But Lindsay still felt stung.

Ginny's mind scrambled for something to say. "Does your nose hurt?" Even in the dim light, she could see that Lindsay had two black eyes and a spectacular bruise that covered most of her face.

Unconsciously, Lindsay wiggled her nose. "Ouch." Her hand shot to the splint, and she slapped herself in the face with the washcloth, stinging her scratches. "Shit!"

Ginny bit her lips to stop an unexpected giggle that threatened to escape. Lindsay lifted an eyebrow at the young woman, inwardly pleased that Ginny was holding back what could actually be a smile. "Yes. It does a little," Lindsay admitted sheepishly. "Not so bad if I don't touch it though." Casually, she shrugged one shoulder. "I'll heal soon and be out of this place."

Ginny swallowed hard as a rush of raw emotion swelled up inside her so quickly that she couldn't stop it. "I need to heal soon too." She blinked several times in rapid succession, sending a cascade of glistening tears down her cheeks. "I can't stay here. God, the boys, Jane, I have to find them. Nobody will tell me where they are." She hiccupped, and her face contorted in pain.

Lindsay's eyes went round, and her hand with the washcloth in it froze, causing it to drip onto her thigh. *She's crying? Not just a few tears, but really crying. Oh, God. Oh, God.* "Don't cry. Please." *I don't know what to do!* She looked around desperately for someone to help, but saw only sleeping patients.

"I… I can't," a sob interrupted her, "I can't help it." Ginny lifted her hands to her face, forgetting about the bandages until she realized she couldn't wipe her tears without getting them wet. Before she could think of what else to do, Lindsay was running the cloth down her cheeks, cooling them with a gentle, almost reverent touch that was at odds with the young rail-rider's rough speech and demeanor. The tenderness was Ginny's undoing, and with her next breath, she broke down in earnest, crying freely and not even trying to stop herself.

Lindsay looked on in horror. Her own hands were shaking, and she felt a little dizzy as her heart rate skyrocketed. "Please," she begged. "It's going to be okay. You'll see. You'll get well and go back to your family."

"No." Ginny shook her head frantically. "There was a fire. And—" she swallowed thickly. Then the words spilled out in a panicky rush. "My parents and two sisters. The nurse came and told me today. You were sleeping. They didn't… I mean Mama and Alice and…" The redhead began to cry harder, and the rest of what she said was lost amidst her broken sobs.

Lindsay didn't know what to do with her hands. It didn't seem right to continue to wipe Ginny's face, so she dropped the rag and hesitantly laid her hand on her companion's shoulder. "I am so sorry," she whispered, truly meaning it.

Ginny closed her eyes as her chest heaved, and when she opened them again, for the first time Lindsay truly paid attention to what she was seeing. She took a long look into Ginny's heartbroken, sky-blue eyes as their gazes locked, and when she did, a pang of sympathy touched her in a spot so deep, so surprising, that she nearly gasped at its intensity.

The comfort Ginny felt from the slender, almost timid hand on her shoulder, squeezing gently, was all out of proportion to the act. Her heart greedily soaked up the compassion like a dry sponge being tossed into the sea, and without thinking, she sat up and wrapped her arms around Lindsay, her body craving another's contact as two days of grief, frustration, and raw fear poured out.

Lindsay bit her tongue, first in surprise, then in pain, as Ginny's body collided with hers. It took every ounce of her willpower not to jerk away. She took a deep breath and did what she'd never done before, never had done to her; she carefully wrapped a lean arm around Ginny's shoulders and allowed the redhead to cry against her unabated. *I think she needs this. She has no one. I can do this.*

Heat was pouring off Ginny, and her sweat soaked through Lindsay's thin hospital gown. *God, she's burning up. Probably delirious.*

"I should have died too," came the raspy whisper against Lindsay's shoulder.

"No." Her voice was unyielding, and Lindsay fought against the irrational urge to shake this young woman, this stranger who was plastered to her, for even thinking such a thing. "Don't say that," she told her emphatically. "It's not true. You survived. They wouldn't have wanted you to die."

Ginny sniffed and closed her eyes. She couldn't keep her teeth from chattering, and between that and her low, scratchy voice, Lindsay could barely make out what she was saying. "But I'm… so, *so* tired." A pause. "My heart hurts."

And that simple statement was something Lindsay had a bone-deep understanding of. Sometimes, when things were so dark and you were utterly lost and hurting, it seemed as though life wasn't worth the enormous effort it took just to live. "Tomorrow you'll feel less tired." She felt her way cautiously. "If not then, the next day or the next."

"I don't know where to find them." Ginny turned her head, and Lindsay could feel small puffs of hot air as labored breaths brushed against her neck.

"You'll find them," Lindsay reassured, knowing full well that might not be possible. Orphans had a tendency to disappear into the system, or worse, onto the streets, never to be heard from again. *Wasn't that what I did?* "You can't look from here. You need to heal *first*." Her arm was feeling more comfortable around Ginny's soft body, and then without meaning to, she began to relax a little into the foreign touch.

"But I don't know where to start! They don't have anyone but me." Ginny's voice cracked, and a fresh wave of tears came along with her next revelation. "I broke my promise to Alice."

Lindsay had no idea what the promise was, but knew from the self-loathing that was so evident in Ginny's voice that it must be important.

Ginny felt as though she might be sick. Abruptly, she pulled away from Lindsay, but she leaned back too fast and automatically reached out to brace herself with her hands. She cried out as soon they touched the bed, and a fat woman several beds down groaned in her sleep, mumbling for everyone to "shudda up."

"Hey. I've gotcha." Lindsay's good hand shot out, and she wrapped strong fingers around Ginny's upper arm, allowing Ginny to take the weight off her hands and lie down more carefully. A fine sheen of sweat glistened on the redhead's brow, and Lindsay uncurled her fingers so she could pick up the washcloth again. Much of the basin's water had spilled onto the towel, but there was still plenty to dampen the washcloth.

Ginny sighed as the cool rag brushed over her eyebrows, cheeks, and chin, wiping away her perspiration and tears.

Lindsay debated with herself, then asked what she was wondering. "What promise did you break?" she asked curiously. This girl didn't seem the sort to lie. Ginny's jaw worked, and Lindsay instantly regretted bringing it up. *Who cares? You don't even know her. It's none of your business.*

Ginny sniffed a little. "I promised not to leave my younger brothers and sister. They're just kids."

The corner of Lindsay's mouth curled upward. "And you're not?"

"I'm almost eighteen." She looked at Lindsay carefully, wishing she could tell what she truly looked like. Behind the bandages, bruises, and splints was someone that Ginny suspected was just about—"How old are you?"

"Old enough. Older than you," Lindsay answered seriously, trailing the cloth down Ginny's neck and wiping away a smudge of soot that had been missed by the nurses.

"How much older than me?" Ginny persisted.

Another small grin twitched at Lindsay's lips at the younger woman's pushiness. "Not much. I'm eighteen… no, nineteen last October."

Ginny blinked, a little surprised that her guess had actually proven to be right. "If I'm a kid, then so are you. You're just like me."

"I'm not a kid." *And I'm nothing like you.*

"What happened to you?" Ginny lifted her bandaged hands to trace the outside of the dressing that circled Lindsay's head, but let them fall back to the bed when Lindsay subtly shifted away. "I'm sorry," she whispered, suddenly very self-conscious. "I wasn't thinking. I…I—"

"No. It's okay." Lindsay's eyes conveyed her regret. She hadn't meant to do that. "I just wasn't expecting that, okay? I'm not mad."

Ginny bit her lip and nodded warily. "Well?"

"Well what?" Lindsay dipped the cloth into the water again and squeezed out the excess into the basin.

"How did you get hurt?"

"Speaking of that…" Lindsay groaned a little for effect. "I could really use some more painkillers. My side is killing me."

Ginny just waited, an eyebrow lifting when Lindsay not so skillfully changed the subject.

When Lindsay glanced up from her task, she noticed Ginny's

expression.

"Oh. I umm… I was run over by a wagon," she lied. *This girl doesn't need to know my business.*

Ginny's second eyebrow lifted, joining its reddish-gold twin. "A wagon with claws and teeth?"

"Absolutely."

"You're lying."

"Absolutely," Lindsay confirmed unrepentantly.

Ginny was tempted to press for information, but could see by the guarded look in Lindsay's eyes that the subject was closed. A tremor passed through her, and she suddenly felt very tired.

As she continued to apply the cool cloth to Ginny's face, Lindsay could see the younger woman growing more and more lethargic. A handful of heartbeats later, and they stopped talking altogether. A comfortable silence grew between them, until all that could be heard was the background noise of coughing and snoring women, and the winter wind rattling the windows. The gaslights at the opposite end of the hall were turned low and emitted a soft haze that barely reached the end of the long, narrow hospital ward.

Several quiet hours passed, and Lindsay's thoughts naturally turned inward to their most accustomed place—the hushed recesses of her own mind. Her head was throbbing, and she didn't have to guess where she'd had her surgery. The area not far below her breast felt as if it were on fire. When she could no longer hold the cloth without her hand shaking, she awkwardly shifted onto her side so that she could watch over Ginny, only occasionally pressing the cloth against a sweat-slicked forehead. *If I can make it till morning, they'll give me something for the pain. They can't ignore us forever. I know it.*

Ginny slept restlessly, her body warring with itself as her fever raged. Finally, just before dawn, she awoke feeling cool and listless. Her shivering had stopped, and her thoughts were once again clear, if grim. Her fever had broken.

Ginny studied the woman who had so tenderly cared for her. The washcloth was still clutched in Lindsay's hand, and her features were slack with sleep.

Dawn's first rays hit ice-covered windows and fractured, casting random patterns of golden light across the walls and beds. Shoulder-length, chestnut brown hair peeked at odd angles from beneath the white gauze dressing that circled Lindsay's head. Lurid purple bruises started at Lindsay's jaw and blended into one another as they worked their way up to her closed eyes, fringed with dark, long lashes.

"Who are you?" Ginny whispered, wanting to know more about this person and wishing she could see the woman behind the bandages and pain. Lindsay's eyes opened at the words, and Ginny met her confused gaze easily.

"What?" Lindsay blinked slowly.

"Who are you?"

"I, um," Lindsay wiped the sleep from her eyes with her good hand. "I thought you heard me answer the nurse yesterday. My name is String—"

"No." That answer wasn't good enough. Not when there was a real one lurking behind the bewildered eyes looking directly into hers. Ginny felt as though she had shared a very personal piece of herself with this sometimes kind, sometimes annoying person, and she couldn't help but crave the same kind of openness in return. "Who are you really?"

They stared at each other for several charged seconds until Lindsay said in a voice thick with sleep, "My name is Lindsay Killian." Ginny smiled, and without meaning to, Lindsay found herself smiling in return. *She has dimples,* her mind laughed.

"Hello, Lindsay." Blue eyes conveyed warmth and strength that wasn't there only hours before, and Lindsay was drawn to their sincerity. "I'm Ginny, and I wanted to thank you."

Lindsay's brow furrowed; she could hear the strain in Ginny's voice and knew every word was painful. "Don't… Well…" She looked away. "It was nothing."

"You're wrong. It was something," Ginny corrected softly. "I um… I need to find my family when I get out of this place." Her eyes twinkled. "And something tells me that you're a very good person to ask for help."

"I am?" The words tumbled out without permission, and Lindsay held her breath, half-expecting Ginny to laugh at her genuine surprise. "You really think so?"

"I really do," Ginny assured her. "Will you? Help me, that is?"

"Yeah," Lindsay whispered back. There was nothing wrong with her throat, but she found herself unconsciously matching Ginny's hushed tone. "I'll help."

They smiled at each other, both feeling a little less alone than they had when they first arrived at Blackwell's Island.

Chapter Four

Twenty-four hours later…

Lindsay clenched her fist as she watched Nurse Goletz feed Ginny a bowl of lukewarm porridge. "That's too fast for her to eat," she murmured under her breath. "Can't you see that?"

In all fairness, the heavy-set women looked as though she were dead on her feet. Even her starched white hat sat askew on her head and the top button of her dress, which was so high that it nearly brushed her jaw, was undone. She had been working nonstop since a building on Mulberry Bend Street collapsed. Because they were short-handed, she was now starting another shift, in addition to the two she'd just worked.

There were several women on the ward who couldn't feed themselves because of injuries to their hands or arms. And the nurse always started at the end, with Ginny, before working her way down the bay. It was a kindness to her young patient, because at least the food would still be warm.

Ginny was swallowing as fast as she could, but her throat was still tender and she always had been a slow eater anyway. In truth, she was starving and mortally grateful for anything she could put in her belly. Unfortunately, during these speed-feeding sessions, she ended up wearing more than she ate. Ginny was, however, bound and determined not to utter a single word of complaint. *I'm not a troublemaker*, she thought petulantly, ignoring a dribble of porridge that trailed down her chin and plopped onto the bib Nurse Goletz had fashioned out of a washrag.

"Stop! Stop. Please. I can't take it anymore."

Two sets of surprised eyes swung toward Lindsay, whose head had been unwrapped. A small bandage had been taped over the lump and gash in her skin just behind her right ear. After cleaning her wound the day before, a nurse had allowed her to have a sponge bath and to wash her hair, which was now hanging loose about her shoulders, the morning sun reflecting off mahogany highlights. Ginny eyed her jealously, feeling ten times grungier because she was looking at someone freshly scrubbed. She could still smell a faint trace of smoke on her skin and could feel the barest hint of grime on her belly and back, and it turned her stomach. She hoped it would be her turn for a bath today. Though she wasn't exactly comfortable with the thought of another person washing her, she knew it had to be done. Lindsay, on the other hand, had pitched such a holy hell-fit over another person touching her that the nurse allowed her to bathe herself—one-handed.

"What is it now, String Bean?" Nurse Goletz asked tiredly. "And be quick about it. I'm in a hurry."

"I can see that," Lindsay informed her bluntly. She stopped when she saw Nurse Goletz's hackles begin to rise and her lips thin. Taking a calming breath, she tried for diplomacy. "How about you let me feed Ginny,"—*so I don't have to watch that disgusting oatmeal concoction pouring down her chin*—"and then you can tend to your other patients?"

The nurse blinked. She hadn't expected that offer from String Bean, who barely said a word to any of the medical staff except for the occasional request for pain medication. She'd been switched to laudanum today. "I don't know…" The nurse rubbed her jaw in contemplation. She'd scolded that new nurse up one side and down the other when she'd found String Bean's and Ginny's beds pushed together the day before. Not only was it wholly indecent in its appearance, but also, even if it was an emergency, a patient shouldn't be asked to assist with another patient's care. That was improper.

Ginny's eyes lit up at Lindsay's suggestion. *I might get to eat like a human being instead of a starving wolf.* "Please, Nurse Goletz," she begged, her voice stronger than the day before. "I know that… um… String Bean would do a good job. And that you have *far* more important duties to attend to than feeding me." Lindsay smiled at Ginny's use of her nickname. She knew the younger woman hated it for some reason, but was inordinately pleased that Ginny hadn't shared her real name with the nurse. It wasn't as though it was a secret. It just wasn't any of the hospital's business who the hell she was. If "String Bean" was good enough for her, it would have to be good enough for them. Besides, she liked the way her real name sounded when Ginny said it, and she didn't have the slightest interest in hearing it otherwise.

"Well," the nurse paused as she looked into Ginny's pleading eyes. She sighed. "I suppose since it's a non-medical task it would be all right. We *are* busy."

"You truly are," Ginny intoned seriously, biting back an enormous grin. "Thank you."

Lindsay began to sit up as the nurse eased herself off her perch on Ginny's bed.

The redhead watched silently as Lindsay bit her lip to keep from crying out as she shifted until she could swing her feet around to the side of the bed and stand. Ginny instantly felt a pang of guilt. *How can I be so selfish?*

The nurse handed Lindsay the bowl of porridge, spoon, and a cloth. "The doctor will be by to see you soon, String Bean."

"You said that yesterday. And the day before," Lindsay grumbled.

"He'll be here today."

"Is it my turn yet?" a woman eight beds down called out to the nurse. Both her arms were in casts, and she had a pitiful look plastered across her face.

Nurse Goletz bit back a nasty retort and began to push her cart filled with bowls of breakfast down the aisle. "Yes, yes. It's your turn, Mrs. Adolf."

Lindsay sat down on Ginny's bed, and Ginny instantly reached out and laid her bandaged hand on Lindsay's arm. "You're hurting this morning," she whispered, her voice full of concern. "I should have told the nurse that she could keep feeding me."

"I'm fine."

"You're sure?"

Lindsay's eyes softened. "My side is just tender, and the stitches are starting to itch," she assured. A smirk began pulling at the edges of her mouth.

"What's so funny?" Ginny questioned suspiciously, sitting up a little straighter and preparing to open her mouth like a hungry baby bird.

"You. There's food all over your chin."

"Well, scoop it up and feed it to me, for goodness sake." She opened her mouth so wide Lindsay could see her tonsils. "I'm starving."

Lindsay chuckled, but ignored the request and took a moment to clean Ginny's face and throw away her food-covered bib. Only then did she give Ginny a fresh mouthful of porridge from the bowl. "Open wide for the choo-choo."

"Funny stuff, Potato Head. Especially… Mmm." Ginny hummed in delight.

Lindsay's face twisted in revulsion. "You actually like this?" She lifted a big spoonful of the gray mixture up to the light and made a loud gagging noise.

Ginny swallowed slowly, sighing at how much better that felt on her throat than rushing it down. "No, this is the most vile porridge I've ever tasted, but I'm hungry so I'm not picky. If you think I'm a messy eater, you wouldn't believe Jane. She—" She abruptly stopped as she realized what she was going to say. *Jane. James and Lewis. Where are you?* She closed her eyes to stop the leaking of the tears she could feel welling up.

"You'll find her, Ginny. You'll find all of them. I know it."

Ginny nodded. *I will not cry. I've already cried enough.* She could hear Lindsay holding her breath, waiting to see if she would be blubbering again, and that was enough to help firm her resolve. She opened her eyes. "Yes. I will." *With your help.*

Lindsay smiled.

The rest of the bowl was emptied in silence, and when Lindsay was done she wiped Ginny's face once more and set the bowl on the floor between their beds, groaning when she straightened. "Now that that's over, I won't lose my breakfast watching you trying to eat your breakfast."

"Very funny." But Ginny couldn't help but smile.

"I… umm…" Lindsay looked around self-consciously. "I have a favor to ask you, Ginny." She licked her lips nervously.

Ginny's eyebrows jumped. "You do?"

Lindsay nodded. "Unless you don't want—"

"No! No. You've been so kind to me," she explained in a rush. "I'll do anything I can." She lifted her hands and looked at them ruefully. "But I can't do much without these."

"You don't need hands for this. I can hold it." Lindsay swallowed and looked down. "It's okay if you laugh. I—"

"Whatever it is, I won't laugh." *I'll bite my tongue through if I have to.*

"Okay." Lindsay reached out with her good hand and pulled her hospital chart from the holder at the foot of her bed, presenting it to Ginny. "Can you tell me what they did to me? They said surgery, but nobody will come and tell me what."

Ginny frowned and turned her concerned gaze on Lindsay. "Your eyes… are they?"

Lindsay shook her head, sending her hair scattering across her shoulders. With an annoyed hand, she pushed a stray lock out of her eyes, wishing for her long-gone cap. "My eyes are fine." She held the medical chart closer. "Please?"

"I can try, but I don't know that I'll understand the medical terms."

"That's okay." Lindsay smiled self-consciously. She knew that Ginny had realized what the problem was now and felt confident the girl wouldn't laugh. "I won't understand any of it unless it's my name, a railway map, or a city name."

"Can you open it?"

Lindsay laid it on her lap and opened the thin metal lid, exposing the lined papers beneath covered in scribbles. "Hey," she pointed to the top line, "that says 'woman.'" She knew that from the signs on outhouses.

"It sure does. Guess that officially rules out jackass, huh?"

Lindsay burst out laughing, causing several women to look up from their breakfasts. "No, Ginny. I wouldn't say that exactly. What else does it say?" she asked anxiously.

Ginny's face went very serious as she read. Several times she visibly flinched.

"Here it says puncture wounds and multiple lacerations, most likely canine in origin."

Lindsay looked confused.

"Dog bites," Ginny clarified, not looking too happy. "And cuts and scratches, I think."

Lindsay rolled her eyes. "No shit. Tell me something I don't know."

Ginny looked around the room as though the police would jump out and arrest them for Lindsay's swearing. "Don't say that!"

"Say what?" Lindsay grinned, unrepentant.

Ginny narrowed her eyes, but continued to read. "Concussion. I think that means your head."

"Cracked open my head. Got it."

"Two fractured ribs, one broken rib. Ouch. And fractures of the third and fourth... meta… meta…" She sighed. "If I had a dictionary…"

"Never mind," Lindsay dismissed. "Gotta be my fingers. They're the only other thing broken that I know of." She held up her hand, showing off scratches that ran from her wrist to elbow that were still red and raw.

"Mmm… true," Ginny acknowledged. "This says a shifting of your broken rib after you arrived at the hospital resulted in a ruptured spleen and then after it—" She looked up from the chart. "Can you turn the page?"

Lindsay blinked. "Yeah, yeah, sure."

Ginny read a few more lines before going very still. Her voice took on a solemn note, and she looked up again at Lindsay before saying, "After ruptured spleen, it says you required a sple… sple… splenectomy."

"What the hell is that?" Lindsay roared in alarm.

"Shhh." Ginny looked around again, wincing at the disapproving frowns thrown their way by several women. "Are you crazy?"

"I dunno. Does having a splenectomy cause that? Because if so, then I probably am!" *I'm feeding strangers for Christ's sake. Isn't that proof enough?*

"Calm down, will you?" She carefully laid both hands over the chart, closing it. "I think it means they removed your spleen."

"You mean cut out my spleen, don't you?" Lindsay corrected angrily. "Then again, if it was something important, I guess I'd be dead by now."

Ginny stiffened. "That's not funny."

Lindsay paled as she thought about what she'd said. "I guess it's not."

"We'll ask the doctor when he comes." She held up a hand to forestall Lindsay's words. "He will come. Eventually." *He has to, doesn't he?*

Lindsay gathered up the chart and moved back to her bed, lying down. Ginny didn't want her to go, but didn't feel as though she could ask her to stay either. She shifted onto her side and looked at Lindsay. "It can't be too bad, Lindsay." Her heart clenched at the thought of something being seriously wrong with the young woman whom she'd come to think of as a friend. "You're getting better, not worse, right?"

There was a hint of pleading in Ginny's voice that Lindsay couldn't help but respond to. Lindsay carefully rolled onto her side so they were facing each other, the two feet of space between the beds all that separated them. She took a deep breath and let it out slowly. "Right. I can move around a little today."

Neither woman could think of anything to say, and Ginny cast around desperately for a change of subject. "What made you think I could read your chart?" Ginny asked finally, fully aware that over half the population—including her parents—couldn't have.

Lindsay thought about that for a moment. Why did she? Ginny was in a charity hospital just as she was, which meant she probably hadn't had the luxury of much schooling. "I dunno." She shrugged. "You just seem smart, I guess."

Ginny smiled weakly at the compliment, but wasn't willing to let it go yet.

"It has nothing to do with being smart, Lindsay. I didn't have to start work until after the eleventh grade. It's just a matter of being taught. Anyone can learn," she hinted.

"I know," Lindsay said amiably, tossing her chart to the foot of her bed. "Maybe I will someday."

Ginny nodded approvingly.

Lindsay's eyebrow lifted. "Now answer me a question. Why did you ask me to help you find your family?"

Ginny didn't even stop to think as the words tumbled out. "Because I'm scared out of my stinkin' mind! You helped me when there was no one else who could."

Lindsay's eyes widened.

"You seemed smart to me too, in every way. Not just smart about living on the street, though I'm guessing you're experienced in things that I'll need to know, seeing as how I'm sure I'm jobless and I know I'm homeless." Ginny's eyes twinkled. "I believe deep in my heart that I can trust you."

"Umm..." Lindsay's jaw sagged. *She thinks I'm smart? How does she know she can trust me? Maybe I'm only being nice so I can steal her coat!*

Ginny flushed at the dumbfounded but pleased look on her companion's face. "Does that answer your question?"

"Yeah." Lindsay could scarcely believe the kind words, and she felt her own skin heat. "That answers my question."

Twelve days later...

Ginny slowly slipped on her coat and leaned against the small slab of wall between her and Lindsay's beds. She was wearing a donated, plain gray dress that was a little too small and a pair of brown leather shoes that were a little too big. The heavy bandages had been removed two days ago, and though they still hurt, her hands were mostly healed and functional. Now only a light layer of gauze covered them.

The doctor had matter-of-factly explained that some scar tissue would remain, but that since she would likely end up working in a factory, squeezing out a dozen children before she was thirty, or washing clothes for a living, the beauty of her hands would be short-lived anyway. He didn't see any reason for her to fret. Ginny smiled a little, recalling how Lindsay had sprung out of bed and berated the doctor for being an insensitive asshole who should be shot. It wasn't until later that night, long after her doctor had gone, that Ginny found out her stubborn, hot-tempered friend had torn several stitches during her spectacular leap from the bed.

She felt worse this morning than she had since she'd first arrived at the Charity Hospital. But this time it wasn't because of her injuries or even the loss of her family. It was Lindsay, and the fact that Ginny was being discharged today while her friend was *not.*

"Buck up, Ginny," Lindsay encouraged mildly, feeling self-conscious in her hospital gown while the other woman was fully dressed.

"I'm all right."

Lindsay sighed at the obvious lie. *No, you're not. Asshole doctor.*

"I'll see you day after tomorrow on the late ferry." Ginny shot an evil glare toward the nurse's station where she could see Lindsay's doctor talking to Nurse Goletz. She privately wondered if, once the man found out Lindsay was anxious to leave the hospital, he'd decided to extend her stay by a day or two out of spite. Of course, her own discharge date had just been decided last night. "I'll wait for you at the docks."

"No, you won't," Lindsay told her seriously. Ginny rolled her eyes. "Lindsay—"

"It's not safe."

Ginny smiled gently. "You forget where I've been living the last six months, Lindsay. And even before that you could hardly call my family's station middle-class. I might not have any experience living on the streets, and I do need your help, but I'm no fool." She pushed herself away from the wall and sat down on Lindsay's bed, causing the springs to squeak loudly under her weight and bringing a hint of smoke to Lindsay's nose. "I won't stand out on the dock, watching the river for two days straight, waiting to be attacked."

"Of course you won't," Lindsay mumbled, embarrassed by her ridiculous assumption, though she couldn't help but feel the surge of relief that flooded through her. *She's not an idiot, String Bean. Don't treat her like one.* "Are you sure?" She was smiling when she said it.

"Humph." Ginny swatted Lindsay's arm with the back of her hand. "Yes, Turnip Green, I'm sure."

Lindsay laughed. "That's String Bean to you, missy." Though she secretly hoped Ginny would continue to call her Lindsay. She was doing her best to ignore the woman in the bed across from Ginny, who was watching them again. The prostitute had one leg in traction and was extremely vocal about what she thought of the two young women's friendship. For some unfathomable reason, she didn't like it. *Nosy skank. And the way she stares at Ginny… I have half a mind to break her other leg. All these prying eyes on me—on her—every minute of the day. This place is driving me mad.*

"I'll be careful," Ginny assured her as her gaze drifted to Lindsay's ribs. "You'll be careful and not tear any more stitches while I'm gone? And be nice to your rotten doctor. If you don't, you'll never get discharged."

"Yes, Mother, I'll try," she grumbled good-naturedly. "But this hospital, and especially Doctor Asshole, is sadly mistaken if they think they can hold me here longer than I want to stay." Lindsay hadn't meant to say that last part out loud, and when she glanced up into Ginny's face, she realized her error.

Ginny's eyes widened. "Oh, no. No, no, no, no. That doesn't mean you're going to try something crazy, does it? Lindsay—"

"Who me?" Lindsay gave Ginny her best innocent look, but most of the effect was lost when her friend actually snorted out loud.

"Lindsay, I'm serious," Ginny persisted. "This island has a prison on it. Do you really think you can just march onto a ferry and not have anyone notice?"

Lindsay's face was suddenly transformed by an expression so wicked that Ginny actually shivered. "God, you are stubborn!"

"Mmm… Miss Chisholm." Lindsay made a clucking noise, but her eyes twinkled. "If I'm not mistaken, blasphemy is the ticket straight to you know where."

Ginny narrowed her eyes. "Just be careful, *please.* You still need those stitches to heal."

That reminded Lindsay that she was uncomfortable, and she shifted in the bed.

Ginny carefully reached behind her and fluffed her pillows.

"You don't have to worry about me, Ginny. You have enough

concerns without one more."

Ginny's hands stilled. "Why shouldn't I worry?" she snapped, truly worried that Lindsay would hurt herself. "There's no one else out there worrying about you, is there?" The words had barely passed her lips before she regretted them.

Lindsay froze for a second, stunned by the unexpected jab. "No," she finally answered, her voice low and dejected. "I guess there isn't."

God. "I'm so sorry, Lindsay." Ginny closed her eyes, her heart in her throat. "I didn't mean it." She sniffed. "I only meant that it's no bother worrying about you." When her eyes fluttered open, she used them to beg Lindsay not to be upset. "I don't mind, honestly. We're friends, right? Best friends, even?" she asked hopefully. *C'mon, please, Lindsay, please don't be mad.*

The look on Ginny's face tugged at Lindsay's heartstrings, and her gaze dropped to delicate lips threatening to tremble. She felt the oddest urge to take Ginny's face in her hands and lean forward and…

"Lindsay?" Ginny was beginning to panic, fearing that she'd finally stuck her foot so far inside her own mouth there'd be no retrieving it. She stood up.

Light-brown eyes snapped up to meet Ginny's. "No. I mean, yes," Lindsay blurted out, clearly confused. She reached out and tugged on Ginny's dress until the younger woman reluctantly sat back down. "I mean…" Lindsay shook her head as if to clear it. *What was the question again? Oh, right. She was apologizing for telling the truth.* "It's okay that you said that. You're right. I don't have anyone who cares what happens to me." She clamped her hand over Ginny's open mouth. "Except you," her mouth shaped a lop-sided grin, "my friend."

Ginny exhaled raggedly, and they both exchanged relieved grins.

"So you'll go to the church I told you about?" Lindsay set her jaw. "And you'll tell them you're Catholic and fifteen and not a day older?"

"I may not be a very good one, but I *am* Catholic. I'm almost eighteen, and I'm not lying to a nun!"

"Huh, I didn't know you were Catholic." Lindsay scratched her chin. "Chisholm sounds English, or something. What makes you not a good—?"

"My stepfather was Irish," she interrupted, "and he insisted that Alice and I convert when he married Mama." Ginny waved an irritated hand and asked defensively, "Do you have something against Catholics?

Does it matter?"

Lindsay blinked. "No. I… I—" She stopped and tried again. "No."

"Good. But I'm not lying."

Lindsay's face suddenly hardened. "Ginny, would you rather sleep outside, alone in the cold? Because that's what you'll be doing." *And I won't be there to look out for you. Don't be a fool, girl.*

Ginny thought about that for almost a full minute. Then she mentally cringed. *Forgive me, Father, but I have a feeling I'm going to be doing a lot of sinning in the near future.* "I'm fifteen. Got it." She looked away. "But after tonight, I'll have the entire day tomorrow to start looking for the kids. I don't think I should just do nothing."

Lindsay knew that the first thing they'd agreed to do when they were released from the hospital was make a trip back to Ginny's tenement. The surviving residents would likely be scattered throughout the same area, and one of them might have seen what happened to the Robson children. "We'll go back to your building tomorrow… together. Okay?"

"Tomorrow?" Ginny's forehead creased. "But you're not being released—"

"When they think I am," Lindsay finished. "I'll be fine. You just need to trust me. I need a little time, but I'll be on the morning ferry tomorrow. We'll go to your building together and talk to your neighbors."

Ginny wanted to argue Lindsay out of trying to leave the island early, but one look into those resolute eyes told her it would be useless. "Thank you," was all she said, but the softly spoken words conveyed more than gratitude.

They were laced with affection, and Lindsay found herself willing to do whatever it took to ensure she'd hear that particular tone in Ginny's voice more often. It had taken her nineteen years, but the rail-rider finally had a true friend. Lindsay wasn't sure which surprised her more, that it had happened at all or how much she loved it. She still craved quiet and the relative solitude of the tracks and a rhythmically moving boxcar. But she admitted that, even though she wanted those things, they would be just as enjoyable if Ginny were there too, maybe even more so.

As their time together in the Charity Hospital lengthened, each woman had appointed herself the other's keeper and the staff had been left with little choice but to back off in deference to that simple reality.

Except for the dispensing of medication, which was by necessity left to the nurses, Ginny and Lindsay each helped the other with the care of their wounds, bathing, and, when need be, other even more intimate necessaries.

What had, at first, caused each woman to blush hotly quickly grew routine. They felt far more comfortable with each other than with hospital staff, and the nurses stopped fighting the inevitable, going so far as to get an orderly to help push their beds together at night so they could continue their quiet conversations and not disturb the other patients.

A nurse walked by and glanced at the number etched into the metal post at the foot of Ginny's bed. She picked up her chart and nodded once. "You're on the seven a.m. ferry. Come with me."

Ginny looked down at Lindsay and licked her lips nervously. "Tomorrow?"

"I'll be there."

Lindsay was shocked to find herself pulling Ginny into a quick but gentle hug. When they separated, Ginny brushed her lips across Lindsay's cheek as she withdrew. "Tomorrow, then."

"Wait!"

Ginny and the nurse stopped. "Umm... let's trade coats. Yours smells like smoke and I know how—"

Ginny's throat closed, but she managed to nod. The smell of smoke on her coat was giving her a headache and irresistibly pulling her thoughts to places she didn't want to go quite yet.

Lindsay reached under her bed and handed Ginny her black woolen jacket.

"The nurses cleaned off the bloo— er... they cleaned it the first night."

"Thank you." Ginny slipped out of her coat and laid it carefully across Lindsay's bed. Her fingertip grazed Lindsay's foot for just a second before Ginny turned away.

She didn't look back at Lindsay as she strode purposefully down the long hospital bay. With every step, a new and nearly overwhelming feeling of loss, that she could neither explain nor understand, threatened to send her to her knees. This wasn't right. She and Lindsay had become a team. *You don't split up a team*, her mind whispered brokenly.

Lindsay lay back down and stared at the ceiling. A plan formed in her mind, and she smiled, biding her time until dark.

When Ginny and three dozen other men and women were finally herded out the hospital's front door, she was greeted with a stiff blast of icy air that smelled like water and tossed her newly shorn hair. She felt naked without a hat and self-consciously turned up the lapels of Lindsay's coat as she boarded one of the wagons heading to the dock. The tattered garment was heavier than her old coat had been and warmer. If not for the slightly long sleeves, the fit would be perfect. She burrowed deeply into it, and closed her eyes, eagerly accepting what comfort it brought.

At the docks, several milling guards moved over to talk to the nurse, who'd escorted the former patients from the hospital. The nurse handed one of the men a folded piece of paper, and he efficiently fastened it to a clipboard.

A line formed, and Ginny was the second to last person to board.

"Name?" a guard barked out.

She fought the urge to tell him none of your business. "Virginia Chisholm." The man nodded, crossed off her name, and began questioning the next patient, all without looking up from his clipboard. The boatload of people was processed in less than five minutes, and Ginny took a spot along the back rail. Her hands ached and the thin, newly grown skin on her palms and fingers quickly numbed in the cold.

As the boat traveled, the Charity Hospital began to appear in the distance, peeking out from above barren treetops. She wondered, would Lindsay really meet her the next day? Or would she forget about the troublesome young woman who had asked far more of a stranger than she'd had any right to expect?

Ginny tucked a lock of blowing hair behind a pink ear, her eyes narrowing and drying from the force of the cold wind whisking off the water. "That's just it, isn't it, Lindsay? We're not strangers anymore," she whispered. Her thoughts turned inward. *I'll be at the docks tomorrow.* "Waiting."

The next morning

Breakfast was being served, and the sound of clinking silverware and tin cups rattling against metal trays echoed through the Women's Ward.

Lindsay pushed away the runny, slightly green eggs in disgust. It was nearly eight a.m., and the ferry would be leaving within the hour. Her heart was already beginning to pound in anticipation. It had taken most of the night, but she'd managed to steal two sets of clothing from the Men's Ward that she was reasonably sure would fit her and Ginny. Now, they were tucked safely into Ginny's coat under her bed.

"Hey, slim," the prostitute from across the aisle called out to Lindsay. "You don't hafta be blue juss cuz your red-haired friend done left this place." The woman smacked her thick, ruby red lips together and made a kissy-face. Then she adjusted her ample cleavage, valiantly tugging down the rounded-collar of her hospital gown in an effort to show off what she considered to be her best feature. The bed creaked loudly, shaking along with the woman's baritone laugh. "Sweet Bertha will keep you company while she's here. Never you worry."

"Shut up, slut." "Disgusting." "Godless trollop," were only a few of the raucous shouts that mixed with not a few catcalls in response to Bertha's invitation to Lindsay.

Dark eyebrows lifted, and at that moment Lindsay gave up her valiant, but likely suicidal plan to escape the island, which involved stealing a wagon, overpowering the ferry's guards, hijacking the boat, and piloting it to Manhattan. *Designs for the future,* she admitted privately, recalling her attempt to recover her flint and eighty-seven cents, *have never been my strong suit. I'm more of a "winging it" sort of girl.* She'd nearly decided to chuck it all and swim for it, hoping the current would help her to the other side, when the streetwalker had given her a better, if more revolting, solution to her problem.

Lindsay swallowed hard and tried not to think about what she was going to do. *Only because I promised you, Ginny.* "Bertha," she shouted, loud enough for everyone in the ward to hear, "I think I love you!" *You disgusting, toothless hag.* "Why don't I just march over there and give you a big fat kiss to prove it?"

"Ooooo, why don't you, girl?" Bertha's enthusiasm was clear, and she chuckled again, low and wicked. "And here I thought you were ignoring me for that sweet-looking little girl who left yesterday. I shoulda *known* nobody in they right mind would have calf when they could have a fine, aged steak."

The room filled with startled gasps and sniggers, and Lindsay was sure she would never eat beef again.

Bertha's coal-black eyes started at the top of Lindsay's head and worked their way down to her chest. Where they stayed. "Mmm mmm! You shore is fine for a skinny thing. C'mon to mama now." Her voice turned playfully scolding when Lindsay failed to immediately jump out of bed. "Lawdy, *lawdy!* Don't you *make* Bertha wait another minute for her kiss. C'mon!"

Out of the corner of her eye, Lindsay could see Nurse Goletz and her doctor rushing down the aisle, their eyes wide. *Heh.* She threw off her sheet and pushed herself to her feet, giving Bertha her best sultry look, the one she usually reserved for that special moment just before kicking some asshole guy in the balls.

Bertha's smile grew so large that Lindsay could have sworn she saw a tooth. She sat down on the fat woman's bed, and Bertha gleefully, but with surprising gentleness, wrapped two meaty arms around Lindsay's waist and pulled the younger woman into her lap, unhampered by the leg she had in traction.

"Oooo… You feel stronger than you look," Bertha exclaimed in delight.

Lindsay wondered if the woman might actually start to drool, and she warred with the urge to knock away Bertha's possessive hands. The pungent scent of body odor caused her stomach to lurch. *I can go through with this. I know I can. Oh, God, but can I do it without puking?*

Nurse Goletz slid to a halt in front of Bertha's bed. "What's going on here?"

"Don't you never mind, Mizz Nurse." Bertha dismissed Nurse Goletz without even a glance in her direction. "This girl is *my* bizness. Not yours." She tightened her grip on Lindsay, and the younger woman stifled a hiss, feeling a tiny trickle of warm blood flow from her incision. *Shit. There go my stitches again.* The nurse's grizzled eyebrows drew together. She knew for a fact that Bertha had been a thorn in String Bean's backside for days.

"What's going on here, String Bean?"

"If my behavior is a problem, then perhaps I should be discharged? Immediately," Lindsay retorted sassily, her eyes narrowing at the doctor, who had finally made it to Bertha's bedside huffing and sweating from the exertion.

Nurse Goletz glared at Lindsay, hoping the young woman would realize the error of her ways before it was too late. String Bean didn't know it, but she was playing with fire.

Lindsay lifted her chin. "Now if you don't mind, I promised Bertha a big," she paused between each adjective for effect, "fat—juicy—wet—heart-stopping kiss. On the *mouth*."

There were more gasps, and the doctor's face turned beet-red as he recognized Lindsay. She sounded less nasal now the splint from her nose was gone, and she looked different now that the lurid purple bruises had faded to yellow. But this was definitely the same woman. "You're the vile woman that called me an a-a…" he intentionally bit his tongue.

"What did my String Bean call you?" Bertha asked cheerfully, refusing to relinquish her grip on her prize. "I'll bet it involved cursing. Or something about that big, block head on your shoulders." Which was fine with her. She didn't like that rude doctor anyway. Couldn't he see that she and String Bean were busy? An idea flashed through her mind, and just to spite him, and, well, because she thought it would be fun, she latched on to Lindsay's neck with massive lips and sucked for all she was worth.

Jesus! Instinctively, Lindsay opened her mouth to scream bloody murder, but managed to clamp down on the impulse just in time. Her eyes widened, and her gaze flicked to the floor. She was surprised not to see eyeballs rolling around on the wooden floor.

Bertha let loose with a long, drawn out, very satisfied moan.

Lindsay's stomach threatened to rebel again, and she could feel her body breaking out in a nervous sweat.

A woman three bunks down crossed herself and promptly passed out.

The doctor's right eye began to twitch, and he tore his glasses from his face with a slightly trembling hand, tucking them safely into the pocket of his long, white coat. "Are you enjoying making a perverted spectacle of yourself with this… this hussy?"

Bertha removed her lips with a loud popping sound. She proudly examined the magnificent hickey for a moment before turning grumpy eyes on the doctor. "I prefers strumpet, if you please." She grinned. "Sounds fancy, maybe even French."

The man visibly grabbed hold of his emotions, and a cool,

professional mask dropped over his face. His hand stopped shaking, and his twitching eye righted itself. "I wasn't talking to you, Bertha." The voluptuous prostitute had a violent pimp and worse husband. She was a regular at the Women's Ward.

Nurse Goletz instantly tried to soothe the doctor's ruffled feathers. "Doctor," she began hesitantly, using her most calming voice, "I'm sure this isn't what it appears. I—"

"Oh, yes it is," Lindsay corrected forcefully, her gaze never leaving the doctor's. "I'm sure you don't want my—" she paused, "*influence* in your hospital ward. I can be on the next ferry."

"Things wuz just gettin' good," Bertha wailed, locking her thick fingers behind Lindsay's back.

The doctor nodded slowly, offering a hand to Lindsay as the young woman pried herself away from Bertha. Lindsay took the hand warily, but allowed the man to help her to her feet. "You're right," he paused and glanced at Nurse Goletz in question.

"Her name is String Bean," the nurse supplied helpfully, wincing.

The doctor scowled. These indigents showed little regard for him or this charitable institution. Their impudence was nearly as appalling as their hygiene.

"You're right, String Bean. I don't believe this hospital ward is the proper place for you."

"Well." Lindsay smiled in surprise. *That wasn't hard. And I didn't vomit. But damn, do I need some fresh air. I can't wait to get outside.* "I'll just gather my things then. No use in waiting for tomorrow's ferry when I can leave now." She padded over to her bunk and pulled Ginny's coat from beneath it, careful not to allow the stolen clothes to be seen. Her feet were near frozen and she slipped them into her shoes, confident that the wide-legged trousers she'd stolen would fit over them.

"I'm having you committed to the asylum right here on the island for treatment," the doctor announced.

Lindsay froze. Her mouth dropped open, and she stared at the doctor, wondering if he was truly serious, or merely trying to frighten her. Her heart began to pound, and a jolt of fear rushed through her veins. "Wh-what?" she finally spluttered.

Nurse Goletz closed her eyes. She was afraid of this.

"You're clearly suffering from a psychological malady, Miss—err—String Bean. Homo-erotic contact is akin to self-gratification in its propensity to devolve into full-blown insanity, rather than remaining the quite treatable mental dysfunction that it is." The doctor's eyes softened, and he laid a sympathetic hand on Lindsay's shoulder. No wonder she had hurled profanities at him. She was deranged. He'd treated several other women with similar symptoms at the island's asylum. "Bertha performs debasing, unnatural acts for profit. As I don't think you're a prostitute, it is clearly in your basic make-up to act this way. We can change that," he assured her solemnly.

The blood drained from Lindsay's face. She hadn't heard a word since he said "committed" and "asylum".

"Huh?" Bertha cocked her head to the side and scrunched up her face. "I don't know what all that man is talkin' 'bout. But if that 'self-grab-ification' is what I think it is, I charge extras for that."

Lindsay cursed inwardly, wishing she'd pirated the boat after all. *The asylum, all because I was going to kiss Bertha? True, no one in her right mind would do that… but still…*

"Doctor, as you've said before, confinement in cases like this is *such* a drain on resources," the nurse reminded him gently. "I think it's a real possibility that String Bean is intentionally trying to get tossed into the asylum so she doesn't have to work."

"Hmm…" The doctor rubbed his chin as he glanced at Lindsay with a clinical eye. Was she that devious? It wouldn't be the first time someone tried to pull the wool over the State of New York's collective eyes.

"Or maybe this was merely a prank, a—"

"Prank?" the man scoffed at the nurse. "I think not. After all, would *you*, a woman clearly in her right mind, tease in such a revolting manner?"

Her hazel eyes went round. "Uhhh… Well, no, but…" The heavy-set woman reached out and wrapped her fingers around Lindsay's lean biceps. "I'll get everything ready for the transfer, doctor. I shouldn't have questioned. I am truly sorry, doctor. I'll await your discharge orders and notify the orderlies of the upcoming transfer."

"Fine. Fine." He puffed up his chest a little and nodded, enormously pleased with his diagnosis. "Carry on, Nurse Goletz."

Lindsay watched in horror as the man turned on his heels and disappeared through the exit. She flicked a panicky gaze at the nurse. *I don't want to hurt her. But*—"I hate to break this to you, but I am *not*—"

"I know you're not, you troublemaker." She let go of one of Lindsay's arms and captured Ginny's coat with a quick sweep of her hand. The stolen men's clothing came tumbling out. "Ugh." She rolled her eyes. "I knew I should have gotten you on that ferry with Ginny." She began tugging Lindsay toward the nursing station.

Lindsay wrenched her arm away from the nurse's grasp. "No. I won't go!"

"I'm trying to help you, you fool," the nurse hissed under her breath. She leaned closer to Lindsay, and she shook her by the shoulders, making it look like the young woman was giving her nothing but trouble and was receiving a firm dressing down because of it. Quickly, she pressed her lips to Lindsay's ear. "Grab Bertha's dress on the way out."

Lindsay blinked. "I—"

"Just do it, or I'll let them commit you!" the older woman ground out from between clenched teeth. Then she straightened, and her mouth shaped a smug smile. "Now that we have an understanding…" Haughtily, she adjusted her apron and turned her back on Lindsay. "Follow me." Without another word, she began marching down the aisle.

She's helping me? Can I trust her? A mental groan. *Do I really have a choice?* Then the rail-rider made her first truly good decision and did *exactly* what Nurse Goletz told her. Lindsay snatched up the stolen clothing from the floor, took a few paces and dropped the shirt when she drew even with Bertha's bunk. A virulent curse escaped her lips, which is what everyone would have expected. And when she bent to retrieve the shirt, she scooped up Bertha's hideous, purple, floral print dress along with it, seriously hoping Nurse Goletz didn't expect it to come close to her bare skin.

"Bye, bye, sweet thang," Bertha crowed as Lindsay disappeared down the aisle. "You come back and visit Bertha, you hear?"

Lindsay was shoved into a supply closet and before she could protest, Nurse Goletz slammed the door shut and held up a single, authoritative finger. "Uh uh. Not a single word, String Bean. I meant what I said, I'll let them commit you."

"I'm not going to the asylum, and anyone who tries to put me there will truly regret it."

The nurse looked into brown eyes that had gone nearly black with fear and anger. Lindsay's pounding pulse was visible against the pale skin of her throat, and for a split second the heavy-set woman was sure she could actually smell danger. In her heart, she believed that String Bean, when pushed, could be a very dangerous person. "I don't doubt you for a second. That's why I'm helping you." The nurse cracked a small smile, hoping to diffuse the tension in the small room.

"As much as I think the doctor is a pompous ass, he truly believes he's helping the patients here. I'd prefer not to see him killed." A beat. "At least not on my shift."

Lindsay couldn't help herself. A tiny grin appeared, and her tightly coiled body relaxed enough for her to let out a shaky breath.

"It'll be okay." Nurse Goletz jutted her chin toward the dress that was tangled with the stolen clothes and still clutched in String Bean's hands. "Put that on."

Lindsay nodded and held up the shirt.

"No, the dress." The nurse reached into her apron and pulled out a small compact. "And you'll need to wear some of this too."

Lindsay's wide eyes darted back and forth between the enormous, tacky, lavender dress and the compact of rouge. "The hell I will," she roared.

The breeze blew a lock of Lindsay's hair into her mouth and she straightened from her place along the ferry's railing. She fumbled with the top button of Ginny's coat, scarcely able to believe she'd made it. As Nurse Goletz had predicted, however, telling the ferry guards that she was a "special" friend of Warden Simmons was enough to get her passage on the ferry without question. Apparently, the warden had a taste for young prostitutes, and a veritable parade of them came and went on the island.

Lindsay winced. The ribs they'd had to cut in order to remove her spleen were still incredibly tender, as was the still-healing incision. But now that she was safe, and out in the cold, fresh air, she felt as if she could breathe. A wave of relief, followed by one of lethargy swept over her, and she longed to find a nice, lonely boxcar somewhere, curl up, and fall fast asleep. *But*, her mind wearily reminded her, *now isn't the time for that.*

As the ferry chugged closer to shore, Lindsay relentlessly scanned the docks. The boat was a half hour late, but surely Ginny would have waited. When realization finally dawned on Lindsay, it was enough to send her sliding down the ferry wall to the floor. There wasn't a single soul waiting on the docks. Not one. *Maybe she found the kids right off.*

Yeah. Lindsay sighed. *That must be it.* Her expression hardened a little and she turned unseeing eyes back toward the murky river. *Not that I can blame her for not coming on any account. She doesn't really know me. And who the hell is she to waste my time? Now that this little adventure is over, I can get on with my own life and give up on playing the Good Samaritan. I have far better things to do. Pockets to pick. Places to go. Things to see.* But she couldn't make herself believe the words, and she felt her heart sink. "I can't believe I did all this for nothing." She chuckled bitterly and rose to her feet. "How stupid am I?"

"You say something to me, ma'am?" one of the ferry workers asked, sidling up to her. His skin was the color of dark chocolate, and his eyes glinted with genuine curiosity as he waited politely for her answer. "You look cold. We have blankets inside. Would you like one?" he asked eagerly.

He couldn't, Lindsay figured, be more than thirteen, though he was tall and well built. "Is this your first day?" she inquired kindly. Either he was too naïve to know that Lindsay was supposed to be made up as a prostitute or too well-mannered to treat her badly because of it.

"Yes, ma'am." He smiled brightly, already thinking ahead to getting paid and taking home food bought with his very own money. Suddenly, he looked a little worried. "Is there something wrong?"

"No." Lindsay smiled gently, melancholy stealing over her. "You're doing great. And I already have everything I need." *Which is nothing at all.*

The boy shrugged then pushed himself away from the rail, off to tie the dock ropes.

She disembarked in silence as the twenty or so men and women passengers scattered across the docks, all seemingly with someplace better to be. She told herself to just leave, that now she was being a fool. But her heart wasn't quite ready to say goodbye to the only friend she'd ever felt close to. She tucked her hands into her pockets and walked a short way down each of the streets that dead-ended at the docks, half of her expecting to see Ginny, the other half knowing she wouldn't.

Lindsay made her way back to the river and stopped alongside the ferry. Her eyes fluttered shut, and she cocked her head and listened, longing to hear the lonely whistle of a train and be well away from the noisy, stinking city.

With several quick strides she was back on the gangway, calling out to the boy who had spoken to her earlier.

The young man was untying the ropes, preparing the boat for the journey back to the island.

"Hey!"

His head popped up from his task and he moved to the railing, sliding a little on the deck's icy surface. "Ma'am?"

"I… I'm thinking I might have got on the wrong ferry."

The boy's forehead creased, and he took off his hat and wiped the sweat from his brow. "This is Manhattan, ma'am."

Lindsay sighed. She was where she was supposed to be. Alone. Feeling stupid she asked, "Is there another ferry?"

"Aren't you even going to say goodbye before leaving?"

Lindsay whirled around at the sound of Ginny's soft, pain-tinged voice. The redhead's clothes were wrinkled, and she was shivering a little. Dark circles ringed her tired eyes, and her hair was disheveled from the wind. But there she was. Just as she promised she would be. Lindsay searched her mind for something to say, but the words wouldn't come.

To her profound relief, Ginny didn't let the awkward silence between them grow. She simply pulled Lindsay into a full body hug and whispered into her ear, "I'm so glad you're here. I was worried sick you'd do something crazy to get discharged early."

Lindsay melted into the embrace, happy beyond reason that at least one of them had the good sense to have faith in the other. She would, she swore to herself, do better next time. The younger woman's heart was hammering, and Lindsay could feel it through their woolen coats. She pressed her wind-burned cheek against Ginny's and hugged her tighter, wondering at her own thundering pulse.

After a long moment, Ginny extended her arms and looked at her friend. Her eyes lit on her neck, and she gasped. Anger, then confusion flickered in her blue eyes. Her mouth opened and closed several times without a sound. An "Oh, my God," finally burst free. "That is the biggest love bite I have ever seen!"

Ginny shook her head as if to dispel the image that she knew would be forever burned into her brain. "What on earth were you doing while I was gone?" She didn't give Lindsay a chance to explain, as her thoughts tumbled directly from her brain and out of her mouth. "Is that makeup? *Lots* of makeup?" She wrinkled her nose in disgust. "You're wearing rouge that looks as though it was applied with a trowel! You look like a…" her cheeks heated, "well, like a strumpet!"

A dark eyebrow arched. "Bertha would be so pleased."

"Huh?"

Lindsay grinned, perversely pleased with Ginny's honest assessment and especially the earlier blasphemy. *She's right*, she laughed to herself. *She's not a very good Catholic girl.* Until that moment, String Bean hadn't realized exactly how much she had missed Ginny and how damn glad she was to see her.

Then Ginny noticed the back of the colored collar beneath Lindsay's coat, and without preamble she unbuttoned it and plucked at the horrendous, enormous, low-cut dress. Her gaze traveled down to her own gray, shapeless dress that she firmly believed had been made by blind prisoners with two left hands and no thumbs. "I'm gone for one day and you become not *only* a strumpet but one with vile taste in clothing?" she asked incredulously, glancing up at Lindsay with shocked eyes.

Lindsay's grin turned sheepish, and she offered weakly, "I've been busy?"

"You'll explain later." It wasn't a question. Ginny exhaled explosively as she wrapped an arm around one of Lindsay's and led her away from the river. "See what happens when I leave you alone for a second?"

Lindsay snorted and gently ruffled her friend's hair. "I have a feeling that Gotham has more to worry about with us together than it ever did with us apart." Her russet-brown eyes glinted in the morning sun. "Let's go get your family back, Ginny."

Ginny's throat closed, and she unthinkingly pulled Lindsay to her again, renewing the embrace she hadn't really wanted to end in the first place. Nothing need be said that couldn't be expressed by that simple, heartfelt gesture, and when two slender arms wrapped themselves tightly around Ginny, they felt so good it hurt.

Some days were longer than others, and some moments necessarily sweeter. For the first time in her short and sometimes brutal life, Lindsay Killian took a moment to savor the sweetness.

Now that she'd had a taste, she wasn't sure she could ever go back.

Chapter Five

Four days later…

It was twilight, that ethereal time when the sky was more purple than blue or black or gray, and New York City's streetlights began bathing the city in a subdued, golden glow.

Fog collected around the glass sconces as they warmed, and lit torches or lanterns appeared on each wagon that rolled along Queens' Thirty-Sixth Avenue. They were still close enough to the docks to smell the water of the East River and hear the blare of horns as boats approached shore.

Lindsay looked over her shoulder for the umpteenth time, watching as Ginny plodded sullenly through the thick, wet snow, a small sack, containing the men's clothing she had refused to wear and two thin blankets, slung over her shoulder. Lindsay sighed but remained silent, unable to think of anything to say. In truth, she felt lousy herself. It had been another day of dead ends, endless searching, and abject failure.

Ginny was beginning to lose faith, and what little optimism Lindsay had had on her friend's behalf had all but evaporated along with their ideas of where to continue looking.

It was as though the Robson children had vanished from the face of the earth. The young women had tried Ginny's neighbors, local hospitals, churches, the fire brigade and police, and several state offices, all to no avail. At one fireman's suggestion, they were now down to visiting homeless shelters and orphanages one by one. And they'd already been to a half dozen of those. A few were so cramped and filthy that tears had welled in Ginny's eyes at the sight. She was torn between praying that her siblings weren't living in such depressing squalor and praying that they were.

Lindsay and Ginny had left the island of Manhattan earlier in the day, after a last-minute stop at a Catholic church not far from Ginny's burnt-out tenement. The old priest had never laid eyes on Ginny before, and Lindsay got an even better understanding of what Ginny had meant when she said she wasn't a very good Catholic. Apparently, actually attending Mass wasn't something Ginny did regularly.

Lindsay squirmed in the high-ceilinged sanctuary, feeling the weight of the statues' stares upon her and hearing their mocking whispers telling her that she didn't belong. Her mind flashed to her father's funeral, the low chanted prayers, the whine of an out-of-tune organ, and the smell of incense. She thought she might be sick.

The priest had generously offered them a place to spend the night, but much to Lindsay's astonishment, Ginny had taken one look at her friend's pale face and refused the offer, explaining that instead they needed to leave the island so they could start their search across the river. Actually getting across proved more of a challenge than Lindsay had anticipated. It had taken three attempts on three different ferries, with Ginny getting caught every single time but managing to talk her way out of being arrested, before they both successfully secured free passage.

On more than one occasion, Ginny eyed Lindsay's trousers enviously, thinking that those covered, lean legs had to be warmer than hers. As she'd reminded Lindsay, however, she needed to appear respectable, or at least as close as she could manage, when she went looking for the children. Dressing as a man would only complicate things.

The bottom of Ginny's dress was soaking wet, and her cheeks were flushed pink from the chill in the air. Large snowflakes continued to drift to the ground, piling up quickly and collecting haphazardly in her soft red hair. She stared at her feet as she walked, only glancing up when she needed to step aside for some passerby. Her throat was nearly back to normal, and if she didn't overuse her voice, she could almost forget that it had ever been burned. Her hands, however, were another story. They alternated between aching, itching, and going totally numb in the frosty January air. She idly wished for a pair of gloves, but settled for tucking her hands under her armpits as she walked.

Lindsay couldn't take it anymore. *Funny*, she thought, *I used to go days without a single word, and now I'm racking my brains for something… anything to say to her.* She slowed her long steps until Ginny drew even with her. "How are you doing?"

Ginny had grown so accustomed to the quiet that her head snapped sideways in surprise at Lindsay's words. "I'm sorry. What?"

"How are you doing?" Lindsay repeated, her worry taking the form of a tiny wrinkle on the bridge of her nose.

"Oh." *I'm hungry, cold, tired, and scared to death for my family.* "I'm fine. You?"

… *Are someone who knows better.* "I'm fine too." She looked hard at Ginny's face, for the first time noticing how much weight the redhead had shed in the past couple of weeks. "Ready for something to eat?"

"God, yes," Ginny blurted out, then she blushed. "I mean—"

Lindsay laughed. "I *know* what you mean." She let her nose guide them three doors down to a bakery/delicatessen. "This way."

Ginny all but pressed her face against the glass and drooled. "Mmm. I dunno, Lindsay," she mumbled doubtfully, her stomach growling despite her words. Displayed in neat rows were sliced meats and cheeses, along with loaves of crusty white and black breads braided into intricate designs. "It looks expensive."

"We have to eat," Lindsay reminded her gently. "And the prices are exactly what you'll find all over the city. No more, I promise." While changing out of Bertha's dress, Lindsay had found a forgotten five-dollar bill tucked deeply into the pocket of Ginny's coat. It was the younger woman's last wages from her job as a feather ripper. But much to Lindsay's disdain, Ginny was doling out the cash as frugally as a miser.

Lindsay clasped Ginny's shoulder with one hand and deftly removed the cloth sack with her other. "My turn." She followed Ginny's line of sight through the lightly frosted window and licked her lips. "We don't have to use your money. I know you want to save that until you find your sister and brothers, but the nearest soup kitchen is at least two miles, and by the time we get there it'll all be gone. I can—"

Unaccountably, Ginny's temper flared. "Steal someone else's wages?"

Both heads turned, and flashing eyes met. Lindsay stiffened in reaction but couldn't disagree, knowing in her heart that, though she had simply planned on offering to shovel the sidewalk in front of the bakery, she was more than capable of stealing the money.

It was Ginny who looked away first. "I'm sorry." She rubbed her temples. "I'm so tired and hungry, I'm not thinking straight." She sighed and her voice dropped to a whisper. "Forgive me, please?"

Lindsay quickly nodded unable to speak after that heartfelt plea. She wrapped her arm around Ginny's shoulder, and the younger woman ignored it, moving in for a hug instead.

Nothing felt as good as this, and Ginny was drawn into it as helplessly as a moth to a flame. The sensation of Lindsay's body pressed to hers stirred something new within her, a curious yearning, at once frightening and utterly safe. Deep in her heart, she feared if she dwelled on the sensation too long, or even gave it too much conscious thought, like everything else she valued in her life, it would be cruelly snatched away.

"They couldn't have just disappeared," Ginny whispered in anguish, her lips near Lindsay's ear. "Where *are* they, Lindsay?"

The cheek pressed tightly to hers felt cold and wet, and Lindsay's heart clenched as Ginny spoke. "I…I don't know. But we won't give up," she promised quietly, closing her eyes against the sensation of their warm bodies pressed tightly together. *We haven't touched since that day at the docks*, her mind whispered. She found herself melting into Ginny's embrace, her mind awhirl. *Why does this feel so damn good? And why do I love to touch her so?*

"Mmm. You're warm," Ginny muttered absently, smiling when she felt Lindsay's cheek grow hotter with her words. She pulled away, offering Lindsay a weak smile. "I'm used to spending all day on my feet, but I feel like we've walked a hundred miles in the last few days."

"My sore legs couldn't agree more," Lindsay said self-consciously, very aware of how her cheek tingled from Ginny's touch. Uncomfortable, she took a step away from her friend and slid off the cap she'd "found" the day before. She slapped it against her thigh to remove the snow, then gently wiped the snowflakes from the top of Ginny's head with slightly shaking fingers.

The unexpected intimacy of the gesture caused Ginny to flush, and she looked away, feelings of bewilderment mingling with a wistful sense of longing.

Lindsay sighed, assuming Ginny was still upset with her. "You don't have to keep apologizing for the truth." The dark-haired woman squared her shoulders. *She already knows you're a no-good thief. Don't hold back now. It'll just come up again later.* "Ginny, I'm a pickpocket when I need to be, and sometimes just when I'm too lazy to be anything else," she informed her with startling self-awareness and honesty. She steeled herself against Ginny's reaction. "I'm a bloke buzzer, mind you."

Ginny blinked stupidly, causing Lindsay to clarify.

"I don't steal from women."

"Ah." She nodded thoughtfully, not sure if that revelation was merely informational, or somehow meant to make her feel better about the situation. "I see." Ginny moved a step, shifting out of the way of an oncoming trio of men. When the men were out of earshot she spoke again. "I do need to apologize, Lindsay. For some reason when I'm around you my foot spends more time in my mouth than on the ground." A small grin twitched her lips before she took on a more serious expression. "I don't have any right at all to judge you. We all do what we need to survive. I need to grow up and accept that. And you're the least lazy person I've ever met."

"Ginny—"

"Please," Ginny bit her lower lip, "just don't steal for me. I'm not insincere enough to pretend I don't want you to do anything in your power to help me find my family, but not just for me, Lindsay. Not if there's any other choice at all."

Lindsay swallowed hard. "Ginny, I can't pro—"

"No, you *can* promise." She reached out and wrapped fingers covered with tattered bandages around Lindsay's. "The question is, *will* you?"

"All right," Lindsay heard herself say, as though someone else entirely was in control of her mouth. *Shit! I wasn't going to do that!*

Ginny smiled a genuine smile, one that showed off rarely seen dimples and made her eyes light up. "C'mon. Let's go inside and buy something hot and filling. If I eat, I won't be such an evil hag." She smiled ruefully. "And I know I have been. Besides, I'm freezing, and if we eat slowly, I might just thaw out before we have to come back out into the cold."

Lindsay grinned affectionately and opened the door. She had already learned that it rarely paid to argue with Virginia Chisholm. As the door was pushed open, the clanging of a small bell heralded their entrance and the yeasty scent of fresh-baked bread and spicy meat wafted out onto the street. Each woman groaned with undisguised pleasure. Apologies, admissions, and promises were filed away for safekeeping as they bolted through the door.

Ginny sat at a small table just inside the bakery door, drinking a cup of steaming black coffee. Between them, they'd consumed a foot-long roast beef sandwich, an enormous kosher pickle that made Lindsay's face scrunch up in an expression Ginny decided was nothing short of adorable, and two large bowls of hearty vegetable noodle soup.

She was pleasantly stuffed, and Ginny closed her eyes tiredly, deciding not to think about tomorrow until it came. They still had to deal with tonight. When had the days grown so long and so cold? *Long before this*, was the answer. Ever since her mother married Arthur and his constant battle with the bottle and ridiculous get-rich-quick schemes led to her already struggling family's gradual financial ruin.

Ginny loved her mother and had long ago reconciled herself to her mother's choice of Arthur, a good-natured dreamer with a heart of gold and a head of wood. She even loved Arthur, who was a kind stepfather even though his life was ruled more by Scotch whiskey and dreams of wealth than by what was best for his family. What she couldn't reconcile was that her parents had taken Alice's and Helen's lives along with their own.

"What are you thinking?" Lindsay asked curiously, noting the look of quiet speculation and anger on Ginny's face.

For a split second, Ginny was tempted to say nothing. But she was too tired to hold it inside. "I'm thinking about how huffed I am with my parents for letting the fire—" she swallowed, feeling a lump in her throat. "For letting the fire claim Alice and Helen." Her eyes lifted and met Lindsay's, and in that instant, she could see that her friend ached for her as though the pain were her own. She reached out for Lindsay's hand, squeezing it to show her thanks since words seemed inadequate.

"Why, Lindsay?" she continued, as her anger bubbled to the surface. "Why didn't Alice come with me? She was always stronger, smarter, faster. She could have made it! Why didn't Mama send them out of the building when she had the chance?"

"Oh, Ginny." Lindsay shook her head sadly, wondering what exactly it was in people that forever compelled them to try to make sense out of the senseless. She got up from her seat across from Ginny and sat down alongside her. "I'm sure she tried to get out. She was your big sister, right? She wouldn't have left you alone to deal with this if she'd had any other choice." *I wouldn't have.*

But Ginny's rational mind wasn't ready to accept that yet. "If she had, she'd be alive now!"

"No. You don't know that."

Ginny's eyes darted back and forth as her mind raced. *Something* could have made this all turn out differently. Her heart twisted in her chest. Or *someone.* "I shouldn't have listened. If I'd only stayed to help, maybe I could—"

"Stop it, Ginny."

"No! If I'd—"

"Stop it!"

The clerk looked up from her work, but Lindsay lifted her hand, acknowledging that, despite appearances to the contrary, everything was all right.

Ginny's mouth snapped shut at the harsh words.

Now it was Lindsay's turn to lose her temper. She leaned forward and lowered her voice, speaking with an almost savage intensity. "For Christ's sake, listen to what you're saying. If you'd stayed, you'd probably be dead too. You said yourself that no one made it out of the building after you did. You couldn't have done anything else that night other than stay behind and die." *Believe what I'm saying,* she willed the younger woman.

"I know. I know," Ginny whispered, squeezing her eyes tightly shut. Her anger melted away as suddenly as it had flared. She felt like a wrung-out dishcloth. "It's not fair. They had their entire lives ahead of them, Lindsay."

Lindsay's dark eyes softened. "So do you."

Ginny gave her a watery grin. "I guess I do." A thoughtful pause. "What would I have done without you these past weeks? It makes me sick even to think of it."

And that caught Lindsay so flat-footed that her mouth worked for several seconds, but she couldn't manage a single sound.

"Don't be embarrassed," Ginny insisted in a low voice, not quite able to meet Lindsay's flabbergasted stare. "I don't expect you to say anything. I… well, I just wanted you to know." Her eyes lifted to meet Lindsay's and she could see that she was making her uncomfortable. She smiled, what she hoped was a reassuring smile, and bumped shoulders with Lindsay. "Go on. Go see if they have some day-old bread or something they'd be willing to part with. We can save it for breakfast." She gestured with her chin toward the clerk, who was diligently slicing a large slab of ham.

"Ahh… Ginny." Lindsay let out a shaky breath. "You… well, it hasn't been any trouble or anything. I—"

"It's okay," Ginny assured her. "Really. Now go be charming, and get us some breakfast."

Lindsay's eyebrows shot skywards, and her mouth curled into a wry grin. "Have you ever seen me be charming?" she asked bluntly.

Ginny laughed, her spirits rising merely from the expression on Lindsay's face. "Well… I have faith in you."

"Well, then, stand back." Lindsay wiped an imaginary piece of lint from the front of her woolen coat. Then she smoothed her lapels with exaggerated care. "I have people to influence."

Ginny watched fondly as Lindsay strolled up to the counter and leaned against the glass, then casually struck up a conversation with the clerk. Her friend was probably the *least* charming person she'd ever known. Ginny still found Lindsay brash, crude, and impatient. But she also found Lindsay… she didn't know exactly what. Captivating, maybe. Or, perhaps, compelling. There was simply something indefinable about her that made Ginny want to stare into those pretty brown eyes and get lost. The mere thought made her stomach flop, and she sighed, giving up on any form of introspection tonight. She was just too tired.

The wind had begun to howl, and the snow had turned to sleet. Ginny could see a layer of ice forming on the metal lamppost across the street. *Being outside is not going to be fun.* For the last few nights, they'd managed to avoid sleeping outside, always finding a church or shelter where they'd been able to curl up on the floor somewhere. *Please let us be that lucky tonight.*

"Ginny?"

Light blue eyes flicked sideways at the sound of Lindsay's voice. Next to her stood the clerk. Lindsay had a strange look on her face, and Ginny quickly pushed herself to her feet. "What's wrong? What is it?"

"Nothing. Nothing," Lindsay promised her quickly. "I just thought you should hear this." She turned to the clerk. "Ester, can you tell my friend here what you told me?"

The middle-aged woman nodded dumbly, her confusion evident from the scowl on her face.

"Look, if this is about the bread, we were just asking—You don't—"

"I can't give you any bread." The woman shrugged. "Sorry."

Ginny shot Lindsay a meaningful look that said, *You brought her over here to tell me that?*

Lindsay shifted impatiently from one foot to the other. "Tell her *why* you can't."

Ginny looked expectantly at Ester, who wiped her greasy fingers on her stained white apron. "Well, I can't give it to you, because I give it to charity."

Ginny's gaze went back to Lindsay. "That's nice?" she hazarded.

Lindsay rubbed her temples. "Tell her more about the charity, Ester. Everything you told me."

"Is this some kind of game?" The woman scowled again.

Lindsay bared her eyeteeth in what Ginny most certainly considered a snarl.

"Fine." The woman shrugged again, not minding being out from behind the counter for a change. "The charity we give it to is an orphanage. It's where we got our little Mildred."

Ginny's ears perked up. "This place is near here?"

"Maybe two miles. Every other day my husband carts over what we don't sell."

Ginny stepped away from the table. "Lindsay—"

"Wait," Lindsay interrupted. "There's more. But for God's sake, I'll tell you so I don't explode. Ester tells me this orphanage is in more need than ever after taking in a few children… sudden like."

Ginny held her breath, her entire being riveted on Lindsay's every word.

"Seems there was a terrible fire in Manhattan."

The redhead's jaw sagged. "That has to be them!" she crowed, grabbing a startled Ester and hugging her for all she was worth. "Thank you."

"Umm…" Ester blinked and pried herself loose from Ginny's embrace, slowly backing toward the counter and away from the crazy person. "No problem."

"Can you tell us the address of the orphanage?" Ginny was already buttoning her coat.

Ester shook her head. "Never was good with addresses. But if you come back tomorrow just after sunrise, you can go with my husband."

"I don't want to wait." Ginny grabbed Lindsay's hand and began tugging her toward the door. "Can you just tell us what street? Which way to go?"

"Won't do you any good, honey," Ester told her. "The manager, a sweetheart of a man who I understand was once an orphan himself, closes the place up tighter than a drum once the sun goes down. Won't even answer the door." She nodded approvingly. "That's one way to keep some of the ruffians in line. A strict curfew and locked doors. The two biddies that help him most days go home at night. How else are a bachelor, washerwoman, and cook to handle all those children?"

Ginny's entire body slumped, and Lindsay couldn't help but curl her arm around those sagging shoulders. "Tomorrow. We'll go tomorrow. If they're there now, they'll still be there then."

Ginny took several calming breaths, desperately trying to grab hold of her scattered emotions, which were making her head spin and tempting her to do something crazy like run outside and stop every person in the street until someone told her exactly where the orphanage was. "Right. I can be patient." She looked a little lost. "I hope."

"Besides," Lindsay's face took on a grim expression as she glanced back out the window. It was raining ice. "We don't want to be wandering the streets in this weather." She leaned close to Ginny's ear and whispered, "You'll need to be rested for them. Tomorrow will be soon enough." *Don't get your hopes up too high, Ginny.*

Ginny sighed and straightened, deciding it couldn't hurt to hope for the best and ignore the worst. That had never worked before in her life, but somehow, she always managed to dredge up the optimism to try just one more time.

"Thank you for thinking about them. You're right. I need to rest. They'll run me ragged for the rest of my life." Relief flooded her as she let the very real possibility of being reunited with her siblings roll around in her mind. She gently patted Lindsay's lower back, and then strode over to the counter. "Ester," she began hopefully, "how would you feel about a couple of boarders here in the store for the night?" She jerked her thumb sideways and smiled. "I'm betting that my friend here wields a mean broom."

"I ca-ca-can't believe sh-she said no," Ginny complained again, ducking her head to avoid the sting of the sleet. "Not ju-just no. But *hell* no." Her teeth were chattering so hard that she was getting a headache, and she'd already accidentally bitten her tongue. Twice. Lamplight reflected off the thin layer of ice covering her coat and hair, and every breath released a haze of fog that was instantly swept away by the wind. She could smell the water again and knew they'd somehow looped around toward the river during their trek.

Lindsay snorted. Her cheeks were bright red, and frosty air made her eyes feel dry and scratchy. "Would you let two strangers sleep in your shop?"

Ginny's eyebrows drew together. "Yes."

"Figures," Lindsay mumbled.

"What was that?" Ginny stuffed her hands deeper into her pockets as they turned a corner and found themselves on the edge of a railroad yard. *No*, her mind corrected, *a railroad graveyard.*

"Never mind. C'mon, we can sleep here."

"Where is 'here'?" Ginny squinted through the rain. Torn up tracks were piled haphazardly and crisscrossed the area, which was surrounded by a tall wire fence. Engine parts and oiled wooden planks dotted the snow-covered ground, and rusted steel boxcars, their doors either missing altogether or partially opened, lay all around. If she looked hard, Ginny thought she could see smoke rising from the openings of several of the metal boxes. She shivered.

Ginny eyed the obstacle before them. "The fence—?" She hadn't even finished her thought when Lindsay grabbed hold of the wire mesh and gave it a strong pull, exposing an unseen slit in the fencing.

"I'll hold this for you." Lindsay shook her head to clear the sleet from her eyes. She was soaked to the bone, and the bandages that held the splint on her fingers were a sodden mess.

"Okay. Thanks." Ginny ducked down and grunted a little as she shimmied through the opening. "I think I can make—Uh oh." Her coat caught on a sharp barb of wire, and she awkwardly tried to free herself, her brain sending urgent messages to fingers that were far too cold to respond quickly. With a sharp jerk, she ripped a small tear in her coat. "Crap."

Lindsay stepped through behind Ginny, tucking under her arm the sack containing Bertha's dress, the clothes that Lindsay had stolen from the hospital for Ginny, and a few things they'd purchased after leaving the delicatessen. She allowed the fence to fall back into place with a clank, smothering a groan at the pain the twisting had caused her ribs.

Ginny pushed soaking bangs off her forehead and waited for Lindsay's next move.

"All right." Lindsay moved directly in front of Ginny and looked her squarely in the eye. "You need to listen to me and do what I say."

A single red eyebrow inched upward, but Ginny's survival instinct kicked in, and she simply nodded. *Anything to be out of the weather. At least I hope we're getting out of the weather.*

"Don't look at anyone as you walk. Keep facing straight ahead. If anyone comes near you, you run. And come right out at this spot. You're smaller than most men here and should be able to get through the fence quickly."

"Is that all?"

"No. If someone speaks to you, ignore them and keep walking. Ignore everybody."

"Even—?"

"Shit! For Christ's sake, Ginny! Please," Lindsay exclaimed, then looked around, hoping nobody had heard. "I'll explain in a minute, but I'm freezing to death now, and I don't have the energy to argue."

"Don't get peevish and swear at me. And I wasn't going to argue," Ginny answered grumpily. "I was going to ask if I should even ignore *you.*"

"Oh." Lindsay brought her shaking fingers to her mouth and blew warm air on them. She bounced on her toes in an effort to send blood to her frigid limbs. "Sorry." Her face was properly contrite, and then her lips curled into a wry smile. "Don't ignore me. I hate to be ignored."

Ginny's smile was playfully sarcastic. "I noticed." She glanced around again, this time worriedly. These were the kinds of places her mother had always told her to walk quickly past, places where strangers lurked in the shadows. But, she admitted, it wasn't nearly as bad as it would be if she were alone. She had faith that Lindsay would be able to handle, and help her handle, anything that came up. Ginny was so caught up in her own thoughts that she started when Lindsay reached out and grabbed her hand.

"Remember what I said."

Ginny nodded slowly and whispered, "All right."

They moved quickly, avoiding the broken bottles and scattered crates that were strewn over pieces of track and broken railroad ties. The sleet suddenly changed to snow, and the flakes instantly stuck to their wet coats and faces. About halfway across the yard the shouting started; disembodied voices came from different boxcars and could be clearly heard above the roaring wind.

"Ooo! Hey, girly, that's a pretty dress. Come over here by me, and keep me warm. It's warm in my box. Yours too, I'll bet."

Raucous laughter.

"Is that you, String Bean?"

Ginny couldn't help it, even though Lindsay's stride hadn't as much as slowed; she turned her head toward the voice.

"Must be. String Bean? I heard you was dead. You got more lives than a damn alley cat! Those biting rats improve your looks any?"

Her looks? What's that supposed to mean? Ginny felt the grip on her hand tighten and knew it was a signal to keep moving, but it did nothing to quell the surge of rage welling up within her, threatening to boil over. With effort, she continued to walk. *They think that's funny? That she was hurt.* "Assholes," she seethed, too angry to be shocked by her own choice of words.

"C'mon, String Bean. I'm sure the rats didn't eat… much. You can come over here and share my fire."

The redhead came to an abrupt stop and whirled around toward one of the boxcars, eyes blazing.

"Ginny." It was a low, almost sub-vocal warning.

Ginny bit her tongue as she waged an internal war over whether or not to march over to that boxcar and rip off somebody's head. But she allowed Lindsay to retake her trembling hand. They moved faster now, the snow wasn't as deep in this part of the yard.

"Here." Lindsay pointed toward a boxcar whose sliding door was partially open.

A few more paces, and Ginny was about to step inside.

"Wait," Lindsay insisted, her voice a harsh whisper. "Lemme check it out first. Someone might be inside."

"Why do you need to check it out?" Ginny asked warily, instinctively moving closer to Lindsay.

"Because someone might be inside," she repeated slowly, as though talking to a dull child. *Didn't I already explain this?* "You should wait here."

"So it might be dangerous then? Someplace you shouldn't go alone?"

Lindsay recognized that challenging expression on Ginny's face, and she jumped up into the boxcar before she had to deal with an argument.

"Lindsay!" she rasped.

Are all women this much trouble? Lindsay's feet thudded against the dirty metal floor, sending a quiet echo through the mostly-hollow structure. She hadn't meant to do that, and before she could lament her error, she was wobbling precariously on the edge of the car. But a second later she'd found her footing and disappeared into the inky darkness.

Ginny narrowed her eyes. They would talk about what Lindsay had done later. She looked over her shoulder, then back into the boxcar. The railway yard had gone eerily quiet except for the pinging of sleet against steel and the pitiful moan of the wind. She waited several seconds, hoping to detect any sound from inside the car.

There was none.

Ginny swallowed and pulled aside a strand of wet hair that was plastered to her cheek. "Lindsay?" she whispered.

Nothing.

Ginny dropped to her knees and reached blindly into an ice-encrusted pile of snow, fishing for anything she could use as a weapon. She found a piece of splintered wood and pulled it from the snow as she rose to her feet and carefully lifted one foot into the boxcar. The wood was icy, and it stung sensitive fingertips as she wrapped her hand tightly around it and climbed inside. She let out a tiny grunt as she pushed herself to her feet. "Lindsay?" she repeated, her eyes widening as she peered into the blackness.

"What?" Lindsay answered in a normal tone, suddenly appearing less than a foot in front of Ginny's shocked eyes.

Ginny gasped. She took a quick step backward and began to slip on the ice. The piece of wood went flying out of her hand and hit Lindsay squarely in the chest. Ginny's arms flailed wildly, and she tried desperately to keep from falling out of the boxcar.

Lindsay's hand shot out, and long fingers wound themselves around Ginny's lapel. "Jesus Christ!" She leaned backward and, adrenaline pumping, yanked Ginny so hard that she sent the woman flying across the boxcar. "I thought I asked you to wait?"

Their voices seemed unnaturally loud after all the whispering.

"What was I supposed to do?" Ginny marched back to Lindsay, until they were nose to nose. "I waited and called your name, but *you* didn't answer."

"I was only gone for ten seconds!"

"Ten seconds where you could have answered!"

Lindsay threw her hands in the air. "Ugh!"

"I was worried." Ginny fought unsuccessfully to keep her frustration from leaking into her voice. "Why did you take so long, anyway?"

Lindsay tiredly tossed down their sack. *Being friends is hard!*

"Sometimes people are sleeping in these cars, Ginny. And if you wake them up unexpectedly, they might just stab you between the eyes. Somehow I thought you might not find an Arkansas toothpick in the brain very appealing. I know I don't."

Ginny blinked.

"I was *trying* to be quiet."

"Oh." Ginny suddenly felt incredibly foolish. She winced. "I thought… What if you'd needed me?"

Ginny's eyes begged Lindsay to understand, and to her surprise, she did. Completely. Lindsay sighed and tucked her hands under her arms to keep from touching her friend again. She was doing that way too much. Surely Ginny would think she was a needy, crazy person, who couldn't keep her hands to herself. "I just didn't want you hurt," Lindsay explained with all the patience she could muster. "Not everyone's as nice as you are, Ginny. You need to be careful."

"I am careful." Ginny looked away. "Usually. But I got so worried," she muttered, knowing it sounded stupid.

"I know what I'm doing. You need to trust me."

Ginny's gaze darted up to meet Lindsay's. "I do," she insisted. "I do."

"I know you've… um… you've lost a lot. So I… I mean I understand that. Maybe I shouldn't have left you outside. I guess. Maybe." Lindsay rolled her eyes at her own inability to communicate. It wasn't usually a problem talking with Ginny. She could, Lindsay knew intuitively, really talk to her. But sometimes when Ginny was looking at her the way she was at this very moment, Lindsay thought her heart might pound out of her chest. The look was a mixture of frustration and raw affection that was both frightening and exhilarating.

Lindsay cast about for something to say that wouldn't make her sound like an idiot. "We're out of the snow," she blurted. *Oh, that was a good choice.*

Ginny's eyebrows jumped at the sudden change in subject. She hadn't really minded the silence, so long as it wasn't because Lindsay was angry. She studied the other woman's face carefully, wondering what in the world had gotten Lindsay so fidgety all of a sudden. "Exactly," Ginny agreed amiably. "No more snow."

Lindsay's head bobbed gratefully, and she let out a shuddering breath. "This will be a good place to stay the night. No wind. No cops who will try to kick us out." Her thoughts drifted back to the offer they'd had to sleep in the church in Manhattan, and a sliver of guilt pierced her heart. "But the church would have been nicer, huh?"

Ginny picked up their sack and untied the top. She pulled out both of the blankets, burying her cold face in them for a moment. "I dunno," she answered noncommittally, her voice muffled. *But you were uncomfortable there. And that was more than enough reason for me to say no.* She lifted her head and looked at Lindsay, wanting to convey that Lindsay's being comfortable mattered to her.

"This place works too. Any place is fine."

Lindsay shifted uncomfortably, knowing full well Ginny was lying.

Ginny read her friend easily. "This really is fine, Lindsay. C'mon, let's go to sleep. I can barely keep my eyes open, and dawn will come soon enough."

"Okay. But first, why don't you put on the clothes in this bag? They'll be warmer than what you're wearing, and dry, and you can change tomorrow before we leave."

The thought of undressing in this strange place and in the bitter cold wasn't exactly appealing. Just being here made Ginny feel exposed. She bit her lip. "Where will… I mean—"

"I need to—I have to take care of some business outside," Lindsay said in a rush, sensing Ginny's discomfort over having no place private to undress. "I'll be right outside and back in two minutes, all right?"

"Two minutes?"

"I promise."

Lindsay climbed back in the boxcar and was greeted by the sound of gentle snores. She carefully laid the armful of wood she'd scavenged on the floor. She smiled affectionately at her friend, who, much to Lindsay's disgust, awoke with the chickens every morning, and could fall into a deep sleep at the drop of a hat. Ginny was curled up into the fetal position, wearing the dry clothes and cocooned in their blankets, her wet coat draped over her legs. She'd found some newspapers inside the boxcar and was lying on them rather than directly on the frigid metal floor.

Lindsay arranged the smallest pieces of wood into a volcano-shaped stack just inside the opening of the boxcar. Then she reached for their bag from which she removed a new flint. She picked up a few pieces of newsprint and balled them up, tucking them into the base of the kindling. Her gaze drifted to her hand, and in a fit of temper she tore off the bandage that was wrapped around broken fingers. Lindsay examined the braced digits with disgust. She had been careless when it came to Albert and those French bastard cousins. She couldn't let that happen again. Not now that Ginny was depending on her.

A few failed tries, and then Lindsay was able to create a spark. The wood wasn't as dry as she'd have liked, but eventually it did burn, producing a fair amount of warmth. The fire was close enough to the door that most of the smoke was drawn outside. She tossed her bandage into the flickering flames, wondering if she should wake Ginny and have her move closer to the warmth.

Lindsay didn't have to wonder for long.

Ginny was in that confusing, murky space between consciousness and dreaming. She could feel the scratchy wool of her blanket against her chilled cheek, hear every gust of wind, but there was a vague detachment from the sensations, as though her brain knew she was experiencing them, but her body couldn't dredge up the energy it took to care.

She pulled the blanket more tightly around herself as her thoughts drifted from the wintry scene at the railway yard to a six-story tenement on Orchard Street. Home. The sensations here seemed more real, tangible. And the smell of old wood and dust washed over her senses, bringing with it the security of family. She climbed into bed next to her sister, her heart bursting with love. There was the faintest hint of smoke in the air, tickling an unhappy memory that was just out of reach, and something about that was vaguely unsettling, but she was so safe and warm, that her mind quickly decided it just didn't matter.

Lindsay poked at the fire and added a few heavier sticks to the flames. They were even wetter than the kindling had been, and they began to hiss and spit, sending a light cloud of smoke into the boxcar as Lindsay fanned them.

Ginny wrinkled her nose at the smell. *My feet are cold. But how can I be cold if there is…?* She rolled over in bed and shook Alice's shoulder. Alice's body flopped toward Ginny, her face shriveled and burned. Too horrified to move, her terror grew when her sister's damaged face dissolved, then reshaped itself into Lindsay's. Ginny's eyes flew open, and a bloodcurdling scream was torn from her throat. "Fire!"

Lindsay nearly jumped out of her skin, and she flew to her feet at the same moment Ginny did.

Ginny tore the blanket from her body and scrambled to the rear of the boxcar on wobbly legs. Her back slammed against the steel so hard that she dislodged several chunks of snow from the roof and they fell heavily to the ground near the door. "Fire," she cried again, her eyes flicking around wildly as her mind frantically tried to reconcile what she was seeing now with her dream and the gut-churning vision of her sister. "Alice? Mama!"

"Ginny, calm down." Lindsay bolted to the back of the car and grabbed hold of Ginny, but the other woman violently wrenched free from her grasp. They both stumbled a few steps, and Lindsay cried out as the splint snapped off her fingers and clattered to the floor.

"Let. Me. Go!" Ginny backed away from Lindsay as though she was terrified of her, but she had no place to go. Their eyes locked and held, and Ginny had a blinding burst of recognition that made no sense. What was her friend doing in her family's apartment? She was burned, but— "There's a fire, can't you see that?"

Ginny's eyes were wild and confused, and even in the dim light, Lindsay could see the furious pounding of Ginny's pulse against her pale throat. Fogged breath escaped her nose and mouth with every harsh pant.

"Ginny, you're dreaming. You—"

"We have to leave!" Ginny darted forward and grabbed Lindsay in a movement so frantic it tore the tattered remains of the bandages from her hands.

"We need to run!"

Lindsay's heart twisted in her chest as the magnitude of her error hit home. *Stupid. The fire. I should have told her.* She swallowed hard to keep from bursting into tears herself. "Ginny," she spoke softly, stroking her friend's cheeks, but quickly realized that wouldn't work.

"No. No! No!" The younger woman was beside herself. Tears welled in beseeching eyes. "You don't understand! You have to get out!"

Lindsay grabbed Ginny by the shoulders and shook her hard. "Ginny! Wake up. Wake up!"

Ginny's entire body jerked as though she'd been slapped. She was so close to throwing up that she wasn't sure she could speak, and she looked around again, this time seeing the dark interior of the of the boxcar, and the small, obviously well-planned fire at its entrance. Her chest heaved, and she brought shaking hands to her face. "Lindsay?" she rasped brokenly.

Lindsay closed her eyes and willed her thumping heart to slow. She felt lightheaded. "Yes." *Thank you.* "It's me." With the smallest of tugs, Ginny's body fell forward, and Lindsay wound her arms around her, feeling Ginny's legs give way.

"Lindsay." Ginny buried her face against Lindsay's neck, greedily absorbing the warmth and scent of her friend's skin, as though it were more vital than the air she breathed. And for that brief moment in time, it was. She began to sob.

"Shhh… you're safe now." Lindsay turned her body so that Ginny's back would be to the flames. "There's no fire, at least not one that will hurt you." *I'd die first.* She unconsciously tightened her hold on Ginny until a soft gasp broke her spell. Lindsay instantly relaxed her arms. "Did… did I hurt you?"

Ginny sniffed raggedly. "No. Feels good," she murmured.

"Okay, then. Let's get comfortable." Lindsay eased them both down to the floor, her back sliding against the cold wall. "I should have told you I was going to build a fire. I don't know what I was thinking. I just assumed—ugh. I am *so* sorry."

"Am I going insane?" Ginny wondered out loud, her voice the barest of whispers. "You're really all right?" She pressed her cheek against Lindsay's throat, feeling the strong pulse against her skin.

"Me?" Lindsay didn't know what Ginny was talking about, but decided it didn't really matter. She pressed her cheek into Ginny's soft, mussed hair, acknowledging deep inside that their friendship had gone far beyond the bounds of anything she'd ever known or understood.

Their embrace was sweet and warm, and in that second, the young rail-rider resolved to take this particular train to wherever it might end up. Going along for the ride, no matter how scary and new, was what she did best. "I'm just great. And you're not insane. You just woke up in a strange place, didn't know where you were or what the hell was going on, and pitched a fit." She waved her hand dismissively and wryly explained, "Happens to me all the time."

A tiny chuckle was forced from Ginny's throat. She pulled back just far enough to see Lindsay's face and gave her a trembling smile as gentle fingers traced her cheek for a split second before tucking a stray lock of red hair behind her ear.

Ginny's glistening blue eyes and tear-stained cheeks tore her friend's heart in two.

On a sudden swell of courage, Ginny begged, "Don't leave me. Please."

Lindsay's mouth worked in vain as she struggled to speak around the lump in her throat. *Leave you?* "I…" a painful swallow. "I won't leave you, Ginny. I swear."

Ginny nodded and closed her eyes as she snuggled closer. Her lips grazed Lindsay's ear, and she whispered through her tears, "I know it's not forever, Lindsay. But… please just don't let go of me tonight. I need—"

"Never." Lindsay adjusted her arms around Ginny, mentally daring anyone or anything to deny them this comfort. Finally, Ginny's breathing evened out as her breaths slowed and lengthened. Lindsay felt the tightly coiled body in her arms relax and go limp. She reached out with one leg and was able to inch Ginny's blanket over to them from the boxcar floor.

The aftermath of the excitement had left her with the chills, and she awkwardly wrapped the blanket over them both, grateful for its added warmth. There would be no sleep for her tonight, however.

The noise they'd made had surely alerted everyone in the yard that there were two women in this boxcar, and although she'd stayed in this very car several times and in places far worse, it was different now that she had someone who depended on her. Someone good, who mattered, and didn't belong in a place like this; someone who listened to her, and laughed with her, and whose smile warmed her from the inside out.

Lindsay studied the small, dancing flames of the fire with unseeing eyes. She was still watching them intently when the last of the embers burnt out and the first rays of the sun began to creep into the boxcar, painting the floor. In those moments of transition between night and day, Lindsay accepted something about herself that was both thrilling and terrifying at the same time. She didn't want to let go of Virginia Chisholm—ever.

Her wistful sigh broke the silence. Nothing, it seemed to Lindsay, was ever simple. "What am I going to do now?" she murmured into the frosty dawn air, pressing her cheek against soft hair and allowing her eyes to flutter closed. *And when you find those kids, how the hell am I going to tell you goodbye?*

Chapter Six

Lindsay roused Ginny with a gentle shake of her arms, dropping her lips to a chilled ear to murmur quietly. She knew the young redhead would want to get back to the bakery as soon as possible so that they could leave for the orphanage, despite the fact that they'd both be starting out exhausted. It was the first time since they'd met that Lindsay had awakened before her friend. It felt odd; their normal routine was already as comfortable as well-worn shoes.

Ginny's body was still plastered to Lindsay when she heard a low hum in her ear, and she awakened reluctantly from a heavy slumber. She pulled away slowly, not wanting to leave the warm safe haven of those slim arms. Bleary eyes tried to focus on the face so close to hers, and she yawned as she got her bearings.

For both women, there was a split second of nervousness when the intimacy of the position of their bodies flashed through them. They froze, and a current of emotion moved freely between two sets of slightly bloodshot eyes. But it passed quickly, and Ginny's face wrinkled into a heartfelt, if tired, grin. "Mornin', Spinach Leaf," she whispered softly, her voice rough with sleep.

Lindsay smiled back, the gentle teasing welcome after the trauma of the night before. "One of these days, you'll run out of vegetables," she warned, opening her arms so Ginny could stand and stretch. She rolled her shoulders, then neck, wincing at their stiffness.

Ginny only snorted. "Too bad for you I happen to love vegetables. They didn't call where we lived Orchard Street for nothing. Brrr." She wrapped her arms around herself, already missing Lindsay's warmth. An object on the floor caught her eye and she moved a few paces, bending to retrieve the splint that had been torn from Lindsay's fingers the night before. She shot a questioning glance at the other woman, who merely shrugged one shoulder as she stuffed their blankets into the sack.

"I'm fine," Lindsay insisted. "I hardly felt a thing." She wiggled her fingers as evidence, her voice cracking slightly at the unexpected twinge of pain the action caused.

A single red eyebrow lifted and stayed.

Shit.

Ginny grumbled something to herself that her friend couldn't make out. If the deep crease in her normally smooth forehead was any indication, Ginny was *not* happy.

"I need to fix it," she told Lindsay in no uncertain terms.

Lindsay sighed as she fought with herself. Though she wholeheartedly enjoyed it when Ginny paid almost any kind of attention to her, which was often, at that moment she was stiff, hungry, and wishing for an outhouse. In short, just not in the mood to be fussed over. "No, you don't. The splint was bothering me anyway." Lindsay made a face. "I burned that nasty bandage."

It wasn't a complete lie. Her fingers were sore, but the bones had knitted, and as long as she was careful, she really didn't think she needed the splint. When Ginny remained almost eerily quiet, she added, "We should get going. Ester said to be there right after dawn, and it's at least a fifteen minute walk from here."

Ginny's gaze strayed out of the boxcar where it stayed for several heartbeats before returning to Lindsay, where it settled uneasily. "I *need* to fix it, Lindsay," she repeated softly, but this time there was a hint of pleading to her voice that Lindsay was powerless to ignore.

Lindsay blew out a frustrated breath, but she wasn't really mad. "Fine." She lifted her hand for Ginny's inspection.

Ginny half smiled and set to work quickly, using a strip of cloth torn from the hem of Bertha's dress, which they'd saved for emergencies. Head bent as she concentrated on her task, Ginny murmured casually that without the splints Lindsay's strong, beautiful fingers might not heal properly. The words fell from her lips as though they were the most natural thing in the world. She was totally unaware of the profound effect they had on Lindsay.

Impulsively, Ginny lifted Lindsay's hand and gently pressed her lips to the long fingers. She swallowed the apology for last night that was on the tip of her tongue, and did her best to ignore Lindsay's surprised gasp at the kiss.

For her part, the stupefied brunette couldn't have been rendered any dumber if she'd been kicked in the head by a mule. An incredulous stare on her face, she watched Ginny stand. *My first kiss*, her mind crowed in a state of shocked delight.

Ginny gave Lindsay's leg a gentle pat, privately thrilling at the slightly dreamy look on Lindsay's face. "All done." She licked her lips, and

Lindsay noticed that she was squirming a little. "Now I need to, um…"

Lindsay chuckled. She'd learned what "um" meant their first day out of the Hospital. "So? Go."

Ginny frowned and spoke between clenched teeth. "So, those men will see me."

"See you?"

"It *is* daylight out." The frown deepened.

Lindsay burst out laughing, showing a flash of the teenager behind the seasoned rail-rider. In fact, she was so happy she felt like singing. *Except* that she couldn't carry a tune. *Hell, I might just do it anyway. Too bad I don't know any songs.* Unperturbed, she said, "Those bums are still sleeping." Gracefully, she pushed herself to her feet then stumbled to the entrance of the boxcar, groaning as the blood began flowing into the leg that had been asleep for most of the night. "Gambling or the cops would be the only things to rouse them at this hour."

Ginny looked a little confused. It was morning, wasn't it? She'd usually headed out well before dawn to begin her trek to work.

"It's one of the few benefits of the lifestyle," Lindsay explained patiently, smirking at Ginny's bewildered look. "We don't live by the clock." She cocked her head to the side. "More like a railroad schedule, I guess. But the when and where we go is still up to us."

"You're sure?"

"About which part?" Lindsay teased.

"Lindsay!" Ginny was shifting from one foot to the other. She looked longingly to the very back of the boxcar, and Lindsay's eyes widened in reaction.

"Oh, no you don't!" A single finger pointed outside. "Out you go."

Needing no further encouragement, Ginny snatched up a piece of old newsprint from the boxcar floor and fairly flew out of the door. Her feet crunched loudly on the snow as affectionate brown eyes followed her exit, then glanced down at tingling fingers in awe.

Ester let the women in through the back door of the bakery, which wasn't open to the public for another ten minutes. Ginny had changed back into her dress in a vain attempt to look as respectable as possible at the orphanage. Lindsay had their sack slung over her shoulder and had, thankfully, been spared the request of changing out of her male attire.

Apparently, Ginny considered Lindsay dressing like a man to be preferable to her dressing like a whore.

Don't think about what you'll do after you find Jane and the boys. Wait until you see them or you'll drive yourself crazy until then, Ginny told herself, the nervousness over the possibility of being reunited with her siblings making her mouth dry.

Both young women moaned throatily as they inhaled the scent of fresh baked bread, strong coffee, and cinnamon when the back door opened. "Lord, have mercy. I think I'm gonna pass out," Ginny muttered.

"Not before me," Lindsay murmured back, her eyes sliding closed in pleasure.

"C'mon in." Ester's salt and pepper hair was covered with a fine layer of bread flour, and her forehead and slightly hairy upper lip glistened with perspiration, which attracted even more flour. "My husband should be here any minute. The old fool is already ten minutes late. These are what we give to the children," she said proudly, pointing a finger that had dough jammed beneath the fingernail toward three large, cloth sacks. The bags bulged with rolls, pastries, and loaves of bread and sat just inside the back door, waiting for delivery.

Lindsay's stomach growled loudly, and her skilled fingers itched to snitch something for breakfast. *She* was an orphan wasn't she? Would it be so wrong to steal a roll or three? *God*, she anguished mentally. *Not stealing is bullshit! How does Ginny stand it?* Lindsay glanced up and caught Ginny eyeing the bags wistfully. She suddenly felt a little better about her moment of weakness when her friend sighed piteously. It was an acknowledgment of the abject temptation before them.

Ester left them waiting in the back room while she shuffled behind the counter to put the finishing touches on her display of sweet rolls.

A loud "meow" drew the young women's attention to the floor, where an enormous, orange-and-white tabby cat stood up from her spot on a blanket in the corner and arched her back, stretching languidly. When she was finished, she plopped back down as though the exertion of standing for those few seconds had been too much for her.

"Aww," Ginny cooed, recalling her long-dead childhood pet who, except for the size, was very much like this cat. "I wish I could have her."

Lindsay stuffed her hands in her pockets, more than a little surprised.

Rocking back on her heels, she wrinkled her nose. "Really? They're not nearly as tasty as they look."

Ginny's head swung around, and her mouth dropped open. "What?"

"I know. It's hard to believe, isn't it? They look like they'd be all juicy and tender. But they're actually stringy and greasy."

"W-wh-what's wrong with you?" Ginny sputtered, placing herself between Lindsay and the fat cat. "I don't want to eat her!"

"Oh." Lindsay smiled brightly, glad she'd convinced her. "Good choice. They're really nasty." She narrowed her eyes at some far tastier prey, and a low growl erupted from the back of her throat. "How about we go for those rolls instead?" She took a step closer to the bags.

Just then Ester walked into the storeroom, brushing the excess flour off her apron. Impatiently, her gaze flicked around the small room. "He's not here yet?" She threw her hands in the air. "I knew that old mule would be nothing but trouble!"

"Mule?" Ginny inquired curiously, wondering whether Ester was referring to her husband or an animal.

"We bought a new one last week and my husband can't control the nag. He's probably halfway to Buffalo right now with the money for the cash register." Ester grabbed her coat from a hook on the back door. "I have to find that fool man." She wrung her hands nervously. "We're opening in five minutes."

Ester was about to shoo Ginny and Lindsay outside, when Ginny piped up, "We'll wait here and tell the customers you'll be right back." She gave Ester her best pleading look. "We wait exceptionally well."

Ester shook her head "no" and Ginny's heart sank. It was freezing out this morning. "I'm sorry but—"

"Or we could stand out front and tell them sewer rats and cockroaches ate all your meat, and that's the reason the store is closed. Because you're out buying more," Lindsay supplied helpfully, lifting a sassy, single eyebrow and pinning Ester with a determined look.

Ginny stifled a gasp with her hand. Ester didn't.

Lindsay hitched her hands onto narrow hips, seeing no reason to mess around with this woman. The bad weather had passed for the moment, and they could always find the orphanage on their own. "Well? Are we staying, or are you booting us out into the snow?"

Ester debated for a moment, then exhaled explosively. "Fine. You," this directed solely at Ginny, "look like the honest sort." Her eyes drifted back to Lindsay. "You. Don't touch anything. Everything is counted. Everything."

Lindsay rolled her eyes and walked out of the storeroom into the deli, intending to get a cup of coffee. "Can't count that, can you, ya skinflint old biddy," she grumbled, her arms crossed grumpily over her chest.

Ginny smiled weakly, not approving of Lindsay's methods, but not stupid enough to want to be out in the cold a second longer than she had to be. Besides, Ester looked too preoccupied with what had happened to her husband and their money to be too upset.

"I'll be back as soon as I can," the middle-aged woman said as she bustled out the back door.

"Okay. Goodb—" The slamming door abruptly cut Ginny off. "That was rude." But there was no one in the storeroom to hear her. Taking off her coat and gently rubbing together hands that were still achy from the cold, she padded back to the front of the store.

Lindsay was sitting at the table, eyes closed, coat and hat off, and feet propped up as she sipped a steaming cup of coffee. She ran her fingers through her tousled hair and didn't bother to open her eyes when she heard Ginny's soft footsteps. "Don't say it," Lindsay warned as she took another drink. "I'm not sorry for taking the coffee. That grumpy old bi—"

"Lindsay?"

"What does she mean, *you* look like the honest sort?" Lindsay ranted. "What about me? It's not like she even knows me."

"Lindsay?"

"What?" Lindsay answered a little defensively.

"Where are the cups?"

"Oh." There was a pause then Lindsay smiled. Okay, so her friend was honest, but not a saint. She could live with that. "Behind that counter next to the pickled eggs."

Ginny sighed. "Great. Because I feel like a train ran over me. Don't get me wrong," she said innocently, her back to Lindsay as she poured herself a cup, "sleeping plastered to your body is far from a chore, but a bed would be a lot more comfortable."

An image of her and Ginny tangled together in a big soft bed, completely naked, flashed through Lindsay's mind, causing a scarlet blush to erupt on her neck and face, and her heart to skip a beat. Her feet slipped off the tabletop and landed onto the floor with a solid thud. *God!* She blinked several times quickly, trying to rid her mind of the shocking thought.

Ginny turned, a small white cup cradled in both hands. Her eyes lifted, and she blinked at the startled look on Lindsay's face. "Wh—Lindsay?" She rushed across the room, setting her mug down hastily as she cupped Lindsay's flushed cheeks. "Are you all right?" She searched her face worriedly. "You didn't scald yourself, did you?"

Lindsay shook her head no and hastily stood up, moving to the door. She already felt like a pervert, and now she felt like a guilty pervert for making Ginny worry. "No," she croaked as she mentally commanded her hands to stop shaking. "I'm fine. Look, a customer."

Ginny frowned, not ready to let the matter drop, but Lindsay unlocked the front door and let the man in, effectively ending their conversation.

A blast of cold air filled the room, and the bell sounded as the door opened.

"Sorry, mac," Lindsay told the man as he walked through the door. "We don't have any money for change, so you'll have to come back later."

The man's dark eyebrows pulled together, and he dug in his pocket, pulling out several coins. "Don't need change." He held them up for Lindsay to inspect.

"I buy the same thing everyday."

Lindsay shrugged and sat back down, studiously avoiding Ginny's inquiring gaze. "Take what you want then, and leave the money on the counter." She put her feet back up.

"Lindsay," Ginny scolded. "We can't do that. Ester said—"

Brown eyes rolled. "Fine. You're out of luck, mister. Get out, we're closed."

Ginny's eyes widened. "Lindsay!" What was wrong with her?

"Hey," he complained. "I have exact change, and I'm hungry." He thrust out his bearded chin. "Who are you two," he sucked in his stomach and sniffed haughtily, "to tell me what I can or can't do? I'm one of Ester's best customers." The man's gray gaze flicked around the room as he searched for the proprietress. Several women hustled through the front door, holding their hats on their heads and complaining about the wind and traffic. They impatiently moved to the register, ready to place their orders.

"Hey!" the man said again. "I'm first in line." He moved quickly, taking his place ahead of the women, who were now squawking about his rudeness.

Half a dozen more people entered the store, and Ginny's mouth dropped open. "Bu…"

"I don't have all day," a woman from the line at the register called.

Ginny narrowed her eyes at her friend. "This is *your* fault for leaving the door unlocked. You'd better not think you can sit there and drink coffee while I work," she informed Lindsay indignantly.

"I have a special order for ten loaves of rye," a man yelled.

"Wait your turn!" was the answer from several patrons. The front doorbell rang again.

Ginny put her hands on her hips and glared at Lindsay. "Well, are you going to help me?"

Lindsay shrugged, totally unconcerned. "I'm really not good at dealing with customers of any kind."

"You are now." Ginny's voice was a growl.

Lindsay bit back a smile of surprise at Ginny's commanding tone and set down her coffee cup. "Attention, everyone!" she yelled over the din of the anxious crowd. "Anyone who doesn't have exact change, get out now."

A chorus of moans, more raucous complaints, and "Where's Ester?" met Lindsay's words.

Ginny marched over to Lindsay and grabbed hold of her ear, lifting her out of her seat with a sharp tug.

"Ouch. Ouch. Ouch." Lindsay squawked as she tried to walk with her head bent sideways. "I'm already missing a chunk of my other ear. I want all of this one!"

"That was not nice, Potato Head."

Several customers laughed as Ginny led Lindsay behind the counter by the ear.

Frowning, Lindsay slapped away Ginny's hand. "What the hell?"

The younger woman turned her back to the customers and faced an outraged Lindsay. "Are you going to be nice now?" She gave her a ghost of a wink, and the tip of a pink tongue poked out between her lips, letting her companion know there was no malice in her actions.

"Why you… you… Ugh." Lindsay felt her anger melt away. For a split second she was frustrated, but she knew it was no use. She sighed. "Do I have a choice?"

Ginny bit her bottom lip and didn't answer, looking at Lindsay from beneath thick lashes.

Lindsay shook her head and chuckled softly, bumping hips with her companion as she moved alongside her.

"Ready to be helpful?"

"Absolutely." Lindsay's answer was delivered with such sincerity and innocence that Ginny's mouth shaped a tiny O.

Lindsay's smile turned devilish. "Okay." She looked out at the waiting customers. "Who was first again?" She pointed to a short fat man who was standing in the middle of the line. "You, right?"

Ginny covered her eyes with her hands as the crowd exploded.

"Careful what you wish for," Lindsay murmured as she reached into the bakery display case.

The next three hours passed in a frantic blur, with a long line of noisy customers packing the small bakery.

"God, I hate New Yorkers," Lindsay grumbled as she locked the door and turned the sign to "Closed." "I don't care if they will want lunch soon; they can go somewhere else."

"I'm a New Yorker," Ginny protested as she settled heavily into a booth. Lindsay snorted. "You don't count. You still have a soul."

Ginny laughed tiredly. "Where in the world is Ester?"

"Probably went and killed herself." Lindsay began rooting around behind the counter. "Can you believe those customers?" Her voice turned whiney in imitation. "I want my bread. I want my bagel."

Ginny's voice deepened, and she affected her best German accent. "Vat do you meeeeean der is no rye bread, girlie?"

"I almost hit that man."

"Why do you think I stepped between you?"

Lindsay emerged from behind the counter with two plates loaded with rolls and slices of seasoned meat. The handles of two coffee cups were carefully looped over her fingers. One of the plates was balanced atop a pot of hot coffee, and the steam billowed around the plate, casting Lindsay in a cloud. She carefully set down her booty, placing the pot between them and the cups and plates in front of them.

Ginny lifted an eyebrow at the solicitous service.

The younger woman's stomach growled as she looked from the

plates to Lindsay. "Payment to us for services rendered, wouldn't you say?" Unceremoniously, Lindsay plopped down next to Ginny and kicked out her feet. A slow smile crept across her face, and she reached into the pile and held up a sweet roll dripping with white icing.

Ginny blinked. "How did you—?"

"You, my friend, telegraph everything you think on your face."

Ginny paled slightly at that idea. Some of her recent mental wanderings that involved Lindsay had been confusing and unsettling and…

"I could practically hear your stomach growling every time you looked at one."

"Oh." Ginny's heart resumed beating. "Okay, that makes sense." Then, on a whim, she opened her mouth.

Responding to the request without thought, Lindsay fed her a bite. When the redhead closed her eyes and moaned low and deep in pure pleasure, Lindsay felt her mouth go dry. She quickly handed Ginny the roll, but the younger woman was so enthralled with the treat that she didn't notice anything but the explosion of taste on her tongue.

"Mmm. This is fantastic, Lindsay. You have to try it." Ginny picked up another of the same type of roll and held it in front of Lindsay's mouth.

Feeling a little lightheaded, Lindsay swallowed hard and leaned forward for a bite. As soon as the sweet, cinnamon flavor hit her tongue she couldn't help but groan.

This time is was Ginny who squirmed a little in her seat. She cast her eyes downward. "I—uh—toldja. Is it hot in here?" She fanned herself with one hand.

"Not really. Mmm." Lindsay licked her lips. "This is the best thing I've ever tasted."

Ginny's gaze shifted to Lindsay's lower lip, which glistened with icing. Unconsciously, she licked her own lips.

"Damn, these are good," Lindsay cooed. *I wonder how many I can fit in my pockets?*

Ginny's head snapped up at the sound of Lindsay's voice, and she let out a slightly shaky breath, wondering what in the world had gotten into her. She couldn't want to— "Uh… Did you ever dream of being trapped overnight in a candy shop as a kid, and being able to eat as much as you wanted?" she said in rush, still flustered.

Lindsay took another bite as she thoughtfully considered Ginny's question.

"Nope." She shrugged one shoulder and smiled affectionately. "But I will now."

A wide, pleased grin creased Ginny's face. "Good."

When Ester and her husband finally hurriedly unlocked the back door of the bakery sometime near noon, they found Lindsay and Ginny pressed tightly together in one of the bakery's booths, powdered sugar and icing on their faces, crumbs sprinkled liberally on their clothes, heads lolling sideways, deeply asleep.

It had been a hectic, horrible morning, and one which both young women would remember with nothing but fondness.

Ginny discreetly lifted the front of her coat away from her body and ducked her head inside to sniff. Unable to come to a firm conclusion, she repeated the process as Lindsay watched with a bemused smile.

They were on the steps of The Society for the Betterment of Children Orphanage, having just been dropped off by Ester's husband Hans, who had gone around back to make his delivery. The dilapidated state of the neighboring buildings, together with the homeless and immigrant population, clearly showed this was a poor section of town. But the snow had been neatly swept from the stairs of the orphanage, and there was a noticeable absence of newspapers, bottles, and other refuse on the sidewalk. Even the street in front of the large brownstone was relatively clear of trash and steaming piles of horse manure, which, in this high traffic area, was an excellent sign that the establishment was well cared for.

Ginny frowned.

"What's wrong? I thought for sure you'd be jumping for joy right now," Lindsay noted, ignoring the vulgar proposition made by a homeless man as he limped down the sidewalk behind them.

"I think I stink."

Lindsay laughed. "What? Don't be silly. You wangled us a bath not three days ago. And I know you brush your teeth."

"Still…" Ginny moved a step closer to her companion and lowered her voice. "I look a mess and have no job. They're never going to give me the children if they think I'm a bummer."

Lindsay's smiled dissolved when she got a good look at Ginny's face and could tell that her friend was truly upset. "You're not a drunk or a vagrant."

"They won't know that," Ginny declared. She held her arms open in invitation. "Just look at me."

Given permission, Lindsay wryly said, "If you insist," and indulged herself in a good long look. She started with shaggily trimmed red hair, windblown and highlighted with streaks of blonde. When her gaze dropped to vibrant sky-blue eyes framed with pale, thick lashes, pink cheeks and a youthful, slightly upturned nose, she couldn't hold back her smile any longer. She was enjoying this in-depth inspection.

Ginny's lips parted slightly, and Lindsay saw a flash of healthy teeth and the beginnings of a nervous grin. Next in the inspection came a slim, delicate neck whose faint scars from the fire didn't even register to Lindsay's eyes; the rest of Ginny was obscured by her woolen coat, but it wasn't hard for Lindsay to recall the womanly curves that lay beneath and the strong arms that gave such wonderful hugs. Lindsay found herself considering doing the most preposterous things just to earn one.

"Well?" Ginny swallowed nervously. She hadn't expected Lindsay to take her time like that, but now that she had, Ginny was dying to know what she thought.

Lindsay shot her a grave look and shook her head slightly. "I'm sorry."

"Wh-what?" Ginny squeaked.

"You're hideous." Lindsay held her hands in front of her eyes to shield them. "I can't believe I didn't notice before."

Ginny stomped one foot and narrowed her eyes. "I am not!"

"Of course you're not." Lindsay grabbed Ginny's arm and began tugging her up the steps. "So why'd you ask me such a stupid question?"

"Well… I mean, it wasn't—"

"Hey!" Lindsay abruptly stopped. "Are you trying to tell me I stink?" Without the slightest trace of modesty, the brunette began sniffing herself.

Blue eyes widened in alarm. "I never said that! You smell—"

"Aha! I smell. You said so yourself. I stink like those b'hoys in the gutter."

"No." Ginny laid her hand over Lindsay's. "Smelling is not stinking," she insisted. "I was going to say you smell like *you*." She thought of the men that Lindsay was talking about, and her stomach roiled. "It's nothing like *that.*"

"I smell like me? What does that mean?" Lindsay demanded, crossing her arms in front of her chest and forcing herself not to laugh, as Ginny tried desperately to reassure her. She was so easy to tease. "I smell like sweat or dirt or something? I brush my teeth too, you know. Most rail-riders just let 'em rot, but not me."

Ginny held up both hands in surrender. "I know, you do. And the smell is not like dirt… I mean, sure you sweat and all, but it's not stinky." She rubbed her forehead with one hand. "I don't know how to explain it. It's all warm and just—" *Please don't make me admit I like how you smell. That's just not something I can explain. Even to myself.*

"I stink. Pheeeewwwwww!" Lindsay crowed.

"You don't!"

"I do."

"Lindsay, you do not!" Ginny's frustration leaked into her words. "I'm the one who has to smell you. *I* would know."

"So you're saying I don't stink, and that I shouldn't worry about it?

Ginny let out a relieved breath, a little surprised that Lindsay suddenly understood. "Yes." *Thank you.* "That's just what I'm saying."

"Ginny?" Lindsay grasped Ginny by the forearms and smiled triumphantly.

"You don't stink. Don't worry about it." Before her moment of victory could be ruined, Lindsay took the final steps up to the orphanage door and rang the bell, leaving Ginny staring open-mouthed behind her.

The doorbell was answered by a man about the same height as Lindsay and Ginny, with thick blond hair and a Roman nose. He was younger than both women had expected, probably not more than thirty, and was wearing dark trousers with suspenders and a crisp white shirt with no necktie. "Come in, come in," he offered politely, stepping aside so they could pass. "I just spoke with Hans out back. He said you were looking for some children?" He suddenly stopped and smiled a little sheepishly. "Where are my manners? I'm Christian Spence." He extended his hand.

Ginny grasped it firmly. "Hello, Mr. Spence. I'm Virginia Chisholm." Both women moved inside, their eyes scanning the interior. The house was inordinately noisy, and children's voices rang out, some in laughter, others in argument. It reminded Ginny a little of the chicken slaughterhouse where she worked and the endless squawking of the birds. *James, Lewis, Jane… are you here?* She licked her lips nervously, the importance of the moment washing over her like a cold bath, leaving her shivering. *You have to be.*

The man's gray eyes turned to Lindsay, who smiled amiably and said, "And I'm Ginny's friend." Slyly she reached out and took Ginny's hand, twining their fingers together tightly and feeling the return squeeze, a thumb brushing gently over her cold knuckles. She marveled at how easy that was and how wonderful it felt. Comfort freely given and lovingly acknowledged. It was so far outside anything she'd ever experienced that she didn't know what to make of it but couldn't bring herself to fight it.

Mr. Spence cocked his head to the side, curious about the person before him, who at first appeared to be a pretty young man but, upon closer examination, was clearly a young woman, an oddly beautiful one at that. Unperturbed by Lindsay's unwillingness to offer more about herself, he pointed at their coats and gently cleared his throat.

"No, thank you," Lindsay answered for the both of them. "We'll keep them if it's all the same to you."

"All right," the man allowed, recognizing instantly the wary attitude of a person who lived by her wits. "I understand you're looking for someone. Hans couldn't tell me anything else."

"I am. Umm…" Ginny glanced at Lindsay. "I mean we are." Lindsay's eyebrows jumped.

"A few weeks ago, there was fire on 84 Orchard Street in Manhattan. A tenement—"

"Yes, yes." Mr. Spence nodded and began walking down a short hallway off the foyer.

The young women followed anxiously, stepping aside as an elderly woman with an armload of frayed white towels shuffled past them.

"It was terrible," he said needlessly. "We took in four children that night. Three siblings in fact, but I'm sorry, none with the last name Chisholm. One is a nine-year-old named Mary." He stopped in front of a door, behind which Ginny could hear the laughter of children playing.

"Yes, Mary Callahan." Ginny's voice grew animated. "I'm so glad she got out. She lived on the second floor. But my brothers' and sister's name isn't Chisholm," she told him quickly. "That's my name. We had different fathers."

"I see."

Lindsay cocked her head toward the door. "They're in here?" Mr. Spence nodded again. "Yes, but—"

Without waiting, Ginny took a deep breath, pushed open the door and stepped inside.

"Wait, Miss—"

Lindsay seized Mr. Spence's arm and held him firm. She had the urge to tackle him for even thinking of trying to stop Ginny, and her hand twitched as she forced herself to relax. "Let her go." She grabbed hold of her temper and gently cleared her throat before sheepishly mumbling, "Please."

In the middle of the floor were two little boys playing with several brightly painted, wooden toy soldiers. When they saw the figure enter the room, their eyes lit up. "Ginny!" they cried out together, jumping to their feet and rushing over to the shocked woman. They wrapped their arms around her legs and hugged her with all their might.

Lindsay let out a shaky breath and closed her eyes. *Yes.* She brought up a hand and scrubbed her face, still not believing that it had actually happened. They'd found the children. It was an honest to goodness, goddamned happy ending.

Her friend's back was to her, but when Lindsay opened her eyes, she could see that Ginny's shoulders were shaking and she was returning the hug. She let them stand that way for a moment or two before quietly entering the room and laying her hand on Ginny's arm. But when tear-filled eyes swung up to meet hers, Lindsay knew that something was terribly wrong.

Lindsay's gaze dropped to the boys, whose dark hair and olive complexions looked nothing like Ginny's. They were small too, and now that she took the time to really pay attention, she figured they couldn't be more than four or five years old.

The redhead straightened her back and wiped her cheeks with a trembling hand. "Leo and Nuncio." She did her best to smile. "How are you?"

"Buenos, Ginny. We good. Do you have treats?" Their faces were hopeful.

"Not today." She sniffed, and her voice dropped to a whisper. "I'm so happy you're all right. You didn't get hurt. That's wonderful." Ginny left any questions about their parents unasked. The fact that they were here was answer enough. Releasing them from her hug, she watched as the boys moved back to their spot on the floor and almost instantly became reabsorbed in their play, bashing their soldiers against one another and making all the required sound effects for a truly good war.

Her chest felt so tight she didn't think she could speak, but Ginny knew that Lindsay was patiently waiting for some sort of explanation. "They're from the fourth floor of my building and don't speak much English. Sometimes when Mama and I would make cookies," she said thickly, "I would go out onto the stoop and share them with the kids." Her breathing hitched. "And—," she stopped speaking and covered her face with her hands as she began to cry.

Oh, Ginny. "I'm so sorry," Lindsay whispered, pulling Ginny into a hug as Mr. Spence, who was standing in the doorway, shifting from one foot to the other, watched the display of comfort and affection.

"That was stupid. Stupid!" Ginny shook her head wildly, scattering her hair across her forehead. "I shouldn't have thought—"

"Shh," Lindsay soothed, her lips near Ginny's ear. "You were not stupid to hope. We'll keep looking. We won't stop. I promise."

Mr. Spence finally moved inside the room. He waved his hand, dismissing the boys; then made the mistake of laying his hand on Ginny's forearm.

Lindsay instantly stiffened, but the man didn't appear to notice.

"I'm very sorry this didn't work out as you'd hoped, Miss. Chisholm. I somehow doubted that these were the boys you were looking for, but—"

"It's all right," Ginny said, giving Lindsay a watery smile that conveyed her thanks before pulling away, her cheeks tear-stained.

Lindsay stared into Ginny's eyes and had to look away. Shining with tears, they were so beautiful and painful that her heart twisted in her chest.

A handkerchief appeared out of nowhere, and Ginny gladly took it from Mr. Spence, who looked pleased that he could finally be of some help.

Ginny wiped her face. "Don't apologize. It's my fault. I just wanted so badly to believe my brothers and sister were here. I—"

He lifted his hand to forestall her. "Enough said. Please. I have a younger brother myself."

Ginny nodded and did her best to pull herself together, drawing strength from the quiet, reassuring presence at her side. *Thank you, Lindsay.* There would, undoubtedly, be more tears later, but for now she needed to get down to business, not fall apart. "I'm looking for Lewis, James, and Jane Robson. The boys are eight-year-old twins, but don't look alike. Jane is three." Her voice cracked a little, but she pressed on. "I'm all the family they have left. Are they here, Mr. Spence?"

The man's gaze softened and to his surprise, his voice was a little rough when he spoke. "No. But for their sakes," *and yours,* "I wish they were."

Feeling a little weak in the knees, Ginny stepped toward the door. "Thank you for your time." Her mind was already spinning out possibilities of where they would look next, and what they would do.

He ran around in front of Ginny, blocking the door with his body and once again laying a hand on her arm. This time he noticed the look that Lindsay was giving him, and he swallowed reflexively. "I'm sorry they're not here, Miss Chisholm." He pushed Lindsay's blazing brown eyes out of his mind so he could focus. "But that doesn't mean I can't help you."

Lindsay's hackles relaxed, and she was glad that for once she'd controlled her temper.

"Another agency took several children from that same fire. I don't know if they're your siblings, but it's a place to start. If you two will wait in the parlor, I'll make some calls." He lifted his jaw proudly. "We had a telephone installed just last year." He held out a large hand to Ginny and wrapped his arm around hers when she took it. With a glance over his shoulder, he led Ginny into the next room with Lindsay following silently behind.

Ginny and Lindsay were barely on the sofa, and Mr. Spence out the door to make his phone call, when a gaggle of girls walked past. A step behind the rest of the crowd, a freckle-faced girl caught Ginny's eye. "Mary?"

The girl stopped and looked and tears instantly filled her eyes. She stood at the door trembling, unwilling to move.

Ginny patted Lindsay's thigh and hurried into the hall, dropping to her knees in front of the small child. Lindsay couldn't hear what they were saying, but she heard the girl's muffled sobs and the soothing murmurs she knew were coming from her friend. In her mind's eye, she could easily picture Ginny on the steps of her building, passing out cookies. She wasn't surprised at all that the neighborhood children knew and loved her. *Hell, I wouldn't have even needed the cookies,* she admitted honestly.

Nearly fifteen minutes passed before Mr. Spence entered the parlor through a side door and joined Lindsay on the sofa. He watched curiously as Ginny tried gently to pry herself away from the little girl. "Mary will be all right," he assured Lindsay. "We found an aunt who's coming in from Florida next week to claim her."

"Lucky girl."

Ginny rushed into the room, looking harried and feeling worse. "Well? Were you able to find them?" She stopped in front of Mr. Spence but didn't sit back down.

He exhaled slowly. "Not exactly."

Lindsay frowned. "What does that mean?"

"Indeed." He stared at the wall. "What does that mean? It's hard to explain, but allow me to do my best."

Lindsay was quickly growing tired of what she considered to be drawn out bullshit. Why wouldn't the man just spit out what he knew? But Ginny was still hanging on his every word, and she couldn't bring herself to disappoint her friend.

"The organization I contacted is called 'The Foundling Placement Society,'" he continued. "It's run by Jeremiah and Isabelle Ward. They're regulars in the society pages. Perhaps you've heard of them?"

Both women looked blankly at him.

"Anyway, their organization is much like this one. It is, in essence, an orphanage that runs on a combination of state and private funding. They operate by placing children on what are commonly called orphan trains. Surely you've heard of those?" he inquired. "The Children's Aid Society, a far better known, and I suspect more reputable, agency than the Wards', has made them quite famous."

The blood drained from Ginny's face. "Are you telling me my family has been shipped out West?"

"No, no, well, maybe."

"Speed up your story, Mr. Spence," Lindsay ground out.

"Of course. This isn't common knowledge, but the Foundling Placement Society is under investigation by the state for allegedly placing children in households where the sole intention is to use the children as workers and nothing more."

"Slaves?" Lindsay speculated, knowing that while New York City was overflowing with unwanted child laborers, other parts of the country were desperate for workers.

He cringed. "In extreme instances, it's not far from the truth. These children are basically sold to those who need workers."

"Jane and Lewis and James are too young to work for some company or farm," Ginny insisted, knowing in her heart that wasn't completely true. Even the chicken-stripping warehouse where she'd been employed had several workers under the age of ten. *God.*

"That's clearly true in your sister's case," Mr. Spence told her, not wanting to argue the case of her brothers. They all knew what went on in factories across the country. There was no need to hammer home the point. He pushed himself to his feet to join Ginny. "The Wards' organization persists in adopting out children of all ages, perhaps in order to gain continued financial support from private donors. Sadly, younger children generate more sympathy while those aged twelve or so are looked at as—"

"Dregs," Lindsay supplied resentfully, knowing society's attitude all too well. Christian's expression intensified as he sensed a kindred spirit in the advocacy for children's rights. "Exactly! Their bodies are nearly adult size, so people believe they should work to earn their keep."

Lindsay's lips curled in disgust, and her gaze went a little unfocused. "Only no one would pay a child an adult's wages, so they can't make a living. So then the children must be *lazy, and worthless...*"

"Lindsay," Ginny interrupted softly. There were still so many things she didn't know about this person who had come to mean so much to her, things she suspected would be hard to hear and harder for Lindsay to say. But just maybe, after all these years on her own, Lindsay needed to say them. And she'd be there to listen.

Lindsay blinked as if snapping out of a daze. "I'm sorry. Please, go on, Mr. Spence."

"That's quite all right." He looked directly at Lindsay. "I'm passionate about the subject myself."

He glanced toward Ginny then back to Lindsay. "If you ladies would call me Christian, I would consider it a personal favor."

Lindsay nodded. He was being far more gracious than most men would to a woman of her standing—or lack of it. "All right."

Sensing that Lindsay was uncomfortable with his attention on her, Christian addressed Ginny. "What I've shared with you and your friend, Miss Chisholm, are merely accusations for which I have no proof."

"But you believe them to be true," Ginny finished grimly. "Please call me Ginny."

He ducked his head. "Yes, Ginny. I believe them to be true."

"And the Robsons are at this Foundlings Placement Society?" Lindsay asked, rising to her feet as well.

He scratched his jaw. "I was told they were not. Of course, I was also told that they did not take in any children from the fire at 84 Orchard Street. And I know for a fact that this is a blatant lie." He scowled, clearly unhappy with his inability to find out more. "If you want to know for sure whether the children are there, I'm afraid you're going to have to go there and check things out for yourself." He pressed a piece of paper into Lindsay's hand. "Here's the address."

Lindsay didn't even look at it before passing it to Ginny.

"Thank you, Christian," Ginny said, unable to contain her excitement at the prospect of another solid lead. "We'll leave right away." She pulled closed the collar of her coat in anticipation of heading out into the cold. "I could just kiss you for how kind you've been."

"Really?" both Lindsay and Christian blurted out in unison.

Ginny blinked, then flushed cherry-red. "Well… I…" Her gaze darted from an open-mouthed Lindsay to the fair-haired man, who was suddenly smiling.

"Lindsay, I—"

Christian let out a laugh that shook his entire body and caused Ginny to jump. "I think it was a figure of speech." He cocked his head to the side and grinned, more than willing to be wrong. "Isn't that right, Ginny?"

Relief melted Ginny's knees. "Yes. Yes, it was."

"Of course it was," he continued, eyes twinkling. "Now that that's settled, you should also know that there is no need to rush out of here. Unless the noise in this place is already driving you mad." He raised his voice over the sound of footsteps running down the hall. "Though I wasn't exactly able to find out what you were hoping, I am rather good friends with Mr. Ward's secretary and I was able to arrange an appointment for you to speak with Mr. Ward in the morning. It was the best I could do."

Ginny and Lindsay's gazes met, and their next plan of action formed in the blink of two sets of determined eyes.

He shrugged and smiled a little. "It also happily allows me the opportunity to offer you a room for the night. Three little boys were adopted out last night, and since we're expecting four more tomorrow, we haven't filled the room yet. It's very plain, I'm afraid. But it is clean, and the bed has fresh sheets." His gaze strayed out the window. "Best of all, no snow."

"I don't know—" Lindsay hedged, not sure what Ginny would want.

"Please," he tried again. "Those are storm clouds brewing again outside. It would be my pleasure for you to enjoy lunch and supper here as well. Our cook makes a mean stew." He cocked his head to the side and smiled. "If you don't mind the absence of meat, that is."

Two little girls chased down the hall. Christian tried to grab one of them, but she just giggled louder as she evaded his hands. "Girls!"

Ginny and Lindsay had to flatten themselves against the wall to keep from being run into. Lindsay grimaced in pain but said nothing, stepping back into the center once the two tiny whirlwinds had blown by.

Christian chuckled softly and scratched the back of his neck. "Sorry about that, ladies. Saturdays are always a little crazy. C'mon now." He gave them his most charming smile. "Don't disappoint me now that I've gone to the trouble of tempting you. I'll throw in a bath all for the same low, low price of nothing at all." Though they hadn't said, he knew they'd be sleeping on the streets if not in the orphanage, and the murder of a local prostitute just the night before had him very unsettled. "Where else can you find a deal like that?"

Lindsay glanced at her friend and shrugged. "Up to you. I'll follow you anywhere, Ginny." Her lips curled into a genuine smile. "But you already knew that."

"I knew that," Ginny confirmed softly, her voice so low that it was meant for Lindsay's ears only. She took a moment to consider their options, which weren't many. True, she was anxious to head to the Wards' orphanage, but she couldn't deny that a night out of the cold would help her and Lindsay recover. It was, however, the dark circles under Lindsay's soft brown eyes that sealed their fate for the evening. Ginny was well aware that her friend hadn't slept a wink in the boxcar. That Lindsay had held her all night instead. A pang of affection for Lindsay pierced Ginny's heart.

Decision made.

"Thank you, Christian," the redhead said firmly. She bowed her head politely. "We accept your most kind offer."

Lindsay grinned, hearing a confidence in Ginny's voice that had been absent only moments before. She stuck out her hand, and the man took it automatically. "I didn't mention my name before," her grin turned slightly sheepish. "I'm String Bean."

Chapter Seven

It was well past bedtime at the orphanage, and the corner room on the second floor was quiet and dark except for the soft glow of light allowed in by the bedroom window. Faintly musty but free from dust, the room appeared to be well cared for, though it clearly hadn't been aired out since autumn. It was nearly eight p.m. when Ginny leaned back on the bed on her elbows and groaned out her delight, purposefully tearing her eyes away from Lindsay's naked legs. *Stop looking at her like that. She's your friend. It's not proper to care what a girl looks like. I think. But I can't help myself. I do care!* "Mmm. This bed is sooo soft. It feels great, Pumpkin Patch."

Lindsay snorted. "From all that moaning and carrying on over there, I can just imagine that it does. And I think a pumpkin is a fruit, not a vegetable."

Ginny shrugged good-naturedly, then burrowed a little deeper into the mattress, lying flat on her back. "You're just jealous because I'm all comfortable here and you're standing over there on the cold floor." She fought the urge to remind her dear friend that the doctor had told her she'd be more susceptible to illness now that she had no spleen. Ginny sighed inwardly, reluctantly acknowledging that it wasn't her place to fuss over Lindsay, once the woman was capable of taking care of herself. Her instincts, however, were screaming otherwise.

"True," Lindsay murmured honestly from across the small room. Her back to Ginny, she gazed out into the night's sky, absently finger-combing her squeaky-clean wet hair with one hand. "It's really coming down out there." She cleared a patch on the frosted glass with her fingertips.

Both women were dressed in borrowed, rough-hewn cotton nightshirts that reached to mid-thigh, gray woolen socks, and nothing else. Christian had kindly seen to having their clothes laundered that afternoon. Much to Ginny and Lindsay's relief, he assured them that his laundress had the tightest clothes wringer in the city and their garments would be dry by morning.

Lindsay idly watched the falling snow. Not a soul was traveling on the road below the window. The normally deep wagon wheel ruts that gouged the streets had been smoothed over by a layer of heavy powder that glistened in the lamplight. "The streets are going to be horrible tomorrow," she mumbled.

"Mmm." Ginny fluffed her pillow, scrunching up her nose as the pillowcase tickled the tender skin on the back of her neck. "I expect it will be difficult. But that won't stop us from getting where we need to go."

Lindsay turned to regard Ginny seriously. "No, it won't."

They held each other's gaze for several long seconds, and Ginny could feel her temperature rising at the intense look Lindsay was giving her. Instinctively, she recognized the darkened, heavy-lidded eyes and the slightly erratic rise and fall of Lindsay's chest as signaling poorly veiled desire. Her mouth went dry, and she felt a vague ache blossom between her legs.

Ginny burrowed beneath the blankets and sheet, yawning, her mind reeling at her body's response; and the fact that deep down inside she not only wanted to see that particular look again, she craved it. *But she's a girl!* her mind blithered. Still, her reaction was something she didn't think she could ignore. *Keep trying*, she reminded herself.

"Aren't you coming to bed?" Ginny asked, trying to scrub what she was sure was a blush off her face. Lindsay was silent for so long that she was forced to glance up from the navy blue blanket and into eyes that twinkled with affection and… fear.

Lindsay frowned a little at Ginny's attentive gaze, and in a moment of uncharacteristic insecurity and despite the fact that she was almost painfully clean, she glanced down at her clothes, then her hands, wondering if Ginny thought she was too dirty to share a bed with. Was she?

Ginny recognized the gesture for what it was, and she felt a tiny surge of anger even as her heart sank. "I wouldn't turn you away if you'd just crawled out of a pigpen, Lindsay." She smiled what she hoped was an encouraging smile. Lindsay was the most self-assured person she'd ever met. "As it is, you're as shiny as a new penny." She inclined her head invitingly. "You don't get a chance at a bed often. C'mon."

A tiny smile edged its way onto Lindsay's face, and she slowly padded across the room, passing a wooden cradle and a short three-drawer dresser as she moved. She licked her lips nervously and lifted the blanket and sheet to climb inside, moving over to the very edge of the bed. It was soft and warm, and an involuntary sigh escaped her lips.

Ginny rolled over so that she was facing her friend. The bed was narrow. *Just like the one I shared with Alice.* But her stomach had never done flip-flops when her sister crawled into bed with her. This was *very* different. Ginny felt as though her senses were heightened; every breath, every heartbeat sounded loud to her ears. Stiff cotton sheets brushed against skin tingling with sensation, and she drew in the scent of lavender soap and wool with every breath.

Lindsay eased over onto her side as well, mindful of her ribs as she mimicked Ginny's position. She fell into Ginny's vibrant eyes, which appeared almost translucent in the dim light. Lindsay swallowed convulsively. "Umm… this is nice."

Ginny nodded, feeling most of her nervousness melt away as she absorbed Lindsay's low, husked words. "It is," she softly confirmed. Ginny lifted her hand to gently reach across the space that separated them, reaching toward Lindsay's face.

Unaccountably, Lindsay flinched.

Ginny's hand froze, and then she slowly drew it back. Even when they'd first met, Lindsay hadn't seemed so apprehensive of her touch. "What's the matter?" she asked, pain coloring her words. She felt a little ill. "You can't think I was going to do something to hurt you?"

There was a quiet disappointment in Ginny's voice that made Lindsay's heart twist in her chest. "No," Lindsay said quickly. "I just um," her eyes darted around the room, restless and anxious, "I usually don't like to be touched… If I don't know it's coming, that is."

"Mmm," Ginny acknowledged. That much she knew was true. She had already suspected that someone—someone whose neck she could wring with her bare hands—had hurt her friend very badly. *Oh, Lindsay.*

Lindsay tried to shrug it off. "I was just surprised, that's all."

Ginny winced inwardly, her eyes softening. "I'm sorry," she whispered. "I should have said something." She gestured with her chin. "I was just going to, well, push back that bit of hair. It was falling in your eyes and—" *And I wanted to see your face.* The thought came unbidden, and for once Ginny didn't fight it. "You are so pretty," she said without thinking, her eyes widening when she realized she'd said it out loud.

"I… I am not!" Lindsay sputtered, unable to believe what she'd just heard.

Ginny narrowed her eyes and set her jaw. "You are so, Lindsay Killian."

An expression dropped over Lindsay's face, so cold that Ginny had to fight hard not to shiver. "You're making fun of me," Lindsay rasped, clearly wounded.

Ginny shook her head forcefully. "No, I'm not." She scooted closer to her companion, reaching out and grabbing hold of her nightshirt before the spooked woman could bolt from the bed. "I wouldn't do that," she insisted gently. "You know I wouldn't."

Lindsay's eyes slid shut. "How can you think that?" Her voice was the barest of whispers and held a note of self-disgust. "Look at you and... well, just look at you." She opened her eyes and pointedly stared at her companion. "We're nothing alike." And she was right. Physically, though they were nearly the same height and close to the same weight, they looked dramatically different.

Lindsay's frame was long and covered with a lean layer of hard-earned muscle. To her eyes, the sharp planes of her face were far too harsh, and though her skin was pale, there was an overall darkness to her features that overshadowed her actual coloring. It didn't matter that the scratches on her face had disappeared with time and that the deeper cuts, the ones that had required stitches and had scarred, were well hidden by her clothing. She felt the way she felt, and missing a good portion of her left ear didn't exactly help her badly battered self-image.

Ginny, however, looked exactly the way Lindsay imagined a woman should. Even though she didn't have much weight to spare, there was a softness to her. Her shape was at once feminine, alluring, and oddly maternal. Hope radiated from behind bright, youthful eyes, and deep dimples creased flushed cheeks when she laughed or flashed a heartfelt smile. The lush curves of Ginny's breasts, hips, and bottom were, to Lindsay's consternation, as inviting as they were beautiful.

"Lindsay?" Ginny waved her hand in front of Lindsay's face. "Hello?"

Lindsay's eyes suddenly darted from Ginny's body to her face. "I... I—"

Ginny pressed her fingers to Lindsay's lips to quiet her. "I have no idea what you're talking about or where you're getting these crazy ideas." In her rush to comfort her friend, she spoke from her heart, forgetting to be bashful about what was so obvious to her eyes. "You are a beautiful woman, Lindsay, and kind and wonderful. *Anyone* who told you differently was a liar."

There was a fierceness in Ginny's words that startled Lindsay. "But—"

"Shh," Ginny crooned, her voice taking on a more tend note. "Just listen to me." Her eyebrows lifted in gentle entreaty. "Okay?"

Lindsay swallowed hard, very aware that Ginny had moved closer. She imagined that she could feel the heat of her skin through their nightshirts, the rhythmic warmth of Ginny's breath brushing against her face. She nodded, closing her eyes and drawing in a ragged breath, when warm, tentative fingers reached out and delicately traced her eyebrows, then cheeks, stopping only to curl under her chin.

Ginny's heart began to pound. In a bright explosion of clarity, her mind finally caught up with the signals from her body and she knew exactly what she wanted to do. She wanted to kiss Lindsay. The thought startled and excited her, and when Lindsay's eyes fluttered open again, she gasped, realizing that while she was nervous she wasn't the least bit afraid. "Lindsay?" Ginny's gaze dropped to Lindsay's lips, and she imagined their softness against hers. She could hear the darker woman swallow.

"Yeah?" came the breathy reply.

"Can… can I kiss you?" A hopeful gaze moved up to meet Lindsay's. "I know I shouldn't." Ginny's voice lowered an octave. "But… but I *really* want to."

Lindsay thought her heart would pound out of her chest. "You did it before," she reminded Ginny, her calm, clear words sounding foreign to her own ears.

A slow smile worked its way across Ginny's face. Lindsay hadn't laughed or been repulsed by her shocking request. "Mmm… I kissed your fingers. I remember." She scooted a tiny bit closer, holding her breath and praying that Lindsay wouldn't move to stop her.

"It was my first kiss."

Ginny's eyes widened a little. "Really?" She didn't try to hide her delight. "Mine too." She ducked her head, a pink flush tinting her skin. "Well, except for Alice."

A bolt of jealously lanced through Lindsay before she realized whom Ginny was talking about. Her eyebrows crawled up her forehead and stayed. "You kissed your *sister*?" she croaked, the last word a note higher than the others.

Ginny nodded, wanting to curl up into a ball and die. Lindsay's face took on a puzzled expression. "On the mouth?" Another half nod.

"Well, bleck!"

"Don't say it like that! It was just one time." Ginny made a face. *God, this is embarrassing.* "She was tired of practicing on her pillow and nervous about seeing Hershel, her beau. And she wanted to… well—"

"Try it on a real pair of lips," Lindsay ventured. She was starting to enjoy the way her friend was squirming.

"Yes." Ginny suddenly had a hideous thought, and her jaw worked a few times before she could utter a word. "You won't tell anyone, will you?"

"I dunno," Lindsay hedged, her own nervousness forgotten. "I *was* planning on taking an ad out in the *Times*."

"Bu-bu—you ca—" Ginny's eyes turned to slits when it finally hit home that she was being teased. "That was not nice! But…" the corner of her mouth quirked and she reluctantly admitted, "It was funny."

Lindsay's body shook with silent laughter. "I thought so."

"You would." Then Ginny recalled what had started this entirely embarrassing conversation, and she wouldn't be distracted. "So can I?" *Oh, please.*

"Kiss me?" Suddenly, Lindsay remembered why her heart had been in her throat only seconds before.

Ginny bit her lower lip and nodded mutely.

"We're both girls," Lindsay told her flatly.

Ginny looked at her like she was a dullard. "I know that!"

"I'm just making sure."

"Does that mean you don't want to kiss me… because I'm a girl?" Ginny crossed her fingers and toes.

Lindsay blushed. Deeply. "No," she said softly. "I mean it's okay that you're a girl. That's good. Very good. And you're sweet too. And—"

"Lindsay?"

Lindsay suddenly clamped her mouth shut, aware she was rambling. "Err… yes?" she said from between clenched teeth.

Ginny looked at her fondly, her heart swelling with every passing second. "I can't kiss you if you're babbling."

Lindsay blinked. "Oh."

With exaggerated slowness, Ginny lifted her head from the bed. To her surprise, Lindsay mirrored her actions, dark hair shifting as she moved. When their noses were almost touching, and she could feel Lindsay's uneven breaths as though they were her own, Ginny tilted her head just a fraction. Two sets of eyes closed, and tentative, trembling lips brushed against each other with gentle passion.

The contact was brief and sweet and so tender that it nearly made up for a lifetime of harshness in those few seconds alone. Lindsay's tongue briefly drew across Ginny's silky lower lip before she pulled away, a breathy sigh escaping her. When the kiss ended, Ginny's eyes remained closed for a handful of heartbeats, as though she were in a trance. Then they popped open, brimming with wonder. Her blood sang through her veins, and the urge to reclaim those silken lips was nearly more than she could bear. She touched her mouth in simple awe, tracing the moistness of her lips. *Oh, my God.*

"Wa—" Lindsay had to stop and collect herself before she could continue. The simple gesture had rocked her to the core. "Was that okay?"

Okay? Ginny smiled brilliantly. "That was very okay, Lindsay. I've—" She shook her head in confusion. "I don't know what to say," she whispered. "I didn't know it would feel like that." She sat up a little, not trusting herself to keep from moving to repeat the wonderful experience. "I didn't think it would be like that." *Wow.*

Lindsay cursed her own clumsiness. "I'm sorry," she said self-consciously, her face creasing into a worried scowl. "I thought—I haven't ever—I never wanted to before, but with you I did, and I mean—ugh!"

Ginny giggled nervously, letting her fingers trail down Lindsay's arm, punctuating the motion with a gentle squeeze when she reached a slender wrist.

"No. No. No. You don't understand." She cupped Lindsay's cheek, enjoying the warmth against her palm, extremely pleased that Lindsay hadn't so much as blinked at the gesture. *I don't want to stop touching you.* So she didn't.

Boldly, she traced Lindsay's slightly askew nose with a single, gentle finger, feeling the bump where it had so recently been broken. She smiled at the contented sigh that greeted her actions. "The kiss was amazing." She gazed into the dark eyes so close to hers for confirmation. "Wasn't it, Lindsay?"

Lindsay could only nod, dizzy with relief. She sighed. "Amazing."

Ginny smiled again and eased back onto her side. She dropped her hand from Lindsay's face, missing the feeling of smooth skin instantly. She felt giddy and tired and happy and as though the small space between them was far too much. Ginny shifted her pillow until it touched Lindsay's. She peeked up at her friend from beneath rusty-red lashes. "Is this—?"

Lindsay laughed fondly. *I want to be close to you too.* "It's good." She lay down facing Ginny, their heads only inches apart. "Good night, Ginny," she murmured, her mind spinning with possibilities, first and foremost of which was when could they do that again?

The younger woman's hand inched forward, and she threaded her fingers through Lindsay's. *I kissed her!* Her eyes slid shut, a wide, obnoxiously happy smile still gracing her face. "Good night, Lindsay."

There would be time for questions and insecurities, doubts and fears, to rear their ugly heads—later.

The following morning, however, when the sun spilled into the small room in an orphanage in Queens, it found two young women fitted snugly together, warm, safe, and dreaming of sweet kisses yet to come.

Ginny yawned, keeping her eyes firmly closed. She could feel the warmth of Lindsay's body pressed tightly to hers, and memories of the kiss from the night before came flooding back to her, sending a jolt of swirling heat to her belly. Reluctantly, she opened her eyes to find Lindsay's unfocused eyes watching her, an intent almost curious look on her face. "What are you thinking?" Ginny asked, her voice still hoarse from sleep.

Something snapped behind dark eyes, and in an instant Lindsay was drawn into the present. "I… I dunno. I was just daydreaming, I guess." She smiled hesitantly, already wondering if the kiss they had shared last night would go unacknowledged.

"Mmm." Ginny stroked Lindsay's palm with her fingertips. "Good dreams?"

"Some."

They could hear the rustle of activity outside their room, but Christian had assured them that getting thirty children dressed and ready for the day meant that breakfast wouldn't be served until nearly eight a.m. They had time, and Ginny didn't want to waste the intimacy she could feel flowing between them on idle chatter. "Tell me about your family," she urged warily, well aware that her previous inquiries had been met with humorous quips meant more to distract than inform. *C'mon, Lindsay. Let me know you.*

Lindsay drew in a deep breath, not especially surprised by the question. Ginny was the curious sort, and her gentle probing over their time together hadn't escaped the older girl. It wasn't really that her past was secret—not at all. There just wasn't much to tell, and a part of her thought that maybe Ginny would find the mystery of not knowing more intriguing than the plain truth. Lindsay exhaled, defeated by the hopeful, blue eyes gazing into hers. "What would you like to know?"

Ginny tried not to show her surprise. "Really?"

Lindsay's mouth quirked. "Really."

"Why are you all alone, Lindsay?" Ginny's eyes filled with unexpected tears, and her throat felt tight. "I can't bear the thought of you not having anyone." She ached for Lindsay in a way she never had for another. And while the rail-rider never seemed downright unhappy with her life, there were times when Ginny could feel the neediness in Lindsay's heart tearing at her own soul. *No one should be alone.*

A hurt expression chased its way across Lindsay's face. "Am I all alone?"

Ginny quickly realized her error. "Not at all. I didn't mean it that way. You have me," she assured before Lindsay could say anything else.

There was a resoluteness in her voice that worked into Lindsay's heart, quelling her fears.

"But is there truly no one else?" She knew how she hurt over the loss of her own kin. Did Lindsay feel the same way?

"No one." Lindsay swallowed thickly, a little surprised that while the thought held only an echo of real pain, saying the words out loud somehow made it seem much worse. More real.

"Why? You told me you've been on your own since you were twelve years old. That's just not right, Lindsay!"

"Shhh." Lindsay brushed away Ginny's tears—tears that were for her. *Will wonders never cease?* "Let me tell you." She tugged affectionately on a strand of Ginny's hair.

Ginny bit her tongue and waited, grabbing hold of her emotions.

"I'm afraid you'll be a little disappointed. I don't have a very interesting story."

"Somehow I doubt that." *I find just about everything about you interesting.* Without asking, Lindsay leaned forward and brushed her lips against Ginny's; hearing Ginny's surprised gasp then a whimper as the contact continued, she moaned.

The kiss tapered off naturally, and Lindsay pressed her forehead to Ginny's. Both young women were breathing raggedly. "I've been wanting to do that since I woke up," she whispered. "Was that all right?"

"God, yes," Ginny breathed, a little unsettled, but mostly excited by her body's response.

"Tsh." Brown eyes twinkled. "Blasphemy again?"

"I've been corrupted." Ginny lifted her chin and nibbled Lindsay's lower lip. *I could do this forever,* her mind whispered. "But I won't be put off." Regretfully, she gave Lindsay a final peck, and then settled back onto her pillow, promising herself that there would be time for more kisses later.

Lindsay chuckled. "I already knew that about you, Ginny. Okay, my life story such as it is. Everything that I know. Are you sure you want the entire boring story?"

Ginny pinched Lindsay, earning a playful squawk. "Quite sure."

"I was born in Plymouth, Pennsylvania. And—"

"Really? Not New York?" Ginny interrupted. Lindsay shot her a look.

Ginny's expression was sheepish. "Sorry, go on."

"My mother is or maybe *was*..." Lindsay paused for a moment. "I'm not really sure which. Anyway, she was from an affluent family in Montreal. Her name is Suzette Mourier."

Ginny's eyebrows jumped. "You're French?"

Lindsay smiled indulgently. Trying to keep Ginny quiet was as useless as fighting the tide. "Half French," she corrected. "My father's name was Jack Killian—he came over from Ireland during the War Between the States."

Lindsay shifted in the bed, getting more comfortable. "Da was a laborer for a lumber yard in Plymouth, and he met my mother when her parents brought her with them on a business trip to Pennsylvania. She was a teenager, pretty from all accounts. He was nearly forty and the roguish sort, if you know what I mean."

"Mmm. Where did they meet?"

"I don't know. Da never said." Lindsay pulled the sheet up a little higher, and Ginny scooted closer until they were touching all along their bodies, jointly warding off the morning chill. "She was only in the States for a week, and because of the difference in their ages and social classes, they met secretly every day when Da finished work. Da asked her to stay in Plymouth when it came time for her to go, but she refused."

Can someone fall in love that quickly? You know the answer to that, Ginny's heart chided. She wondered what Lindsay thought about that and asked, "Were they in love?"

Lindsay snorted. "Does it matter? She left him."

That, Ginny admitted to herself, was something she didn't have an answer for.

"My mother returned to Plymouth six months later, alone and very pregnant, after being thrown out of the house by her parents. My Da married her, and sometime later I was born."

"Nothing interesting happened in between all that?"

"Not as far as I'm concerned."

Ginny sighed and tried to lighten the mood by mumbling, "Some storyteller you are."

A smile eased over Lindsay's face. "Toldja." Then she became more somber. "My mother was always unhappy. Always. And even in the best of times, Da never did more than eke out a living. Mother went back to Canada when I was four, and I've never seen or heard from her since."

"Oh, Lindsay." Ginny closed her eyes, furious with a woman she'd never met, her heart crying out for her friend who'd missed so much. "That's awful."

"Not really." Lindsay tried to shrug but it wasn't possible with Ginny plastered to her side. "I don't really remember her, other than the fact that she had brown eyes."

Beautiful ones, I'll bet. "Like you."

Lindsay nodded. "Like me. Da's were the color of cornflowers," with effort, she turned onto her side and tweaked Ginny's nose, "like yours."

Ginny smiled weakly.

"Da was never the same after she left. Over the next few years, he lost his job at the lumberyard, then he started staying out all night. He never drank, or beat me, or anything like that. He just wasn't there. No one bothered to make me go to school or do much of anything. And by the time I was ten or so, he'd be gone for days at a time." Her brow creased, and she wondered for the millionth time where he'd disappeared to. Deep in her heart she wondered if it wasn't to Canada to visit her mother. Maybe the reason her mother had left had been her and not her father. The thought had haunted her since childhood and did nothing for her already battered self-image.

"Days?" Ginny could scarcely believe it. "You were just a little girl. How did you survive?" How could any man do that? Even Arthur, who had been a dreamer and a drinker—a dangerous mix—had loved his children and stepchildren. Ginny always knew that. Always.

Lindsay's voice was flat, as though it were someone else's life she was talking about. "We lived on the skirts of a shanty town mostly full of drunkards, kids, and veterans who couldn't work because of broken bodies or minds. I learned from a boy who lived a few shacks down that I could jump on one of the passing trains and hitch a ride into the city."

She wistfully recalled the feeling of freedom she felt the first time she'd tried it. How the wind ruffled her long dark hair, and how the endless miles of tracks had stretched invitingly before her, taking her away from where she was, promising her an unknown future that could only be better than her present. "So I did it. In the city, I worked selling flypaper and matches to buy food. Men liked buying from little girls, and I sold more than the boys my age who were just as hungry."

Tears filled Ginny's eyes again. "Lindsay—"

"It's all right," Lindsay whispered tenderly. "There's not much more to tell. In eighty-five the typhoid epidemic hit Plymouth." She closed her eyes. "I had been living on the streets in the city for nearly a week, not bothering to go home, when I finally decided to make my way back in the middle of the night. The shantytown was deathly quiet, and I knew something was wrong." *And the smell. God.* It turned her stomach just remembering. "I found Da on the davenport… He was hunched over and pale as a ghost. He was—" Her voice cracked, and she stopped.

Ginny squeezed Lindsay's good hand, her own eyes leaking. "I'm so sorry."

No. I can't think about it. I won't get through the tellin'. "He was dead. Musta come home while I was gone. Most of the neighbors were sick or dead themselves, so I gathered up a few things and hopped onto the next train east." Ginny wiped her wet cheeks. "You never tried to contact your mother?"

"Nah," Lindsay scoffed, though the idea wasn't a foreign one. "I didn't have an address, and even if I did, she had plenty of years to contact me… to get to know me. She chose not to. Besides, she was no goddamned mother to me. And Da wasn't much better. I raised myself." *And a fine job you did too, thief.*

A quiet anger filled Ginny. "You shouldn't have had to do that, Lindsay. No child should."

"It's in the past, Ginny. Fretting now can't change a damn thing." Lindsay suddenly sat up, got out of bed, and marched across the room. With her back to her friend, she stepped into her trousers, which she found piled in the doorway. The laundress must have left them there last night. She cursed the tears she could feel welling in her eyes.

Ginny followed Lindsay, crossing the room and watching as the rail-rider's back stiffened in reaction. Without hesitation, she wrapped her arms around Lindsay from behind, hugging her as tightly as she dared. She felt the involuntary flinch run through the lean form in her arms, and knew there was more to talk about—but not now. She pressed her face against Lindsay's shoulder and whispered, "I'm so, so sorry. You aren't alone anymore, Lindsay." Lindsay's shoulders began to shake helplessly as silent sobs racked her, years of pent-up grief bubbling to the surface. Her knees went weak, and she felt Ginny supporting most of her weight.

"Let it out."

Her sobs intensified.

Ginny sniffed and held on for dear life. "I won't let go."

At nine a.m. sharp, Ginny and Lindsay stood on the sidewalk outside a three-story brick building. A bronze plaque near the front door read:

The Foundling Placement Society
Founded by
Jeremiah & Isabelle Ward
1888

Ginny twitched her skirt. She turned to Lindsay. "What if they tell us the kids aren't here?"

Lindsay kicked a bit of snow from her shoe. "If these big bugs can't tell us, we'll find out for ourselves, Ginny. There are ways. If I have to, I'll sneak into the orphanage at night and check every goddamn bed."

Ginny smiled. "I hope that won't be necessary."

Lindsay's look, however, was grim. "So do I."

Fifty minutes later, the young women were still waiting outside Mr. Ward's office. Just when Lindsay had lost all patience and was about to push her way inside, the office door opened and a tall man emerged, his shiny black shoes clicking on the wooden floors. He was rail thin and in his middle forties, with black curly hair cut close to his head on the sides and left longer on top, and thick, mutton chop sideburns. His dark green eyes were close set and nearly obscured by his bushy eyebrows. The man's gaze flicked briefly to Ginny and Lindsay, dismissing them, before traveling to his secretary.

Lindsay suddenly wished she were here to pick his pockets clean. *Smug bastard.*

"Wendell?" Mr. Ward questioned. "Who are these…? Who are they?" His tone was firm. Wendell knew better than to waste his time with beggars. His gaze slid sideways. *Adult beggars at that.*

Wendell was a large, round black man with tiny hands so smooth and feminine that Ginny found herself a little jealous. Unconsciously, she pushed her own scarred hands into her coat pockets.

Wendell jumped to his feet, taking care to set down his ink pen carefully despite his jittery hands. "This is Miss Chisholm and… and… her… uhh…" He threw a panicked look Ginny's way.

Ginny mouthed "friend," and Wendell repeated the word to Mr. Ward.

"They're your nine a.m. appointment, sir. A referral from Mr. Spence; I cleared it with you yesterday."

"Spence," Mr. Ward spat the name as though it were a curse, "should know better than to bother me on a Sunday." But he had accepted the appointment, assuming it had something to do with the investigation of his foundation. And now the time he'd spent in his office, making his supposed opponent wait, had been nothing more than a waste. With jerky motions, he pulled his pocket watch from his vest and frowned at the time. He finally looked up at Ginny and Lindsay. "Won't you come into my office? You have a few moments before my next appointment."

Lindsay rolled her eyes, but refrained from comment as they were led into a plush office. Inside, a tiny woman in an expensive green dress, with brightly colored feathers woven through its collar, sat behind a large mahogany desk, which was strategically placed in the very center of the room. From the lines around her eyes, she looked to be nearly the same age as Mr. Ward. An enormous pile of golden curls sat atop her head, bouncing a little as she drew in a deep breath to speak. "Jeremiah—?" Her gaze lifted from the ledger book in front of her. When she saw who was accompanying her husband, she froze.

"My dear. This is Miss Chisholm and her associate."

Isabelle Ward lifted a pale eyebrow at Ginny and Lindsay. With a slight turn of her head, her second rapidly lifting eyebrow was directed at Mr. Ward.

"They were sent here by Christian Spencer," he clarified, clearly annoyed that he'd agreed to the meeting in the first place.

Isabelle sighed. "I see." She stepped out from behind the desk, deciding to conclude this meeting as quickly as possible. "I'm Isabelle Ward." She smiled a sugary smile. "How can we help you?"

Ginny cleared her throat, suddenly nervous in the presence of these two imposing figures.

Lindsay was less impressed.

"I'm looking for my brothers and my sister," Ginny said.

"Orphans?"

Ginny's mouth worked but no sound emerged for several seconds. "No," she announced crisply, surprising everyone in the room. Suddenly she felt very tired that she had to go through all this to reclaim her family. She'd done nothing wrong. "An orphan is someone who has no one to raise them. That's not the case with my siblings."

"Hmm." Isabelle tapped her chin. "I see. Pity we can't help you. Your brothers and sister aren't here." She pushed herself off the desk. "Now if you'll excuse us. We have work—"

"Do you know Lt. Robert O'Malley of the one-hundred-eleventh Manhattan Police Precinct?" Lindsay asked loudly.

Three heads turned toward her, and Ginny's eyes widened. *What are you doing? There is no one-hundred-eleventh Police Precinct in Manhattan!*

Jeremiah Ward took a step closer to Lindsay, studying her with a critical eye. "I'm afraid we don't, Miss…?" He waited for Lindsay to supply her name. She didn't.

Lindsay crossed her arms over her chest. "We spoke with him

yesterday. It seems he was at the scene of the fire at 84 Orchard Street several weeks ago. And he personally saw an employee of yours load the Robson children into a wagon. Are you saying you did not take them into custody for your care?"

"That's exactly what I'm saying," Isabelle snapped. Who was this person to question her?

Lindsay scratched her jaw. "If they weren't properly taken and aren't under the care of your orphanage, then I'd say we need to report a kidnapping by this agency." She turned to Ginny, whose mouth had dropped open. "Wouldn't you, Ginny?"

The redhead's brain kicked into gear, and she mimicked Lindsay's defiant stance. "I would. We know you have them." *Please, God, let us be right.*

"Hold on just a minute!" Isabelle's gaze flickered with anger that ratcheted up to rage when she saw that both young women were deadly serious.

"Wait. Wait." Mr. Ward held up both hands. "Let us check our records again, won't you?" He grabbed his wife's arm and retreated behind the large desk, whispering in her ear as they went. He pulled out a thick book from the bottom drawer and thumbed through until he had reached the last page that contained any visible writing. "Robson, you say?" he asked Ginny, glancing up.

Ginny nodded, her heart climbing into her throat.

Mr. Ward nodded. "Yes, it seems we were… in error before. We did collect three *orphans*," he emphasized the word, causing Ginny's back to stiffen, "from a burned-out slum. Our records indicate that both their parents were killed along with two sisters." Next, he slid open the drawer of a deep-red, mahogany file cabinet that sat alongside his desk, pulling out a stack of certificates. He took the one that was second in the pile and handed it to Ginny.

Isabelle smiled cruelly. "In case you can't read, Miss Chisholm, that certificate was issued by the State of New York, giving us full custody of Jane, James, and Lewis Robson." It was dated two days after the fire.

"How could this happen so quickly?" Ginny handed back the heavy paper, her hand shaking. "They have family. You can't just turn them out to strangers!"

"Not according to the State of New York." Mr. Ward made a show of raking his eyes over Ginny's plain dress. "And even if they did have family, which you have not adequately proven, that person would have to be able to demonstrate that they qualify to be the children's guardian." He smirked. "You have to be at least eighteen years old for that."

"So?" Lindsay told him. "She's eighteen."

"Uh huh." It was clear neither Isabelle nor Mr. Ward believed that lie. Jeremiah rubbed his heavy sideburns. "And even if she were eighteen, she'd have to demonstrate that she could support the children."

Ginny visibly winced. She had known that would be a problem, but had hoped that the State would allow her time to get a job. Two if she had to.

A victorious smile tugged at the corner of Isabelle's mouth. "If your husband had accompanied you, we might have been able to assist you."

"Husband?" Ginny was dumbfounded. "I… I…"

"You're not married?" Isabelle's gaze softened for just a split second before turning to granite. "Did you really expect that three small children would be handed over to an *unmarried* girl with no visible means of support? Foolish child."

"Get out of this office," Mr. Ward ordered them plainly, pointing a thick finger toward the door. "You've wasted enough of our valuable time." He made a shooing motion with his hand. "And be glad that a stupid farmer somewhere is shouldering the *burden* that you so clearly cannot."

Ginny's face flushed with anger. "Burden?"

Lindsay took a menacing step toward Mr. Ward. "Where are they?" Her voice was a dangerous growl, and the tall man took a step backward at the sound. "Answer me!" Lindsay curled her good hand into a tight fist.

Jeremiah backed up until his shoulders hit the cool, paneled wood wall. Lindsay followed him step for step. His face paled.

"I won't ask you again," Lindsay warned, her violent intent clear as she leaned so close to Mr. Ward she could smell the salty bacon he'd had for breakfast on his breath.

"Out… out West," he blurted.

"Jeremiah!" Isabelle gasped. "Shut up!"

"What does that mean?" Ginny stalked across the room, shouldering her way between Lindsay and Mr. Ward. "Where? Where are they?"

The man wiped his forehead with the back of his hand, regaining a bit of his equilibrium now that he wasn't facing Lindsay, who to his eyes resembled a rabid dog, ready to strike. He glanced over at his wife who was shooting daggers at him. Shame washed over him. "What does it matter?" he told her. "What's done is done." He refocused on Ginny. "They were put on an orphan train heading West nearly three weeks ago. The train hasn't returned, so I can't say where or by whom they were adopted."

"And even if we *did* know," Isabelle piped up, moving to the wall to stand next to her husband. Discreetly, she brushed her fingers against his hand. But when he moved to grasp hers, her hands just as casually moved away. "The adoptions would still be binding, and irrevocable."

"Irrevocable?" Ginny whispered incredulously. "How can that be? I'm their sister!" She all but bared her teeth in a snarl. "You as good as stole those children. No one checked to see if they had family." Her eyes darkened. "No one did anything at all, did they? You just collected them to sell them off to the highest bidder."

Mr. Ward's green eyes flashed. "If Mr. Spence told you that, I'll sue him. I'll—"

Lindsay's powerful hand darted out, and long fingers wrapped themselves around the man's skinny neck. "You won't do a damn thing." Each word was said slowly, giving Mr. Ward ample time to digest them. "We'll go to the papers. We'll stand in front of this building if we have to. You won't see another dime in donations once the press gets a whiff that this place is nothing more than a trussed-up child farm."

Perspiration trickled down Lindsay's forehead, and she tightened her grip until Jeremiah's eyes began to bulge. "You filthy pig. I should break your neck this very instant." Her heart began to pound, and in her mind's eye she could see herself squeezing the life out of this man who had so casually shattered Ginny's family. Then a hand on her back, moving in a slow steady circle, caused her to go very still. She remained motionless except for her heaving chest and raging eyes that flicked sideways, their gaze landing on Ginny's face.

"No," Ginny said simply. Her heart was slamming against her ribs with such force that she was surprised she hadn't passed out. Outwardly, however, she appeared perfectly calm. She wasn't sure which frightened her more: what Lindsay was doing or that she'd seriously contemplated not trying to stop her. Lindsay's eye twitched and she drew in a shaky breath. Slowly, her grip on Mr. Ward's now sweaty throat relaxed, and she took a step backward, adrenaline coursing through her and threatening to send her to her knees.

Mr. Ward sucked in a large lungful of air, then moved to straighten his necktie.

Isabelle turned away from her husband, disgusted.

Her expression wasn't lost on Mr. Ward, and the resulting look he gave Lindsay was one of pure hatred. "I… I'll have you arrested for that, bitch."

The relationship between Mr. Ward and his wife crystallized before her eyes, and Ginny dismissed the man with a look of her own, focusing instead on who was really in charge of The Foundling Placement Society. "We'll be back, Mrs. Ward. I won't give up on my family. *Ever*."

Isabelle nodded very slightly, and something wordless passed between them, an acknowledgement of sorts. *Enemies*, Ginny's gut whispered in warning.

Lindsay wrapped her arm around Ginny's shoulder, and the two young women exited the office with hurried steps. Ginny's pallor told Lindsay that she was about to throw up. And Lindsay would be damned straight to hell before she'd give the Wards the satisfaction of knowing they'd rattled her friend so. She admitted to herself that she wasn't feeling much better. Her rage at Mr. Ward had flared so quickly that she wasn't sure she could have stopped it even if she'd wanted to.

And *that* scared her.

Ginny and Lindsay were barely out of the office, when Isabelle moved to her desk and pressed a button. Within seconds, a rather nondescript young man entered the office through a side door.

"Ma'am?" he inquired eagerly.

"We just had visitors, Delano."

"Yes, ma'am." He'd seen two people in the waiting room earlier.

"Follow them."

"Find out about the brunette," Mr. Ward commanded brusquely, still fussing with his collar. "I want to know *everything*. I'll take care of finding out about Miss Chisholm myself."

There was a pause, and the young man shifted from one foot to the other, unsure of whether he should leave now or wait for further instruction.

"For God's sake, go! Or you'll never find them," Isabelle exploded.

He raced out the door, causing Wendell's head to jerk up in surprise as he passed.

The office door slammed shut, its boom echoing in Jeremiah's ears. He turned to his wife. "Bella, what if that bitch…?"

Isabelle knew which young woman he was referring to. The one who had left with his balls in her pocket.

"What if what she said is true… that they'd go to the press?"

"Then it's all over," Isabelle said. Keeping the investigation of their foundation out of the papers had proven nearly impossible already, not to mention ridiculously expensive. Donations came in from the wealthy who wanted to be associated with a fashionable charity. Public perception meant everything. One bad article in the press at this critical time would be like a strong gust of wind to a house of cards.

Jeremiah threw his hands in the air. "Those children won't make us a dime; we only added them to the bunch going out West for appearances' sake anyway. They're too young to command a price. Couldn't we just find the brats and turn them over to Miss Chisholm?"

"And have the adopting parents do exactly what those girls are threatening to do by going to the press?" She shook her head. "No. Besides, what's to keep Miss Chisholm from going to the press anyway?" Isabelle rubbed her throbbing temples. She could feel a migraine coming on.

Slowly, waiting to be rebuked, her husband moved his hands to her shoulders and gently rubbed them. He sighed when she permitted his touch.

"What then, Bella?"

Isabelle closed her eyes and leaned into his hands. She loved her husband, but he was insufferably weak. "Something… more permanent may have to be arranged." *I've worked too hard to let two mangy street urchins ruin it all.*

Jeremiah nodded and continued his massage, smart enough not to question his wife on such matters.

Isabelle knew best.

Chapter Eight

The younger woman had been beside herself ever since they'd left The Foundling Placement Society Office. "I'm too late," Ginny whispered in anguish. They carefully traversed the icy sidewalk, often having to venture into the street to move around small groups of people, apple sellers pushing their rattling carts, or merchandise displays that hogged the sidewalks even in the winter. "My God, they could be anywhere." She suddenly felt as though she couldn't breathe, the enormity of trying to find three small children "out West" hitting her like a sledgehammer.

"Ginny," Lindsay said, in as soothing a voice as she could muster. "It doesn't matter where they are. We'll still find them. You have to truly believe that, or we're wasting our time and might as well stop right now."

Ginny's face showed every ounce of the incredulity that she felt. She stopped abruptly, and a man who had been walking behind them grumbled an insincere apology when he bumped into Lindsay, then stepped around her and disappeared into the pedestrian traffic. "Stop? Never, Lindsay," Ginny hissed, resuming her steps at a slightly faster pace than before, her feet crunching on the crusty snow. She tucked her chin down into the warmth of her coat, murmuring into the scratchy wool that smelled faintly damp. "I meant what I told that horrible woman. I'll never stop looking for them." *I mean to keep my promise, Alice. Wherever you are, you know that, don't you?*

Lindsay nodded, having heard enough for her to have no doubt about Ginny's intentions. Not that she'd ever really had any concerns to begin with, but after receiving the sort of bad news they just had, she figured Ginny could use a little reminding. "Then let's figure out where to go from here."

"Well, we only know one person who seems to be an expert on this orphan train business."

Lindsay exhaled slowly, sending a stream of fog into the air, as her mind raced ahead to what she knew they'd have to do. *We're going to be following that train, Ginny. And for that we'll need some traveling money, even if we hitch most of the way.* She mentally sneered. *And I know just where to get it.*

"Then that's our next stop, The Society for the Betterment of Children Orphanage."

Christian Spence leaned forward a little on the davenport in the study of his orphanage as he looked into Ginny's confused face. "I don't know what to say other than I'm sorry. I was truly hoping the children wouldn't have been sent out West yet. I'd hoped that, if that were the case and if you kicked up a fuss, it wouldn't be worth it for the Wards to fight you for the children." His eyes conveyed deep sadness over his next statement. Child welfare was his life. "It's not like there aren't plenty more orphans where they came from. Jeremiah and Isabelle do work quickly." He shook his head. "I'll give them that."

Lindsay closed her eyes. She was afraid of this. *God, this day has just turned to shit. Ginny*—Her mind paused as she savored the myriad of emotions the name alone aroused. *My friend, so sweet and kind, you're the first person I've met whose luck was as piss poor as mine. We make quite a pair.*

"Ladies," Christian's voice was tinged with regret, "if they showed you a certificate of guardianship awarded by the State, then I'm afraid they have every right to do what they're doing."

"Bu… But you said they were selling children," Ginny sputtered. She tightened her grip on the hand she was holding. "That can't be legal." She knew the words came out louder than she'd intended by the slight widening of Lindsay's and Christian's eyes.

"Yes, yes, that is illegal." Christian patted Ginny's knee. "But what I believe they're doing is selling older children as laborers. I have no proof, mind you, but the adoption services business community is relatively small, and I'm not wholly without contacts. My educated guess is that your siblings are part of the few children the Wards adopt out to keep up the appearance of a legitimate organization. These adoptions would basically be like any other adoption, and it's highly unlikely that they would be nullified wholesale. They would be looked at case by case."

Ginny stood angrily, and Lindsay joined her. "Are you trying to tell me that the fact that my brothers and sisters were stolen out from under me and sent West was somehow legitimate?" *That can't be true.*

"Ginny, please." Christian rose to go over to her. "If you find them-"

"When," Lindsay interrupted in a low, serious voice. "*When* she finds them." Christian licked his lips and nodded quickly. "Of course. *When* you find them, you can petition the State to have their adoptions nullified on the grounds that a reasonable attempt at placement within the family wasn't made. I'm sure the children themselves explained they had a living sister."

Ginny nodded glumly, her anger bleeding away. "Lewis and James wouldn't let this happen without a fight." She smiled wryly, thinking of James, an old soul for such a young child, intelligent and willful; and Lewis, who was boisterous and loving, but just as headstrong as his twin. "I suspect they were more than a handful."

Christian relaxed a little now that it was clear that Ginny wasn't going to shoot the messenger. "I have a lawyer friend who I'm sure would take on your case pro bono."

Lindsay and Ginny exchanged confused, slightly embarrassed glances.

"That means for free," Christian clarified delicately, not wanting the young women to feel stupid. "I only learned the phrase myself recently." He winked. "I'm afraid it's become one of my favorites." His face sobered a bit as he weighed whether or not to mention more potential obstacles. His internal debate, however, was a quick one. These women were serious, and knowledge was power. "You do understand that finding them is only the first step. If you expect to take *legal* custody," the words were said slowly and pointedly and the implication was clear—legal, while preferred, was only one way to do things— "there are guardianship requirements."

"The Wards made those very clear," Lindsay told him, her mind already spinning scenarios in which she could help Ginny financially. Unfortunately, they all included her having a dime to spare, which she didn't.

Ginny swallowed hard. She wasn't very far from her eighteenth birthday so the age requirement, at least in her mind, was a not a problem. Besides, she'd been born at home and never had a birth certificate. And she'd changed schools so frequently, sometimes attending one for only a few weeks before moving, that she doubted any records were kept on her at all. Money, however, was going to be a problem. "I understand I'll need to meet an age and financial requirement."

"Yes. I'm glad you understand. And of course, you'll have to be deemed morally fit. But that won't be an issue," Christian said confidentially. "It's mainly to ensure the children don't end up with criminals, those who fail to understand the importance of Christian teachings, or perverts."

Lindsay looked at Ginny and the redhead glanced back, biting her lower lip. Then they both blushed beet red.

Christian blinked. "Is… well, is there something I should know in order to help you?" He looked back and forth between Ginny and Lindsay, and impossibly, their blushes deepened.

"No," both young women mumbled guiltily, not meeting Christian's gaze.

"Are you sure? I could—"

Out of the blue, Lindsay exploded. "Assholes have children every single day! In fact, some folks do nothing but breed more assholes. The world is *full* of assholes. They can treat their kids like shit, beat 'em, or stay dead drunk for a solid month, and the State of New York, which can, might I add, kiss my ass to begin with, doesn't give a goddamned lick. These children are Ginny's *family*. She's not some stranger who wants to take them. I don't see how this is anybody's business but hers! And as for all these requirements—"

"Lindsay?" Ginny said softly, chewing the inside of her cheek to keep from laughing at her friend's colorful tirade.

Christian looked as though he'd swallowed his tongue.

"What?" Lindsay glanced at Ginny, annoyed at being interrupted.

Ginny smiled affectionately, taking the sting from her words. "We get the idea."

"Oh." Lindsay cleared her throat a little sheepishly. "I mean… err…" She focused on a red-faced Christian. "You know everything you need to know, but we appreciate the information." A gentle squeeze of her hand from Ginny was her reward.

Christian coughed a couple of times. Then he leaned a little closer to Lindsay and whispered so that Ginny couldn't hear his shocking admission.

"This isn't the first time that these walls have heard someone curse the State of New York."

Lindsay fought not to smirk or roll her eyes. She examined Christian with a curious eye, finding his statement hard to believe. He was, she suspected, exactly the wholesome do-gooder type he appeared to be, genuine and kind, the go-to-church-three-times-a-week-and-take-a-bath-just-as-often sort. But she wasn't going to argue the point, so she just shrugged and amiably said, "If you say so." She felt her heart pick up a little in anticipation of what she had to do next.

Lindsay didn't dare look at Ginny as she continued to address the blond man. "I have to attend to some business this afternoon." *Now for the hard part.* "Maybe Ginny could stay here and talk with Mary again, or those two boys from her building? She was so good with them before."

Ginny's eyebrows crawled up her forehead. "What?"

"Ummm." For a second, Lindsay's mind went blank.

Ginny's voice was incredulous. "You're abandoning me for the afternoon?" *She never said she had someplace to be today—never once.*

Lindsay sighed. Ginny was nothing if not direct. "Awww, Ginny, I wouldn't put it that way. Exactly."

"You never mentioned this before. Why not?" Red brows knitted. "Where are you going?" Bewildered, a feeling of general unease began gnawing at her guts.

An annoyed look flitted across Lindsay's face. She didn't want to lie, but Ginny was making it so damn hard. "Look," she finally risked a glance at Ginny's face, "I just have something to take care of, that's all. Some old friends I was thinking of meeting up with." She forced herself to stop fidgeting. "C'mon, Ginny, it's not like we're joined at the hip or anything. I have important things to do." The words were barely out of her mouth before she realized her mistake. "I won't be long," she added in a rush, her eyes pleading with Ginny to understand that she hadn't meant that the way it sounded. The surprised, hurt look on Ginny's face nearly made her give up the entire idea. But Lindsay held firm.

"I see," Ginny said slowly. Though she clearly didn't.

"I'm glad that you do," Lindsay answered, but didn't move to leave. Instead, she stood there awkwardly, not wanting to leave while Ginny was angry, but at the same time unwilling to explain herself.

Ginny remained silent as well. She had, she knew, no claim on Lindsay's time. Still, she didn't appreciate being passed to Christian like a troublesome puppy that needed to be watched. Her eyes took on an inner fire that screamed, "I'm a grown woman who can take care of herself, Lindsay! I don't need you!" Lindsay looked away.

The tension between the young women grew until Christian couldn't take it anymore. He gallantly jumped to the rescue. "I'd be most honored if Ginny would stay for the afternoon and join me for lunch. She can meet with the children afterwards, and I would be most pleased to explain to her how the adoption process on these orphan trains works. If that's acceptable, that is." He looked questioningly at Lindsay, not because he sought her approval over Ginny's, but because she was closer. A split second later, when his gaze swung to Ginny, he realized his grave error. Ginny's eyes shot him so full of daggers the man was honestly surprised he wasn't bleeding.

Lindsay smiled gratefully at Christian. "I'll be back before dark." She slipped her arms into her coat, pretending to be too occupied in her task to notice the angry flush of Ginny's cheeks. "Then we can find a place to stay for the night."

"Please," Christian insisted, "I don't have a proper bedroom to offer you tonight, but you can bunk down in my office or here in the parlor. We can put blankets on the floor and—"

"Thank you, Christian," Lindsay accepted quickly, not giving Ginny a chance to say differently.

Ginny's back went ramrod straight in reaction.

Lindsay tried to fasten the top button of her coat, but gave up quickly when the task proved difficult. "We'll take whatever room you have."

Wordlessly, her face a mixture of anger and confusion, Ginny stomped out of the room, slamming the door behind her.

Lindsay and Christian both jumped at the sound, and the pictures on the walls rattled wildly. "Uh-oh," Lindsay muttered, rubbing her forehead with the fingertips of one hand.

Christian let out a low whistle. "She's got quite a temper, hasn't she?"

"Whatever gave you that idea?" Lindsay answered wryly.

The man stuck his hands in his pockets and rocked back on his heels. "You will be careful, won't you?"

"I… well—"

Christian snorted. "Just be careful. I suspect whatever it is you're going to do is something I wouldn't really want to know about anyway, correct?"

"Probably," Lindsay admitted, a little surprised. Maybe the man was more savvy than she'd given him credit for. "Frankly, I can't believe I'm doing it myself."

It was on the tip of his tongue to tell her that maybe she should just stay here then, but he didn't. Ginny was already madder than a wet cat, and by any estimation, one angry woman was more than enough to deal with. "If she doesn't punch me in the nose for my efforts, I'll try to keep Ginny busy this afternoon so she doesn't spend it watching the clock." *And stewing over being separated from you.*

Lindsay's mouth curled into a grateful, lop-sided grin. Sometimes, she admitted, you find allies in the strangest places. *Now, String Bean, you get your ass back here this afternoon in one piece so that you can explain things to Ginny yourself.* She extended her hand to Christian. "I owe you one."

"Nonsense," the man scoffed good-naturedly, giving her hand a firm shake. "One can never have too many friends. And helping my friends is always my pleasure. If you'll excuse me now, I have another friend to attend to, who I fear is not very happy with me at the moment."

"You and me both, buddy," she mumbled unhappily, as she stepped out into the hall.

Across the street and down a few buildings from the orphanage, Delano restlessly paced the sidewalk, trying his best to stay warm. His alert eyes never left the Society for the Betterment of Children's doorway as he waited for his quarry to emerge.

The last of the afternoon sun was just beginning to disappear when Lindsay carefully approached the alleyway. Even if she left now, she wouldn't make it back to the orphanage until well after she'd told Ginny to expect her. This was her last stop, and if she didn't find them here, she'd be forced to admit that she simply couldn't find them at all—at least today. She'd hitched a ride on several trains as she searched, and her ribs and fingers ached from jumping in and out of boxcars that usually posed no problem at all.

The temperature had risen to a few degrees above freezing, and the afternoon sun had begun to melt the heavy layers of ice that blanketed nearly every surface. Long icicles that hung from the buildings' gutters and roofs shone blue in the shifting light, their constant dripping making it sound as though the city were being drenched in steady rain. Shallow puddles of smelly water had formed on the sidewalks and streets, and Lindsay waded through them gingerly, knowing that sometimes ice still lay hidden beneath. The last thing she wanted was to be jarred by an unexpected fall.

Then she heard them, and her mouth shaped into a feral grin.

"Shut up, Wop. I said *two* bits. The bet was *two* bits," Jacque barked.

"Fine. Fine," Albert conceded ungraciously, throwing his coins on the ground with a petulant hand.

Jean laughed.

The alley was lined with crates, strewn with stinking garbage, and dotted with empty metal drums that had rusted beyond use. Lindsay hid behind one as she watched the men shoot craps.

"Dammit. Snake eyes," Jacque hissed, kicking his coins closer to Albert.

"Pick 'em up, fat fuck."

A fourth man stood behind Albert, his hands in his pockets, apparently a bystander rather than a player in the game. Lindsay's eyes narrowed. He looked familiar. But then, so did a couple dozen rail-riders she'd run into over the last decade. *No matter*, she told herself. *I've come this far. Nothing is going to stop me, including him.*

And then she waited.

It was full dark, the moon and streetlamps providing the only illumination, before the game began to break up.

"That was a seven. I saw it! Look." Jean reached down and picked up the dice. He held them up for Jacque and Albert's examination.

His cousin shoved him hard, causing him to drop the dice. "Bullshit. You cheated and turned the dice when you picked them up. Don't cheat me, Jean."

"Whatever," Albert groaned tiredly. "It's too dark to play. I want something to eat." He scooped up his change and began to exit the alley in Lindsay's direction. The man who'd only been watching moved ahead of a lumbering Albert, his step light in comparison. They both walked right past Lindsay, oblivious to her hidden presence.

She let them get a few paces in front of her, then followed behind them quietly, picking up a large, heavy icicle that lay half submerged in a puddle as she moved.

The cold stung her palm, and her grip slipped a little as her fingers tightened around the icicle. Just before Albert reached the entrance to the alley, she took several large strides, until she was right behind him. Her upper lip curled into a snarl as she raised the icicle high above her head, bringing it down against his skull in a blow so vicious the ice shattered into dozens of small pieces.

Albert dropped like a sack of potatoes, his body thumping to the ground with a dull sound.

The other man walked on a few more paces before he realized that he was alone. He turned around and blinked in surprise at what he saw. He peered uncertainly through the shadows at Lindsay, deciding whether or not to bolt. She was crouched over Albert, and her cap was pulled down tightly over her head, leaving her face a mystery.

Lindsay was panting, and with trembling hands, she rolled Albert's hefty form over onto his back. "Go away," she hissed at the other man, sensing his continued presence, but not bothering to look up as she rifled through Albert's pockets. "He owes me money, and I'm collecting it. That's all. This is none of your business."

The man stood frozen, and Lindsay tilted her head upward, her eyes appearing an eerie black in the moonlight, as she gazed up from beneath the brim of her hat. "Are you deaf?"

The man lifted his palms in surrender and shrugged. He didn't want any trouble. "Nope. Not deaf. And it's not like I'm pals with that useless carcass Rat Face." He spared a look at Albert. "I was just bored today, so I tagged along for some action." The man grinned, but the lamplight was at his back and his smile was lost on Lindsay. "I don't have any money. I lost it all in the first five minutes to those crooked Frenchmen."

"I don't want your money. I told you, I'm not stealing from Rat Face; I'm only taking back what's mine." *What's coming to me.* Lindsay's eyes narrowed. The man's voice sounded vaguely familiar, but not enough to place it. "Then I guess you didn't see a thing, right?"

"Not a blessed thing," he agreed softly, before nodding and exiting the smelly alley. He disappeared around the corner.

Lindsay breathed a shaky sigh of relief. She checked Albert's pulse, not sure whether or not she was truly glad to find one. "Bastard." He had nearly two dollars in change, and she took it all, along with her pocketknife, before she dragged his body over to the wall and propped it up against one of the cool metal drums. *God, you weigh a ton! One down. Two idiots to go.*

Jean and Jacque were still arguing over their last bet when Lindsay crept deeper into the alley, hiding behind the same metal drum she'd used only moments before. She searched for another handy weapon, but there was none to be found.

Her pocketknife was small, and she doubted it would do much damage, considering the thick coats the men were wearing. But it was all she had, and so she carefully extracted it from her trouser pocket and opened the razor-sharp, three-inch blade. The thought of actually stabbing the men made her sick. *I won't let things get to that point*, she promised herself, all the while knowing how easily things could spin out of control. She was playing with fire, but she was willing to get burned if she had to.

Now what? This is what you came for. Think. Albert, she had known, wouldn't pose much of a problem. Lindsay had bested him before. Jean and Jacque, however, were another story. She was grateful it was only craps they were playing, and she shivered, remembering the dog's nasty breath against her face as he tore into her with deadly intent.

Deciding that her best chance of success was a sneak attack, she waited impatiently for the cousins to move in her direction.

Jean said something in French, and Jacque laughed, then lewdly adjusted his crotch. Jean cursed at his cousin in English, then spat at him. Jacque dodged the glob of spittle, his laughter increasing.

Lindsay made a face, glad she couldn't understand most of what they were saying.

When Jacque drew even with the drum Lindsay was hiding behind, she sprang to her feet, her hand darting out and tangling itself in his greasy black hair. Jacque's hat fell off, and he screamed as he was yanked to his knees, ice water splashing on him and Lindsay when he crashed to the ground. She moved in behind him, dropping to one knee and tightening her grip on his hair. She pressed the blade of her knife under his chin with enough force to draw a thin line of blood.

"Hello, boys," she said in a low voice. "Bet you're surprised to see me."

"Who?" Jacque choked out, his eyes bulging with fear. "See who?"
Jean wrinkled his nose. "It's that girl. The one the dog killed."

"Do I look dead, idiot?" Lindsay snapped.

Jacque swallowed carefully, feeling a trickle of hot blood trail down his neck.

"String Bean, right?" He licked his lips. "That… Well… that was just a little joke. Isn't that right, Jean?"

"Oh yeah. A joke," the other man dutifully answered, taking a large step backward.

"Uh-uh," Lindsay chastised, pressing the blade deeper into Jacque's skin, ignoring his high-pitched scream. "I guess you've noticed by now that I'm not laughing. It's payback time."

Jean shook his head sadly. "Adieu, cousin."

Lindsay rolled her eyes. "Not that sort of payback." She gave Jacque's head a firm tug for emphasis. "Not unless you make me."

Jacque's heart resumed beating.

"Empty your pockets," Lindsay instructed Jean, jerking her chin in his direction. "I figure that since you made money while you watched me get mauled by that evil dog, it's only fair that I get in on the action. After all, it was my blood."

Jean chewed at his scraggy, newly grown mustache. In his pocket was a shiny ten-dollar gold coin. Even Jacque didn't know about that. And there was no way in hell he was going to surrender it to some girl. "No," he said finally, thinking of how bossy his cousin had been lately. "Go ahead and kill him."

"Bastard!" Jacque wailed, causing the knife to nick him again.

Lindsay jerked his head back and repositioned the blade lower against his thick, sweat-slicked neck, not wanting to accidentally slit his throat. "I said, I'll kill him! I'm not bluffing, Jean," she warned, all the while inwardly cursing her rotten luck.

Jean shrugged again.

Jacque began to cry. "My mother is your mother's sister and your Godmother, and this is how you treat me? Your own blood?"

Broken sobs filled the alley, mingling with the endless plinking sounds of water droplets striking metal drums.

Jean's eyes softened. "No more bossing me, Jacque?" he asked warily, his hand sliding into his coat pocket.

"No more," Jacque sobbed. "I swear to the Holy Mother. No more."

Jean nodded, and pulled a pistol from his coat pocket. He drew in a deep breath and pointed the weapon straight at Lindsay and Jacque.

"Oh shit," Jacque and Lindsay breathed in unison, shocked.

"You had a gun?" Jacque questioned, suddenly indignant. "And you were still going to let her kill me?"

Lindsay didn't loosen her grip on her captive; instead, she ducked down a little behind Jacque's bulky body, using him as a shield.

Jean told Jacque bluntly, "You shouldn't pick on me so much,

Jacque." His gaze swung round to Lindsay. "Now, bitch, let him go before I shoot you."

"No," came the immediate response. "I'll slit his throat before you can shoot me."

Jean considered that. "I don't think so." He re-aimed the gun.

Jacque wet his pants. "No! No!" he screamed, heedless of the blade. "You'll miss and shoot me, you—"

BANG!

"Arghhhhh!" Jacque crumpled to the ground, howling and grabbing at his thigh. "Dieu! You son of a whore!"

The knife was torn from Lindsay's grasp by the force of Jacque's fall, and she hit the dirt the same time he did. It took her a few seconds to realize that she wasn't dead and that Jacque's prediction had proved true.

"You shot me! I can't believe it." Jacque's chin was bleeding from where the knife had sliced him when he fell, and dark blood was pouring from his thigh, blending with the icy water of the puddle he was lying in. "Jesus Christ!"

Jean stood paralyzed, staring with an open mouth at his writhing cousin. "Uh oh. That was an accident, Jacque."

Lindsay pushed herself to her feet and hurled herself at Jean. Her shoes left the ground as she tackled him, sending the gun skittering across the ground.

"Ugh." Jean barely avoided a wild punch. "Bitch, I'm gonna kill you."

She managed a single blow to his mouth, feeling his front teeth give way under her fist. The skin covering her knuckles split, a jagged flap of skin exposing the bone. The pair separated, both managing to stagger to their feet. He stumbled toward the gun, and she jumped on him again, ramming her knee into his ribs, and crying out herself when he grabbed her hand and twisted her barely healed fingers out of shape.

They fell to the ground in a tangled heap, rolling several times and drenching themselves in frigid, dirty water that had chunks of fish carcasses from the fishmonger next door floating in it. They cursed and grunted as they scratched and fought, exchanging blows to the face and chest. Lindsay managed to grasp the gun first. She turned it on Jean and fired without looking, sending the bullet zinging into the alley wall behind him. He scrambled to his feet and backed away.

"Take it easy, eh, String Bean?"' He sounded funny with no front teeth.

Jacque moaned, not so caught up in his own agony that he couldn't laugh at his cousin. "Kill him, you cowardly bitch. Shoot him for me!" he roared.

"No hard feelings, okay?" Jean tried again.

"Yes, hard feelings, you asshole," Lindsay muttered darkly. "You're just lucky there's nothing here for me to feed you to. Because I would." Her lip and nose were both bleeding sluggishly, and she cradled her damaged hand against her chest. The pain was making her nauseous, and she was starting to shake. She waved the gun recklessly at Jean, whose lip was split all the way to his nose. She needed this to be over quickly, before she passed out. Every breath hurt, and she could feel her ribs grinding against each other whenever she moved. "Empty Jacque's pockets. Now! Or I'll shoot you and do it myself."

"Here," Jacque said, holding out a handful of coins and two tattered bills to Jean. "Give it to the bitch." Jean hesitated again.

"Hurry up! I'm dying here." But the bleeding from Jacque's leg was starting to slow. The bullet had passed through the meaty portion of his thigh but missed his femoral artery. "For God's sake, asshole, you can't spend the money if you're dead."

Begrudgingly, Jean took the money and turned to face Lindsay.

"Set it down." She motioned to the ground in front of her. "And keep the cash out of the water." Lindsay shook her head a little, trying to clear away a shock of dark, wet hair that was stuck to her cheek.

Jean did as she asked and took a step backward again.

"Not so fast. Now yours," she instructed, her finger tightening on the trigger. This was the first time she'd ever held a gun. It was heavier than she expected, and the blast from both shots was still ringing in her ears.

Jean's eyes narrowed, but he did as she asked, pulling out a small handful of pennies and nickels.

"Keep going," Lindsay encouraged, knowing by the pissed-off look on his face that couldn't be the last of it.

Jean dug into his other pocket and pulled out a single coin. Its shiny gold surface glinted softly in the moonlight.

Jacque's eyes went wide as saucers. "Dammit! You were holding out on me?"

"Drop it. Hurry up!" Lindsay's eyes darted around nervously, and she wondered if someone would call the police because of the gunshots. Not to mention the fact that Albert should be coming to soon. She didn't need any more complications. Gagging, she spat out a warm mouthful of blood.

Jean let out a string of curse words and bent down to set his money alongside Jacque's. At the last moment, however, he couldn't do it and dove for Lindsay.

Lindsay jerked away, involuntarily squeezing the trigger several times. She heard the bullets hit the barrels and wall behind Jean, then the man fell to the ground screaming and wildly trying to reach the back of his shoulder with one hand.

Jacque laughed. "Stupid. She didn't even hit you straight on, and you still missed the gun. It was a ricochet. Hurts, doesn't it?" he taunted.

"Shit! Shit! Shit!" Lindsay chanted. "Why did you do that? I have a *gun*, you asswipe!" she shouted, her hands shaking so badly she was afraid she'd drop the pistol.

"'Cause he's stupid," Jacque told her, not even trying to move to help Jean. "Let him bleed to death."

Lindsay's face looked pale, even in the moonlight. *What have I done?*

Jean turned raging eyes on her. "You shot me!"

Jacque laughed again. "Hurts, don't—"

"Shut up! Just shut up," Lindsay ordered, wiping her eyes awkwardly with the back of her throbbing hand. She smeared blood across her face. "I need to think." She bent down and scooped up all the money, hastily shoving it into her pockets with her injured hand. Hot tears streaked her bloodstained cheeks from the pain the action caused. She stood, feeling queasy. "Stay here." She staggered a step closer to Jacque and picked up her pocketknife. "Don't follow me. And remember this next time you think it's a good idea to throw a person into the rat pit."

Jacque and Jean glared at her. "Don't worry, String Bean, we'll see you again," Jacque stupidly said.

"Not if I see you first." Lindsay glanced down the alley, seeing the outline of two men in the distance. She tried to focus. The men were getting closer. Limping slightly, she took off running in the opposite direction.

Ginny pressed her forehead against the moist windowpane as she stared down onto the street. Waiting. As the temperature dropped, shallow puddles that dotted the sidewalk were beginning to grow a thin layer of ice that reflected the moonlight and streetlamps. Following a lights-out custom an hour after dinner, the entire house was dark and quiet.

Far from being able to sleep, Ginny had lit a single beeswax candle some time ago, casting the room in long shadows. Christian had insisted she and Lindsay stay in the same room they had the night before, deciding that the three little boys, who were slated for that room, would feel more comfortable with other children on their first night in the house. Blankets and pillows had been laid out in Leo and Nuncio's tiny room, and all five boys were already getting along famously, their animated chatter finally quieting an hour ago.

"Lindsay," she whispered, her eyes rooted on the sidewalk below, "where are you?"

"Right here."

Ginny gasped, and spun around, her heart in her throat. "Lindsay?"

"You weren't expecting someone else, were you?" Lindsay teased weakly. She'd thrown up twice on the way home and, despite her shakiness, felt a little better than she had when leaving the alley.

"How did you get in?" Ginny rushed forward, her socked feet sliding on the smooth, cool wood as she came to a halt.

Lindsay looked down at her wet shoes. Her hands were stuffed deeply into her pockets. "I picked the lock on the service entrance. I—"

"Oh, my God." Ginny stepped closer, peering carefully at her friend. Lindsay smelled of foul water and fish bits, mixed with an unmistakable metallic scent. *Blood?* Lindsay stepped closer to the candle, and Ginny could see that her dark hair was matted and her face stained with crimson streaks. "What on earth happened?" Her voice was rising along with a surge of panic.

Lindsay's eyes fluttered shut. She suddenly felt very tired. "Ginny, can I—?"

"You're hurt." Ginny reached out and grabbed Lindsay by the biceps to steady her; the older woman was swaying a little. She looked as pale as she had in the hospital, and a new smell was released as Lindsay moved. The redhead got a whiff of—her mind raced as she tried to place the scent. Then her eyes went round. "Gunpowder," she whispered in disbelief. At one time, before he'd had to pawn them, her stepfather had amassed an impressive gun collection. She and Alice had been taught to clean and care for them, and the bitter scent of black powder was one she could place anywhere. Her heart began to pound as she searched Lindsay's body with frantic hands. "Are… God, are you shot? Where, Lindsay? Tell me!"

"No," Lindsay answered softly, pulling away from Ginny's seeking hands.

"I'm not shot. But, Ginny, I really need to sit down. It's been a long walk."

Ginny guided her over to the bed so she could sit down. "Sit. Bu— How did…? You're all wet." She blinked several times in confusion. It wasn't raining.

"Did you fall in the East River? That, at least, would explain the smell." Her tone was curt, but Lindsay could tell it was only because she was worried. Ginny shook her head in dismay. "Let me take this off." She began tugging at the sodden coat, but couldn't remove it with Lindsay's hands still stuffed deeply in its pockets.

"What time is it?" Lindsay asked dazedly, feeling chilled despite the fact that the house was well heated.

"Way past bedtime. Near nine, I think," Ginny answered, not really paying attention to the words. "You need to… here." She gave a gentle tug on one of Lindsay's arms, insisting that she remove her hands from the pockets, so she could take off her coat.

Gingerly, Lindsay tugged one hand free, groaning softly in pain. Picking the lock had nearly sent her to her knees in agony.

Ginny could see instantly that her fingers were broken again. She winced, her heart aching for her friend. "Oh, Lindsay."

Lindsay's second hand emerged significantly more slowly than the first, and was tightly wrapped around the handle of a black pistol.

Ginny forced herself not to jump back.

Lindsay's knuckles were still sluggishly bleeding, and a white bone peeked through the stained, torn flesh.

Frightened, tear-filled eyes ventured upwards to judge Ginny's reaction. Lindsay swallowed thickly. "Things…" She shook her head, her throat closing for a moment. "Things… they… they didn't go right."

Ginny own eyes brimmed with tears as she pushed a strand of dark hair from Lindsay's forehead, noting the swollen, cut lip. "I can see that, honey," she whispered tenderly, putting the weapon out of her mind for the moment. "You need me to help you?"

Lindsay's breathing hitched at the kindness in Ginny's voice, and she managed a quick nod. Then the words poured out in an almost incoherent stream. "It happened so—so f-fast. I didn't mean for it to. I swear. They're not dead, I don't think." She sucked in a shallow breath. "I'm sorry about this afternoon… so sorry. I didn't mean what I said. I *am* joined at the hip with you, Ginny. Like those poor Siamese bastards I once saw a picture of—that's us." She stopped, and gave her stunned friend a watery smile. "Just your luck, huh?"

Ginny gently cupped Lindsay's cheeks, stroking the dirty skin with a tender finger. "Just my luck," she repeated solemnly, making it very clear that that proposition was just fine by her. "Now, you need to give me the gun."

"No!" Lindsay shook her head frantically. "It's dangerous… Oh, God, I didn't mean to shoot—"

"Shhh. It'll be okay," Ginny soothed. *Dear Lord, she shot someone?* "I know guns are dangerous. I'll be very careful. Please, Lindsay, I can't help you until you give it to me."

Lindsay's hand was shaking so hard that Ginny had to steady it; then carefully, one by one, she pried Lindsay's fingers from the blood-drenched handle.

She deftly opened the cylinder and dumped the remaining bullets onto the bed. Then she snapped it closed and quickly placed it on the dresser. She paused, biting her lip, and grabbed the pistol again. Their bag would be a safer place.

Lindsay didn't hide her surprise. "How—?"

"You don't know everything about me yet, Lindsay Killian," Ginny said absently as she began rummaging through their bag for the remains of Bertha's purple dress. "Wonder if Bertha has any idea she turned out to be so useful?"

Lindsay decided to get up and help. "Ginny, are… aren't you," she paused, grunting in pain and changing her mind about getting up. Now that she was thawing out, she was starting to hurt more. "Aren't you going to ask me again what happened?"

"Suppose you save me the trouble, and just tell me instead." Ginny poured water from a pitcher, which Christian had thoughtfully placed in their room earlier that evening, into a small washbasin and carried the basin over to the bed. "I need something to cut the dress."

"Knife's in my coat pocket," Lindsay told her tiredly. *God, I'm an idiot. Only an idiot would be hurting this bad. I should have stayed away from those insane rat-bastard cousins.*

Ginny reached into the pocket, and her fingers brushed against a cool pile of coins. She glanced up at her friend in question.

Lindsay sighed. "Some guys I know owed me some money." She tried to shrug without moving her ribs, but it was impossible and she gave up quickly. "Only they didn't want to pay me back, and things… Well, things…" She carefully covered her eyes with dirty palms. "I dunno what happened."

Ginny bit her tongue, suspecting that Lindsay would tell her *everything* if she could only clamp down on her natural inclination to nag the information out of her. "I see," she said noncommittally, extracting the knife from the other pocket. It was hard to open, and she realized why when she saw the blade, which was covered in half-dried, sticky blood. Ginny's stomach roiled, but she forced herself to cut several long strips of material.

"It's not mine," Lindsay whispered, seeing the color drain from Ginny's face. "I just got a good old fashioned ass-kickin'." She groaned inwardly, more than a little disgusted with herself. "Again."

"We should get a doctor. You look awful."

Lindsay's eyebrows jumped. "Gee, thanks, but I don't want a doctor." A memory of her most recent experiences with a doctor, including herself sitting in Bertha's lap ready to lay a big wet one on the large woman, flittered through her mind. She wanted to grin, but her heart wasn't in it. "I don't want to end up in the asylum."

"I have no idea what you're talking about," Ginny said testily. "Did you get hit on the head again?"

Lindsay pursed her lips. "Probably."

Ginny let out an unhappy grunt. "You swear you're not seriously hurt? I've never known somebody who gets in as many scrapes as you do."

"Sadly, I think I'll live." She trembled a little, feeling chilled.

Ginny expelled a shaky breath, lightheaded in her relief. *Thank you, God.* "Where are you hurt the worst?"

"I think my ribs are cracked… hurts to breathe." Ginny began tugging at her shirt until Lindsay stopped her. "Leave it. There's not a damn thing you can do about it now. My fingers need to be re-splinted though, or I'm gonna end up with gnarled paws like an old woman." She slowly extended her cut hand, and Ginny nodded at the sickening sight. "This, on the other hand," she chuckled weakly at her bad pun, "needs something."

"All right. I'll be right back." Ginny rushed out of the room, taking great gulps of air as she exploded into the hallway, then leaned back against its cool wooden panels, closing her eyes. "What have you done, Lindsay?" A gun, a bloody knife, a pocket full of money she didn't have before—all had Ginny's mind spinning. Much to her surprise, however, she composed herself quickly, knowing that right now her attention was needed elsewhere. After wiping the blood off her hands on a dirty towel in the laundry room and rousing the half-asleep washerwoman who lived in a small room on the first floor, she concocted a lie and obtained a needle and thread.

When Ginny returned to their room, she found her friend half-undressed and awkwardly running a damp washcloth over her face. The white cloth was stained red, and the water in the basin already needed to be changed. Ginny swallowed hard. *Okay, a change of plans.* "Can you make it downstairs to the basement on your own? Because there is no way I can carry you." She didn't want to drag Christian into whatever it was they were involved in, but she would if she had to.

Lindsay blinked. "I made it up here from across town. I suppose I can get downstairs." Though the thought of traversing the stairs wasn't a pleasant one. "But I don't—"

Ginny set the needle and thread on the dresser and gently closed the door behind her. "You're filthy and covered in blood. This tiny washbasin won't be enough. You need a real bath. You've got… Lord only knows what in your hair, and I need to clean your hand and lip." She sounded worried. "Lindsay, you're more likely to get an infection now. You need to get cleaned up. Properly." Her demeanor brokered no argument, and despite the overwhelming desire to do nothing more than curl up in a ball and go to sleep, Lindsay caved in quickly.

"All right."

Ginny's nervous gaze strayed to the window. "Should we be expecting the police?"

"I…" Lindsay couldn't help but glance in that direction too. "I don't think so. I don't think I was followed." She paused so long Ginny figured that she was finished when Lindsay quietly said, "I think I'd better tell you what happened."

Finally. "It might help, Lindsay."

"C'mon, I'll explain while I'm getting cleaned up." Lindsay leaned forward, tense lines of pain marring her face as she moved. She stopped, sighed, and gave Ginny a long-suffering look. "Will you help me?"

Ginny was already at her side, helping her onto her feet. "Silly question." She pulled a sheet from the bed and wrapped Lindsay in it, hoping they wouldn't run into any of the children, who were all supposed to be in bed, on the way downstairs.

They were in the first floor washroom and Lindsay had climbed into one of the large tubs. A huge wood stove was kept well-fed twenty-four hours a day in the winter, its vents heating several of the first floor bedrooms. The washroom itself was toasty warm, and Lindsay felt herself relaxing in the moist heat as Ginny drained the tub, whisking away most of the grime and blood that had been on Lindsay. Her hand and lip had stopped bleeding, but a large mottled bruise still covered her ribs below her left breast.

The redhead refilled the tub three-quarters full with steaming water and moved behind Lindsay, kneeling to wash her hair. She was wearing the trousers and man's shirt her companion had stolen from the Charity Hospital for her and was glad for the ease of movement the garments allowed. Ginny's face was covered with a light sheen of perspiration from the steamy air, and she pushed her own hair out of her eyes with the back of one hand, before she lathered her hands with a large bar of white soap. "Dunk," she ordered, hearing the crack in her own voice. She worked quickly, wanting to attend to Lindsay's hand.

"Feels good," Lindsay murmured, her eyes closed in pleasure. This almost… almost made the ass-whippin' worth it. "Thank you." Things didn't seem so desperate now that she was here with Ginny. She felt her panic subside and the nausea that had been plaguing her ease.

"What happened next?" Ginny wasn't at all sure she wanted to know.

"Then I came back here."

Ginny let out the breath she'd been holding. "Thank God. Do you know how close you came to getting killed for the sake of a few dollars?" The righteous indignation she'd been holding in all day came flooding back, and she began scrubbing harder, her movements jerky and abrupt. "Hard as you might find it to believe, you're worth more than twelve dollars."

"Ginny," Lindsay spoke through gritted teeth. "Don't get huffed, please."

Ginny's hands slowed. "I'm sorry," she murmured, taking the time to lean forward and place a soft kiss on Lindsay's cheek. She couldn't help but smile when she saw that cheek flush.

"S'okay. That was my money," Lindsay said, examining both her hands. She could wiggle the index finger on the hand with the damaged fingers and figured that one must only be bruised. "Besides, we'll need that money for traveling and food."

"Lindsay." Ginny cupped Lindsay's chin from behind, asking her to turn her head. The young women locked eyes, and their faces were so close together that Ginny only needed to whisper. "I've lived nearly my entire life in a household where trying to find a way to get another dollar was more important than anything else. It came before our health, our safety, our comfort, even our love. Though in my heart, I don't think Arthur meant it to or even understood that it did. And Mama never once tried to change things."

Ginny licked her lips, fighting the urge to break Lindsay's intense gaze. "They're dead now." She felt a lump grow in her throat. "And I won't live that way again. *Ever.*" *Not even to be with you, Lindsay.* "There has to be a better way." She searched her eyes. "Do you understand?"

Lindsay nodded slowly. *Shit.* "I think so." She turned away, feeling well and truly chastised. "It wasn't that the money was more important than you are, but it was *my* money," she repeated, the statement having the same pathetic impact it had the first time she'd said it to Ginny.

"Dunk."

The brunette did, and when she emerged, she felt another bucket of water dumped over her head. She sputtered and coughed, cursing at the pain that caused her split lip. "Hey," she complained weakly. Next she felt hands rinsing the remaining soap from her hair.

Ginny ignored Lindsay's protest. Her feelings were so raw right now, she didn't trust herself to keep things civil. *Of all the stupid… careless… dangerous—* "Lindsay?"

"Hmm?"

"What did those men owe you money for? Were you playing craps too?"

Lindsay snorted. "Hardly." She mulled this next part over. It was pretty embarrassing, but this was Ginny. "One of them robbed me and pushed me out of a moving boxcar."

"What?" Ginny screeched.

"And then when I went to try to get my stuff back from him, his two asshole pals beat me senseless"—Ginny's hands stilled—"and tossed me into a pit, where they bet on how long it would take a mad dog to kill me."

"Bu—that's why you were in the Charity Hospital? The cuts and your ear and everything else? *They* did that?" Ginny was truly stunned. She'd assumed Lindsay had been in some sort of accident, or maybe attacked by a rabid dog.

"Them and the dog, I guess."

Ginny pulled her hands from Lindsay's hair. They involuntarily shaped themselves into quivering fists. Her face flushed, and her pulse began to race as a wave of rage crested within her. "They tried to kill you."

Lindsay shrugged one shoulder. "Well, yeah, so I figured the money they were betting, and then any more money they made off that money, was mine." Something didn't sound right in Ginny's voice, and she turned around, her eyes widening at the look on Ginny's face.

"Bastards," Ginny spat, shooting to her feet.

Lindsay winced. Ginny was picking up her colorful vocabulary.

Ginny wiped her hands on her trousers. "If I'd known… They're lucky it wasn't me in that alley tonight, or they'd be dead right now." She picked up a towel from a stack on the table next to the tub, wringing it with strong hands as she silently seethed, both at the men and at Lindsay.

"You're a better shot than me, huh?" Lindsay teased weakly, the thought of the gun making her sick to her stomach again. She hated guns. Just the sound of one going off, which had been a regular occurrence in the shanty town where she'd lived as a child, scared her witless.

"This is not funny!" Ginny snapped. "They tried to murder you once and they almost killed you again!"

Lindsay bit off a groan as she leaned forward onto one knee and rose to her feet, sending a sheet of water cascading down her body.

The younger woman's rant derailed, and her mouth went cottony-dry in a heartbeat as she stared at her friend's wet body. She had never been presented with anything so overtly gorgeous in her entire life. The friends had helped each other wash in the hospital to be certain, but they were never alone there, and they'd always had towels and hospital gowns to protect their privacy as best they could—unlike now. Steam was rising from Lindsay's skin, that was tinted pink from the hot water, and her hair was slicked back off her face. "Lord have mercy," Ginny said out loud without even realizing she'd spoken.

Lindsay held her injured hands out slightly in front of her, and looked down at the lurid bruise below her breast, deciding it was ridiculous to be self-conscious about her nakedness at this point. She couldn't see the bruise as well as she wanted to; so with the hand whose knuckles were cut, she gently shifted her breast to the side.

Ginny gasped, surprised she hadn't passed out at the sight.

"Looks pretty bad, huh?" Lindsay narrowed her eyes at the purple skin. "Ugh."

"Bad?" She licked her lips. "Are you blind?"

Confused, Lindsay blinked a few times. Her eyes seemed okay. "What are you—?"

"Nothing," Ginny said quickly, snapping out of her reverie and thinking that perhaps she could use a bath herself—a nice cold one. "Here." She extended the towel to Lindsay who only looked at it and then back up at Ginny.

"Umm… Could you?"

"I'm sorry," Ginny shook her head and chided her unruly thoughts. "Of course." *What's wrong with me? She's hurt, and I'm drooling over her like one of the pigs from the rail yard.* As carefully as she could, she set to work drying Lindsay; the task banished all dark thoughts of finding Jacque and Jean and finishing what Lindsay had started. Outwardly, she did her best to maintain a detached air. To her heart, and most especially to her body, the simple chore amounted to delicious torture. She was extra careful with Lindsay's ribs, frowning at the bruise, and knowing how badly it must hurt.

Lindsay closed her eyes at Ginny's ministrations. They felt wonderful, making her feel not just well cared for, but cherished. She sighed. *If I didn't feel like crap, I'd never be able to keep from moaning at how fabulous her hands feel on me.* Ginny gently dragged the towel down her back, lifting her hair and giving it a good squeeze before drying her neck. The towel moved lower, caressing the skin on her bottom before reaching her thighs.

Lindsay moaned. *Okay, I was wrong.*

Ginny grinned to herself at the sound. When she was finished, she drained the tub and tossed the towel and sheet from their bed into a laundry hamper, grabbing a fresh sheet for Lindsay to wrap up in.

"Thank you, Ginny."

"You're welcome. C'mon, let's get your hand taken care of and you in bed. You've got two days to rest up before we're catching a train out West. That's the next time we can duplicate the stops the orphan train made without losing too many days." She and Christian had spent the latter part of the afternoon on his phone with the stationmaster's office, mapping out a schedule.

"Wonderful. I… um… I probably shouldn't hang around Queens or the entire State of New York for a while." She couldn't be sure that the police weren't looking for her.

"Mmm. Probably not." Ginny couldn't help but smirk. "And now it looks like we'll have money for two tickets."

"What? Tickets?" Lindsay exploded. She reached up to touch her split lip, which was stinging from her sudden outburst. "Ouch." She tasted blood.

Ginny waggled her finger at Lindsay. "Don't yell." Lindsay made a face. Ginny sighed. "Or pout. Not that you *can* pout." She crossed her arms over her chest. "We're buying two tickets and sitting with the other passengers. You are *not* jumping on and off trains."

"But—" Ginny's glare silenced her. Lindsay gulped. "Fine." She wanted to say more, but she didn't dare. She did, however, roll her eyes in a last, rather pitiful show of defiance. If the boys at the tracks heard about her buying a ticket, she'd never live it down.

"Let's go. Here," Ginny wrapped her arm around Lindsay's for balance. "Yeah, that's it. Lean on me." And so Lindsay did.

Chapter Nine

"Well, here we are," Christian said. He gave a tug on the reins, and the buggy carrying him, Ginny, and Lindsay rolled to a stop. Dozens of wagons were packed in around the station, crowding the street. Horses' hooves stamped, splashing in the icy mud as the beasts snorted in the cool, smoky morning. Several teams were clearly agitated by the throngs of New Yorkers determinedly pushing their way to and from the platform. Steam engines arriving and departing hissed loudly, and their wheels screeched. Conductors, who controlled the crowds with whistles and booming voices, shouted out various train numbers and destinations, but even their voices were drowned out by the long wail of train whistles that sounded off regularly.

It was deafening.

Ginny grabbed their bag and allowed Christian to help her out of the buggy. The young woman was wearing men's clothing and a new cap they'd purchased the day before, the kind the paperboys wore. "Thank you," she said in a raised voice so that Christian could hear her.

He smiled and offered his hand to Lindsay. When it became clear she couldn't take it, he moved forward and put his hands on her waist, helping absorb some of the shock as her feet hit the wooden boards that had been placed over the sidewalks so people wouldn't have to wade through the deep mud. Two days of temperatures above freezing had the streets looking more like pigsties than roads. The stench of horse dung and mud filled the air.

"Thanks, Christian," Lindsay told him sincerely, a little embarrassed that she'd needed his help. Her ribs protested her every move, but her fingers and the crookedly sewn cut on her knuckles had already begun to slowly heal. Her lip was no longer swollen, and the cut had scabbed over, though the skin around it was still tender.

The trio stood awkwardly. They had become good friends in a short time, and this was goodbye. "Christian," Ginny began, not knowing quite what to say. "I can't ever repay your kindness. From the bottom of my heart, thank you."

Christian flushed with pleasure. "You're welcome."

Feeling uncomfortable, Lindsay clasped Christian's shoulder and offered her own thank-you, before pushing her way up onto the platform and heading toward the ticket office. In her pocket was a list of the cities they needed to stop in.

Christian blinked, watching Lindsay hurry away. "Well, I didn't expect that."

Ginny sighed a little as Lindsay disappeared. "I don't think she's had a lot of friends, Christian. She doesn't know what to do."

"Ahh." He wrapped his arm around Ginny's shoulder and led her to the corner of the station, where they could talk without having to constantly move aside for passersby. "Saying goodbye is always hard, especially when you know you won't be seeing the people again."

A tiny crease appeared on Ginny's forehead. "You don't know that."

"Don't I? There's nothing here calling you back. I should imagine the lures of the West will capture both your fancies." His gaze drifted back to where Lindsay had been swallowed up by the crowd.

Ginny gave him a fond, somewhat sympathetic look. "She's easy to care about, isn't she?"

He shrugged one shoulder, acknowledging a simple truth. "You both are." Before Ginny could answer, Lindsay reappeared with two tickets. She looked a little lost, which for some reason Ginny found endearing. Here was a person who'd spent most of her life in boxcars and around train stations and who'd never ridden with the other ticketed passengers, even once. This was going to be an adventure.

Lindsay extended her hand to Christian, and the man took it in his but didn't squeeze.

"Be safe, String Bean."

Lindsay nodded. "You too. And thanks for the nightshirts." Then, on a whim, she leaned forward and pressed her lips gently to his ear. "What you're doing with the children is more important than you know. If the world had more folks in it like you… well, it would be a better place is all."

A little self-consciously, she pulled away and stepped aside, so that Ginny could say goodbye.

The redhead boldly gave Christian a peck on the cheek. She pulled back and looked him dead in the eye with smiling, but serious eyes. "Take care, Christian, and thank you again. I won't forget you."

With that, the women turned and arm in arm began weaving their way through the crowd.

Stunned, Christian lifted a hand to his cheek, feeling its flaming heat against his fingers. Just when he was certain he was falling for one woman, the other would do something sweet, or interesting, or funny, and make him reconsider. He shook his head and chuckled as he walked to the buggy, admitting to himself that he simply couldn't choose and had been left with a hopeless crush on them *both*. "Timing," he muttered to himself, "timing, Christian, is everything. And yours stinks."

Jeremiah scrubbed his face and spoke through his hands. "This happened the night before last, you say?"

"Yes, sir. I couldn't believe it myself. It was too dark for me to see who did the shooting, but the dark-haired one they called String Bean was the only one who left the alley without a bullet in her. She went back to Spence's orphanage and didn't come out all day yesterday." What Delano didn't mention was that, after he'd heard the first gunshot, he'd been too frightened to get close enough to find out what had really happened in the alley.

"Bella, Bella, this is more serious than we suspected." He made a fist. "Not that I needed any *more* proof that the woman is unbalanced. I knew that sniveling fool, Christian Spence, had to be involved somehow!" Jeremiah Ward paced the floor in front of his wife, who was sitting at the desk in their office. The Wards had been out of town the day before, and this was the first time that Delano had had an opportunity to give them the shocking news.

"Both the young women are dangerous," Isabelle said, tapping the desk with a pencil. Steam rose from the small china cup in her other hand, sending the aroma of fresh coffee into the air. "Spence won't do a thing without proof."

"Yes!" Jeremiah agreed instantly, laying his palms on the desk as he leaned closer to his wife. "Much too dangerous to ignore." *What if she comes back here after me?* He'd thought gun-wielding women only existed in those ridiculous dime novels. "We must—"

Isabelle silenced him with a raised hand. She turned to Delano. "And the man, the one you told us about earlier?"

"Rat Face?"

Isabelle rolled her eyes. "If you say so. He said he knew her."

"He said a lot of things after I paid him a few coins."

A nod. "And what sort of man is this Rat Face? A friend of… String Bean?" Just having to say these ridiculous names was making her angry. She set down her cup. Its base had a tiny chip in it, and she frowned, turning the cup slightly, so that only she could see the imperfection.

Delano's eyes narrowed as he thought back, wondering if he should repeat the coarse language in front of a woman. "He's a… he's a rough sort, ma'am, part criminal, part beggar. He cursed the woman many, many times and told me what he'd do if he ever saw her again. He's no friend of String Bean's."

"Interesting," Isabelle pointedly commented. She took a final sip and set the cup aside along with her pencil.

Jeremiah turned around and sat on the edge of the desk. He felt Isabelle's hand come to rest on his back, the comforting warmth of her palm seeping through his thin woolen vest, starched cotton shirt, and undershirt.

The small woman stood and moved alongside her husband, leaving her hand where it was. Virginia Chisholm and this String Bean woman were a team. She had seen the subtle give-and-take between them when they'd confronted her and Jeremiah. It was something she understood quite well. Partnerships were about balance. Upset the balance and you upset the partnership, thereby weakening the team. Alone, String Bean had no business with them. Alone, how much of a problem would Virginia Chisholm really be? *Let's find out.* "Well then, Delano, perhaps if we… *encouraged* this Rat Face to find String Bean, some of our problems would start to take care of themselves."

Jeremiah smiled. "That's an excellent idea." His pride was still smarting, and the thought of some harm coming to the brash young woman who'd bested him in front of his beloved filled him with a quiet satisfaction. He reached into his vest pocket and pulled out two silver dollars. Then he moved around to his desk and unlocked the bottom drawer. He glanced up at Isabelle, who nodded. In the drawer was a locked cash box. It opened with a sharp click, and he removed a crisp ten-dollar note from the bottom, idly wishing he hadn't had to reach through the few tattered singles above it. Business could always be better.

Delano's eyes widened slightly. He hoped he was being rewarded for his diligence. Mr. Ward was holding a week's pay.

"Delano," Jeremiah ripped the bill neatly in half, ignoring the other man's shocked gasp, "perhaps this will encourage Rat Face to follow String Bean and… bring her to justice. You followed her and Virginia Chisholm this morning. It's clear they're going after the children. Even someone named Rat Face should be able to find them."

Rat Face had said over and over what he'd do to String Bean if he ever saw her again; though privately, Delano didn't believe the man had enough nerve to follow through with his threats. "You want him to hurt her?" he asked casually, trying not to show how nervous just saying the words made him.

"Of course not!" Isabelle snapped, her eyes flashing. "We never said that. *Never.*" Then she visibly calmed herself and smoothed the fabric on her dress.

"We're doing nothing more than encouraging the victim of a robbery to reclaim his stolen property and inform the police of String Bean's whereabouts. You did say that he believed String Bean robbed him, correct?" She waited for him to nod dutifully. "But Jeremiah and I are realists, and we do know that things— sometimes unfortunate things—happen."

"Yes, they do."

Jeremiah rolled the silver dollars around in his palm. "If Rat Face locates String Bean, and she somehow ends up in jail or otherwise incapacitated, he can come back here and collect this reward." He turned to his wife and reached out to stroke her cheek. "I consider it our civic duty to promote the hunting down of criminals, don't you, Bella?"

She leaned into the touch. "Absolutely, Jeremiah. And the fact that Miss Chisholm and the ever-pious Mr. Spence consort with people of such obvious ill repute only serves to discredit them. Which is exactly what we need."

A contented chuckle escaped from the back of Jeremiah's throat.

Delano scowled. He had thought he was sure what they wanted, but now—

"Mr. Ward, I don't think Rat Face will go anywhere near the police. I think once he finds her he'll—"

"Enough," Isabelle warned him firmly, her eyes glinting with anger. Why did Jeremiah employ this idiot, who clearly had no appreciation of the type of discretion required to carry out business in the modern world? She expected more from her husband. "I don't want to hear speculation, Delano. I don't want to know about things like that." She slowed her speech. "*Ever*. Do you understand?"

Delano nodded quickly, recognizing from the look on her face that he'd made a serious error. "Yes, ma'am." He stepped closer and glanced nervously at Mr. Ward, whose face was set in granite. "My apologies to the both of you."

"Then here." Reaching out, Jeremiah pressed the coins and half the bill into Delano's hand. "I expect Rat Face will be leaving immediately. The two dollars are for his expenses."

Delano looked at the money doubtfully. "But the cost of a ticket alone is—"

"None of our concern," Isabelle interrupted. She strode across the room and opened the door, effectively dismissing him. "I believe you have someone to find, don't you?"

When the door slammed behind Delano, Isabelle whirled around and raised a sharp eyebrow at her husband.

He looked down at his shoes guiltily. Delano needed a lesson in discretion—a severe lesson. "I'll speak with him privately, Bella."

"See that you do," she said crisply as she moved back behind the desk. There was work to be done.

Lindsay shifted uncomfortably in her seat. The padded wooden bench was covered with a thickly napped red fabric and was barely big enough for her and Ginny. In fact, their thighs and shoulders were touching. That however, was not what was bothering Lindsay, who had decided if Ginny wanted to sit on her lap the entire trip that would be fine too. Problem was, the train was cramped and crowded.

Several men in the back of the car were smoking cigars, and the smoke wafted over them in great clouds. People were staring at the way she was dressed, and Lindsay realized for the first time why Ginny had chosen to dress in a similar fashion. *Now they'll look at both of us and not just me, huh? Ginny, Ginny, what am I going to do with you?* Her mind sighed contentedly, and her chest tightened with a surge of affection for her companion.

Ginny noticed the odd expression on Lindsay's face and leaned over to whisper in her ear. "What's the matter, my Bruised Tomato? Hurting today?"

A laugh bubbled up from deep inside, and Lindsay shook her head, laying one of her bandaged hands on Ginny's knee and giving it a gentle squeeze.

"Bruised is right," she acknowledged wryly. "But otherwise I'm really good, Ginny." *Better than you know.*

"Good." Ginny's delighted grin showed off her dimples, and she glanced down at Lindsay's hand, placing her own atop it. Her spirits were higher than they'd been in days. Lindsay was healing slowly but steadily, and though there hadn't been too much kissing, in deference to her friend's injuries, she hadn't been able to resist giving her a few.

They'd both grown slightly bolder, and she found herself flushing just thinking about it. She tried not to do that too much, though. It was not only unbelievably distracting, but still a little bewildering and scary. And as if that weren't enough to keep her mind spinning, they were finally on their way to find James, Lewis, and Jane. They'd all already been through so much. She couldn't help but think that things could only get better from here.

The train whistle blew, drowning out the constant hum of conversation around them. A black cloud erupted from the smokestack, and the train lurched forward.

The wooden cars squeaked with the steady movement of the wheels, and Lindsay began looking around. The men in the seat directly across from her and Ginny were already asleep. She wondered idly if they knew just how easy it would be for her to lean over casually and relieve them of the burden of their wallets. She snorted to herself, suspecting that they didn't.

Lindsay didn't like the way it smelled in here and felt an irrational jolt of anger at having to purchase a ticket, when they could be traveling in an airy boxcar, stretched out on their backs with warm blankets as they watched the world go by. No one would be around to look down their noses at Ginny then. Of course, she didn't dwell on the fact that they'd have to take three times as many trains to get where they were going, and that she'd probably kill herself trying to get in and out of them. And there was always an element of danger. Many times you weren't alone in a boxcar. Still, the air in this car was a sickly combination of wet woolen clothing and leather shoes, sweat, cloying perfume, and food.

"Ugh." Ginny wrinkled her nose. "Is that fish I smell?" *For breakfast?*

"Do you really want to know?"

"Good point."

Lindsay didn't move her hand from Ginny's knee for the next couple of hours—even when it fell asleep.

They changed trains in Jersey City and settled into a second-class car, much like the first one they'd been in. A thin Negro man, dressed in a starched, navy-blue uniform, with a black necktie, a leather-billed black hat, and the shiniest shoes Lindsay had ever seen, approached them with a hole-puncher in one hand and a pencil in the other. He politely asked to see their tickets and confirmed that they were, indeed, proper passengers on the Pennsylvania Railroad, train number 8704 to Washington, D.C. He punched a tiny square out of the tickets next to the name of the city, before moving on to the next passenger and the passenger after that.

Their next stop wouldn't be for four more hours, and Ginny could tell that Lindsay was bored and anxious, still struggling with her unaccustomed role as a regular passenger. Her dark-haired friend was so used to hiding from railway employees that she visibly flinched every time one walked by.

This experience wasn't wholly new to Ginny. When they were little girls, while her father was still alive, she and Alice would take the train every summer to upstate New York and visit her father's parents. She considered those visits the sweetest, golden time of her childhood, and she and Alice had recalled the fond memories often. But first her grandfather passed away, then her father the following year. When her grandmother died six months later, there was no one left to visit.

"Lindsay?" Ginny began, pulling herself out of her memories, "I've been thinking."

Lindsay perked up a little. Ginny's voice sounded serious. "Yeah?"

"We need a plan to fall back on if the family that has the children doesn't want to give them up. I was thinking we—"

"Family?" A crease appeared in Lindsay's forehead. "You do realize that chances are they didn't all go to the same family? We could be dealing with three different families in three different cities."

Ginny stared at Lindsay for a second, the words not penetrating her brain. Finally she began to sputter. "Bu-bu—" She squeezed her eyes tightly shut. *Why didn't I think of that before? Of all the stupid—* When she opened her eyes again, they glistened with unshed tears. "Who would do that?" she whispered harshly. "Who would split them up? The boys are twins, for God's sake; and Jane… she's only a baby, they're all she has!" Her voice rose as her emotions spilled over. In her mind, she'd always allowed herself to be comforted by the fact that they would at least have each other. Her guilt made her sick. What if they were truly all alone with strangers?

The outburst caused Lindsay to pull back, her eyes wide. Why was Ginny so upset over the obvious? Some of the passengers were staring, and she returned their glares hotly, daring them to continue to stare. "What are you lookin' at?" she growled at the gaping man in the seat across from them. He wasn't even pretending not to be listening avidly to their conversation.

The man blinked stupidly, unable to believe that one of the strange women dressed like men was addressing him. Then he stiffened in his seat and jerked his newspaper out of the leather satchel at his feet. He shook it open loudly and promptly blocked out the view, though Lindsay could hear him grumbling behind the business section.

"That's what I thought," the rail-rider said under her breath. Ginny's face was red, but Lindsay couldn't tell whether it was from embarrassment or because she was upset. *Guess it doesn't matter.* She gentled her voice. "Ginny?"

Feeling foolish, Ginny hesitantly swung her eyes up to meet Lindsay's.

"Don't tie yourself in a knot, okay? I'm sure they tried to place them in a home together." Ginny's shoulders sagged, and Lindsay quickly moved to reassure her, sorry now that she'd said anything in the first place. "Hey, we don't know exactly who has them for sure. Maybe they all three went to a family at the very first stop." She lifted her eyebrows and cocked her head slightly to the side. "We can still hope, right?"

The words transported Ginny back to a snowy night on Orchard Street when Lewis, his little face stained with soot and his cheeks streaked with tears, looked up with all the hope and faith a child could possess and uttered the exact same thing. Even now, she could feel the cold wind ruffling her hair and the sting of tiny snowflakes as they melted against her hot face, while she had stood there, helplessly watching her life go up in flames. *Stop it*, she told herself ruthlessly. *Was it only a few weeks ago… a month?* It seemed like ages.

"What's your plan if the folks who did the adopting don't want to turn the kids over to you?" Lindsay asked her, desperately hoping to steer the conversation back to safer ground.

With a sad smile, Ginny allowed herself to be dragged back into the moment. "Don't worry. I'm all right. I don't know why I hadn't thought of that before. Stupid, I suppose." A grim look chased its way over her normally bright features, making Ginny appear much older than her seventeen years. "Okay. I've been thinking about this for days." And she had. She'd imagined some sweet, loving couple, who had tried to start a family but couldn't. They would have taken in all her siblings to give them a loving home. And now she was coming to rip the couple's beating hearts from their chests.

"I see," Lindsay said gravely, adjusting her coat, which was wadded up against the window in a vain attempt to keep the cold air out. The look of guilt in those blue eyes next to her was unmistakable. It was an emotion Lindsay saw little use for.

Ginny's eyebrows jumped. She leaned forward and propped her elbows on her knees, resting her chin on her fist. "What exactly do you see, Miss Mind-Reading Rutabaga? You don't know what I'm going to say."

Lindsay stuck out the tip of her tongue at the younger woman, relieved that Ginny's good humor seemed to be making a reappearance. So much had happened to both of them, so fast, they were prone to the occasional outburst. But that was okay. They had been working on that together.

"Well?" Ginny prompted again, giving Lindsay's chest a tiny poke with a challenging finger. "What do you see?"

A single brown eyebrow lifted. "I see someone who feels guilty that she's about to claim what's already hers—her family."

The look on Lindsay's face dared her to disagree. "Wh-whoa." Ginny let out a long breath, a little unnerved at the other woman's ability to read her so clearly.

"I'm that obvious?"

"Mmm-hmm."

"But, Lindsay—"

"No buts. Your brothers, at least, know you're out here... somewhere." A fond, slightly wry smile tugged at the corner of Lindsay's lips. "If they're anything like you, then they're not shy about saying what's on their mind. Whoever's got them knows about you,

Ginny. And they have to know it's only a matter of time 'til you turn up."

Ginny sat back in her seat and forlornly gazed out the window. "I just don't want anyone else to get hurt, Lindsay." Her eyes remained fixed on the passing scenery. "I know I'm putting the cart before the horse, but there's been enough hurting to go around lately, don't you think?"

Lindsay followed Ginny's line of sight, watching the trees and snowy landscape speed by. Finally, she sighed and said, "Someone might get hurt." She felt her way carefully through the sensitive issue. "But if they do, it's the Wards who are to blame for this mess. Not you. The guilt rests on their shoulders, Ginny. Let it go."

Ginny turned her head and gave Lindsay a weak smile, trying to adopt her friend's attitude, but failing quickly.

"Now, what about your plan?"

Ginny's expression grew determined. "If they won't give them back voluntarily, I'm taking them anyway, Lindsay. They can't have my family. They just can't. The law can call it kidnapping if they want to, but it's not true. We belong together." She paused, not wanting to continue. Her next words were physically painful, though she knew they needed to be said. "You could probably get into a whole lot of trouble if you do this with me and—"

"Oh, for fuck's sake!" Lindsay exploded, rolling her eyes. "Do I seem to be concerned about the law?"

"Lindsay!" Ginny hissed, glancing at the other passengers, who were shooting her companion disgusted looks.

"You clearly have me confused with someone else." She snorted then questioned Ginny impatiently. "What?" She gave Ginny a pointed look. "You were going to tell me something stupid, like I'd better not help you because I could get in trouble." Ginny opened her mouth to speak, but Lindsay plowed ahead, undeterred. "I know you, Virginia Chisholm. Don't try to lie your way out of it. This is the part where you make some selfless statement about how I'll be better off not helping you. Let's get this out of the way here and now, I'm in this mess and not getting out of it anytime soon." She nodded firmly. "I don't want to get out of it. So there." Lindsay lifted her chin, a little proud at the way she'd handled that.

Ginny threw her hands in the air and groaned. "You make it sound like a bad thing that I don't want you getting into trouble!"

"It's not bad." She gave Ginny a ghost of a wink. "Just not realistic in my case, or yours either, for that matter. Besides, when the shoe was on the other foot, I seem to recall you giving me 'what for' until I ate crow like a starving woman."

Ginny's exasperation melted away in the space of a single heartbeat. "It's not the same thing," she argued gently, but even as she said them, she didn't believe the words.

"Sure, it is," Lindsay responded knowingly, thinking of what had happened the day before and how she'd nearly gone insane with worry. But Ginny would not be deterred.

The look on Lindsay's face told Ginny exactly what her friend was recalling.

Ginny had announced to Christian and Lindsay that she needed to go someplace that afternoon and wouldn't be back until after supper. Ignoring their curiosity and Lindsay's outright concern, she'd left the orphanage alone and walked the several miles to the East River. Once there, she'd followed a path along the shore until she found a spot secluded behind a cluster of trees, their dry branches extending over the water.

Ginny had stood there for a long time, waiting for dusk and thinking. Her hand closed around the pistol in her pocket, and she remembered how her grandfather had taught her and Alice to shoot, using empty bean tins as targets. Despite his time and care with her, and the cleaning lessons she'd received from Arthur, she never really liked guns and was never able to move beyond the overwhelming sense of dread that something terrible was going to happen just by being around one. She pulled the bloodstained gun from the pocket of her coat and hurled it as far as she could, watching it disappear into the murky, fast-flowing waters with a small splash.

It wasn't much, but it was all she could do to help; and she realized at that moment, still standing on the riverbank, the dirty water lapping at her feet, that there wasn't anything within her power she wouldn't do to help Lindsay.

Now that same type of bone-deep loyalty and devotion was being offered back to her. The same fierce affection and concern was mirrored in warm brown eyes. Ginny understood the overwhelming desire to help and protect so completely that she couldn't find it in her heart to begrudge Lindsay that. Though she sorely wanted to.

The redhead scrunched up her face in defeat. "I hate it when you're right. You know that?"

Lindsay chuckled, wishing she could kiss those smiling lips. "Lucky for you it doesn't happen very often."

Delano carefully negotiated his way through the muddy railroad yard, ignoring the wary looks and unhappy murmurs from several men who were standing around small fires, warming themselves, and talking. It was late afternoon, and this was the place Rat Face had informed him he'd be most likely to find String Bean if she hadn't taken to the rails yet. Of course, it wasn't Lindsay that Delano was here to find. His shoes sank deep into icy-cold mud with every step, making sucking noises as he lifted his feet. The cold stung his ankles.

There was a larger fire at the very end of the yard, near the fence, where half a dozen men idly stood around the flames. Several were drinking from dark bottles, their vulgar words and laughter carried across the yard by the wind. Delano pulled his collar up around his neck and continued on his course, shooting each man a surreptitious glance as he passed.

When he finally made his way to the largest group of men, he sidled up to them, trying his level best to appear casual, though his clean-shaven face and clean coat were enough to make him stand out like a sore thumb. He pulled his hands from his pockets and focused on them for a few seconds as he warmed them over the hissing flames. Then his eyes rose to meet Albert's.

"Well, lookie who's here," Albert said, not hiding his surprise. "This is the guy who was so interested in our String Bean." The words were laced with venom, and he brought his bottle to his lips, sending a few droplets of cheap beer splashing onto his shaggy beard as he swigged down the last swallow. He wiped his mouth with the back of his hand and tossed the bottle over his shoulder without looking. It shattered against a boxcar, sending shards of glass into the mud and remaining snow, the loud crash echoing through the yard.

The men around the fire all laughed when the boxcar's occupant poked his disheveled head out of the car and hurled profanities at whichever prick had interrupted his nap.

"Shut up and go back to screwin' Bug Eye's ass!" the oldest of the men at the fire yelled over his shoulder. There was more general laughter, with men from several other fires joining in this time.

Delano was hard-pressed not to gag.

The head disappeared back into the boxcar with another even louder string of expletives.

Delano recognized Albert instantly, but there was another man present who was familiar too. The wheels in his mind turned until finally something clicked. The man with the mustache and black hat was the one he'd seen leaving the alley just before the shooting. They hadn't spoken, but they'd glanced at each other as they passed on the sidewalk beneath a street lamp.

Albert followed Delano's gaze and sneered. "Yeah, that bastard Bo was there." His gaze shifted into a nasty glare.

Bo was on the tall side with a naturally broad build, despite needing a little more meat on his bones. His head was covered with a thick crop of wavy, reddish-brown hair that curled around his collar and ears and stuck out wildly from the sides of a dirty black Derby. He was barely out of his teens, and his slight harelip was mostly hidden by a dark mustache that needed trimming.

For the umpteenth time, Albert recalled the events of the evening he was attacked. "Amazing that you didn't get bashed on the head or shot, isn't it, Bo?" His voice dripped with contempt, but Bo merely shrugged.

"I didn't owe her any money. And you're a fat *loser*."

"Shut up, asshole!" Albert boomed, jerking his coat closed over his protruding belly as he tried to act indignant. "I didn't owe her squat."

Bo sniggered. "Not according to her."

The other men laughed. String Bean, whom they taunted as cruelly as they would any in their ranks, was begrudgingly respected. Rat Face, on the other hand, was about as popular as the pox, though his presence was tolerated out of laziness as much as anything. No one was completely shunned: not Negroes or foreigners, though they were undeniably given a harder time than other riders; or String Bean, who most knew to be a woman, though she didn't advertise that fact; not even Jacque and Jean who were exceptionally violent. The community was so loose, its members so transient, that they didn't bother trying to weed out the bad ones. That tended to take care of itself—like it had with Jacque and Jean who hadn't been seen since the shooting. Personal alliances were few and far between.

Delano wanted to pull Rat Face aside to make his proposal, but he didn't know how the other men would react. Unsure of what else to do, he ignored them. "I, um… I have a job offer for you, Albert." His eyes darted to Bo, and he made a split-second decision that he hoped the Wards would applaud. He had not performed as well as he should have earlier in the day. The Wards knew it, and so did he. Now was his chance to rectify that. Albert couldn't be trusted, but perhaps with another man watching over him, he would manage to get the job done. "Job's for Bo too, if he's interested."

At the word "job," the other men scattered like roaches in the sunlight. Albert was about to do the same when Delano stopped him with a firm hand on his arm. "I think you'll want to hear my offer." Bo began edging his way to the other side of the fire, away from the stranger. "You too, Bo," Delano told him, his eyes requesting that the young man stay put for the time being.

Bo reluctantly held his ground, ready to bolt if need be. Folks just didn't come down to the tracks and offer people jobs out of the blue. Still, this man had been asking about String Bean, and that piqued his curiosity.

Albert looked around nervously, hoping the other riders didn't think he was turning snitch for the cops, or getting religion, or something equally despicable.

"Whaddya want?" he said in a hushed voice. "And make it quick."

"It's simple really. I want you to find String Bean and—"

Suddenly, Albert's anger flared. "If I ever meet up with that rotten bitch, I'm going to break her in two!" he barked, his heart beginning to pound.

Delano nodded slowly, then carefully stoked the flame burning in Albert's dark eyes. "She stole from you. She attacked you, and she should be"—he paused for effect—"punished."

"Hell yes, she should." Albert narrowed his eyes, and absently pulled a hand-rolled cigarette from his pocket, and crouched down. He tugged a slender twig from the flames. The stick's tip was smoldering, and he used it to light the cigarette, puffing heavily. "Why should you care what happens to her? You never did say why you were sniffin' around after her the other night either. I don't even know your name."

Delano's expression went cold. *No link back to the Wards. No matter what.*

"That's none of your business." He shifted from one foot to the other. "All you need to know is that there is someone out there who believes String Bean should get what's coming to her." He stopped, allowing both Albert and Bo to absorb his words. "Maybe justice will come from the cops." The look on his face, however, made it clear that he wasn't impressed with that option. "Or maybe it will come from—"

"Me." Albert finished. He smiled, showing off stained teeth. "Maybe from me."

"Either way, you benefit financially, Rat Face." Delano handed each of the men a shiny silver dollar. Next, he held up the ten-dollar note Jeremiah Ward had torn in half. "Find her; conduct your business; come back with proof that you did it; and you'll get the other half of this as a reward." He passed over the note.

Albert's eyes widened. He'd never had ten dollars at one time in his entire life.

"What about me?" Bo asked, warily. "I don't have anything to do with what's between Rat Face and String Bean."

Delano corrected him quickly. "You do now. Your job is to see that Albert does his job."

His eyes flashing with anger, Albert scowled and kicked mud at Delano, who stepped aside. "Bullshit! I ain't splittin' the money. I can-"

Delano held up his hand at Albert, but addressed Bo. He forced himself to take a calming breath before he continued. He found himself wishing String Bean had hit Rat Face hard enough to crush his worthless skull. "If you do this, Bo, there'll be several more dollars in it for you." He only hoped that the Wards would agree, because he sure as hell wasn't going to give either one of these men a penny of his own money.

"And I don't have to do anything else?" Bo asked, scratching his jaw as he considered it.

"Not a thing," Delano promised. "You're just my back-up security when it comes to Rat Face."

A cloud of cigarette smoke wafted from Albert's mouth. "Where is she?" he asked, picking a tiny piece of tobacco off his tongue with stubby fingers. He wasn't happy about having Bo reporting back on him. But then again, once they got paid, he intended to rob Bo and beat the shit out of him because he could. So things could be worse. He regarded his new partner carefully, wondering if Bo was already planning to do the same thing to him. *Probably, the bastard. Can't trust nobody these days.*

Delano dug into his coat pocket for a folded piece of paper. He gave it to Albert. "That's a list of the towns she'll be stopping in." Albert blinked. "She's already left New York? Shit."

"There's a telephone number on the back. Call me when you've done what I've asked, and we'll meet." He'd been careful to leave the number of a fancy hotel where his brother worked. There'd be no way to trace that to the Wards. "Leave a message, and I'll get it."

Albert shoved the paper back toward Delano's face, causing the other man to stumble backward a couple of steps, but he managed not to land flat on his ass.

"Can't read and never used no damn phone. Just tell me where she went."

Bo crossed his arms over his chest. "Same for me, mister."

Delano had to stick his hand in a deep mud puddle and brace himself to keep from falling further. He stood angrily, his hand already achingly cold and dripping. "You men now have two dollars between you." His face twisted into a snarl. "Pay someone to read it and have them make the call if you're too *stupid*."

"Hey! Who you callin' stupid?" Albert took a step forward, but was restrained by Bo.

Bo shot Delano an evil look before turning to Albert. "Can't kick his ass, Rat Face. He's our new boss." He smiled boyishly and slapped Albert's back in a gesture that was a little too hard to be entirely friendly. But finally, Albert relaxed and grinned back at the younger man.

"That's right." Albert chuckled smugly. He took a long drag from his cigarette and intentionally blew the smoke in Delano's direction. "Never had me a boss before. I forgot myself. Kickin' him in the ass is probably not a good thing to do on your first day."

Delano nearly bit his tongue through, half hoping the fat rail-rider would try it and give him an excuse to throttle him. "My boss expects you to leave immediately," he ground out. "Do it and don't fail."

And with that, he whirled around and began stomping out of the railroad yard, blocking out the sound of Albert's laughter as he went. *Maybe*, Delano thought moodily, *it's time to find a new job.*

Chapter Ten

The next afternoon…

"Finally," Ginny mumbled as she stepped down off the train and was greeted with a blast of fresh air. A light snow was falling, and she tugged on her cap, moving away from the door so that Lindsay could join her on the platform.

"Where are we really?" Lindsay climbed down the three steps, jumping off the last one, her shoes thudding lightly against the wood. There was a teasing glint in her eyes as she awkwardly tried to button her coat.

"Here." Ginny guided Lindsay a few paces away from the door, so that other passengers could disembark without running into them. But there were none. She blinked a few times, her eyes scanning the platform. "Huh. Popular place. There's not even a stationmaster. Folks must buy tickets in town someplace." She set their bag between her feet then began working on Lindsay's buttons. The skin of her palms was still thin and sensitive, but it didn't ache as much as it used to, and most of her manual dexterity had returned.

A loud hiss escaped the train's smokestack.

Lindsay briefly covered one of Ginny's busy hands with one of her own. "Thank you," she said softly. "Now say it… You know you want to."

"I do not." Ginny spoke without looking up from her task, a tiny smile creasing her cheeks. "And you're welcome." She enjoyed doing things for Lindsay and only wished she had opportunities to help her that didn't come about because her friend was hurt. When she was finished, she gave Lindsay's chest a little pat.

The whistle wailed, and with a puff of black smoke, the train began to slowly inch forward, gaining speed and momentum with each passing second.

"Ginny," Lindsay pleaded.

"Tch. I've read you the name of this place three times already."

"What's your point?" Lindsay smiled.

Ginny rolled her eyes, but dutifully repeated herself. "We're in Big

Ugly, West Virginia."

A snicker met her words.

"Mercy, Lindsay, how old are you again?" She laughed. "You remind me of the boys." Then the happy sound came to an abrupt stop, and Ginny's face fell as she remembered why they were here. Her tone grew melancholy. "I'll bet they laughed when they saw the name too." *Please,* she prayed silently. *Please let them be here.*

Lindsay's eyes softened, and she opened her arms. "C'mere."

Ginny stepped forward and wrapped her arms around Lindsay's solid, strong body, sighing a little at the contact. Even though they'd sat next to each other on the train, she'd missed this more intimate contact.

Lindsay's entire body felt stiff, and she was bone-tired from not being able to sleep while sitting up in front of two-dozen strangers, but she melted into the embrace now, feeling herself relax and her heartbeat slow. Her eyes slipped closed of their own accord.

There wasn't another soul at the station, and they stayed pressed tightly together until the chugging of the train disappeared into the distance. The world went blessedly quiet, except for the occasional clinking of dry, ice-covered branches when the wind blew.

Ginny gave a final squeeze to the sturdy body against hers, smiling a little when Lindsay's eyes fluttered open, a disoriented look replacing her normally alert gaze. "Tired, Lindsay?"

Lindsay frowned. She was used to far more activity than this, but clearly her body still hadn't recovered from Jacque and Jean and that damned dog. She refused to give Rat Face any credit at all for her current state. "No, I'm not tired." But it was a half-hearted lie that earned her a slightly raised eyebrow and a smirk.

"It's so quiet here." The hush in Ginny's voice reflected the surroundings. She could see a few small wooden buildings and a church with a tall steeple a block or two down the road. There wasn't a wagon in sight, and she couldn't remember the last time silence actually thundered around her like this. In the distance, several plumes of smoke disappeared into the gray sky, probably, she mused, from the town's few houses. *What an odd place for the train to stop and try to place children.*

"Ahh." Lindsay breathed in a deep breath of cold, fresh air. "Smell that?"

Ginny bent to retrieve their bag and sniffed the air as they began walking toward the buildings. The breeze was scented with the sweet, pungent smell of pine and wood-smoke and… nothing else. "Wow." Clearly impressed, she gazed at the mature trees that lined one side of the street and the snow, so blindingly white it hurt her eyes. Deep green, pine-covered hills shone in the distance. "If they call this 'Big Ugly,' New York City would give these people a seizure."

The snow on the street was deeper than it looked and came halfway up the women's calves as they trudged forward. Lindsay snorted. "Gotham is enough to give *anyone* a heart seizure. Even tough-as-nails New Yorkers!"

"Hideous… but home," Ginny muttered wryly, knowing even as she said the words they weren't really true anymore. Christian had been right. There was nothing left for her there. When she found her family, she had a new life to create—for all of them. She desperately wanted Lindsay to be a part of that new beginning, but fear kept her from mentioning it to her friend. They'd never spoken about what would happen later, though Ginny knew things couldn't remain unsaid between them for too much longer.

"Where are we starting?" Lindsay scanned the buildings, knowing by the shape of the large one in the middle of the street, and its wide picture window, that it was the town's general mercantile. "The store or the church maybe?"

Ginny's stomach growled. They hadn't eaten since their pre-dawn, several hour stopover in a tiny town, whose only industry had appeared to be feeding hungry railroad passengers. The food sold in the dining car on the train was ridiculously expensive, so they'd gone without, trying to stretch every penny. She sighed. It was nearly suppertime, but they could always eat later. They needed to begin searching before the last of the afternoon light disappeared. "First the church, I think. Christian said that the adoption committees were usually sponsored by one of the local churches or Ladies Leagues."

They crossed the street and headed toward the small, steepled building. "Tell me about these committees," Lindsay said, her thumb fiddling with the bandage on her hand. Maybe tomorrow she could remove it. The cut to her knuckles was healing nicely.

"The committee puts up notices around the town, and when the children arrive, the committee makes sure the people wanting to adopt them are fit. The committees also do all the paperwork, and then mail it back to New York. I guess every orphanage does it a little differently, but the trains usually take different routes when they leave New York every month or two. That way a town won't see another train for at least a year, and there's a chance by then that folks will want more children."

"Mmm. I've seen groups of orphans at a few different railroad stations. They get their own car and don't sit with the other passengers."

Ginny cocked her head to the side and drew in a surprised breath, the cold air stinging her lungs a little. "You never mentioned that before."

Lindsay shrugged one shoulder. "Nothing to say really. I suppose I've seen just about everything that goes on around trains. Never have seen bunches of kids like that except in New York, though." She didn't mention that many of the children had been sobbing, and that she'd seen some forcibly carried onto the trains. "I guess if they'd had them in Pennsylvania, it might have been me on one of those trains…" She chuckled humorlessly. "The State couldn't have held me though, unless they'd tied me up the entire trip… Even then, I'd have just run away when they finally untied me."

Ginny smiled a little at that, acknowledging that her strong-willed friend probably couldn't have been controlled unless they'd gotten her as a very tiny child. She imagined what Lindsay had been through over the years, growing up cold and hungry, truly alone in a world far too cruel to be navigated by a stubborn little girl. Even before Lindsay had taken to the rails, her father had abandoned her emotionally if not physically. As near as Ginny could tell, she'd been robbed of her childhood completely. *Maybe, just maybe, my friend, you'd have been much better off on one of those orphan trains.*

Lindsay glanced sideways and shook her head at the pensive look on Ginny's face, easily guessing what she was thinking. "I wouldn't change the past even if I could. Besides, if anything had happened differently, I probably wouldn't have met you." She didn't dare turn her head to see the expression on Ginny's face as the unexpected words tumbled out. But she heard a sharp intake of breath next to her and felt her heart begin to pound, as an unexpected silence grew between them.

Ginny reached out and grabbed Lindsay's sleeve, pulling them both to a stop. Lindsay felt her stomach drop as she looked at Ginny's deadly serious face, and their eyes locked. "Lindsay—" Ginny paused when a man exited the barbershop door only a few feet in front of them, and they caught sight of their first citizen of Big Ugly. His skin was tanned and weather-beaten, and he wore a wide-brimmed hat. He was dusting small clippings of white hair from his coat when he stepped outside, nearly bumping into Ginny and Lindsay.

"Afternoon," he said absently as he sidestepped the women. Then his ancient eyes met Ginny's, and he did a double take, nearly stumbling as his brain tried to reconcile the pretty girl's face attached to a body dressed like a man. Confused, he hesitantly reached up and tipped his hat—just in case. The redhead smiled her hello, while Lindsay politely answered back, "Afternoon," and took a small step forward, putting a respectable space between her and Ginny.

Scowling, the man lengthened his stride. The voice was clearly female. And women didn't have any business dressing like that. He began mumbling something about that train and the queer sort of folk it brought to town as he disappeared down the street.

Lindsay rocked back on her heels and let out a low whistle. "Lucky that man didn't see us at the depot."

Ginny cringed. "I need to change into something more respectable. My dress is wrinkled but clean." Her eyes flicked from place to place, finally landing somewhere that would do. "I can use the outhouse behind the church."

Lindsay shrugged as they began to walk again. "To hell with respectable." But her soft voice wasn't angry or even defiant. "You look fine to me."

Ginny's lips twitched, and her blue eyes twinkled affectionately. "I know I do. And you look fine to me too." A light pat on the arm reaffirmed her words. "It's other folks I'm worried about."

Lindsay paced outside the outhouse while Ginny changed. "Ginny?" She took a step closer to the thin wooden door.

"Almost finished. Ugh… It's cramped in here."

"I'm going back down the street to… um…" Lindsay cast about for an excuse to leave. "To find out if there's a place to stay in this town." *Yeah, that's it.*

The movement inside the outhouse stopped. "What?"

"I'll meet you later. Don't worry, I'll find you… I promise."

"Lindsay, wait." There was a loud thump as Ginny kicked off her shoe so that she could pull her leg out of her pants. "Stupid… trouser leg… stupid."

The older woman laid her bandaged hand on the door and softly said, "Good luck."

Ginny's eyes widened. *She's serious?* "Lindsay, don't you dare leave before I finish!" Ginny grunted in frustration, as she buttoned the top of her dress with one hand and scooped up the clothes at her feet with the other. She burst out the door, her face flushed and hair disheveled as she stepped into the snow. She scanned the area around the outhouse. Lindsay was gone and a new set of footprints led back toward the town. "Argh. Lindsay." Angrily, she stuffed her clothes into their bag. When she straightened, she gazed down the street unhappily and combed through her hair, which was growing damp from the falling snow, with one hand. She let out a tiny sigh and whispered into the wind, "Please, Lindsay, stay out of trouble."

Lindsay scowled fiercely at the items in the picture window and was about to step inside the general store when the sound of girlish giggles caused her to turn her head. "Mmm-hmm. What do we have here?"

Two pretty, teenage girls about the same age as Ginny approached her shyly, smiling and blushing the entire time. Reflexively, she smiled back, feeling a little guilty at the thoughts that instantly flooded her brain. *What would Ginny think?* she wondered, but just as quickly her rebellious side reminded her that Ginny wasn't here at the moment, and now she wouldn't have to resort to paying for it. She couldn't remember the last time she'd been forced to sink that low, and now maybe she wouldn't have to. Just the thought made her sick.

But they're just girls, her more reasonable side reminded, only to be shot down when Lindsay got a good look at the taller of the two. She was slim, but definitely full-grown, with long legs and broad shoulders. *Oh, yeah. This could work out perfectly.*

The bolder of the girls said hello, and Lindsay responded in kind, certain that this obvious flirting was only taking place because the girls thought she was some wet-behind-the-ears buck and not a woman. With a wicked internal grin, she decided to use the situation to her advantage. They'd figure out she was a woman eventually. But with any luck, by then they wouldn't care. And Ginny would never have to know exactly what happened. "Hello, girls," she said again, grinning roguishly.

"You're not from around here, are you?" The taller blonde girl found her voice again.

"Noo," Lindsay drew out the word smoothly, leaning against the store wall and tucking her bandaged hands into her pockets. "I just came in from New York City." She purred the last word, hoping to add a little mystery and sophistication to what in her mind was a cesspool.

The quieter of the two girls blushed hotly and stammered, "Mercy. Th— that's a big place. Or so I've heard tell."

"Oh, it is. Very big," Lindsay agreed, eyeing her critically, and then deciding in favor of her friend. Still, it never hurt to have a backup. She glanced around until her gaze lit upon a spot that would afford them a little more privacy than in front of the town's biggest store. She briefly considered taking them back to the room she'd already secured for the night. But the alley would do in a pinch. This shouldn't take long. "Care to take a walk with me? I could tell you all about the city."

"Yes!"

"Oh, I don't know," the shy one demurred, shifting uncomfortably from one foot to the other.

"You're smart not to trust strangers," Lindsay complimented the girl sincerely, a tiny sliver of guilt digging into her gut. "But we could always introduce ourselves. Then we won't be strangers anymore."

"I'm Angie," came the anxious reply from the blonde, her voice brimming with excitement. "And that's Greta." She indicated her red-faced friend.

"Pleasure to meet you both," Lindsay said, reserving judgment on whether or not to give her own name for later. She began slowly walking toward a narrow alley that separated the barbershop from the bank.

Angie followed her without question, skipping along in the snow.

Not to be left out, Greta reluctantly trailed after them both, looking around worriedly to see if anyone was watching. She lifted the hem of her dress and jogged the few steps necessary to catch up with her friend. Carol-Ann Johnson's wedding, which the entire town had attended, had ended just a few moments ago, and now people were starting to filter back onto the streets. Her papa had warned her about strangers, but this boy seemed so nice. Still, it was best to be cautious; her father wouldn't understand that the local boys were so boring that she craved conversation with anyone new.

The trio ducked into the alley, and Lindsay steeled her resolve, reminding herself that she did, indeed, want this. She gave the girls what she hoped was a charming grin. "How would you ladies like me not only to tell you about New York City, but also show you something I learned there?" Her smile turned inviting. "I can *guarantee* you'll like it."

Angie squealed with delight, and a wide-eyed Greta nodded, wondering what fantastic tales this beautiful young man had to tell.

Lindsay steered them deeper into the alley, forcing herself not to look over her shoulder for Ginny.

Ginny stepped into the church, not surprised to find its sanctuary empty. If she hadn't seen that old man outside the barbershop, she'd swear Big Ugly was a beautiful ghost town. There were, however, several candles lit around the room.

"Anyone here?" she called out, carefully shutting the door. She brushed the snow off her shoulders, spinning in a circle as she took in the simple but well-kept room. "Hello?"

A middle-aged woman shuffled out of the preacher's office, tucking a strand of brown hair back into her bun. She jumped back a step, obviously not expecting to see anyone in the church. "Oh, hello." She laughed a little at herself. "I'm sorry, I didn't hear you come in."

Ginny breathed a sigh of relief. "That's fine, ma'am." She smiled warmly, and the woman seemed to relax. "You don't know how glad I am to see you. I was beginning to think there wasn't but one person in this entire town."

The woman laughed. "That would be on account of the big Johnson wedding at the fancy church across town. It's bigger and more suitable for a large crowd. I think just about everyone in town was planning on attending. I was using it as a good excuse to get some work done here." She continued to fiddle with her hair. "My husband Arnold and daughter Greta went to represent the family though," she added quickly, not wanting Ginny to think she was rude enough to snub Carol-Ann.

"I see. That's very—err—neighborly of you." Ginny set her bag down on one of the pews and sucked in a nervous breath. This was it. The time had finally come. She threw her shoulders back, lifting her chin a little as she said, "Ma'am, my name is Virginia Chisholm and-"

"Oh, my." The woman anxiously crossed the room and stopped in front of Ginny. "You're the one looking for her brothers and sister, aren't you?" Ginny blinked. "You… you know who I am?" *Uh oh.*

"Oh, yes. I received a cablegram yesterday from a man who runs an orphanage. We don't have a phone for the church, but the general store can send and receive cables, of course. He warned me you might be heading here and—"

Ginny's blue eyes flashed with sudden anger, and her fists clenched convulsively. "You can't believe what Mr. Ward says." She could feel her hackles rise. "He's a liar who can't be trusted."

"A liar?" The woman looked confused. "Who is Mr. Ward?" She frowned and shook her head in exasperation. "I'm afraid I have no earthly idea what you're talking about. The cablegram was from a Mr. Christian Spence." Her face suddenly relaxed, easing the tiny creases that surrounded her mouth and eyes.

"Even from his few words I could tell what a wonderfully polite man he was. I wonder if he's single." She touched her chin with her index finger as she pondered. "My Greta just turned seventeen last month."

Ginny's knees went weak with relief, and her eyes fluttered closed for a moment. *It wasn't Mr. Ward. Thank God.* She hadn't imagined, until now, what harm a few simple cables could do to her search. She only hoped Mr. and Mrs. Ward hadn't thought of it either. "Christian is very kind, ma'am."

"No need to be so formal," the woman assured Ginny kindly. "I'm Mrs. Arnold Watts, the church secretary, but please do call me Josephine." She glanced back at the door by which Ginny had entered and then around the church. "Where's your friend? The undercover agent for the Child Protection Agency of New York?" Just saying the words gave Josephine a little thrill. She whispered conspiratorially to Ginny even though there was no one else around to hear, "Mr. Spence said she'd be posing as a man; that her work was so secret she couldn't even reveal her name." Her eyes lit with glee, and she clasped her hands together. "How terribly thrilling."

Ginny bit back a laugh. *How long was that cablegram? Oh, Christian, do we ever owe you one.* "Yes, Lind—agent—er—well, the woman helping me is frequently in disguise. It's best not to call her anything at all." She cleared her throat a little, wanting to get back to the matter at hand. "I'm here for my family, Josephine. My sister and two brothers—the Robsons."

"I'm afraid they're not here." She gave Ginny a contrite look, watching uncomfortably as the young woman absorbed the unhappy news.

Ginny closed her eyes and mumbled something under her breath that Josephine couldn't quite hear. All the same, the woman was sure it wasn't appropriate language in the House of the Lord—or anywhere else for that matter.

"I couldn't give the information to Mr. Spence, you see—privacy and all that. But seeing as how you're their sister, I can't think it would hurt you to know. No one ended up choosing them." Her forehead wrinkled. "Sort of."

A wave of nausea hit Ginny, and Josephine encouraged her to sit with a quick motion of her hand. Ginny's eyes filled with tears, and she swallowed hard.

"No—" she paused and swallowed again, irrationally angry that no one found her siblings worth adopting. "No one wanted them?" She shook her head fiercely. "There's nothing wrong with them! They're smart and beautiful and..."

Unconsciously, Josephine fed off Ginny's distress. She quickly pulled a handkerchief from the pocket of her dress and offered it to Ginny. Her voice was a little panicky. "Oh, it's not that. I'm sure your brothers and sister are all those things." Ginny still hadn't accepted the cloth, so Josephine pressed it into her slightly trembling hands. "You look like you could use this. No, it wasn't that there was something wrong with the children, but in the end, no one came forward to adopt them. And we would have stopped it even if they had."

Ginny took the small cloth and wiped her cheeks, resentfully wishing Lindsay hadn't abandoned her. "But you said—"

Josephine dropped down onto the pew next to Ginny. "Let me explain, dear. Do you know how these children find families once they get here?"

Ginny shook her head.

"All right. Then if you'll be patient, I'll explain that too. This is only the second time a train has come to Big Ugly carrying orphans. Why, only last spring eight children found homes here," she stated proudly. "Five girls and three boys. This year folks were looking for boys, probably because the mines have been short of little fellows or very young men for the past few months. For some reason the mines can never seem to have enough short men to do"—she waved her hands in the air—"whatever small men do in coal mines."

Ginny paled a little at the thought of James or Lewis working in a dark, dank coal mine. Suddenly, she wasn't so upset they hadn't ended up in Big Ugly after all.

Josephine picked up a Bible that had been left on the pew and neatly stowed it in the holder on the back of the next pew. "So, because it was boys that people were after, your sister wasn't chosen." She smiled. "I remember the little blonde girl myself."

"How'd she seem?" Ginny asked softly, desperate for any scrap of information.

"Fine. Fine." Josephine patted Ginny's hand, wanting to reassure her any way she could. "The girl didn't shed a tear the entire time; she was a chubby little thing, if I recall."

Ginny let out a half-sob and nodded. "She is chubby. Mama's arms used to ache from holding her, so then me and Alice—umm—she is—was my sister— well, we'd take turns. I don't think Jane's feet touched the ground for more than a minute for the first two years of her life. It's amazing she learned to walk at all." The women shared watery smiles, each lost in their own memories of the children in their lives.

Ginny sniffed. "Bu-but what about the boys?"

Josephine tried not to grimace. Their story was somewhat more distressing.

"After everyone inspected them—"

"What do you mean inspected?" Red brows knit together.

Josephine blinked, shocked at the banked flames she could see flickering behind Ginny's eyes. Like dry tinder, Ginny's anger was itching to combust.

"Oh, my," Josephine breathed. "That was perhaps the wrong choice of words. You see, the children walk up there." She pointed to a ten by ten platform behind the pulpit, where the town sometimes held children's plays and the church's choir stood to sing. "And then everyone can see them without descending upon the children all at once and frightening them," she explained. Ginny's eyes strayed to the stage as Josephine spoke. She imagined her brothers standing there, as men and women looked them over like pieces of meat.

"If they see a child or two they want, they come to us, the Ladies' Committee. I'm the treasurer this year." She smiled toothily as though that last bit was a grand announcement. "We're the ones who determine whether prospective parents are fit to adopt."

Ginny's voice was low and controlled. "Let me understand this. You march the children up on stage to be inspected like *livestock* at auction or perhaps *slaves,* so that people can decide whether or not they want them? And what about the homely or skinny child? Do they have to stand up on some stage in every town, wondering why no one wants them?"

Josephine's back went ramrod straight. "That's not fair. How else are folks supposed to decide?" Her cheeks flushed. "We don't see a picture or know anything about the children before they get here. The citizens who come to this church for those children are taking strangers into their homes, sometimes to live alongside their own flesh and blood children. I think it's a little much to expect them to do that sight unseen. Is it so different from how any orphanage works where people come to see the orphans?"

Ginny didn't have an answer for that, and she ducked her head, a little ashamed of her outburst, though her blood still ran hot at the entire process.

"Some of the children were living on the streets back in New York. They were outside in the cold. Can you imagine that?"

Ginny's head snapped up, and her jaw worked. "I can imagine it."

Josephine continued, undaunted. This young woman wasn't the first person to criticize the way the Ladies' Committee did things. "Other children don't speak a word of English. Because of what we do, some of those children have families of their own and roofs over their heads." She wrung her hands together, truly upset that this young woman didn't see the good in what she and the other women were trying to do. "I understand that the process can seem a little… harsh. We aren't perfect, Virginia. But isn't the result the most important thing?"

"I… You're right, of course," Ginny said quietly, sinking deeper into the pew. Most of these orphans came from places exactly like Orchard Street. It was hard for her to remember that she and her siblings had been very lucky—even in that harsh place where she'd scrounged for every nickel and worked until she could fall asleep standing up—she'd always had what mattered most. Who was she to criticize a woman who was trying to give that to total strangers? She glanced up at Josephine, heartsick. "I'm sorry."

Josephine let out a deep breath. It had been a long day, and that had been building up inside her for far too long. "It's all right, dear." The tips of her ears reddened when she realized how rude her defense of the Ladies' Committee had been. "I didn't mean to snap. If I were in your shoes—Well," she sighed. "I'm just glad I'm not."

"My brothers?" Ginny reminded.

"There were two families interested in each of those boys."

Ginny nodded in understanding. "But they didn't qualify to adopt."

"No, actually they did. They were all Christian families with some visible means of support."

Ginny shot to her feet and glared at Josephine. "That's it? You let people take children based on that alone?"

"You did hear the part about how we make them swear to be Christians?"

Ginny dropped her face into her hands. "Oh, boy."

"Like this?" Angie asked a little uncertainly, dragging her eyes up to meet Lindsay's.

"Oh, yeah. You're a natural," Lindsay praised. "Just… umm… Not quite so hard."

"Remember what String Bean said," Greta prompted her friend as she began buttoning her dress. "Don't use your entire arm. It's all in the wrist." She smirked at Angie, delighting in torturing her friend over the fact that she'd gotten to go first. Of course, they were both undoubtedly going to hell for this. But she'd kissed Mickey Jackson only last week and was, most likely, already on her way there anyway. "You'll be hard-pressed to do better than me, Angie."

Lindsay had to nod. Greta had been surprisingly spectacular—especially for a beginner.

"Shut up, Greta. You've had your turn," Angie said crossly.

Lindsay laughed, not quite knowing how to deal with her sudden popularity. *Maybe paying for it would have been easier. Sure would have been quicker.* "Now, girls, no need for that."

Greta stuck her tongue out at Angie and tried not to think of the horrible sin she'd just committed. Of course, String Bean had been right. It was fun. Now she knew what all the boys had been grumbling about behind the schoolyard. If she'd only known then…

Lindsay rolled her eyes and focused on the taller girl. "Are you ready, Angie? I'm playing for keeps here," she warned seriously. "I don't want you do something you'll regret tomorrow." For all her bravado, it had been Greta, not Angie, who'd insisted on participating, even when she didn't know what to do. Angie had been content to stand back and watch.

Angie bit her lip, then squealed delightedly. "I can't believe I'm going to do it. Can you, Greta?" she asked her friend, her excitement practically bubbling over.

Greta gave her a bored look. "No."

An expression of steely determination swept over Angie, and she tossed her coat onto the snow and began to unbutton her dress.

Lindsay smiled and started at the buttons on her trousers, the motion a little difficult with her hands in bandages.

"And this is how men do it?" Angie inquired curiously.

"Basically," Lindsay said. Greta had figured out that she was a woman almost immediately, so Lindsay came clean. To her surprise, instead of frightening the young women, it intrigued them even more. Who knew the girls of Big Ugly were such rascals?

Greta finished buttoning her coat and stuffed her hands into her pockets.

"Ever done it with a woman before, String Bean?"

"Not before today," she admitted honestly. Then her thoughts turned to Ginny. "But damned if I haven't wanted to."

"Ready," Angie told her nervously, rubbing her hands together.

A predatory look washed over Lindsay's face. "So am I, Angie. So am I."

"I'm sorry, I don't recall which boy was which," Josephine told Ginny. The women were both seated and looking much calmer than they had only moments before. "A couple approached one of the boys on stage"—she paused to cluck her disapproval—"and, right there in front of God and everyone, the boy started screaming that he was a *Catholic* and that he wasn't going anyplace without his brother and sister."

She felt uncomfortable telling Virginia this next part, but obligation was, after all, more important than comfort. "After that, the poor boy burst into tears; I'm afraid we had to take him outside and calm him down." She sighed. "While I'm sure there are plenty of Catholics in New York City, there are none in Big Ugly. The two families were no longer interested."

The words were said so matter-of-factly that Ginny didn't take offense. She was too tired to bother. "That would have been Lewis." Her guts were churning full-force at the thought of her brother's tears. *You little stinker, you're too smart for your own good.* She knew, however, that it wouldn't take long for the Wards' employees to make certain he never did something like that again. *No one had better lay a single finger on him*, she thought darkly. "And James?"

"Ahhh." A heavy eyebrow arched. "The second Robson brother *also* refused to be separated from his siblings. When one of the prospective parents didn't seem to be taking his request seriously, he—umm—well, he kicked him in the… you know," she murmured delicately, glancing down between her legs and waggling her eyebrows.

A tiny laugh exploded out of Ginny. Her hand flew to her mouth as more tears welled up, threatening to spill over. Her emotions were all over the place, confusing her even more. She couldn't tell whether to be glad that her brothers were fighting to stay with each other and Jane, or furious at them for being so stubborn. As it was, she was probably going to have to traipse across the entire nation before she'd find the family crazy enough to take them in. Despite herself, she chuckled, a sad smile on her face. "That would definitely be my brother James."

Having told Ginny everything she knew, Josephine stood. "We're not in the business of placing children in homes where they don't want to be. And it was clear your brothers wouldn't be happy with anyone here." She wiped her palms against her skirt, wondering what was keeping Greta. Surely the wedding was over by now. "I'm sorry I couldn't have been more help." Her gaze softened.

"May God bless you and your journey, Virginia."

Ginny stood as well and gathered her bag. She sniffed a little as she backed toward the door. "Thanks to you, I at least now know they're all right. And with or without God's blessing, I intend to find them."

The older woman inclined her head slightly. "But a little help and a lot of luck never hurts."

"No." A genuine smile played at the edges of Ginny's mouth. "It never does." She was grateful for what little information she'd been able to glean. "Thank you, Josephine." Turning away, she pushed open the door to be greeted by a blast of cold air. It would be dark soon, and she needed to find Lindsay and a place for them to stay the night.

They had a train to catch early in the morning.

After asking a man on the street what her options for accommodation in Big Ugly were, Ginny was directed to the local boarding house, a narrow, two-story building just off the main street. To her surprise, the plump proprietress told her that her friend had already paid for a room for the night.

The room was dark and cool, and Ginny did nothing more than toss their bag on the bed before heading back down Main Street in search of Lindsay. As she walked, two young women approached her, too absorbed in their own conversation, which consisted mostly of shrieks of laughter and nervous giggles, to notice anyone in their path.

The redhead stepped out of their way and walked slowly backward, her eyes going round as she noticed that one of the girls was wearing Lindsay's hat, and the other was carrying—

"Ahh!" A scream was torn from Ginny when a pair of hands shot out from the alley and dragged her inside. "Ginny," was whispered in her ear, but her heart was pounding so loudly she couldn't hear it. Off balance, she began to fight and kick, and the hands instantly fell away from her coat. She whirled around to fight back at her attacker and raised a fist. Eyes already the size of twin moons grew even larger. "Lindsay?"

Lindsay backed up a step, panting. "Jesus Christ!" she hissed under her breath. "It's me, not the boogieman. And did you have to try to kill me?" Grimacing, she clutched one of her hands to her chest. "I was just trying to get your attention without letting the entire town know I was here."

Ginny's mouth dropped open, and her jaw dangled in the breeze. Now she knew what it was that one of the girls who'd passed her on the street was carrying. Her temper exploded as a tendril of white-hot jealousy intertwined with the anger she was still feeling over being ditched by Lindsay at the church. Together they formed a vise around her heart—and squeezed. "What the *hell* happened to your pants?"

"Don't you swear at me!" Lindsay blinked a few times, startled by her own statement. "Something is wrong with this entire conversation."

"What's wrong is that you're naked!" Ginny wanted to stamp her foot. Instead, with jerky, angry movements, she shrugged out of her coat, and hurled it at Lindsay, hitting her squarely in the face, doing her best to ignore her churning belly.

Lindsay peeled it off her head, throwing Ginny an icy look of warning, which Ginny promptly ignored.

"Wrap it around your legs, Lindsay, before you catch your death."

Lindsay's teeth were starting to chatter, and she prayed for it to get dark quicker. Still refusing to take Ginny's coat, she said, "But-but what about you?"

Ginny hugged herself, already feeling the chill as snow pelted her dress and stuck to the thin cloth. "*My* legs aren't blue and hanging out in the wind." Then she saw Lindsay's snow-covered head and sighed, a little of her anger and hurt giving way to worry. "You're just trying to get sick, aren't you?" she whispered thickly.

"'Course not," Lindsay protested feebly, shaking her head to dislodge the snow. There had been several times in her life when she wished the earth would open up and swallow her whole. Those times, however, paled in comparison to the misery and embarrassment she felt at this very moment. There was no use in praying for a tornado to come and whisk her away. She wasn't that lucky.

"Come on," Ginny said quickly. "It's dark enough so that no one will see you. I hope."

Lindsay shook her head grimly. "A few more minutes yet." She peered out onto the quiet street. "I don't want to get thrown in jail."

Ginny crossed her arms and snorted.

"It's not what it looks like, Ginny." Brown eyes begged the younger woman to believe her.

Twin red eyebrows disappeared behind windblown bangs. "It looks like you're standing in an alley half naked, and somehow, two pretty young twits ended up with your pants and cap."

"Oh. Okay, it's exactly what it looks like," Lindsay said glumly.

Ginny didn't bother to disguise her hurt or confusion. "Why? I don't understand. I thought—" She lifted a hand, then let it drop to her side. She closed her eyes. "I don't know what I thought."

"Damn, Ginny, it's not like it was that horrible," Lindsay protested. "The girls had fun."

"Well, in that case!" Ginny shouted, not caring at that moment if the entire town caught Lindsay in her underpants. "Everything is just terrific!"

"I was shooting craps for a dress."

Ginny blinked. "Wh—"

"And I lost," Lindsay added needlessly, not making eye contact.

Ginny looked at Lindsay as though the rail-rider had lost her mind. "I don't believe it," she murmured.

"I know!" Suddenly, Lindsay was inconsolable. "But, Jesus Christ, Ginny, the dresses in the store window were three dollars. Three dollars! For a *dress*. A pair of waist overalls only cost ninety cents and denim is stronger!"

"You were playing craps for a dress?" Ginny clarified with exaggerated slowness, still quite sure she'd heard Lindsay wrong.

"Yes," Lindsay repeated, clearly frustrated at having to do so. It all seemed rather obvious to her. "Don't make me mention the losing part again, all right?" she pleaded.

"You talked those girls out of their clothes?"

Lindsay kicked at the snow. "They were ready to turn 'em over." *Shit, here I go again.* "Only I'm the one who kept losing."

A tiny incredulous smile began to twitch at Ginny's lips as the weight of the world lifted from her shoulders and her upset stomach began to ease.

Lindsay noticed the change immediately and breathed a heavy sigh of relief.

"They won your pants off you, eh? Oh, Lindsay." Ginny began to laugh. "That's pitiful."

Brown eyes narrowed. "If you breathe a word of this to anyone… I'll… I'll…" A triumphant look finally swept across her face. "I'll tell everyone we meet that you kissed your sister."

Ginny gasped, then her mouth formed a tiny O. "What crap game?"

"Smart girl."

By the time they both darted out of the shadows, Lindsay was reasonably sure that she wasn't going to be sleeping in the local livery stable.

A small box of matches sat next to a kerosene lamp, and Ginny picked it up with cold, clumsy fingers.

"I'll light the stove next-next," Lindsay chattered. "Damn." She began jumping up and down. "This floor is like ice." She tossed Ginny's coat over a small chair in the corner of the room before heading straight for their bag and the blankets inside. She grabbed them both and dropped one onto the bed as she shook the other out and began to wrap it around Ginny's shoulders.

Ginny fitted the globe over the lit wick and back into its holder, illuminating the room with a golden glow that caused the ice crystals in her hair and eyebrows to glitter like diamonds.

Lindsay's hands froze mid-motion as she stared, utterly transfixed.

"There." Ginny flicked her gaze sideways and saw Lindsay standing with the blanket held open for her. "Oh, yesss." She would have smiled gratefully, had her cheeks not been blocks of ice. "Brrr. Just a minute, okay?" Her hands set to work on the buttons that went up the top half of her dress. "I don't want to get the blanket wet."

Lindsay nodded and remained stock-still, torn between looking away and staring at Ginny. Her heart began to beat a little faster, sending a rush of warm blood through her.

Ginny removed her dress, shoes, and underclothes in a matter of seconds. Any nervousness about being naked in front of Lindsay had long since faded as the trust between them grew. She kicked away the wet clothes and steadily met Lindsay's penetrating gaze. "Lindsay?" She began to rub her arms.

"Oh," Lindsay murmured, as Ginny's voice pulled her from her thoughts. She wrapped the blanket around the shivering body and pulled it close, pressing her cold cheek against Ginny's. "I'm sorry I stink so bad at craps."

Ginny laughed at the unexpected apology that was just—so Lindsay. "Me too. Tomorrow we'll b-buy you a dress and a p-pa-pair of pants." She felt Lindsay draw in a breath to speak and cut her off by simply saying, "We will."

Lindsay's protest died on her lips, and she tightened her hold, absorbing the comfort of having Ginny in her arms. "I'll put on your trousers and light the fire then. I can go down to the kitchen and bring up some food. The room comes with bread and soup."

Ginny's stomach grumbled again at the mere thought of food, but her chilled skin demanded more immediate attention. Her hand snaked out from behind the blanket, and she gave a sharp tug on Lindsay's shirt. "Nuh uh." She shook her head, scattering a few drops of water onto Lindsay. "Too cold. Take this off, and come to bed first."

"Bu—"

"Please."

And as easy as that, Lindsay willingly gave in again. Unfortunately, her conscience was starting to kick up a fuss. It was time to face the music. "I shouldn't have left you this afternoon."

No hesitation. "I needed you."

Lindsay's heart ached from the beautiful, awful words. *And I wasn't there.* "I'm *so* sorry. I won't do it again. I promise." She felt Ginny's answering nod against the side of her face and pulled back, but not before her long arms gave a final, heartfelt squeeze. She quickly stripped out of her coat, shirt, and stockings, leaving her as naked and exposed as the day she was born.

Ginny reached out and pinched her, relieving the tension in the room and letting Lindsay know that she was forgiven. Again.

Both women scurried into bed and under the blankets, giggling a little as they wiggled around, settling in. They stopped moving with their bodies facing each other, less than a foot apart, with the blankets pulled up to their ears.

Lindsay reached out and placed her hand on Ginny's forearm. The bandages wrapping her fingers were cool to the touch but not wet, and only the tips of her fingers peeked out to feel soft skin. "Better?" she burred, low and concerned.

"Mmm." Ginny nodded a little. "Much."

They shared slightly nervous, expectant smiles. The night before leaving New York, when they were alone like this, safe and warm, had been filled with soft, tender kisses, and increasingly bold touches. It was something they both desperately wanted to continue.

Lindsay lifted the fingers that were now grazing Ginny's arm to the fairer woman's face. She traced her jaw and cheekbones and pushed back a lock of silky hair.

Ginny sighed and leaned into the touch. She was calm and yet at the same time alive with sensation, as the slightly rough woolen blanket peeked out from behind heavy cotton sheets and brushed against her bare skin. The tips of Lindsay's slightly rough fingers left goosebumps in their wake as they skimmed her face.

"What about your brothers and sister?" Lindsay whispered, half-knowing the answer by the simple fact that Ginny hadn't said anything about them sooner. *I should have asked earlier.*

Pale eyes closed, and Ginny gave her head a tiny, pained shake.

"Aww… Ginny. I'm so sorry." Her voice was the barest of whispers. "Soon."

"Soon," Ginny agreed, not opening her eyes. Licking flames, broken promises, and crying children still invaded her dreams. It was time to reclaim her waking hours. She consciously let herself feel the warm rush of Lindsay's breath against her face as she spoke, and imagined that she could hear the strong heart beating so close to her own.

The quiet moment between them lengthened, and Lindsay found herself mesmerized by the feel of Ginny's skin and the deep, almost overwhelming sense of longing that gripped her. Suddenly, she wanted more of everything. More of the gentle passion she so often saw lurking behind soft blue eyes. More of what they could be to each other, if they only knew what to do or what to say.

Lindsay leaned forward, bridging the small gap between them and brushing her mouth against Ginny's. As the sweet contact grew firmer, lips parted easily and eager tongues explored and mapped, drawing breathy moans and sighs from each woman as the kiss stretched on endlessly. With her entire body, she leaned closer still, until Ginny was on her back and Lindsay was perched carefully atop her, using her forearms to support most of her weight.

Ginny gasped at the unexpected sensation of bare skin on bare skin, as they touched with the entire length of their bodies. Her eyes flew open, as a searing bolt of desire tore through her and settled in her groin to smolder. "Lindsay," she breathed hotly, scarcely knowing what else to say, her eyes darkened with arousal. She opened her mouth, unsure of what was going to come out, only to be stopped by the slightly rough pads of two fingers pressed against her lips. *She's so soft!*

"I'll move if you want me to," Lindsay whispered, willing Ginny to want this more intimate connection between them as much as she did. "I don't want to frighten you."

There was an urgency to Lindsay's voice that captured Ginny so completely she forgot how to breathe.

"I-I love you, and I just wanted to be closer to you." Her brown eyes looked amber in the lamplight as she anxiously searched the youthful face below hers. "I wanted to feel you. To feel *us*, Ginny." She paused and swallowed hard, waiting for the lump that had grown in her throat to ease, placing feather-light kisses full of affection and wistfulness on Ginny's eyebrows and cheeks. "I don't think this is wrong. At least it's not for me."

Lindsay's heart was thumping wildly against Ginny's chest, and the other woman knew that hers was pounding just as fiercely. Helpless to do anything but respond to the spirit calling out to hers, Ginny ignored her momentary panic and allowed herself to experience fully the sensation of soft breasts and firm nipples that tickled when pressed against hers. An involuntary moan was wrung from her. There was instant heat as smooth bellies met and legs tangled together.

"I knew you loved me," Ginny explained quietly, a look of wonder shimmering in her eyes. "I could feel it in my heart."

Lindsay nodded as her vision swam.

Ginny smiled as she whispered, "I love you too."

Simultaneously, they let out deep breaths. Tiny smiles made a surprise showing through the tears when they each relaxed a little, and their bodies melted into each other even more completely, making it hard to tell where one ended and the other began. They memorized the precious moment, tucking it safely away deep inside to be taken out later and savored slowly.

"Do you really think it's," Ginny paused and lifted her head to brush her lips across Lindsay's, "all right for two women to feel this way? To want *this*?" she asked softly, not quite understanding how she could know something deep in her bones, but still feel the need to question it.

Lindsay thought about that for a few seconds before she answered, knowing how important her answer was to her companion. A sigh. "I… I don't know what's right for other folks. And except for how it makes you feel, I don't care." She watched as Ginny's brow furrowed. "I don't have anyone to disappoint," she reminded her gently. "Anyone except you."

Following an urge too strong to deny, Ginny leaned up and kissed Lindsay again. This time with a gentle intensity that decimated the darker woman's ability to think. "Mmm," she hummed a little as they separated, utterly entranced by this sometimes crazy, funny, tough, and tender woman. "I'm far from disappointed in you, Lindsay. You mean everything to me."

They kissed again, slowly, deeply, asking time to stand still as they greedily indulged in each other. "And you mean everything to me," Lindsay finally murmured against moist lips, her body thrumming with excitement. "I don't think being together this way"—she trailed her fingertips over Ginny's lips—"is wrong." Her voice grew steely. "Even if they try, other people can't tell me the right way to feel about you, Ginny. It… it…" she searched for the words to express what being with Ginny meant to her; how her life now felt different and happy and whole. Finally, she simply settled on, "It just is."

And *that* was something that resonated so clearly within Ginny, she was able look beyond her fears and embrace what she knew, deep down inside, to be the purest of truths. "It's good that you said that, Lindsay."

Lindsay licked her lips and her eyes widened. "It is?"

"Mmm-hmm. Because my heart's already decided on you." She shook her head a little. "I-I don't know how, but I do know why." She nearly laughed at Lindsay's shocked but undeniably lovesick expression. Then Ginny sobered, her voice lowering even further. "I'm still… I'm still a little scared, I guess."

Lindsay's eyes softened. "Me too."

"Let's be scared together."

Lindsay leaned forward and very gently rubbed noses with Ginny. "A team then, you and me. We stick together no matter what."

Ginny's smile rivaled Lindsay's, and she felt her breath catch when she tried to speak. She lifted her hands and cupped cheeks flushed pink and bathed in soft lamplight. She drew her hands through dark hair. "Through thick and thin."

When their lips met again it was more than a showing of devotion or even heartfelt passion. It was a promise.

The tension in the room plummeted, and Lindsay scooted down a little and shifted, so that she could lay her head just above Ginny's breasts. She sighed softly at the feeling of warm skin against her cheek.

Ginny grinned and wrapped her arms around Lindsay, feeling as though she held a very precious gift.

"Ginny?"

"Hmm?"

"Ca-can we go slow?" She laid her hand on Ginny's stomach, its concave shape making her frown. They were missing too many meals. "I'm not… well, I'm not sure what to do… exactly." *Oh, that was smart.* She winced internally, feeling her cheeks flame. Then she remembered one or two things she liked to do alone that were bound to be better with Ginny, and she blushed even hotter. "I'm an idiot," she mumbled, lifting her head to gauge Ginny's reaction.

Ginny blinked, never having seen a human being that particular shade of red before. Even the low lamplight couldn't hide it. A relieved smile curled her lips, and she drew her hands down the gentle slope of Lindsay's back. "You're not an idiot, sweetheart."

Lindsay's face brightened perceptibly at the endearment. "Sweetheart?"

For a second, Ginny's courage faltered. She'd used the term many times in her head. But this time it had tumbled out before she could censor herself. "Is that okay? I mean when we're all alone?" she asked quickly. "I'm sorry if—"

"No!" Lindsay corrected just as quickly. "It's fine. It's really good."

Ginny let out a deep breath. "Slow is perfect. We don't have to do everything all at once. Even though… Well, with two women I'm not sure what *everything* even is." Though her mind was spinning with possibilities. Her expression turned impish. "I'm *more* than willing to try to figure things out together, if you are."

Ginny's words were met with a wicked chuckle. Lindsay nuzzled the soft skin at the swell of Ginny's breast, then kissed it, pulling a surprised groan of pleasure from deep in the other woman's throat.

"Ooo, nice sound." Lindsay's voice was a sexy purr, and Ginny gulped, wondering what she'd just gotten herself into. Glad beyond measure that she'd finally made the leap, she moaned again, responding instinctively to Lindsay's tender, inquisitive touch. "Oh, Virginia Chisholm, you've got yourself a deal."

Chapter Eleven

Late the next afternoon…

"Welcome to Talking Rock, Georgia." Ginny pointed to the sign she was reading as she and Lindsay stepped out of the railroad station and onto the street. "Population… What?" The last two numbers on the sign looked as though they had been recently painted, and she wondered idly whether a few new adoptions might be the cause. "I can't believe they'd bother to stop someplace so small."

Lindsay shouldered their bag and chuckled, already doing her best to unbutton her coat in deference to the fifty-degree weather. "Christ," she scoffed. "I could spit off the roof of a building in the Lower East Side and hit more people than that."

Ginny turned her head to face her friend and raised a playful eyebrow. "What a lovely mental picture."

"My pleasure." Lindsay smiled brightly. "C'mon." She gently grasped Ginny's sleeve and steered her toward the building in her sights. "I can't believe it, but it looks like this place has a city hall, or courthouse, or something." She gestured with her chin to a three-story wooden structure that proudly flew the American and Confederate flags from its twin flagpoles out front.

Ginny gave a satisfied nod. "Perfect. We can start there."

Lindsay absently pushed a lock of blowing hair from her face. She scowled, hating that she'd lost her hat. Not to mention that the circumstances under which she'd lost it were still too horrific to contemplate.

Ginny saw the motion and sighed. Before leaving Big Ugly, they'd purchased Lindsay the least expensive dress in the store, which still cost two dollars and twenty-five cents, and a pair of denim pants. She wanted to buy her a hat as well, but her friend insisted that they couldn't afford to spend the extra forty-five cents. Ginny pulled the cap from her head. She bumped hips with Lindsay, and her friend's eyes shifted sideways. "Here." She held out her hat.

Lindsay stared at the cap in confusion. "You want me to hold it?"

"Nuh-uh. I want you to *have* it." She held up a hand to forestall the protest she could already see forming on Lindsay's lips. "It's not the kind I'm used to wearing anyway, Lindsay. And it looks stupid when I'm wearing a dress." *And what's mine is yours.*

"I'm wearing a dress," Lindsay reminded, a small smile playing on her lips.

"True," Ginny allowed, "but I'm quite certain that you'll be back into your beloved trousers as soon as you can."

Lindsay gave her a slightly worried smile, a little insecurity bleeding through her normal confidence. "Do I look that all-overish when I'm all slicked up?" She tugged unhappily at the brown skirt. "It's just been so long since—"

Ginny stopped their progress with a hand on Lindsay's shoulder. "You look *beautiful*"—she smiled fondly—"Like always." Though privately, Ginny had to admit that she'd grown rather fond of her gangly companion wearing men's attire. It reflected her friend's free spirit in a way a plain dress never could.

"There's nothing wrong with you being more comfortable in what you're used to." She held up the cap again. "Please take it."

Hesitantly, Lindsay reached out and relieved her of the hat, accepting it for what it was—a simple gift from the heart. "Thank you," was all she said, delighting Ginny, who had been bracing herself for more of a fuss. Lindsay reached out and playfully tugged a lock of hair, enjoying the fact that it wasn't hiding under a cap. "It's growing out."

Ginny's blue eyes twinkled, reflecting the fading glints of the afternoon sun. "Thank goodness." She knew she'd developed a habit of pushing aside her bangs with impatient fingers, and she had to force herself not to do it now. "It must have been singed to pieces to have earned me this shaggy cut."

Lindsay shrugged. "I like it," she said honestly, as they resumed their trek. It seemed a little odd to be having this conversation after all this time. But Ginny, she knew, tended to jabber when she got nervous.

"Really?"

"Really," she confirmed. "Would I lie?"

Ginny snorted. "Yes."

A burst of laughter exploded from Lindsay. "True. But I'm not."

They grew quiet as they approached the building. Unconsciously, Ginny eased herself a little closer to Lindsay as they walked.

"Don't worry," Lindsay told her, breaking the short silence.

Ginny let out a deep, frustrated breath. They had been disappointed so many times already, with each time more crushing than the last. It made her physically ill just thinking about it. Her jaw clenched against the sensation.

"How can I not?"

Lindsay thought about that for a moment. "All right," she conceded. "Be a little nervous." Her voice deepened. "But you don't need to be scared."

Ginny smiled through the tension roiling in her guts. *My protector.* Unobtrusively, her hand drifted sideways a few inches and gently grasped Lindsay's.

They'd thrown away the bandage covering the rail-rider's hands the night before, though her last three fingers on one hand remained splinted and taped together, and a smaller bandage was still taped over the knuckles of her other hand.

"We're going in together, right?" Ginny asked softly, knowing the answer but craving the reassurance just the same.

Lindsay knew better than to make the mistake she had the day before. "Count on it."

An hour later, a very pale Ginny pushed open the tall doors of the Talking Rock City Hall and stepped outside. Lindsay followed immediately, laying her palm on the small of Ginny's back as they descended the steps. The sun traveled behind a curtain of wispy clouds, and it seemed a little cooler than when they'd gone inside.

"I can't believe it," Ginny said, her voice shaky. "We found one of them." She wondered briefly if Lindsay could hear her pounding heart. "Lewis is here."

"It was bound to happen sometime." They had, Lindsay admitted, finally gotten lucky. It was such a foreign sensation she almost didn't know how to cope. Ginny had explained her situation to the clerk, who had processed three adoptions from the Wards' passenger car of orphans. The clerk had eagerly given her the names of the family that had taken Lewis in. Now, armed with directions, a wish of good luck, and the sincerest apologies on behalf of the City of Talking Rock, they set out to hike the three miles to the country home of Jon and Erika Bergquist.

Lindsay regarded the sky thoughtfully as they walked. "Ginny?"

"Hmm?"

"Should we get a room first? It'll be well past dark before we get there, much less make it back into town for the night." Though she was more than happy to find a place to sleep outside, especially in this more temperate climate, she didn't know how Ginny would feel about doing that, particularly with Lewis in tow. "Then again, if we end up having to snatch him, it won't be safe to get a room in town. Maybe we should buy an extra blanket and some food just in case?"

Ginny stopped walking and rubbed her temples. She hadn't thought of any of those things, and she suddenly felt overwhelmed. "I— Maybe— Yes— Or—" She groaned at her own inability to make a firm decision. "I don't know."

Lindsay sighed and wrapped her arm around her. "Okay, first things first. We meet the Bergquists and then decide. Maybe we could come back for him in the morning?"

"I don't want to have to steal him away," Ginny said bleakly.

"I know," Lindsay answered softly. "But you will if you have to?"

A solemn nod was her answer.

"Let's go."

The Bergquist home sat on the edge of a narrow dirt road that wound its way through the Georgia mountains. They hadn't even had a dusting of snow this winter, and tall, brittle blades of grass blew gently in the breeze. The women could smell the smoke from the chimney long before the house came into view. It was dark, but the moon was full and bright, illuminating their surroundings in bluish-silver hues.

And then they saw it, nestled between a cluster of creaking, leafless oaks. The house was small but well-kept with a split-rail wooden fence that enclosed a good-sized yard. Fifty feet or so behind the house stood a narrow red barn, an outhouse, a well house constructed of stone, and a tiny shack. The sounds coming from inside the shack indicated that it served as a chicken coop. The latch on the coop door was loose, and the thin wooden slab rattled helplessly against the frame with every gust of wind.

"It looks… nice. In a country sort of way," Ginny said, stopping at the mouth of a short path that led to the front door. She spun in a circle, absorbing the outdoors and feeling as out of sorts as she had in Big Ugly. "God, Lindsay, it's so quiet here and still so noisy. You can hear *everything*." Her thoughts turned inward. "I can hardly believe he's in there. I think I'm afraid to find out that he's not, and that this has all been some sort of horrible mistake."

"Ginny—"

Before she could utter another word, the door to the house opened up, spilling firelight and the sound of childish laughter into the night. Three little girls, all in pigtails, and ranging in age from four to twelve, ran outside. Two of them carried wooden buckets. Hot on their heels was Lewis, giggling right along with them as he jumped off the porch.

Ginny's hand flew to her mouth, and her knees weakened at the sight of her brother.

Lindsay reached out to steady her, unconsciously holding her breath, in equal parts anxious and afraid at how the scene would unfold.

The children caught sight of the strangers in their yard, and the oldest of the girls ran inside the house yelling, "Papa, Mama, we can't go get water— somebody's here!"

Lewis froze.

From across the yard, Ginny could see his wide eyes.

Lindsay studied the boy curiously. Other than his red hair, he didn't really resemble Ginny. *Must look like the da.*

Ginny drew in a sobbing breath. "Lew—" The word broke, and she was forced to swallow a few times before she could try again. She felt Lindsay take her hand and squeeze it gently. "Lewis?"

The boy blinked stupidly, his feet seemingly rooted to the ground.

"It's me, Lewis," Ginny forced out, too afraid to step forward lest he fade away like a ghost in the mist.

An enormous smile lit the boy's face, and his cheeks creased into dimples so familiar Lindsay felt a tug in her heart. "Ginny!" He sprinted across the yard as fast as his feet could carry him, the bottoms of his shoes slipping on the grass every few feet, nearly causing him to crash to the ground on several occasions.

Thank you. Lindsay felt her heart resume beating and let go of Ginny just in time for the young woman to drop to her knees and open her arms.

Lewis flew into them. The impact sent Ginny sprawling onto her back into the dirt. She couldn't have cared less. Crying, she pulled him close, squeezing him so tightly the boy could hardly breathe. "Oh, Lewis."

"Ginny!" he squealed enthusiastically, returning his sister's embrace with equal fervor.

Lindsay looked away, a little surprised at the tightness in her throat, and feeling very much like an intruder on this special familial moment. Then she noticed the outline of a man and woman in the doorway of the small house. Even in the shadows, she could tell that they were an older couple—and not happy. She stepped forward to intercept them, bound and determined to give Ginny the sweet reunion with her brother that she deserved.

Oblivious to Lindsay's absence, Ginny sat up, taking Lewis with her. She pressed several sloppy kisses on his face, which he endured with good humor, not squawking out his usual "eww" at the attack of sisterly affection. Then she held him at arm's length and took a long, hard look at him.

He was sporting a slick new haircut and wore a new coat over plain but clean homemade clothes. One of the questions that had been making her guts roil for the past month was finally answered. He didn't appear to have any lingering physical effects from the fire

"You're all right, Lewis?" Ginny nodded vigorously to herself, continuing to eye every inch of him critically. "You're all right," she repeated in a hushed voice, more to reassure herself than to pose an actual question to her brother.

He regarded her curiously, almost as if seeing her for the first time. He blinked a few times, wearing the most serious expression she'd ever seen on his young face. "You look like Mama."

The stark words hung between them, piercing both their hearts and unerringly reminding them both of everything they'd lost.

Suddenly, Ginny couldn't meet her brother's eyes. *Oh, Lewis.* "I know," she whispered brokenly.

"I told them you weren't dead," he explained quickly, thinking that perhaps Ginny was angry with him. "I told them!" And with that, tears finally began to shimmer in pale gray eyes. "Nobody would listen." His face began to crumble, and his voice took on a panicky edge. "They took James and Jane. I'm sorry. I promise, I tried to stop them—"

"Shhh," Ginny soothed, gently stroking his cheeks. "We're going to make it, Lewis. You'll see."

"I tried to tell them—"

He began to cry in earnest, quiet tears that Ginny felt more keenly than her own.

"No." She grabbed him by the shoulders and gave him a tiny shake. "You don't have to apologize for anything. This is *not* your doing."

He stilled, gazing at her doubtfully as he processed the words, willing himself to stop crying. Only babies or girls cried. But to his shame, he'd always been prone to tears. "Where were you?"

The voice held more curiosity than recrimination, but the question still tore at Ginny's heart. She didn't bother to try to stanch the tide of hot tears streaming down her cheeks. "They took me to the hospital on Blackwell's Island," she explained patiently, sniffing as she spoke and praying that he'd understand. "The fire, or I guess just the hot air from the fire, burned the inside of my throat, and I was having trouble breathing. I was there for a long time, Lewis."

At the word "fire," Lewis's skin took on a noticeably green pallor and Ginny instantly regretted she'd brought it up. "I'm sorry," she whispered, pulling him close again, feeling his small chest meld to hers and slim arms wrap tightly around her.

He frowned. "That m-must have hurt."

Ginny squeezed her eyes shut, fairly bursting with love for this sensitive, young boy. "It did a little," she admitted, not wanting to lie. "But it's important for you to know that I didn't *want* to leave you. The moment I was released from the hospital, I started looking for you and James and Jane."

"I knew it," he muttered against her neck, the skin moist from tears. "I *knew* you wouldn't leave us."

Ginny gently pried him from her. Looking him squarely in the eye, she cupped his chin with a steady hand. "Never," she swore. "I would *never* leave you on purpose." She paused and willed her pounding heart to slow. "We're family forever," she whispered, causing him to fling himself at her once again. "Nothing is more important than that."

Her gaze drifted to Lindsay, who was standing on the porch, talking with the Bergquists, the other children gathered around them anxiously. She closed her eyes again. "Nothing."

Erika Bergquist crossed her arms over her ample chest and turned her back on Ginny, Jon, and Lindsay. They were in the barn, discussing Lewis's fate. Ginny and the Bergquists had been arguing for so long that they'd all lost track of the time. Erika sniffed and wiped at her face angrily. Both she and Ginny had been reduced to tears several times already. "No," she whispered brokenly.

Jon sighed and wrapped his arms around his wife from behind. He didn't want to give the boy up either, but it wasn't right to break up an intact family. He rested his chin on her shoulder. "Erika… honey."

"No! She's just a girl herself. She can't take him," her voice trailed off and, "We've waited so long for a son," was barely audible.

"You were younger than Virginia when our Katherine was born," he reminded softly, smiling a little at the thought of his oldest daughter, who was now a teacher in Atlanta and the mother of two beautiful girls herself. They had tried and tried for a boy, but after their last baby, the midwife informed them in no uncertain terms that another delivery would kill Erika.

Lindsay leaned close to Ginny and pressed her lips gently against her ear to whisper, "We've been out here for a while. Would you like me to go inside and check on Lewis and the other children?" She winced internally, knowing that she hadn't done a very good job of keeping the hopefulness out of her voice. Confrontations like she'd had with Jean and Jacque, or Albert, or even the Wards were something she could handle. But this—with Ginny and Erika looking like they were both about to fracture apart at any moment and Jon barely keeping it together for his wife's sake—it was all too much.

Ginny wiped her cheeks with shaky fingers and nodded. The tension around Lindsay's eyes was so painfully evident that she felt a little sick to her stomach at the sight. *She hurts for me as much as I do.* She hadn't acknowledged Lindsay's presence since the adults had adjourned to the barn to talk in private. But the silent support the rail-rider had offered Ginny—the casual, warm palm that came to rest against the small of her back, the eyes that promised they would work things out somehow—meant everything. And now her friend needed some air.

"That's a good idea."

She patted Lindsay's side gently, her eyes drifting to a small window. Ginny frowned. The moon was high in the sky. "It's been longer than I thought."

"You sure?" Lindsay questioned softly.

Another sniff. "I'm sure."

In a much louder voice, Lindsay announced she'd check on the children and be back in a few minutes. Before she was out the door, Ginny had asked about the farm and Talking Rock, and the Bergquists eagerly shifted topics in favor of something more benign.

Lindsay pushed open the door and took a deep breath of cold night air that whisked away the earthy scent of hay and livestock. She absently pulled the edges of her coat together, trying not to feel guilty for leaving the barn. *They seem like nice enough folks, but why do they have to talk about this endlessly?*

She stood out in front of the house and lifted a hand to knock at the door. Deciding that the children were most likely asleep, she let her hand drop and quietly stepped inside.

It was dark, the orange coals in the fireplace providing the only light. It took a few seconds for her eyes to adjust, and then she spotted Lewis sitting nervously on the davenport.

"Hi," Lindsay said quietly as she shut the front door. She held up her hand. "One minute, okay? I want to check on the other kids."

Lewis nodded and silently led Lindsay to a large back bedroom that the three girls shared. Lindsay peered at the bed that contained the sleeping children. Not knowing what else to do, she placed her fingers in front of each little mouth so that she could make sure they were all breathing.

Lewis muffled a snort.

Lindsay lifted an eyebrow at the boy, then padded quietly out into the living room. She fed the fire several short logs from a wooden bin along the wall, being careful not to use her injured fingers. When she was finished, she straightened and dusted her hands on her skirt before turning to Lewis.

He was staring at her, and it made her uncomfortable. "Who are you? Someone from the orphanage?" he asked curiously, hoping that wasn't the case.

"'Course not," she answered, dropping down on the davenport with a soundless sigh. "I'm a friend of your sister's."

Lewis's face suddenly brightened. "I'm Lewis," he said happily, extending a small hand.

Lindsay smiled. "Pleased to meet you, Lewis. I'm—" She paused, not sure exactly what to say. "I'm Lindsay, I guess." It sounded so strange coming from her own lips.

Lewis scratched his chin. "You guess?"

"No," she corrected with another smile. "I'm pretty sure."

"Good." His gaze slid sideways to the door. "Is Ginny talking to Uncle Jon and Aunt Erika?"

Lindsay's eyebrows jumped. "Uncle and aunt?"

Lewis shrugged one shoulder and brought his stockinged feet up onto the davenport to sit Indian style. "They asked if I wanted to call them Ma and Pa, but I said no."

"Mmm. Were they unhappy that you didn't want to?" She picked at a tiny piece of the davenport's fabric, well aware that she wasn't very good at fishing for information. "Maybe they were even mad enough to give you a whippin'?"

"No!" Lewis looked horrified. "They don't do that. Annie said—well, she's eight and is always trying to steal my biscuits—Annie always—"

Lindsay stifled a chuckle. Like his sister, Lewis could hold his own in the conversation department. "Lewis," she said gently, her voice reminding him what they were talking about.

"Oh. Right. Anyway, my first day here I dropped a plate." He winced. "I was sure I was gonna get it." His own parents used spanking quite frequently as a means of punishment, or a way to control the boys when they got too rambunctious. "But she told me they've never spanked her once. They don't believe in it." He didn't quite know what that meant, other than his backside would be safe.

Lindsay looked a little surprised, idly wishing that her father had had similar beliefs when it came to child-rearing.

"As for them being unhappy about what I said… Well—" Lewis considered that for a moment. "A little, I guess. So I said that, since I didn't have any uncles or aunts or anything, I could call them that, if they wanted."

Lindsay nodded slowly. "And they wanted?"

"Yup."

Lindsay leaned forward and rested her elbows on her knees. *I might as well make the most of my time. I need to go back soon.* "Are you happy here? Would you rather stay than come with your sister and me?"

Again, Lindsay was surprised when Lewis hesitated. She hadn't really considered that any of the children could bond with their new family so quickly. Which was a little ridiculous, she privately admitted, considering how she felt about Ginny.

"I do like it here," he said carefully. "Uncle Jon is a vet-vent-vat—" He scowled and tried again. "A vent-vet-vent—"

Lindsay narrowed her eyes as she tried to decipher what the boy was saying. "A ventriloquist?" She shivered. "God." She'd seen one of those once in a saloon in Kansas City. After the show, the crowd had demanded their money back, attacked the performer, and ripped that queer little head clean off his dummy.

Lewis snapped his fingers. "That's it. And I'm his apprentice," he informed her excitedly, his pride in the announcement written across his elfin features.

Lindsay made a face. *They have apprentices?* "What the hell do they need apprentices for?"

Lewis glanced around nervously. "Shhh. Girls aren't supposed to cuss!"

Lindsay couldn't help but smile. She'd heard this lecture from another redhead. "Sorry," she offered with as much contriteness as she could muster. "So you're going to make a puppet or doll or whatever talk when you grow up?" *We're stealing him tonight!*

Horrified, Lewis scrunched up his face. "Girls play with dolls!"

"Some girls."

"When I get bigger, I'm gonna fix hurt cows, and horses, and stuff."

"Ohhhh." The light of understanding finally dawned on Lindsay. *Maybe Georgia isn't as odd as I thought it was.* "A veterinarian."

"Right. That's what I said. Didn't you hear me? You talk normal so you should be able to understand me. Everyone else here talks funny."

Lindsay nodded. "I know." Her jaw worked silently for a moment. This was going to kill Ginny. "I guess now we need to tell your sister you don't want to come with her." *And then see if she's willing to let you go.*

"No!" Lewis shot to his feet. "I love it here, but I love Ginny more!" Desperately, he looked around the room, ready to bolt if need be. "She hasn't left yet, has she? She promised! I—"

Lindsay reached out and grabbed Lewis by the sleeve, tugging him back to the davenport. "Shh. Relax. You'll wake the girls. Ginny's still here," she promised, feeling bad that she'd unintentionally frightened the boy so. She let out a raspy breath and mentally crossed her fingers. "So you do want to leave?"

"I don't *want* to leave Uncle Jon and Aunt Erika or leave Ginny," he clarified miserably. "If I stay here, I'm going to be an apprentice in just a few more years. It's not the same as my real folks, but Uncle Jon and Aunt Erika are nice and listen to me when I talk—like Ginny does. And I have my own room, and Aunt Erika makes the best blueberry pies."

Lindsay leaned back against the sofa with an unhappy grunt. She let her head fall back, and her eyes fluttered closed. "Then I guess we've got to think of a plan so that we can all be happy." *And this plan had better be a hell of a lot better than your last one, String Bean.*

Fifteen minutes later, Lindsay and Lewis headed to the barn with their hearts in their throats.

Two men jumped from a moving train, tumbling down a rock-strewn embankment and coming to a violent halt at the bottom.

"Damn," Bo cursed. He stood up and brushed off his coat, drawing in a deep breath of pine-scented air. He glanced down at Albert, who was sitting back on his heels trying to catch his breath. "Here we are."

Albert shook his head. He was going to make String Bean suffer twice as much for making him chase her ass out into the middle of nowhere.

Bo took off his Derby and scratched his head. "What's the name of this place again?"

Albert made a face. "In Big Ugly, they said the name on the paper was Talking Rock." The men had counted piss-poor, whistle-stop towns for hour after hour until they'd hit the twelfth town.

Bo laughed humorlessly and began to walk toward the flickering lights of houses in the distance. "Can't believe a damn thing that comes out of people's mouths nowadays."

"Ain't that the truth."

"It's too late to find String Bean." Bo extended his arms in front of him, stretching his sore back. "Let's go get a drink."

Albert grunted and unconsciously patted the railroad schedule in his coat pocket. He'd already planned on nabbing her when she tried to board the next outbound train in the morning.

"You're buying."

"No." Albert chuckled and fell in step behind Bo. "The guy who I'm going to rob is."

Ginny tucked the thick quilt up under Lewis's chin. She smiled and pushed back bangs the same color as her own. The tiny room was dark, except for a sliver of moonlight that painted the narrow twin bed.

The boy flashed her a brilliant, if sleepy, smile. "Can I really come back here and still be an apprentice?" he asked, a big yawn interrupting his question.

"Every summer," Ginny confirmed. "Once school gets out." She wasn't sure how she was going to manage it, but she planned on keeping her promise to the Bergquists. Lewis wouldn't disappear from their lives. "We'll find a way… somehow."

"Maybe James can come too and—" Lewis began excitedly, then abruptly stopped. His voice cracked, and his eyes fluttered shut. "I miss everyone."

Ginny continued to stroke his forehead. "So do I," she whispered, her chest tight. "We'll find them, Lewis. Just like we found you."

He continued to speak with his eyes closed as he tumbled toward sleep. "I knew you'd come someday."

A tiny bittersweet smile appeared on Ginny's face. *Better late than never, little brother. I'm so sorry it took me this long.* "Shhh," she crooned quietly and drew her thumb along the smooth skin of his forehead. "Go to sleep."

"I'm not tired," he protested weakly, instantly reminding Ginny of the many nights she would lie quietly next to him, trying to convince the little boy that he actually *was* tired—he just didn't know it. That hadn't worked then, and she didn't bother trying it now. Instead, she schooled herself in patience. And she didn't have to wait long. Within seconds, Lewis's breathing evened out and soft snores filled the quiet room.

When Ginny was sure he was asleep, she straightened the covers once more and stood. "Goodnight, sweetie," she said quietly.

A small hand shot out from under the blanket and wrapped slender fingers around hers. "Don't go." He began to whimper. "Don't leave me."

Ginny sucked in a surprised breath and dropped back down on the bed. She resumed her gentle stroking of his forehead with her fingertips. "Oh, Lewis," she began, her heart twisting painfully in her chest. "You don't have to worry anymore. I'll be here when you wake up."

The skin she was touching drew together as the boy frowned. "Promise?" he begged.

Ginny nodded and swallowed thickly. "Promise."

The magic word did the trick, and the boy visibly relaxed. "Mmm…'kay." Ginny gently kissed his cheek the way their mother did when she tucked her and Alice in during their childhood. Years later, on many nights when one of the babies was fussy, she and Alice took over that duty for the boys. Alice gravitated toward James and she to Lewis. She'd end up telling him a story or discussing something that had happened during the day; they would laugh quietly and dream together of a new life where there was green grass to play on, and where he could have the puppy he'd always longed for. Innately, she understood his giving, sensitive nature, which was much closer to her own than his sometimes stoic, often mischievous twin. Ginny spared a thought for the other half of this pair of boys who meant so much to her, vowing never to stop looking.

She stood to make her way to the door, her legs stiff from being perched on the edge of his bed for so long, but before she could turn around she heard her brother's fuzzy mumble again.

"Ginny?"

She narrowed her eyes and peered through the darkness, trying to determine if he was talking in his sleep. "Yes?"

"Lindsay's." He smacked his lips together a little and burrowed deeper into the mattress. "She's nice."

This time Ginny's grin stretched her face. "She is." A little jolt of happiness bubbled up inside her. He was just a child, but his opinion, she admitted to herself, and James's too, mattered to her.

He rolled over and tucked his hands under his cheek. "Night."

"Good night." She watched his chest for a few moments, reluctant to leave. Finally, she let out a soft sigh and opened the door to find Lindsay waiting patiently for her. Her friend was holding their coats and two feather pillows the Bergquists had loaned them.

Ginny pulled the door shut and scanned the small, fire-lit living room curiously.

Lindsay leaned against the back of the davenport, emotionally and physically exhausted. "They went to bed a while ago. Said to say goodnight and asked us to join them for breakfast."

"Mmm." Ginny yawned and stepped closer to Lindsay, invading every inch of her personal space without a second thought. "Can't blame them for that." Too tired to be self-conscious, she nuzzled

Lindsay's neck, dropping several small kisses on the warm skin she found there. She hummed happily, reveling in the pure hedonistic joy the action brought her.

Lindsay nearly jumped out of her shoes. "Whaa!"

Ginny laughed quietly and glanced up to innocently bat her eyelashes at Lindsay. "What?"

A single eyebrow rose as Lindsay eased past the initial surprise at Ginny's sudden burst of semi-public affection. "You're certainly not as shy as you were when we first met."

"I was never shy, Lindsay. I just didn't know you. And—" A faint blush worked its way up from her neck to her cheeks, but Ginny pushed out the words, which were new, delicious, and terrifying at the same time. "I didn't love you— then," her voice dropped an octave, and Lindsay felt the words resonate all the way in her toes, "The way I do now."

Lindsay reached up with one hand and cupped a pink cheek. "Me too," she whispered, unable to keep what she was sure was a goofy smile from overtaking her face.

Ginny grasped Lindsay's wrist and gave it a little tug. "Let's go to bed."

"In front of the fire?" Lindsay tilted her head toward the low burning, hickory-scented flames. "Or in the barn?" She wanted to be completely alone with Ginny, away from the prying eyes of curious children, but left the decision up to the younger woman.

Ginny didn't hesitate. "The barn. It shouldn't be uncomfortably cold. Not with the horses and that big cow and you—"

"Hey," Lindsay protested in mock irritation, opening the front door. "Are you comparing me to the *cow*?"

"Keeping me warm," Ginny finished, her eyes dancing. The day, she reflected, had been hard and tiring and wonderful. She wasn't sure she could live through too many like it. At the same time she prayed for more—two more, to be exact.

Lindsay draped their coats over one arm and wrapped the other around Ginny. Their bag containing their blankets and nightshirts was still in the barn. The outside air was frosty, but the wind had died down to a gentle breeze. Every breath sent a stream of fog disappearing into the night sky, and their feet crunched on the dry grass as they walked. The barn was so close they didn't bother to don their coats, and for a few paces they moved along in companionable silence, their eyes adjusting to the moonlight as they breathed in the fresh air.

Ginny turned her head as she walked, Lindsay's arm comfortably wrapped around her waist. "Have I said thank you?"

"You don't have to thank me, Ginny." But the redhead could hear the smile in Lindsay's voice.

"That's not true," Ginny disagreed gently. "You came up with a solution that none of us thought of. You kept me from having to steal Lewis away and helped give him a future that I could have never given him on my own." She bit her bottom lip and fought off tears that were still lurking dangerously close to the surface. "You saved us." She stopped walking and turned to regard Lindsay's profile. Intelligent brown eyes glinted in the moonlight, and white teeth showed faintly when soft lips curled into a smile. Ginny's heart skipped a beat. *She's smart and beautiful. I'm so lucky.*

Lindsay's brow creased, and she couldn't stop herself from squirming a little. "Ginny?"

"Mmm?" Ginny said, eyes, glossy with unshed tears, turning dreamy.

"You're staring."

"I know."

Lindsay gave her a fond look and shook her head, chuckling. "I think you're about to blow, and it's making you crazy." *Not that I mind.*

The metal handle felt cold against Lindsay's palm as she opened the door. It wasn't much darker inside the barn, but the smell of the animals and sweet grass was much stronger. The door rattled on its hinges when she pushed it closed, using her weight to secure it tightly, as she slid a plank into the brackets that served as a lock.

Ginny began to look for their bag. "Lindsay, I—Yow!" she squealed when Lindsay hugged her from behind, causing the pair of black horses and the milk-cow to snort and stir in their stalls.

The darker woman rested her chin on Ginny's shoulder and pressed her cheek into the soft hair above Ginny's ear. "When you look at me like you did outside," she whispered, emotion gripping her heart. "It feels, I mean, I feel like—" She paused, unable to put voice to the sensations churning inside her. In frustration, she shook her head and closed her eyes. "Ugh."

"S'okay, Lindsay," Ginny soothed. She let the pillows drop from her hands and covered the arms wrapped around her waist with her own, giving them a comforting squeeze. "I know just what you mean." And deep in her heart, she did.

They stood that way for a long time, each absorbed in her own thoughts and letting the rhythmic breathing of the animals, the light sound of the breeze rustling nearby branches, and the warmth of their bodies pressed tightly together lull them into a relaxed haze.

Suddenly, Lindsay jerked backward, and Ginny grasped the arms around her waist tightly. "Careful." She unconsciously widened her stance for better balance. "Don't fall."

On unsteady feet, Lindsay straightened and rolled her eyes at herself. "I haven't fallen asleep standing up in forever."

Ginny turned and studied her seriously. Lindsay's face looked pale in the silvery light. She sighed. "You're tired and need to rest." Latent resentment flared unexpectedly. "If you had been in the sort of hospital rich people go to instead of the Charity Hospital, they never would have released you so early. You weren't ready, Lindsay." *She left because of me. They probably would have kept her longer. Her incision and ribs weren't even healed all the way.*

"I'm fine, Ginny. I'm just tired from traveling in a way that I'm not used to. I'm not accustomed to keeping any sort of schedule at all." *And getting my ass kicked twice took more out of me than I realized.*

"You needed more time."

"We didn't have more time," Lindsay pointed out gently.

Ginny's jaw worked. She knew Lindsay was right. But she still didn't like it.

"You're worn out."

Lindsay cocked her head slightly to the side and reached up to trace the dark circles that were visible even now. "Yes. And so are you," she reminded her.

Ginny closed her eyes. "I know. But I'm so happy too. Something with my family finally went right." The feeling was so foreign she almost didn't know how to deal with it. In the last handful of hours, she'd experienced the full spectrum of emotions, and she wasn't sure how much more she could withstand. Her body and mind seemed to be at odds, neither one knowing whether to be giddy or pass out from exhaustion. "I don't know what to think or do," she admitted, rubbing her eyes.

"I do." Lindsay leaned over and brushed her lips across Ginny's. Her actions were immediately rewarded by a breathy sigh from her companion. "C'mon, it's bedtime." Lindsay padded over to their bag, which was propped up against a bale of hay near the barn wall. Careful to give the big gelding in the stall next to it a wide berth, she passed quickly in front of the horse, swiftly bending and snatching up the bag.

Ginny watched in mild surprise. "You're afraid of horses? Why?"

Lindsay scowled as she crossed the barn and extracted their blankets and nightshirts from the dirty cotton sack. "I just like trains better is all," she said a little defensively. "They rarely bite. Horses are okay—I guess—if they're tied to one end of the wagon and I'm at the other."

"Uh huh." Ginny raised a skeptical eyebrow.

"So I wouldn't say I'm afraid—exactly."

"What would you say then?" Ginny moved to help her, spreading one of the blankets on a pile of fragrant, loose hay. Then she set to work removing her dress.

Lindsay smirked as she began untying her shoes. "Nothing." Ginny stuck out her tongue. "Smarty pants."

"I'm wearing a dress."

"Smart ass then," Ginny corrected boldly. Though some of the effect was lost when she blushed despite herself.

Lindsay snorted in surprise, but didn't dare disagree. But she couldn't resist a tiny jibe. "Tch. Ginny, don't you know that girls don't cuss?"

Their eyes met, and they both dissolved into tired laughter. It was already an old joke between them, one that they would happily carry on for two lifetimes.

It wasn't long before both were tucked under their blankets, heads on pillows, snuggled closely together.

"Shit!"

Ginny jumped. "What?" She sat up and looked around, her eyes darting wildly. "What's wrong?"

"I have to use the outhouse, and I just got comfortable," Lindsay admitted sheepishly.

Ginny blew out a disgusted breath. Then, unexpectedly, a devilish grin twitched at her lips. "And here I thought that big bad horse gave you a scary look." Her smile grew. "But I could use the necessary too."

Brown eyes turned to slits. "Just for that, I'm using the last of the Montgomery Ward's Catalog." Lindsay got up as quickly as her ribs would allow and stuffed still-socked feet into her shoes. She began to chuckle wickedly.

"What?" Ginny gasped, mortified. Her fatigue vanished as she delighted in the rare moment of pure play. "And leave me with none?" She jumped up and began wrestling on her own shoes, groaning when Lindsay snatched up the blanket, wrapped it around herself, and headed for the barn door. A chill swept over her, causing goosebumps to erupt over her bare legs. "Get back here, Brussel Sprout!"

Ginny's giggles mingled with Lindsay's until both sets of laughter faded away into the night.

Chapter Twelve

It was just before sunrise when Ginny opened her eyes. The inside of the barn was cast in grayish-blue hues. She blinked a few times to clear her vision. They couldn't have gotten more than four or five hours of sleep, and her body protested that fact when she tentatively stretched. She could feel Lindsay's side pressed firmly against her back, and she smiled. She'd been right. She wasn't cold—all except for her toes, which despite being covered with socks, felt like ten tiny lumps of ice attached to two bigger lumps of ice.

Ginny carefully scooted away from Lindsay and rolled over so she could face the sleeping woman. She propped herself up on one elbow and ran her fingers through sleep-tousled brown hair, enjoying the feeling as coarse strands tickled the sensitive skin.

Lindsay, she had learned, usually slept like a rock, not waking up until she, or something else very loud, prodded her. Today, however, Ginny was especially loath to wake her. *She needs this rest. She looks pale.* But she also figured that it was likely the Bergquists would be up within the next half-hour or so, and that someone would be coming into the barn to relieve the cow of her bulging supply of fresh milk.

Just a few more minutes, then we'll get going, Ginny promised herself. Something, she wasn't exactly sure what, compelled her to touch Lindsay. And Ginny wasn't of a mind to even try to curb that urge.

"Mmm." Lindsay shifted a little under the blanket, and her hand brushed against Ginny's. Feeling the warm body, she let out a small sigh, and the corners of her lips shaped the barest of smiles before going slack again.

Ginny gave her a fond look, feeling a rush of affection for the woman sharing her journey. Her eyes swept over the relaxed face so close to her own, admiring its strong lines and the way light played off the peaceful features. *She looks younger when she's asleep.*

Perhaps it was the now-familiar scent of warm skin that she found more intoxicating than any liquor she'd ever tasted. Or maybe it was the tranquil sound of deep, even breaths that lulled her into slumber every night. Or maybe it was just that she felt safe and happy and loved. Whatever the reason, a good portion of the lingering nervousness she felt over their budding physical relationship melted away.

Ginny dragged her fingers lightly down Lindsay's cheek and across a section of collarbone, which was exposed by the "V" in the front of the nightshirt, amazed, once again, at how soft and inviting Lindsay's skin was. Suddenly, she wanted to touch her everywhere. She snuggled closer and dropped her hand down to the hem of Lindsay's nightshirt, which had worked its way up her hips in the night. A tentative smile crawled across Ginny's face and settled there. This was going to be good.

She gently pushed the blankets down to Lindsay's knees, feeling a rush of cool morning air sweep across her skin. She touched a bare hipbone, admiring its lean shape. Several bands of muscles crisscrossed Lindsay's stomach, though in this position a soft layer of flesh hid them.

She traced the pink scar on Lindsay's abdomen, and her eyebrows contracted. But she forced her thoughts past that and onto happier things. Ginny recalled what a shock it had been to learn that Lindsay didn't own any underclothes. Her smile shifted into a faint smirk, and she admitted to herself that, even then, she'd been more intrigued than anything else.

Her hand moved lower still, and her entire body shifted along with it until she was lying with her head pillowed on Lindsay's shoulder, stroking the silky skin of a slender, naked thigh with idle pleasure. *I could get used to this. Oh, yeah. I really could.*

Lindsay groaned in her sleep, clearly enjoying the delicate, phantom caresses. The primal sound tore through Ginny, and her innocent affection gave way to arousal. The heat seared her fingertips and caused her lower belly to twist in anticipation, though she wasn't quite sure what she was waiting for. Still uncertain of what she was doing or how Lindsay would react, she swallowed and forced her eyes upward, allowing her gaze to caress Lindsay's flat belly and finally the soft curve of her breasts. Mesmerized, Ginny's hand began to follow the same path her eyes had taken.

"What are you doing?" Lindsay burred, her voice low and rough with sleep. Ginny's hand froze, and she bit her lower lip, feeling her face heat until she thought she might faint. "Touching you."

Lindsay sighed. "Good."

Ginny laughed, still feeling a little embarrassed after being caught with her hand someplace a little more intimate than a cookie jar.

Lindsay leaned upwards and gently drew Ginny's mouth to hers for a tender but thorough kiss.

The kiss lasted forever; when they paused and pulled far enough away to look at each other's faces, Ginny's pupils, dark and glassy, were dilated with desire. When she looked into Lindsay's half-lidded eyes, she licked suddenly dry lips, and with a slightly shaky hand she cupped Lindsay's breast, hearing Lindsay's sharp intake of breath.

"That feels—" Lindsay couldn't even think of a word to describe what Ginny's touch did to her; she could only hope that Ginny would understand the depth of what she meant. "It feels really, *really* good."

"Good." Ginny grinned, laying her hand flat against the valley between Lindsay's breasts and feeling the thrumming heartbeat beneath her palm. "Have I told you I love you this morning?"

"Nope." Lindsay wriggled her eyebrows. "But I'm waiting."

A soft laugh. "I love you." Ginny lifted her hand and affectionately raked her fingers through the thick, mussed hair that surrounded Lindsay's face, taking time to tickle her ear.

Lindsay's smile lit up the barn. "I love you too." Then, without warning, she launched her own attack, playfully returning Ginny's tickles, but mixing hers with heartfelt kisses.

Then there was a banging on the barn door.

Lindsay couldn't believe her ears. The time together this morning had been so intimate she wasn't nearly ready for it to end. She nearly burst into tears. Ginny's irritated groan mixed with hers.

"Are you girls coming?" Mrs. Bergquist called. "It's nearly time for breakfast."

Ginny bit her tongue to keep from saying something awful.

Lindsay wasn't inclined to mind her manners; she whimpered when Ginny gave her one last regretful kiss and rolled over to begin rooting for their clothes. "If I had a gun," she murmured darkly.

Ginny chuckled. "You'd shoot yourself in the foot or wet your pants." Lindsay scowled and pinched Ginny hard on the bottom, earning an indignant squawk.

Mrs. Bergquist tried the door again, giving it a slightly annoyed shake. *Why would they lock the barn door?* "Virginia? Lindsay?"

When did the sun come up? Ginny blinked at the golden light pouring through the dirty windows above the stalls. "We'll be out in a minute," she called, noting that her hands were trembling. She crawled back over to a dejected-looking Lindsay, who had just sat up. Their eyes met and held. "I want more time with you," Ginny told her earnestly.

Lindsay sighed and pulled Ginny into a heartfelt hug. "I want that too." She buried her nose in soft red hair and murmured, "I love you." It still felt a little new and odd to say, but she found it falling from her lips so naturally she didn't stop to think about it.

"I love you too." Ginny closed her eyes and held on to Lindsay as tightly as she dared. *My life is meant to be spent with you,* her mind whispered, though her heart had reconciled itself to that happy fact quite a while ago. "We'll get more time—like this. We just have to be patient."

Lindsay managed to smile through her frustration. "You know," she began wryly, "I'm really beginning to *hate* that word." The body in her arms shook with silent laughter.

Ginny turned back and pressed her forehead to Lindsay's. Unable to stop herself, she kissed her again, uttering quietly against moist, slightly parted lips, "Me too."

The trio was walking down the road toward town. Jon and Erika had offered them a ride, but Ginny, hoping to avoid a teary scene at the train station, had suggested they walk off their breakfast instead. The Bergquists had been livid over the Wards' nonexistent attempts to reunite Lewis with Ginny before adopting him out. And the look on Erika's face, after she kissed Lewis goodbye and told him she'd see him again this summer, told Ginny that Jeremiah and Isabelle had angered the wrong Southern woman. There would be hell to pay—Ginny's mouth twitched in a malicious grin just thinking about it. *Couldn't happen to a more rotten couple of swindlers.*

It was beginning to cloud over, and the *Farmer's Almanac* predicted rain for the rest of the week, but they were certain they could make it into town well before it began to fall. It was colder than the day before. Their coats were buttoned to the top, and frost covered the dry grass. They had walked nearly the first mile in silence, and it was Ginny who tried to break them out of their funk.

"Oh, my," Ginny groaned, patting her stomach. "Breakfast was incredible." Lewis and Lindsay could only nod.

"I'm as full as can be. One more bite, and I'd have exploded right on the spot." Lindsay made an explosion sound just to see Lewis smile.

Casually, she reached down to the waist of her pants, wondering if she could undo the top button without anyone noticing.

Ginny, who was thinking the very same thing about her trousers, and who was holding one of Lewis's hands as they walked, turned to her brother. "Do you eat that well everyday?" They'd enjoyed hotcakes and maple syrup, along with eggs, thick slices of ham, and hot coffee. It had truly been a feast.

"Mmm-hmm." Lewis smiled. "It's great."

"No shit," Lindsay mumbled, receiving an elbow jab to her arm from Ginny. "Ouch!"

Lewis got a far-off look in his eyes. "I'll miss the food."

Lindsay frowned. "What do you mean… miss it?" She gestured sideways to the boy's sister. "Can't she cook?"

Lewis covered his mouth with one hand and snorted wildly, sounding amazingly like a piglet.

"Thanks a lot," Ginny muttered good-naturedly to her brother, her eyes narrowing with fake menace.

"But I sold three doorstoppers—I mean biscuits—to the neighbors," the boy sassed back.

The siblings looked at each other and grinned, happy to be back together. Lindsay, however, was still nonplussed. "That was a joke, right?"

Lewis's eyebrows jumped. "A joke?"

"The part about her not being able to cook, I mean."

He shook his head sadly. "Nope. I *really* wish it was."

Lindsay's mouth dropped open in horror. "Well, Godda—"

"Lindsay…" Ginny's voice was filled with warning. She smiled inwardly when the darker woman's mouth snapped shut with an audible click.

Lewis laughed again.

Lindsay resettled their traveling bag on her shoulder, her face a picture of confusion. "But you lived with your parents and had a *mother*." She gestured wildly with one hand. This was serious. There were no delis around here! "You're, well, supposed to know how to cook," she explained somewhat petulantly. "Everyone knows that!"

"Everyone knows that I'm supposed to be able to cook?" Ginny clarified in a slow, incredulous voice.

Lewis nodded and kicked a rock out of his path. "She's right, Ginny.

Alice and Mama could cook. You were the only one who couldn't."

"Hmph." Ginny let go of Lewis's hand so she could cross her arms over her chest. "It's not like I didn't try. I can cook—" She winced, and her voice trailed off. "It's just not fit to eat."

Lewis nodded again, more vigorously this time.

"Besides," Ginny continued, giving Lindsay a pointed look, "you've been on your own for years; you should be able to cook better than all of us."

Lewis glanced back and forth between Ginny and Lindsay as they bantered, thrilled they were including him in their conversation. And James, he was certain, would just love Lindsay.

"I can roast… *meat*," Lindsay paused and smiled wickedly, "over an open flame."

Ginny visibly shivered, deliberately refusing to ask what sort of meat Lindsay was referring to. "Good," she praised sarcastically. "Then *you're* the new cook."

Lindsay took one of Lewis's hands in her own. With a smile so wide Ginny thought his face might split in two, he glanced up at Lindsay. "Lewis," Lindsay said, "is it okay if I come back this summer to Talking Rock with you?"

Both Ginny and Lewis blinked. They froze mid-step.

"I figure by then," Lindsay let a twinkle enter her eyes, "I'll be near starved to death and need to put on some weight."

"Sure!" Lewis exclaimed, starting to jump up and down. "You can come. Ginny can stay with James and Jane; we can bring 'em back some food to keep 'em all from dying."

Lindsay and Lewis shook hands. "Good plan, little man."

Ginny rolled her eyes and increased her pace, leaving a laughing Lindsay and a confused Lewis behind her. The growing friendship between her brother and Lindsay warmed her heart, and with that, she realized her goals were changing. Was it possible to knit together the shattered pieces of all their lives into something different, but even stronger than they'd known before? She wasn't sure. But with a brave heart and a happy grin, Ginny was ready to find out.

"Ugh. Christ." Albert lay in the fetal position on the ground in the alleyway behind the local saloon. His head was pounding, and he still felt like he was going to puke, though he'd already done that. Several times. A half a bottle of rotgut whiskey and an empty stomach turned out to be a wicked combination.

"Shut the hell up, Rat Face," Bo grumbled. He kicked weakly at the other man from his position flat on top of a pile of garbage. "I'm trying to sleep." He pushed his Derby down over his eyes. "Stupid light."

Albert struggled to make sense of what Bo was saying. *Light?* There couldn't be light. It was nighttime. Bloodshot eyes popped wide open. "Damn!" He shot to his feet, and then fell over a bucket of rancid grease that had been carelessly discarded by a nearby restaurant. His knee plowed into the bucket, sinking deeply into the vile, soft substance. "Arghhh…"

With his index finger, Bo slowly tipped up his hat and glared at Albert. "What is wrong with you?"

Albert pushed the bucket off his knee, the sucking noise making his ears ring. "Look around, dumbfuck." He threw the bucket aside. "It's morning."

Reluctantly, and with slitted eyes, Bo gazed up into the gray, but clearly daytime, sky. "Huh." He shrugged and closed his eyes again. "So it is."

"We've got to find her before she leaves town," Albert ground out, leaning against the cold brick wall to get his bearings.

Bo sighed. "Fine. Fine. Don't have a fit."

"I want to find her," he paused, not wanting to say what he was planning on doing, in case Bo had a crisis of conscience at the last moment. "And go back to New York City to collect my reward. This fresh air is killing me."

Bo pushed himself to his feet and wrinkled his nose at Albert, who was covered in food scraps and rancid grease. "Fresh air?" He smiled derisively. "String Bean must have broken your nose the last time she kicked your ass."

Albert's jaw clenched. "Shut up," he barked. "And get your ass to the local boarding house to see if she's there. I'll go to the train station so she doesn't get past us."

Bo stalked the few feet to Albert and poked his chest with an irritated finger. He'd finally had enough. "You"—another poke—"Mr. Fat-Fuck-Rat-Face"—a third poke—"are not my boss. I'm here to watch you find String Bean. Not to be your slave."

Albert's dark eyes flashed, though he remained deathly still. *After I use you to help find String Bean, I'm gonna break your legs and leave you for the dogs to eat. This is the last day you're going to be a pain in my ass.* "You're right," he said suddenly amiable, and surprising Bo. "Do you want me to go to the boarding house instead?"

Bo blinked slowly, not sure what to say now that he had a choice.

Albert looked down at the pocket watch he'd stolen the night before, taking a moment to blow on the glass and shine it against his coat. "Well?"

Bo brushed the finger that had been touching Albert against his coat. Haughtily, he straightened his hat, wishing he'd stuck to beer the night before.

"No. I'll go to the boarding house." Confused, he stormed off, scanning the streets for String Bean as he moved.

Albert pulled a tattered copy of the railroad schedule from his trouser pocket and sniggered, glad to be rid of that pest. In the distance he could hear the faint whistle of a train. "Ready or not, String Bean"—grungy yellow teeth made an appearance—"here I come."

Frustrated, Ginny pulled off her brother's cap, so she could look into a pair of sheepish gray eyes. "You were supposed to put it in the bag. I know that Mrs. Bergquist set one out for you. I saw her do it myself."

He twisted a toe into the ground and stuffed his hands in his pockets. "I forgot."

Ginny sighed. "I can see that, Lewis." She and Lindsay exchanged glances. A blanket wasn't an optional item, considering they never knew what their sleeping arrangements would be from one day to the next. "Don't worry," she reassured her brother in a calm voice. "We'll buy one when we arrive in Alabama."

She mentally calculated their finances, not liking the result. "C'mon, we need to get to the station. The train's due to leave in a few minutes."

As if on cue, a large puff of smoke exploded from the waiting engine's smokestack, sending a black spiral into the sky.

Lindsay shook her head. "Ginny, by the time we stop for the night, the stores will be closed. The boy needs a blanket. We just passed a store." She began digging in her pocket, pleased to feel a silver dollar in the bottom. "I don't need to eat again today." She held up a hand to forestall what she knew would be Ginny's objection. "Really. Let me go buy one, and then I'll meet you." She winked at Lewis, trying to make him feel a little better for having forgotten to put the blanket in. "Save me a seat." *I never will get used to sitting with the paying passengers.*

He nodded. "Okay, Lindsay."

"No." Ginny tried not to take their bag, but Lindsay was pressing it into her hands. "No, Lindsay. The train is about to leave. You'll miss it."

A dark eyebrow arched. "I'll be back in time if we stop jawing about it and I get going. I know trains. I'll be fine."

But Ginny wouldn't be dissuaded. "We change trains three times before we get to our next stop. We can buy a blanket later. Or he can have mine." A hint of panic crept into her voice. "If we miss this train, it's two days before we can catch another. We can't buy different tickets, and we can't afford to stay here. We—"

"We won't have to." Impulsively, Lindsay leaned forward and gave Ginny a chaste peck on the cheek. "I'll be right back." She affectionately ruffled Lewis's thick, rust-colored hair before turning for the store.

Ginny reached for her, but Lindsay pulled away and broke into a light jog, causing Ginny's fingertips to do nothing more than graze her coat. "Lindsay!" She fought the urge to stamp her foot. "Argh. Lindsay." Her voice was quieter this time.

"Get our seats, or we won't get to sit next to each other," Lindsay called over her shoulder.

Ginny took a quick step forward and drew in a deep breath, as though she were going to bolt after the other woman. But she didn't, and let out an angry exhale instead. She shook her head. "Stubborn," she muttered hotly.

Lewis looked back and forth between Ginny, whose eyes hadn't left the retreating rail-rider, and Lindsay's rapidly retreating back.

Lindsay grabbed her side and slowed her jog to a fast walk.

"Your ribs, crazy," Ginny whispered, grimacing as she imagined what the jarring motion would feel like with ribs that were still tender.

"Ginny?"

Ginny handed Lewis his cap and gave him a reassuring smile, though an uneasy feeling had settled deep in the pit of her stomach. A rather shabby clock mounted on the depot roof heralded the time. "C'mon. Lindsay's right. We need to get our seats."

"She said she'd be back in a minute," he reminded his sister, trying to make her feel a little better. "Don't worry."

They made their way to the depot, hand in hand, with Ginny looking over her shoulder frequently. She squeezed his small hand. "Easier said than done." She felt his fingers tighten around hers, lending her his silent support.

With a loving smile, she squeezed back.

Lindsay drew in a painful gasp. "God. I forgot about those." Her ribs had been healing nicely and were only painful if she twisted awkwardly or jarred them. Running, apparently, did a little of both.

She scanned the shop windows, until she saw one with brightly colored bolts of cloth and several pairs of boots in the window. When she pushed open the heavy wooden door, a bell clanged loudly and the scent of cinnamon hard candy rushed up to greet her. Despite being stuffed like a prize hog, she moaned her appreciation at the scent that she associated with the Christmases of her very young childhood. Soon the scent mingled with tobacco and cured meat. The store had a little of everything.

"Blankets?" she asked the clerk quickly, noting the time on the cuckoo clock above the register. She had eight minutes.

The older woman smiled. "Right this way." She led Lindsay to the back of the store and a table that held blankets, linens, and a few towels.

There was a fair selection, but one blanket caught Lindsay's eye. She picked it up and rubbed the cloth between her fingers, testing its thickness. "How much?"

"Mmm… Nice choice. That one is seventy-five cents."

"For a blanket?" Lindsay exploded. "You've got to be kidding. For this?" The woman jumped back a step, her hands coming up defensively.

Ginny didn't pay that much for the blankets she'd bought after they left the Charity Hospital, "You're crazy, lady."

"I-I—" The woman babbled, aghast.

Lindsay tapped her foot and looked at the blanket. "Well?"

The woman was too shocked to speak, and Lindsay chastised herself. *You're not in Queens anymore, String Bean. Stop bein' an asshole and scaring the locals.* She softened her voice. "Look, I'm really sorry. I'm in a hurry. I'm about to miss my train and my… well, my… I have people waiting for me."

The clerk visibly relaxed and glanced at the clock. "You have seven minutes," she said crisply. She made a dismissive gesture. "Conductor won't leave early. The train never leaves early."

A tiny smile etched its way across impatient features. "I know."

Her wariness forgotten, the clerk tentatively stepped forward to show off her wares. "It's a warm blanket," she said, her tone holding only the slightest hint of guardedness. "I have another for fifty-five cents, but we sell lots of these blankets to the boys who run off and go hunting for a few days. It's all wool and plenty sturdy." She petted the fabric as though she'd spun it herself. "Not a thread of cotton in the entire thing."

Lindsay's brow contracted as she ran her hands over the slightly rough cloth.

"Boys, you say?" The tightly woven, navy blue blanket had a picture of a golden anchor in its center and did seem like a good choice for a young boy. She supposed. Unsure, she suspiciously asked, "You really think an eight-year-old would like it?"

The woman's smile was genuine. "Absolutely."

"All right then," said Lindsay, admitting to herself she really didn't have time to dicker. Not that she knew how anyway. "I'll take it."

"Wonderful. You won't be sorry." The woman plucked the blanket from Lindsay's hand and took it back to the counter. "Shall I wrap it?" Lindsay shook her head and gazed out the store window. "No time."

The woman took Lindsay's silver dollar and refolded the blanket. Then she looked hard at Lindsay and said, "Wait a minute."

"I don't have—" Lindsay stopped when she saw what the woman was doing. She licked her lips.

The clerk put a small sack of cinnamon candy on top of the blanket and passed it back to Lindsay along with her change. "No charge."

Lindsay beamed. Free candy. Dear God, the shop owners in Gotham would rather pull out their own teeth. "Thanks, lady!" Lindsay headed for the door and the train.

Four minutes.

She opened the door, the bell clanged, and two small children ran in, knocking the candy and blanket from her hands. Lindsay bit off a curse and bent to pick it up. The older of the two girls bent to help her. "Sorry," the child mumbled.

Lindsay glanced up quickly from her task and winked. "S'okay, kid."

At the same moment, a man in a black Derby, with a dark, scruffy mustache, walked through the door, bumping into Lindsay's upturned bottom as he moved.

Lindsay lurched forward, shot daggers at the man's back as he continued to march toward the register, and decided she didn't have the time to care. As quickly as she could, she scooped up the bag of candy and draped the blanket over her shoulder; taking the time to a press a cinnamon ball in the helpful girl's hand before disappearing out the door.

"Thank you!" the girl cried out, her brown eyes wide with delight. "Look, Agnes, I've got candy!" Her friend darted from her hiding spot in the corner, looking on with envy as the girl showed off her unexpected treasure.

Bo turned from his place at the register to see what the commotion was about. All he saw was the closing of the door and a dark-coated, fast-moving figure vanishing around the corner. He shrugged and turned back to the clerk.

"Can you tell me where the boarding house is?"

Ginny kept her eyes glued to the window. Another few seconds, and she was going to gather up Lewis and get off this train. There was no way she was leaving town without Lindsay. Then once she caught up with her, she was going to kill her.

"I gotta go," Lewis whined for the third time. Ginny ground her teeth together. "Lewis—" He winced inwardly, knowing that tone.

"You should have gone before we got on the train."

He gave his sister his most pitiful face. "I didn't have to go then. But I do now." He squirmed a little to make his point. "I really do, Ginny."

Ginny sighed. "We're getting off the train. You can go then."

"But they have a little room like an outhouse. I used one on the other train. I don't need to leave."

Ginny stood up, grabbed both their coats, and took Lewis's hand. "Doesn't matter. Lindsay's not back yet. We can't leave without her." Then she saw her through the window, weaving her way through the traffic about thirty yards down the street in front of the depot.

Lindsay caught sight of Ginny at that same moment and waved. Her smile was unrepentant, and she was relieved to see Ginny's slightly irritated grin that quickly turned indulgent. A stab of guilt assailed her. *You're a shitsack, String Bean.* She was worried. Lindsay resolved on the spot to ply Ginny with her candy, deciding that her partner and the cinnamon balls were a lot alike. *Sweet, but packing a deceptive jolt of heat. Heh.*

Ginny's body went weak with relief, and she plopped back down in her wooden bench seat. It creaked loudly, and she kicked out her feet in front of her as she sighed. Her eyes, however, never left Lindsay. "Finally."

Lewis followed Ginny's line of vision. He smiled, as brightly as a boy whose back teeth were floating could, and said, "I knew she'd be back. She said she would, didn't she? Can I go now? Puhleeeeeeeez?" His wiggling grew worse, and his hand began to creep down.

Chuckling, Ginny slapped his hand away from its destination. "Go, for goodness sake." She wrinkled her nose. "Otherwise you won't be sitting near us today." But her smile took the sting out of the words.

"Yes!" Lewis's eyes rolled back in his head in anticipation.

"Do you know where—?"

But he was already bolting for the next car, which held a tiny room that contained a seat with a hole in its center that led directly to the tracks.

The train whistle blew again, and Lindsay increased her pace, ignoring her immediate discomfort. *It's my own fault for cutting things this close,* she told herself. Then her world spun around as she was grabbed from behind by the collar and thrown to the ground with stunning force.

Several wagons passed between Ginny and Lindsay; and for a moment the younger woman lost sight of her partner.

Lindsay's face and chest hit the ground at the same time, knocking the wind out of her and digging her front teeth into the dark soil. "Uff!" Red cinnamon balls exploded from their sack and scattered onto the dirt.

"Going somewhere?" Albert asked, pushing hard on Lindsay's back.

She was still seeing stars, and her first thought was that she'd been hit by a wagon. She gasped, trying desperately to pull air into her lungs.

"Aww. Did that hurt?" His voiced dripped with sarcasm. "Good." He laughed cruelly. "Here, let me help you," he said much louder for the benefit of the few people on the street and in front of the shops.

Dazed, Lindsay blinked with exaggerated slowness and spat out a mouthful of dirt. She tasted the metallic tang of blood. "Ph-Ph-Phft." Lindsay's eyes went round as the voice finally started to register. "Ra-Rat Face?"

"That's my name. Don't wear it out." He punched her in the kidney just for the hell of it, and then hauled her to her feet, smiling at several curious passersby, who weren't sure what was happening. "My friend here went out and got roostered up last night and tripped." He gave Lindsay a good shake and grinned stupidly. "Don't you just hate a clumsy drunk?"

The women grimaced at his grungy appearance, and wrinkled their nose at the smell of putrid grease that clung to Albert's pants. A prim-looking blonde pulled her small son closer to her skirts as they scurried away.

"Nice to know you remember your old pal," Albert said, once they were out of earshot. He grabbed a handful of the brown hair sticking out from Lindsay's cap with one hand and a chunk of the back of her coat with his other. Then he forced her off the road and away from prying eyes.

Ginny rose to her feet, her eyes scanning the street. "Lindsay?" A light rain began to fall, pelting the passenger car and sending dirty rivulets of water down the window. *Where is she? She was just there!*

A depot worker stuck his head out of his ticket booth and waved to one of the porters, who called out in a strong voice, "All aboard! Last call!" The town was a small one, and they didn't bother to dispatch a car knocker to check the boxcars.

The train hissed and lurched forward, then stopped. Ginny began to panic. Her eyes shot to the door in the far end of the car, then darted out the window.

"Lewis," she yelled, causing the other passengers to lower their newspapers, or stop their murmured conversations, to stare. She scrambled to pick up their coats and travel bag and ran toward the far door, nearly tripping over her own feet in her haste to grab Lewis and get off the train. She crashed against the outer door of the lavatory, shoved it open, and then began furiously banging on the lavatory door with her fist. "Lewis!" Her voice was rising with every word, but she could hardly hear it over the painful thumping of her heart. "Get out…

now!"

"Huh?" came the muffled response.

The train lurched forward again, and this time it kept going.

"Now!" Ginny flung open the door and caught the boy in the middle of pulling up his pants. "We've got to get off." She grabbed hold of his hand and yanked him from the small stall. Kicking the outer door open, she began running down the aisle between the seats, dragging Lewis behind her.

Outside, Lindsay began to fight. "Let me go!" Albert jerked her head back and pressed his lips against her ear, his coarse, dirty beard scratching her neck. The foul smell of his breath made her gag. Peripherally, she was aware that the train had started to move, and her struggle intensified. She slammed her elbow backward and connected with his stomach, but his grip on her hair remained tight.

"No," Albert growled. "You're not going anywhere."

Before Lindsay could say a word, Ginny's frantic scream rang out.

"Lindsay!" Ginny and Lewis were standing in the outdoor, railed-space between cars. The train's whistle blew again as Ginny desperately took in the situation. *We need to jump,* her mind cried. *We need to do it now.* With each passing second, the train began to pick up more speed. She quickly turned to her brother, trying to look past the terror in his eyes. She dropped their coats and bag and lightly gripped his shoulders. "Lewis—"

"No!" The boy grabbed onto the railing and shook his head wildly, scattering the raindrops that had collected on his face onto Ginny's damp shirt. He knew what she was thinking and couldn't do it. "I'm afraid."

Their eyes met and held, and for a split second, Ginny considered scooping him up and jumping anyway. "Lewis, please!" she begged, wanting to scream out her frustration. "It'll be okay if we go right now."

He began to cry and tightened his grip on the railing until his hands hurt.

"I'm sorry, I'm sorry," he chanted. His fear was palpable, and he was visibly trembling. It began to rain harder. "You go."

Ginny's heart seized up in her chest. "No," she whispered.

Her eyes bore into his, and in that second he knew deep in his soul that his sister's promise was gold. She would never abandon him—even if it meant leaving Lindsay behind.

Ginny whirled around, but all she could see was a building that blocked her view of the depot, and the street in front of it. The wind tossed wet hair into her eyes, and she pushed it back as she called out desperately again, "Lindsay!"

Lindsay heard Ginny's scream and elbowed Albert a second time. This time his grip faltered, and she was able to tear herself away.

With meaty hands he grabbed, but came away only with the navy blue blanket. He cursed furiously and threw it down.

Lindsay bolted for the tracks. Every step was agony as her injured ribs ground mercilessly together. It felt as though a hot knife was slicing into her, and tears sprang to her eyes, her face twisting in anguish.

She rounded the corner of the depot, and up ahead, she could see Ginny and Lewis standing outside the car and leaning against the cold metal railing. She scrambled up a rocky ravine until she was running along on the flat, narrow area alongside the track itself.

Lewis's arm shot out, and his eyes widened. "Look!" He pointed. "She's coming!"

Ginny's heart leapt into her throat. Lindsay was gaining speed. "Come on, Lindsay, you can make it!"

Lindsay's cap flew off as her arms pumped and her feet pounded the wet ground, a blur of motion. Faster and faster she ran until she had nearly drawn level with the last car. There was no caboose. The last car was Ginny's.

Albert was lumbering behind Lindsay; and for a few seconds she could hear his labored breaths and heavy footsteps, but they faded from her consciousness well before they did in reality. He didn't matter. All that mattered was catching this train.

"Run!" Ginny's hands were white-knuckled fists, and her throat hurt from yelling. "Run!" She could see the strain in Lindsay's face and the steam that flew from her mouth and nose with each panted breath. She could hear the crunch of rocks under her feet, even over the whining of the locomotive's wheels. Lindsay's chin was covered in dirt and blood, and raindrops splashed against her face, etching clean lines through the soiled mess.

"Almost!" Ginny leaned over the railing as far as she could and extended her hand. "C'mon!" She could see the look of steely determination glinting in Lindsay's eyes. She was going to make it.

Lewis screamed, afraid Ginny was going to tip headfirst over the railing. He lunged for his sister's legs, using his body weight to help anchor her and holding on for dear life. He screwed his eyes tightly shut, knowing this was his fault. His tears had stopped, but he was still shaking. "Please. Please. Please."

Lindsay stopped gaining ground as the train's momentum grew. Ginny knew it; the look of sheer panic on her face forced Lindsay into a final burst of speed. She threw her head back and forced herself forward, pushing herself faster and harder than she ever had before. "Argh!"

Impossibly, Ginny reached out farther, extending herself dangerously over the tracks that flew by beneath her. "Take my hand, Lindsay. More! Reach! Almost. Almost!"

Lewis screamed again as one of his sister's feet left the floor. Even using his entire body, he couldn't hold her down.

Lindsay's heart was trying to burst free from her chest. She leaned forward and threw out her hand. Her breaths were coming in sharp gasps. She was no longer aware of the pain in her ribs or the burning of her lungs. Only Ginny's face. With a final push, she lunged forward and their fingers touched. Their eyes met, and the cool feeling of Lindsay's fingertips registered with Ginny for the barest of seconds before—

Lindsay's hand fell away—

The terrain changed, sending her sprawling headfirst to the ground.

"No!" Ginny howled, watching Lindsay slam to the dirt, then disappear down the ravine along the side of the tracks. She blinked the rain out of her eyes, hardly believing what had just happened.

Lewis grabbed great handfuls of Ginny's trousers and leaned back, pulling her away from the railing. She crumpled onto the wet metal floor next to him and stared unseeing down the tracks.

"G-Ginny?" Lewis said in a small voice. The look on her face was scaring him.

She opened her arms, and the boy surged forward, needing her acceptance and love like he needed air. Ginny's eyes slid shut, and she heard her brother's breath catch. She pressed her lips to his wet hair and left them there for a long time, her chest too tight for her to speak.

They both began to cry.

Chapter Thirteen

Lindsay lay on the cold ground panting, her eyes gazing dully at a growing mud puddle, as the last sounds of the train carrying her heart faded into the distance.

Something inside her snapped.

"Rat Face, you bastard!" she roared, shooting to her feet, then immediately faltering as a wave of dizziness swept over her. She dropped down to all fours once again. Her hands sank into the sodden soil, so cold it burned. Her stomach chose that moment to rebel, and she heaved up the bitter remains of her breakfast. "Ugh."

She stayed on her hands and knees, breathing shallowly, as icy rain washed sweat from her face and blood and dirt from her chin.

Lindsay waited to hear Rat Face's heavy footsteps with a grim sense of anticipation. Seeing him again was no accident, though she couldn't imagine what had induced him to follow her all the way from New York. He wouldn't cross the street to see his own mother. Not that it mattered. This would be the last time she ever dealt with the miserable excuse for a man. *The next time we meet, only one of us is going to walk away,* she promised herself darkly.

But all she heard was the uneven pitter-patter of the rain and the mournful whistle of the wind through the spindly branches. An unknown time later, she opened her eyes and willed herself not to dissolve into tears. "Goddammit," she whispered.

She felt cheated of the satisfaction of pummeling Rat Face. Lindsay slumped back on her heels, her hands making loud sucking noises as she extracted them from the mud. She wondered how this could possibly hurt her heart so badly—how she could possibly feel this lost—when she knew exactly where she was. *In the middle of Hicksville—Without her.*

Lindsay wiped her hands as best she could on a nearby tuft of grass. It didn't help much, but at least they weren't dripping slop anymore. With a groan, she stood and slowly climbed back up to the flat strip of land alongside the tracks. "A plan. That's what you need, String Bean. You always need a plan." She thought for a moment, her coat growing heavy as it continued to absorb the falling rain.

"Okay, first things first. Get my goddamn blue blanket back and kill

Rat Face if I see him along the way." Pleased with both ideas, she nodded and smiled to herself. "Then I've got to find a way to Ginny."

Mentally, she ran down the list of cities where Ginny and Lewis would change trains. *Atlanta, Macon, Columbus.* They would stop at a dozen other tiny places but stay on the train, or perhaps only step off to stretch their legs. Her eyes narrowed as she continued to puzzle out Ginny's next move, which would determine her own.

"She'll continue on to the stop where the orphan train tried to place the children. Her ticket won't let her turn around, and even if it did, she'll keep going. She knows I'll find her." Lindsay looked skyward for guidance and reassurance; what she got for her troubles was a boom of far off thunder.

"Figures." She sighed, then whispered, "Please let her know I'll find her."

Much to Lindsay's disappointment—and relief—Rat Face was nowhere to be seen when she made it back to the depot. The rain had shifted to snow, and Talking Rock was getting its first dusting of the season.

Her blue blanket lay crumpled in the street. Groaning quietly, she picked it up and shook off the snow before slinging it over her shoulder. How was she going to get to Alabama before Ginny? A brief conversation with the stationmaster had proved fruitless. No other passenger or even supply trains would be by today. And the coal train that would pass tomorrow would be heading in the opposite direction.

There was a bench outside the depot, and dejected, Lindsay plopped down on it. She began fiddling with her hat, which she'd picked up on the way back to the depot. Finally, she put her head in her hands. "Christ."

"Lindsay?"

A familiar female voice caused Lindsay to turn her head. A woman and little girl approached her, both with odd looks on their faces. The girl waggled her fingers shyly at Lindsay.

Unable to stop herself, Lindsay grinned and waggled her own back.

"I thought you were taking the train with Virginia and Lewis," Mrs. Bergquist said, her slender eyebrows pulled together in distress over Lindsay's dirty, drenched appearance.

Lindsay smiled weakly. "I… um—" She gestured with one hand, then looked down at her muddy shoes. "Something—well, something happened, and I missed the train."

"Oh, dear."

"You could say that." *Although to say, "I'm fucked" would be more fitting.*

The younger woman looked as though she was about ready to burst into tears, and Erika laid a comforting hand on her shoulder. "Come on, our wagon is over there. We're done with our business in town. Let's go back to the house."

Lindsay shook her head. "No thank you, ma'am. I have to get to Ginny. There won't be another train for two days, and I've got to find another way to southwest Alabama."

Erika smiled kindly and used the hand that was resting on Lindsay's shoulder to cup her chin. With her thumb she wiped away a stripe of dirt as she thought of what kind of help she could offer this young woman. She expected to be a part-time mother to Lewis for many years to come, and Ginny had treated Lindsay as though she were kin, so Erika assumed that this dark-haired woman, who dressed like a man, would also be part of her extended family.

Lindsay found herself leaning into the unexpected, maternal contact.

"You can't go anywhere soaking wet." She hauled Lindsay to her feet. "We'll find a way to get you to Ginny and Lewis."

"But—"

Erika gave her a scolding look. "Sometimes, young lady, you need to just do what you're told and stop fighting."

Lindsay's nape hairs bristled, and any trace of warmth melted from her face. She was about to pull away when Erika dropped the hand from her arm, realizing that, if she truly wanted to help Lindsay, she'd started off all wrong.

Erika had seen the anger brewing in those intense brown eyes the night before, when she had initially refused to hand over Lewis. She'd also heard the softly spoken, gentle words Ginny had used to calm her. Perhaps the redhead had the right idea when it came to dealing with this headstrong northerner.

The older woman's face flushed with embarrassment. "That came out all wrong. I, well, I—"

"Can you help me?" Lindsay asked, her initial resentment quickly replaced by an earnestness that made Erika blink.

"I can try."

"Why?"

Erika was a little surprised that Lindsay had asked so directly, but she found herself liking her simple honesty. "Because you are important to Virginia. And Virginia is important to Lewis." Her voice deepened. "And Lewis is important to me."

"Then let's go."

"A horse?" Lindsay looked like someone who had just stepped in what comes out of the hind end of a horse, rather than someone being asked to ride one. "You've got to be kidding," she said flatly.

She was dressed in a pair of Jon's trousers and a shirt, while her own clothes hung drying in front of the fireplace. She was freshly scrubbed and sporting a tiny bandage on her chin.

Jon looked up from the map spread out on their kitchen table. "It's the only way. Look." He pointed to the dot that represented Atlanta. "You can ride here, and then catch a train straight to Montgomery and the south. You'll be maybe twelve hours behind Virginia, if you're lucky. Your route will be more direct. She's going all the way down to Columbus and then west." He drew an "L" on the map with his finger.

"What if I walk?"

Jon and Erika stared.

Lindsay rolled her eyes. "*Really* fast." At this point she didn't think she was physically capable of running more than a few feet.

"To Atlanta?" Erika laughed. "Honey, even taking the back roads, that's near on fifty miles. Take our gelding, Diablo—"

"Diablo?" Lindsay croaked. "You want me to ride a huge beast named after the *Devil*?" Lindsay didn't know more than a word or two of Spanish, but somehow that was one she'd picked up somewhere. Her eyes widened as what she'd just said registered.

"He's a sturdy boy," Erika continued, trying not to smile. "You can leave Diablo at the northern train station. I'll wire our daughter, Katherine, and she'll pick him up. It's the only way."

Lindsay cursed inwardly. Through gritted teeth, she admitted, "I… I don't know how to ride."

Jon and Erika exchanged worried glances. "Well." He scratched his jaw. "If it's any consolation, you will by the time you reach Atlanta."

Lindsay paled. "I was afraid you were going to say that."

Albert jerked as the toe of Bo's shoe tapped his sagging head.

"Finally. I've been looking for you for hours. Get up." Albert blinked stupidly and lifted his head. "Ugh."

"Oh, boy." Bo's jaw dropped when he got a good look at Albert's face, which wasn't exactly pretty to begin with. "What the hell happened? Did String Bean do this to you?" he asked incredulously. "Damn."

"Wasn't her," Albert muttered. He was leaning against the back wall of the depot—without his coat—or shoes—or anything else except for his shirt, pants, and stockings.

One dark, beady eye was swollen shut, and his lips were nothing more than bulbous, bloody masses that hung sadly from his face.

"Uh huh. Sure it wasn't."

"It wasn't! Ouch!" Albert's face twisted in pain, and his hands shot to his mouth. "Now look what you made me do," he mumbled pitifully.

"Who then?"

"Some guys. I found that bitch String Bean and pulled her off the road." He poked at his mouth with a dirty index finger, knowing something was seriously wrong, but unable to see the damage. "Some bitch walking by told her husband I was hurting a girl, and he tackled me and dragged me back here, the country bumpkin asshole."

"And he kicked the shit out of you for grabbing String Bean?"

Albert's expression darkened. "No, dummy. A few of the guy's friends followed us, and one of 'em noticed my new watch."

Bo leaned against the wall and slipped off his Derby. He ran his fingers through his wavy brown hair, then gently tapped the rainwater from the brim of his hat. "The watch you stole?" He dropped his hat back atop his messy hair and gave it a tug. "Why'd he notice that? Nothing special."

"It was his."

Bo's eyebrows lifted. "Oh." He cocked his head to the side, as he glanced down at the other man, thinking Rat Face had gotten exactly what he deserved.

He stared at the holes in Albert's stockings, which were so large that all his toes, except for his pinky, hung out in the breeze. "Eww. Your feet are disgusting. Aren't you cold?"

"Too numb to be cold," Albert grumbled.

"Guess we're heading back to New York then," Bo said in a chipper voice, relief coursing through him. This much hell wasn't worth the money; when was Rat Face going to realize that?

"The fuck we are." Woozily, Albert pushed himself to his feet, heading to the local store intent on shoplifting a pair of shoes. With every step across the cold, wet ground, he let out a curse. "I'd kill String Bean for free now."

Bo groaned inwardly. He let out a slow deep breath and stuffed his hands in his pockets as he followed Albert toward the fat man's next crime spree. "String Bean, you're gonna be the death of me yet."

The moon hung high in the sky, illuminating the land in a soft, golden glow. Diablo whinnied softly and stamped his front hooves. He smelled water. His steady walk increased to a trot, and quite without permission, he turned off the road for a nearby trickling stream. "Hey!" Lindsay squawked, the sudden movement shocking her out of a light sleep. She grabbed on to the saddle horn to keep from toppling off. "Stupid. I… whoa… I told you about that," she grumped, her voice cracking after hours of disuse.

Seeing where the gelding was heading, she felt a little of her moodiness dissolve. "Thirsty?" She yawned, then grimaced at the dry, scratchy feeling in her throat. Her hand stroked her neck. "Me too."

The horse stopped a few feet from his destination, and Lindsay took the hint; she slid off his back, landing heavily on the soft soil with a protracted moan. "Oh, God." She looked down. "My legs," she whined. "For the love of God. I'm alone, I'm getting sick, my arse will never forgive me for this, *and* I'm bowlegged?"

The horse lifted his nose out of the water and swung his head in Lindsay's direction, his large liquid eyes gazing at her intently as water dripped from his lips.

Lindsay studied his expression. "Are you saying I'm not alone? Wouldn't it be something if you actually answered me? Then I could add bein' crazy to my list of woes."

Ignoring her rhetorical question, the horse dipped his nose into the stream again and began sucking water into his mouth.

"That's what I thought." Gingerly, she padded the few steps to the narrow stream and dropped down onto her belly, so she could stick her mouth directly into the water. Her hands were already cold, and she couldn't bear the thought of plunging them into the icy stream. The water was so cold it burned going down, but she drank her fill and pushed herself back to her feet. The water stung the small cut on her chin, and she spared a violent thought for the man who had caused her so much trouble. *Where did you go, Rat Face?*

Diablo finally finished and turned back to her, burrowing his nose in her coat and letting out a loud snort.

A tiny smile creased Lindsay's cheeks, and she carefully reached up and stroked the velvety skin of his nose. "Yeah, I guess, you're all right," she allowed, acknowledging the tenuous understanding they'd come to during this long journey. He was in charge, and she was along for the ride. Once she'd reached that conclusion, she admitted ruefully, things had gone much smoother.

A far-off sound caused Lindsay's head to whip around. In the distance, for the first time, she saw the hazy outline of Atlanta. *Yes.* The faint, plaintive sound came again and Lindsay's grin grew. The noise wound its way around her brain, gently tugging the cords of her subconscious with aching familiarity.

A train's whistle.

Her world righted itself a little as she began walking toward the road, Diablo's reins held loosely in her hand. Despite her exhaustion, her pace quickened. An hour or two more and she'd be back in her world and on her territory.

The tracks.

Squinting, Lewis stepped off the train first. The morning sky was dull gray and spoke of rain yet to come. He shielded his eyes from the subdued light, having spent so many hours enclosed in the shadowy railcar. He had slept against Ginny, his head pillowed in her lap, and it was surprisingly comfortable, given the situation.

At first, he'd been afraid to sleep, afraid he'd dream of the fire and hear the imagined screams of his parents and sisters, which tormented his sleep nearly every night. But Ginny had stroked his hair and spoken in the soothing tones that had unerringly reminded him of the best parts of home. Not the smoke or fear or anything else. It was as though an enormous weight had been lifted from his small shoulders.

Lewis yawned and moved away from the steps, so that Ginny and the passengers behind him could exit the railcar.

She gently cupped his cheek and peered at him with worried eyes. "How you doing, Lewis?" Ginny handed him his coat, and he slipped into it quickly, already shivering in the cool morning air.

"Fine." He couldn't meet her eyes. "I guess," he murmured.

"Mmm." Ginny frowned at her brother's guilt-ridden face. "I can see that. Lewis, honey, I told you it wasn't your fault. Lindsay missed the train… on her own." Not quite the truth. But she wasn't sure what she'd seen; there was no use frightening the boy and making him feel worse than he already did.

"But the blanket—"

"Was an accident," she finished kindly but firmly. "She'll find us." *She has to.* Ginny wrapped her arm around his shoulders and steered him away from the depot to where the crowd was thinner. "I'll never give up on Lindsay. Just like I'd never give up on you or James or Jane. But if we backtrack, we might spend days or even weeks and still not find each other. Your brother and sister need me now, and Lindsay is a grown woman—"

"Who can take care of herself?"

A faint, wistful smile crossed Ginny's face. "I didn't say that."

Lewis took their traveling bag from his sister and slung it over his shoulder as they walked. "If she's gonna find us, why are you so sad?"

Ginny swallowed hard, acknowledging the ache in her chest that hadn't stopped since they left Talking Rock. "I don't know," she whispered truthfully. "I guess I just miss her."

Lewis was about to say something when a short woman, with a head of thick white hair streaked with blonde and a slim face with pointy features, hurried over to them. Ginny guessed the woman to be in her late sixties and thought her remarkably well kept for her age. Despite the cool temperature, she was perspiring and her wrinkled face was pink.

"Virginia?" she drawled, coming to a stop next to Lewis. "Virginia Chisholm?"

Ginny and Lewis looked at each other in surprise, and then back at the woman. "Yes," Ginny answered hesitantly. "May I help you?"

"Thank you, Jesus!" The woman fanned herself dramatically, looking as though she might pass out from sheer relief. "Yes. Yes, you can."

Uneasily, Ginny offered her hand. "Hello." She grasped the old woman's hand gently, feeling the paper-thin skin beneath her fingers. Her brow creased. "Do I know you?" Ginny asked doubtfully.

The woman smiled brightly at Lewis before turning her attention back to his sister. "No, Miss Chisholm." But that didn't stop the woman from smiling at Ginny as though she were her long lost granddaughter. "If you knew me, you'd remember me."

That, Ginny silently agreed, *was the God's truth.*

"I've been coming every day to meet the train in case you were on it. You look exactly as you were described." Twinkling brown eyes drifted to Ginny's pants. "Except for those, of course. Lordy, what won't you Yankees do?" Her voice held more curiosity than censure. "Next, your men folk will be wearing petticoats."

Still at a loss, Ginny looked down at the old woman blankly. "I'm sorry… I—"

In one long breath the woman informed her, "I'm Edith Pigg, of the Montgomery Piggs, widow of Captain Eustace Pigg of the Forty-Fifth Alabama Regiment. God rest his Rebel soul." She waited for the usual awe her words inspired. Getting nothing but a confused look from Ginny and a snort from Lewis that his sister quickly muffled by clamping her hand across his mouth, she plowed ahead at the same rapid speed. "Come with me. Trudy is waiting." Edith wound her bony arm around Ginny's and began walking.

"Yeow," Ginny squealed, her eyes nearly popping out of her head when Edith blithely began to drag her along. Lewis, who was even more bewildered than Ginny, had to run every third step just to keep up.

Edith prattled on happily, as though she were taking a breakneck Sunday stroll with a dear friend. "I got the most lovely telegram from a fine man named Christian Spence."

"Ohhh," Ginny drew out the word as things suddenly started to make more sense. *You're always looking out for us, my friend. Meeting you was so lucky.*

Ginny nodded, starting to think that Edith might not be insane. Though she was reserving judgment on that matter.

"He told me about your search." Abruptly, Edith stopped, causing Lewis to run a few steps past them. She turned and stared at Ginny with regret-filled eyes. The look on her face was enough to make Ginny hold her breath for a second.

"I'm so sorry. Had I known he had any living kin… well, I don't know what I could have done." She pursed her lips. "But something, surely."

Ginny blinked. "Who?" Her eyes went round as realization hit her squarely in the chest. "Do you mean James?" *Please.* "He's here?" Her heart leapt into her throat, and the two or three seconds Edith took to answer seemed to stretch out for a lifetime.

"Yes, of course." Edith's forehead creased deeply, and her voice held a note of irritation at having to explain. "Why else would I be waiting for you at the train station, dear?"

"God." Ginny was scarcely able to believe her ears. She closed her eyes. Her knees felt like water, and if it weren't for the deceptively strong arm curled round hers, she was sure she would have crumbled to the ground.

"Are you all right?" Edith gasped, using her slight form to steady Ginny.

Next came her brother's worried voice. "Ginny?" He dropped their bag and grabbed onto Ginny's coat to steady her.

The redhead scrubbed her face with one hand. She felt dizzy. "I'm sorry. I-I—" She scrubbed her face again and let out a shaky breath. "I wasn't expecting that."

Edith smiled kindly. "No, I don't suppose you were." Her gaze seemed to sharpen and she "tsked" Ginny, as she began tugging her toward a shiny black buggy parked in the front of the milliner's shop. "You're exhausted. How long since you've eaten or slept?"

"A long time," Lewis piped up, earning a glare from his sister but a pleased nod from Edith. Encouraged, he continued to tattle on Ginny. "She didn't sleep at all last night, or eat anything for lunch, or dinner yesterday, or breakfast this morning."

"Mmm." Edith gave a small nod. "Just as I suspected. Don't worry. We'll take good care of you. You'll be staying with us, of course. And we'll fatten you up in no time."

"With you and James?" Ginny asked hopefully.

"Me and—? Oh, my." Edith's voice softened with regret. "I didn't mean to give you that impression."

Ginny's mood sunk like a rock. "I was just hoping—" She shook her head and chastised herself for setting herself up for another likely disappointment. "I should know better by now. I was just hoping is all."

Edith looked truly distressed at the woebegone look that had settled over Ginny's young face. "I'm sorry, but the boy isn't with me."

"And my sister? Jane?"

Edith shook her head. "She wasn't adopted in Troy. I'm truly sorry."

Ginny's heart sank a little further, and she swallowed a few times before answering. She managed a weak smile, mostly for Lewis's sake. His eyes were glued to her face, and he was hanging on her every word. "Not your fault, Mrs. Pigg." She relaxed a little into their brisk walk and let her hand rest on Lewis's shoulder, forcing herself away from the looming depression her mind seemed so hell-bent on embracing. "So James is here somewhere, but you don't know where?"

"I didn't say that either, Virginia. I do know who took him in."

Thank goodness. "Who?"

Edith made a face. "His name is Milo Porter. I'll explain everything on the way home." Imperiously, she stood alongside her buggy, waiting, until Lewis realized that he was expected to help her in.

"Oh." His cheeks flushed, and he scrambled into the buggy, tossing their bag onto the floor, and turning to extend a courteous hand to Edith. "Ma'am?"

"Thank you, young man," she praised gently.

Ginny's eyes widened at Lewis's polite tone. *He's getting so big. Mama would be so proud; she'd just die.* She cringed at the sick feeling caused by the accidental words.

"Well?" Edith daintily picked up the reins and wrapped the white-gloved fingers of one hand around them. Lewis settled in next to her. Edith retrieved a reed-thin riding crop from the floor and absently arranged her carriage blanket about her knees. She lifted a snowy eyebrow at Ginny. "What are you waiting for, Virginia?"

Ginny glanced back at the tracks longingly before pushing down her emotions and boarding the buggy.

Everything.

Ginny stood outside Smokey's Saloon, feeling vaguely dirty for even considering going inside, and nervously wiping her sweaty hands on her dress.

"Okay, Ginny, be firm. This is your brother. Don't mess this up. It doesn't have to be a fight if you explain yourself reasonably."

But her thoughts were quickly derailed. *What sort of man spends his afternoon in a saloon? Didn't Edith say he worked for the city?* She'd never actually been inside a place like Smokey's, though she'd waited outside one for her stepfather on several occasions.

She had changed back into the plain dress the Charity Hospital had given her and shed her coat in deference to the afternoon temperature, which had climbed into the upper fifties. It felt wonderful to shed the heavy garment that she had worn so much it now felt like a second skin—a dark, itchy, somewhat grungy second skin.

Edith had introduced Ginny to her younger sister Trudy, who was her spitting image, if you erased a half dozen years. She filled her in on what had happened with James, while Lewis was taking a much-needed nap. Both elderly women were on the town's adoption committee and swore up and down that what happened with James was far from the ordinary; so far, in fact, that the sisters had written to the Wards protesting James's placement. Not surprisingly, the Wards never responded.

On the afternoon that the orphan train came to Troy, Milo Porter had shown up trying to get a boy, any boy over the age of six, just as he had last year when the committee deemed him unfit to adopt. He was unmarried, had no chance of marrying in the future because he was as appealing as a leper, didn't attend church services, and lived in a squalid shack, whose stench was bad enough to make even his white trash neighbors cringe.

True to form, when James was literally dragged out in front of the prospective parents in Troy's Town Hall, he'd been such a holy terror that none of them would come near him. Edith's face had colored when she explained to Ginny that the town's adoption committee had been at a loss as to what to do with the boy. No one wanted to force an adoption or separate James from the sister he seemed so attached to. But the sad reality was that the town's committee didn't have any real legal authority. The most they could do was make recommendations to the Wards' employees.

Milo had approached one of those employees, as the children who weren't selected for adoption were herded back onto the train only minutes after leaving the Town Hall. Edith wasn't sure what had actually transpired at the depot. All she knew was that Milo left the train station dragging a kicking and screaming, eight-year-old boy behind him.

Ginny shook her head to clear it and pushed open the saloon's door. Not surprisingly, it was smoky inside, and she suppressed a cough. Feeling the weight of a room full of curious stares, she headed for the bar. "Excuse me."

The bartender stopped drying the glass in his hand and glanced up at her.

"Can you tell me which man is Milo Porter?" She glanced around the room uncomfortably, her eyes quickly moving past the faces wreathed with drunken smiles.

"I'll be Milo for you, honey," a loud voice from the back of the room called, causing the place to erupt in raucous laughter.

Ginny ignored it.

The bartender draped the rag he was using over his shoulder. "Who wants to know?" But the words were still hanging in the air when his eyes swung in the direction of the dusty piano. A man sat at the table next to it. Alone.

Ginny didn't wait for confirmation that this was Milo. She drew in a deep breath and marched across the room, not stopping until she stood in front of a small, table that held several empty shot glasses and beer mugs. "Mr. Porter?" Her voice rose a little at the end, betraying her hope that this was *not* the man who had adopted her brother.

Milo was in his late forties, though he looked at least fifteen years older. Even with him seated, she could tell he was tall with wiry, whipcord muscles. His skin was pale and sallow, and what was left of his greasy black-and-gray hair was worn long and hung limply around his shoulders. A cigarette was perched on thin lips and emitted a thick cloud that hung around his head. The rank, stale smell of liquor and smoke that oozed from his pores told Ginny that this was his normal, pitiful state.

Milo eyed her warily. "How much?" His voice was scratchy, as though he'd just awoken.

Ginny blinked a few times at a loss. "How much what?"

Milo took a long drag on his cigarette, then adjusted it so it was hanging out of the corner of his mouth, barely stuck to his lower lip. "For a poke in the whiskers, girlie. What else? Hurry up, 'cause I ain't got all day."

Huh? "Poke?"

Milo let his gaze drift up and down her body, making his intent crystal clear. Ginny's eyes nearly popped out, and she suddenly craved a very hot bath— in lye. Her mouth worked silently for a moment before she ground out, "You must have me confused with someone else." *Eww. I'd rather tie rocks around my waist, and then jump off the Brooklyn Bridge.*

Milo's face went very still. "Then get the hell away from me," he mumbled, obviously dejected. He dismissed her with the wave of a dirt-stained hand. "I'm busy."

Ginny paid no attention to his rebuke and lifted her chin a little as she spoke. "I'm here for James Robson."

Milo swallowed his mouthful of warm beer hastily and wiped the foam from his stubbly chin with the back of his hand. "If I ain't getting a poke, that runt boy sure as hell ain't." He leaned way back in his chair, causing it to creak in protest, and once again ordered Ginny to get the hell away.

The young woman wrung her hands together. "I *can't* just go away. You don't understand. James is my brother."

Milo narrowed his eyes, for the first time looking at her as something other than a quick, and probably very expensive, lay. She had a passing resemblance to the boy. Though he had darker features. Even in the dim light of the bar, Milo could see that Ginny's worried eyes were a vibrant, pale blue; he idly wondered if James's were the same. After a moment, he shrugged one shoulder. "So, he's your brother. What do I care?"

Ginny ground her teeth together. She leaned forward and planted her palms on the sticky tabletop. This man was nothing but a rotten drunk. "You adopted someone who already had family who wanted and loved him."

Bored, Milo rolled his eyes.

"It was a terrible mistake. And I'm sorry that it happened; I can tell how attached to him you are." Try as she might, she couldn't keep the sarcasm from her voice. "But he's my family, and I want him back."

Milo flicked his spent cigarette to the floor, wishing he had another. "Fine."

Ginny's mouth abruptly closed. "D-did you just say "fine"?"

"Take him. The little bastard is nothing but a pain in my ass. He's all yours."

Ginny's eyes flashed dangerously, and her voice turned to ice. "He's not a bastard."

"Ha! Then you don't know the little shit like I do."

"Where is he?" she hissed, her temper flaring, and her livid glare burning a hole into Milo. She'd had enough of this man. All she wanted to do was collect her brother.

"How should I know?" Milo stuck his nose in his drink, which he found infinitely more interesting than this annoying stranger. Sure, she was young and pretty enough, but he'd never cared for uppity women.

Ginny could feel her ire rising. Milo was ignoring her, and she fought to keep her voice even, realizing that her anger was getting her nowhere. "Where's James's school then? I'll get him myself. You can stay right here." *And drink your miserable life away.*

Milo laughed and shook his head, causing several long strands of oily hair to stick to his face and stay there. "What the hell does that boy need more schoolin' for? I'll tell you what I told him. Once you can read, any more learnin' is a waste of time. My time."

Ginny pushed herself away from the table, her back going ramrod straight. A heady rush of adrenaline sang through her blood, and she was on the verge of doing something very stupid. *Easy. If you kill him, you'll just end up in jail.* "Mr. Porter—"

"Enough talk." Unsteadily, he rose to his feet. He leaned heavily to one side. "Pay me eight dollars, and the boy is yours. I never signed those damn papers the orphanage people gave me anyway." He sniggered a little, exceedingly proud of himself for having found a suitable use for them. "A better ass wipe a man could not ask for."

Ginny's lips twisted in revulsion. "Pay?" She re-thought her decision not to do something stupid. "My brother is a human being, not a cow," she sputtered. *Oh, James.* "He can't be bought or sold!"

"Oh, really?" Milo challenged, his voice dripping with condescension. "Tell that to the orphanage folks. The way that boy was acting, I figured they'd pay me to take his worthless hide off their hands." He paused to let out a loud belch, smiling when a man across the bar raised his glass to him in silent salute. "As it was, I paid four—no, five dollars for that worthless shit." He spread his hands in entreaty. "Don't I deserve to make a profit for my troubles?"

Ginny gave him an incredulous look, any pretense of civility long gone. "What are you talking about? You shouldn't have been able to get him in the first place. I'm not going to pay you!" But even as she said the words, she was calculating what little cash she had left. It wasn't nearly enough.

"Then we got nothing else to talk about." Milo took several ragged steps toward the bar, and for the first time, Ginny noticed that beneath his trousers was a wooden leg. Not an uncommon feature for men his age, who had cruelly had bits of themselves blown away in the War Between the States. Ginny blocked his path with her body.

He towered over her, and fearlessly she looked up into his glazed eyes. "Yes, we do."

In a flash of motion, Milo grabbed Ginny and threw her down on the nearest table, face up. Bony fingers wrapped around her wrists, pressing them firmly into the tabletop just above her head.

She cried out in surprise.

He shoved his face so close to hers that tiny bits of saliva sprayed her as he hissed, "Do not sass me, you short-haired Yankee bitch." In a much calmer voice he added, "I don't like it."

Wisely, Ginny clamped her mouth shut. Her heart was pounding so loudly she was surprised he couldn't hear it. She nodded meekly, hoping that would ease his violent temper. His breath smelled like a brewery and rotten teeth; in that instant, she realized she'd been a fool to even try to reason with a drunk.

Milo smiled cruelly. "That's more like it. I can tell you're kin to that bastard. He *used* to sass me too." His smile grew as he saw his chilling words register on Ginny's face.

Her blood ran cold, and she swallowed convulsively, her mind instantly giving her visions of James being hurt. "Wh-what did you do to him?"

He chuckled and moved his lips closer to hers. "Wanna find out yourself?" Ginny couldn't find her voice. She closed her eyes and shook her head as her mind desperately tried to come up with a way to escape. He was far stronger than she was, and rather than fight him, she let her body go limp under his.

"Aww." Milo seemed genuinely disappointed. "Too bad." Abruptly, he released his captive and called out to the bartender, "Put the drinks on my tab."

"Milo," the man behind the bar growled, suddenly paying attention now that the subject was his money, "you still owe me from last week."

Milo grumbled to himself as he hobbled toward the door. "Got me a visitor tonight," he slurred, fumbling for the handle. "You'll get your damn money."

The door closed behind him, and Ginny let out a shaky breath. That could have gone better. After a long second, she rolled off the table and onto wobbly legs. Her hands were trembling, and she wrapped her arms around herself in mute comfort as she dropped down into Milo's chair. "No, no, no. This can't be happening. James, what has he done to you?"

A young man in worn overalls hesitantly walked over to Ginny's table and gently cleared his throat. "Are you all right, Miss?"

Ginny looked up into shame-filled eyes, rubbing wrists she was sure would be badly bruised. "No," she said honestly. "I don't think I am."

"I'm sorry, I didn't—" He winced, his excuse for doing nothing seemed much more cowardly now that he wasn't in actual danger. He rocked back on his heels. "Milo's got a really bad temper. I didn't want—"

"It's okay," Ginny assured him quietly. Though in truth, it stung more than a little. She wondered briefly if the patrons in Smokey's would have calmly continued to sip their drinks and watch if Milo had started beating her—she shivered—or worse.

Having said his piece, the young man turned to walk away.

Ginny's hand shot out, finding a fistful of his sleeve. She gently tugged him to a halt. "Wait," she said eagerly. "Do you know Milo?"

"I reckon."

"Can you tell me where he lives and works? Things like that?"

The young man's brows drew together as he considered her request. It wouldn't be smart. But— "Well, I don't know."

"Please," she begged, not above bestowing him with her most innocent smile. His eyes softened and she could see that he was wavering. "I could buy you a drink?" Her smile turned inward when she saw him lick his lips at her enticing offer.

His gaze flicked to the bar, and he chewed his bottom lip. "Maybe we could talk for just a minute."

"Exactly. It'll only take a minute. I promise." Ginny motioned for him to sit in the empty chair next to hers. She couldn't pay for her brother, and she didn't want to risk bringing in the police or a state agency in case Milo was lying about the paperwork. Though she had no doubt they'd find Milo unfit as a parent, there was still the chance they'd decide the same thing about her and put her brother back up for adoption.

She waved to the bartender, wishing with all her heart that Lindsay were here. Things never seemed as desperate or dark when they were together. It had been less than a day and a half, and she already missed her companion badly. Tonight, she would need Lindsay's strength and support more than ever, because she wasn't going to allow James to spend one more miserable day with Milo Porter.

Tonight she was stealing back her brother; somehow, she just knew all hell was about to break loose.

It was well past dark by the time Ginny started on her way to Milo's dilapidated house. She'd learned more than she'd expected about the man who had her brother and had listened interestedly when she was told that, over the years, Milo had tried to quit drinking several times, only to be lured back to the bottle each time. As it had many soldiers, the war had changed Milo. And the townsfolk in Troy gave him a wide berth. Despite what he became later in life, he'd started out as an earnest young man, who had fought valiantly for his home and way of life. He had simply lost more than he could bear, and for some reason, the only place he believed he could reclaim a tiny sliver of it was at the bottom of a bottle.

Edith and Trudy had prepared Ginny and Lewis a hearty dinner, which Lewis inhaled and Ginny picked at with her fork. Her stomach was in knots, and eating at this point was not an option. After a long argument with Lewis, Edith, and Trudy, that had reduced the boy to tears, she headed out to reclaim James.

A thick fog clung to the ground and enveloped the city in a cloying mist. The streets took on an eerie, haunted quality that made Ginny shiver. She drew in a deep breath of air that smelled of burning wood and moist soil, as she slowly moved down the deserted streets of Troy in a buggy she'd borrowed from Edith. Troy was a mostly sleepy town, and its residents had long ago banked their stoves and extinguished their lanterns, settling themselves down for the chilly night.

The rhythmic clippity-clop of the mare's hooves mixed with the sounds of buzzing insects and the faint howling of an occasional gust of wind, as Ginny guided the buggy onto a smooth, but lonely, side road. The burning lantern that hung securely from a pole mounted to the buggy's front barely cut into the fog. She was concentrating hard, as she peered into the haze, trying to make out the road in front of her and the houses alongside, which were set back from the traffic.

Ginny's hands unconsciously tightened on the reins. She suddenly felt very alone, her craving for her partner so overwhelming that she nearly stopped the buggy and turned back for Talking Rock. *But not without my family.*

To her right, a heavy thicket disappeared and was replaced by a tall black, wrought iron fence. Through the fence, she could see the damp tops of granite tombstones peeking out of the fog as the haze shifted and rolled with the breeze. Feeling a chill wash over her, she pulled together the edges of her coat and buried her nose in the cloth, her breath sending a swirl of fog into the air. She had changed back into her trousers and shirt, but despite their warmth, goosebumps chased up and down her legs.

"Whoa," she whispered, tugging back on the reins. The dappled gray mare snorted once, puffs of steam escaping her large, black nostrils. She swung her head twice, agitated by the command to stop. Ginny pulled back again, this time sharply, and the mare dutifully came to a halt. Ginny set the hand brake and unhooked the lantern, gently stroking the thick muscles along the horse's sleek neck as she passed. "I'll be back soon." *I hope.* She gave her a pat. "Be ready to run."

The gates of the cemetery creaked loudly when Ginny pushed against them with one hand. The cold, wet metal caused a shiver to run through her, and she wiped her hand on her coat, before setting the lantern down and using her body weight to force her way in. Reclaiming the lantern, she began carefully traversing the path she assumed would lead to the gravedigger's shack. Milo's house.

The young man in the bar had explained in great detail that most folks believed the old cemetery was haunted, and though the city had hired several men as gravediggers over the years, none of them had lasted as long as Milo, whose demons weren't, apparently, of the ghostly variety. He was well paid for his trouble, receiving a dollar fifty for every grave he dug and free boarding in the small, shabby house that doubled as a supply shed for the cemetery and nearby church.

The flu had hit Troy in the winter of 1888 and 1889, and it was treating the town to a morbid curtain call this year. Milo had a steady stream of business, but was too cheap to hire someone to help him when he got busy. Instead, he'd taken on James.

"Yeow!" Ginny jumped out of her skin as a rabbit darted across the path and right over her feet. "God." She covered her face with her hand, her heart pounding so wildly little spots danced in front of her eyes for a few seconds. *Stop it, stupid,* she told herself. *It was only a rabbit.* A shuddering breath. *Only a rabbit. Relax.*

She didn't have much of a plan, Ginny admitted to herself as she walked silently down the uneven dirt path. Wait until Milo fell asleep; sneak into the house; snatch up James; and run like the Devil. It was simple, but she liked that. Her smile became slightly predatory.

Tombstones lined the path that began gradually sloping upward, and with a shift of the wind, the fog separated to allow a thin sliver of moonbeam through; she could see the house nestled between two creaking birch trees. It was a little larger than she expected, and the wind carried the strong smell of rotten wood, smoke, and rancid hops. *He's trying to make his own beer. And doing a lousy job.*

The house was dark, but she could see the outline of smoke as it drifted up from the chimney. Ginny felt a little thrill stir inside her. She wouldn't have to wait. It was time.

She carefully used her sleeve to wipe grime from one of the front windows, but it was no use. The glass was still so filthy that moonlight couldn't penetrate it, and she couldn't catch even a glimpse of the interior. Not wanting to face any surprises when she entered the house—like a vicious dog or Milo or a shotgun— she slowly circled around behind the house to try again.

Halfway there, her head slewed sideways at the faint sound of voices coming from the fog. She cocked her head as she listened, hearing Milo's raspy voice and that of another person, a child. *James?* She mouthed silently. *Please let it be him.* Ginny moved toward the voices, taking care to keep from tripping over the gravestones and roots that protruded unevenly from the ground. She caught sight of a dimly glowing lantern in the distance, which disappeared and reappeared as the wind swirled the fog.

Ginny opened the door of her own lantern and blew out its flickering flame. She stopped dead in her tracks, her mind racing and eyes blinking rapidly as they adjusted to having as a guide only the barest hint of moonlight that had fought its way through the mist. She crept forward, taking care to keep herself low to the ground and out of sight. She could see Milo plainly, his face illuminated by the small lantern sitting next to him. But Ginny still couldn't see clearly with whom he was talking.

"Keep diggin'." Milo paused to take a drink. "Or we'll be all night."

Another shovelful of dirt was tossed out of the hole. "I'm tryin'."

Ginny's throat closed as the voice wrapped itself around her heart. *James.*

Tears welled so quickly, she couldn't stop them. *At last.*

James's head suddenly emerged from the partially completed grave.

Ginny ducked behind a tree, close enough to see their faces and smell the dug rich soil. James's hair was longer than she'd ever seen it, and it hung in his eyes. He looked smaller than she remembered.

Milo's words were slurred. "Try harder." He sat at one end of the grave, a half empty bottle dangling loosely from one hand, his feet hanging into the pit as James continued to dig.

Ginny felt around the ground at her feet. The grass was damp but still brittle, and after a moment of silent fumbling, she found a rock the size of a large apple. She set the lantern down and held her breath, waiting for the right time. She jumped when she heard a loud snap.

"Aww, shit, boy!"

James scrambled out of the hole, tossing the shovel on to the ground just outside it. "I'm sorry. Really. I'm sorry," he said shakily, visible flinching when Milo rose unsteadily to his feet.

"You snapped the shovel!"

James took another step backward and raised his arms to protect himself.

Ginny felt a wild surge of anger over the defensive gesture, knowing in her heart he'd been beaten by this man. Her knuckles turned white as she gripped the stone in her hand so tightly it was painful; she imagined silencing his cruel voice by crashing the rock into Milo's head. The feeling scared her, but instead of pushing it away, she embraced it. She needed it now.

James took a tentative step toward Milo, who was turning the shovel over in his hands, examining it with jerky, angry motions. "It was an accident, I swear. M-maybe I can f-fix it." His terrified stutter tore a hole in Ginny's heart, and more tears blurred her vision.

Milo grabbed the shovel out of James's hand and lifted it as though he was going to hit the boy with it.

Ginny's eyes widened, and she drew in a deep breath to spring from her hiding place. Before she could take a step, however, Milo lowered the shovel, then let it fall to the ground.

He took a long pull from the bottle still in one hand, emptying it and pointing it at James. "You stay here. I'll get another shovel." He looked down at the lantern but decided against taking it. He knew every inch of the graveyard, light or no. "If I send you, it'll take too damn long," he murmured, hobbling back toward the house.

The redhead had only a second to decide what to do. She bit her lower lip so hard she tasted blood, as her heart demanded that Milo be made to pay for ever touching James. But to her dismay, her head commanded she wait. It was one of the hardest things she'd ever done, and a light sweat broke out on her face and neck as she warred with herself. But in the end, she allowed the more reasonable part of her nature to triumph—and Milo to pass.

The fog closed in around him in just a few seconds, but she waited until she could no longer hear his ranting curses and heavy footsteps before leaving her hiding place.

She licked her lips nervously. "James?" she said quietly, hoping her voice sounded steadier to him than it did to her own ears.

The boy whirled around, and his eyes shaped twin moons as he gaped at his sister.

Ginny could see that he was terrified, and she stopped walking toward him, afraid he'd bolt if she took another step. "James, honey," she soothed, "it's me. You don't have to be afraid. I've been looking everywhere for you."

James shook his head wildly, scattering his dirty bangs into his eyes. "No! You're dead!"

"Shhh!" Ginny pressed her finger to her lips. "He'll hear you." She extended her hand to him. "I'm not dead. I've come to take you away from here. C'mon," she prodded gently. "I'll explain it all later." Quickly, she checked over her shoulder and swallowed nervously. The house wasn't far. They didn't have much time. "We need to leave before he gets back."

"You're a g-gho-ghost."

She turned back to James. "No, I'm your sister. And I'm very real. Plea—"

He began to scramble away, falling almost instantly and screaming in terror. "Stay away from me!"

Christ. Ginny dropped the rock and surged forward, grabbing his dirty coat with both hands before he disappeared into the fog. "It's me, James. I'm not a ghost. I won't hurt you!"

"It can't be you!"

Ginny was at a loss. "It is me."

He began to fight, his thin arms and legs flailing in all directions. He picked up the broken shovel and used it as a weapon, slamming the metal head against Ginny's thigh.

Ginny cried out in pain, as the powerful blow dropped her to her knees and sent James crashing to the ground with her. "Stay away from me!" he howled, still trying to break free from her grasp. He knocked the lantern into the grave, snuffing out its tiny flame and sending them deeper into horrifying darkness.

"You can't take me into the grave. I won't let you!"

Ginny sucked in a quick breath, shocked at the strength of his unexpected, stinging blow, but somehow she maintained her grip on his shaking body.

"James, stop!" she barked authoritatively, causing him to freeze in mid-strike. The graveyard went silent, and for a second, the world stood still.

They were both panting, hot breath rising from their open mouths.

James began to whimper, sure he was going to be dragged down into a grave by a ghost. Just like Milo had said.

Even in this light, Ginny could see his pulse pounding against his pale throat. She hesitantly let go of his coat with one of her hands and gently, but firmly, cupped his chin, and lifted, forcing his head upward so that he would have to look at her face, her eyes. What she saw through the gloomy moonlight made her as physically ill as furious. "Oh, sweetheart." Her gaze softened, and a faint, worried smile flickered across her face. "I'm so sorry. It's going to be okay now, I promise."

His face was covered in a myriad of bruises—old and new. And his cheeks were sunken and sallow. Like a cornered animal, his fear-filled eyes darted from side to side, as he looked for a means of escape. She was sure he hadn't seen the sun for days and a good meal for longer than that.

"James," she whispered, the lump in her throat making speech painful. "It is me." She sniffed, and hot tears streamed down her cheeks, tiny wisps of fog rising from each wet trail. "See?" Tenderly, she ran her thumb across his trembling cheek. "I'm not a ghost." Her voice broke, but she pressed on. "I'm your sister."

Something clicked behind his eyes, and she could see the dawning of recognition spark there. She opened her mouth to say more when she heard Milo fast approaching.

"Who's there?" the man called out through the fog, his wooden leg and the shovel he was using as a walking stick thumping loudly against the ground, as he moved closer and closer.

Ginny pushed herself to her feet, wincing when she leaned on her thigh, and lifting her brother up along with her. "We've got to go, James. Right now."

He stared at Ginny, still not convinced that she was real. "Bu-but the orphanage said—"

Ginny let out a frustrated breath. "They lied. This has all been a lie. C'mon." She began tugging hard on his sleeve. "We need to go now!" The words unerringly reminded her of Lewis and the train out of Talking Rock. She was determined that this would go better and was about to scoop him up and carry him off when Milo exploded out of the mist, not five feet in front of her, catching James between them.

The man glared at Ginny for a moment, trying to place where he'd seen her before. There was something different about her now—the men's clothes.

"You're that whore bitch from Smokey's," he finally accused, his face twisting as the fuzzy memory came into focus.

James bristled at Milo's hateful words. Even if Ginny was a ghost, nobody should talk to his sister that way. "She is not, you bast—"

His words were cut off when Ginny wrapped her arm around him and pulled him behind her as she stepped forward, putting herself between James and Milo.

"We spoke this afternoon, Mr. Porter," she said evenly, hoping to forestall the inevitable until she could get James out of there. A direct confrontation wasn't what she'd wanted, but now that she had no choice, an eerie sense of resolution flooded her, leaving her more confident than she'd felt when she first walked into the graveyard. She could do this. She *had* to do this. "I told you I was here for my brother." Her voiced deepened and took on a menacing edge James had never heard before. "I meant it."

Unaccountably, a grisly laugh exploded from Milo, harsh and low. "I can see that, girlie." He lifted the shovel in his hands a little, making sure she saw it. "But you aren't taking him. He's mine, bought and paid for." Unflinching, their eyes met and held.

"James," Ginny said after a few charged seconds. "Go out the front gates. There's a buggy waiting there for us. Get in the buggy, and if I'm not there in one minute, you drive it into town. I'll find you."

He clutched her coat as his voice rose in panic. "Ginny?"

"Don't you move, boy!" Milo rasped, pointing an angry finger at what little bit of James wasn't hiding behind Ginny. "*She* is not your boss."

Ginny reached around and patted James's hand, then gently pried his cold fingers from her coat. "You go now. I'll be right there." It was a lie, and they both knew it. She was going to make sure Milo couldn't follow him out of the graveyard. There was only one way to do that.

The boy took a tentative step away from his sister, stopping when he saw the look on Milo's face. To James, he looked like a demon, surrounded by thick fog and bathed in a sickly light.

"One more step, boy, and you won't be able to move for a month when I'm through with you," Milo warned darkly, his eyes flashing with rage.

Slowly, James turned his head. He didn't know what to do; he looked at Ginny in question.

She gave him a watery smile and brief nod. "It'll be okay, James. I'll make it that way." *And this time I won't mess it up.* "Go."

All hell broke loose.

As James took a giant step to run away, Milo roared and lunged toward the boy. Ginny surged forward to intercept him, and at the same moment another figure burst from the shadows, startling them all.

James screamed, his feet glued to the ground as he watched in confused horror.

Milo crashed against Ginny. When she moved out of the way, his body just kept on falling, until he dropped limply to the ground. When he fell, Ginny could see a very drained-looking, disheveled Lindsay standing behind him, the rock that Ginny had dropped earlier clutched tightly in her hand and dripping crimson blood.

Ginny blinked a few times, and her mouth dropped open. "Lindsay?" Without thought, she jumped over Milo's fallen body, and propelled herself into her best friend's waiting arms.

Lindsay pressed her face to Ginny's chilled cheek and closed her eyes, rocking her slowly. "It's me," she whispered, greedily drinking in their closeness with a sense of relief and contentment so profound she felt it all the way to her toes. "Didn't think you'd get rid of me so easily, did you?"

She tightened her hold on Ginny, who was rapidly progressing from crying to sobbing. "And you say I get into trouble?" she teased weakly. She pressed her lips to Ginny's ear, first softly kissing it, then begging in a whisper so low Ginny barely heard it, "Please don't cry. I hate it when you cry." Her own eyes glinted with unshed tears.

Ginny pulled back to look at Lindsay, but kept hold of her coat, not daring to let her go. "I knew you'd find me." She looked her up and down, assuring herself of Lindsay's presence. "But I still can't believe you're here." She pressed her palm to Lindsay's cheek. When the darker woman leaned into the touch with longing and happiness written all over her face, Ginny's mouth erupted into a genuine, if tired, grin.

Milo began to stir, and James picked up the shovel at his feet. He studied the man's face for a long second, his hands flexing against the wooden handle. With effort, he lifted the shovel high over his head, intent on crushing Milo's worthless skull. He closed his eyes and swung with all his might…

Only to have the tool stopped in mid-swing by Lindsay's iron grip. "No." She licked her lips as she quickly pulled the shovel from James's hands. She purposely didn't look at Ginny. "I'll do it."

James didn't know who this woman in trousers was, but one look at the determined set of her jaw and the fierceness in her eyes; and he knew she meant what she said. He shrank back, ready to let her finish off Milo, but too faint at heart to watch.

Ginny's eyes went round. "Lindsay?"

Lindsay raised the shovel high into the night sky, heaving as she twisted the tool in her hands, turning the shovel's sharp head into an axe with her intent. The blade sang through the air as she put her back into its downward motion.

"Lindsay, no!" Ginny reached out, trying to stop her, but it was too late.

The sound of the strike rang out into the night, causing both Ginny and James to jump. "Lindsay… uhhh." Ginny nearly fainted with relief when she realized that Lindsay hadn't chopped the man's head clean off, though a big part of her wasn't sure she could have blamed her if she had.

Milo moaned as Lindsay began prying the deeply embedded shovel blade out of his wooden leg.

Just as he woke up, Ginny threw her body across his to pin him down.

"Again!" she blurted, and Lindsay swung, this time severing the peg leg at the knee.

Disoriented, Milo began to thrash and scream. James dragged Ginny off him before he could figure out what they'd done.

Lindsay distracted the tall man by throwing the shovel hard against his chest.

"Uff!" The wind was forced from his lungs, and he wheezed raggedly.

She dropped to the ground and used her feet to give him a strong push that rolled him right into the half-dug grave, his body landing with a muffled thump.

"It's not nice to hit women and little boys," Lindsay hissed as she stood.

Ginny's stomach clenched, and she spoke over Milo's enraged, half-coherent cursing "You're not going to—" She glanced at the grave, then back at the shovel in Lindsay's hand.

Lindsay tossed the shovel aside and shook her head. "I might be a bitch, but I'm not crazy."

Her companion gave her a stern look. "You are not a… you know, Lindsay Killian."

Ginny's eyes spoke volumes, and Lindsay smiled back at her, hoping hers did as well.

Ginny shook her head in amazement. "How did you get here?"

Lindsay held up her hand. "I'll tell you once we get out of here."

Ginny nodded. There would be time for explanations and a more private reunion later. Right now, she needed to see to a very frightened little boy. She reached out for James, and he flinched away from her touch. She blinked.

"Wh—? Honey, what's the matter? Milo is loud,"—she gestured vaguely to the grave containing the cursing man—"but he can't come after us now. It's just me. I—"

James's face was a mixture of anger, hurt, and fear. "I'm going to the gates." And without another word, he disappeared into the fog.

Lindsay grasped Ginny's hand and squeezed. They looked at each other, then turned and ran after him, neither one willing to let go of her grip on the other.

"Lindsay?" Ginny panted as they jogged toward what they hoped was the dirt path that led to the gates. Lindsay nearly tripped, and Ginny pulled her back upright with their linked hands.

Her eyes closed briefly as a sharp pain shot through her ribs. "Thanks. What?"

"Don't even think of getting out of my sight for a good long while."

Lindsay smiled. "I love you too."

Chapter Fourteen

The buggy ride back was mostly quiet, with James sitting next to Lindsay rather than Ginny and refusing even to acknowledge his sister's presence. The lantern had been forgotten at the graveyard, so the ride through the fog was slow, dragging out the painful silence.

This was not the reunion Ginny had longed for. *But I found him*, she told herself as she guided the wagon up the long winding drive that led to Edith and Trudy's antebellum home. *And he's alive and okay.* She glanced sideways at her brother's pale face. She let out a heartfelt sigh. *At least mostly.*

Lindsay wrapped her hand around Ginny's, feeling the reins tangle with her fingers. She leaned sideways and bumped shoulders with the younger woman.

"It's gonna be all right," she whispered. Ginny nodded, but Lindsay could see her heart wasn't in it. A change of subject was in order. "So," she began, "where are we going?" She received a gentle squeeze of her hand as thanks.

"We're going to Edith Pigg's house."

Lindsay snorted, drawing a surprised burst of laughter from Ginny.

"God, Lindsay, that's the same reaction Lewis had." Her gaze turned fond. "I should have known you'd do the same thing."

James's head shot up at the mention of his brother's name. He licked his lips, trying to sound casual but failing miserably. "Lewis is here?"

Ginny bit back a smile, at least that much she'd done right. "He sure is. We found him and brought him with us." She paused for a moment, gathering her thoughts. "We've been looking for you for weeks. For all of you."

We? James was dying to ask, but held his tongue. He wouldn't give her the satisfaction of talking to her. Not after she'd left them and allowed them to be ripped apart.

Ginny waited patiently, seeing the question on his lips. He never voiced it and she felt her irritation rising along with the pain that was twisting her guts into knots. If she'd learned one thing from the fire that nearly destroyed their family, it was that time was fleeting and sometimes there were no second chances. Never again would she allow things to go unsaid to the people she loved.

"Whoa." She pulled the horse to a stop so she could focus on her brother. Lindsay sat back a little so Ginny could easily look across her.

James squirmed under Ginny's serious stare, but didn't dare look away.

"I know you're mad at me, James," she began softly. "And I know you don't understand what happened or where I went after the fire. I'll explain it all. But for now you have to know that I didn't leave you on purpose." She swallowed convulsively. "I wouldn't do that."

Tears filled his eyes, but he stubbornly refused to let them fall.

Lindsay watched the battle of two strong wills, knowing who would win eventually, but equally sure that the victory wasn't going to happen tonight. She knew what James was feeling all too well. No sweet words, no matter how heartfelt or even true, would fix that.

Ginny pressed on. "I'm doing my best to put us back together again, James." A heavy weight settled on her chest. She could see that he either didn't believe her or didn't care. She couldn't tell which. "I love you and I'm so sorry that all this happened," she said quietly, turning back toward the big mare, and giving the reins a firm snap.

The wagon jerked forward, and Ginny's thoughts turned inward. Time, that's what they all needed, she decided. Time to heal. Time to forgive. And time to look forward and face the future with more anticipation than fear.

James barely held himself in check. The emotions inside him were churning wildly, and he didn't know whether to scream or run and hide. He was furious, and hurt had piled upon hurt until he didn't think he could hurt anymore. After several minutes, he finally mustered a noncommittal, "Oh."

Even in the dim light Ginny could see the dirty creases on his forehead ease; and hear the creaking of the seat as he relaxed a little against it, unconsciously responding to his big sister's comforting words. It was a small victory and one she greedily grabbed hold of with both hands.

The silence between them thickened again, but it was less tense than before. Suddenly, Lindsay tapped James on the arm and stuck out her hand. "I'm Ginny's friend, String Bean. Pleasure to meet you."

Ginny eyes widened. Hadn't she introduced them? *Crap*. "Sorry," she muttered sheepishly.

The boy blinked a few times, startled by Lindsay's voice; the stranger hadn't done more than whisper to Ginny once or twice since they'd left the graveyard. He reluctantly reached out and shook her much bigger hand.

James studied her curiously, wondering who she was and why Ginny seemed to be stuck to her like glue, and mostly why she was here at all. Finally, he made a face, deciding that the vegetable nickname was stupid. "She"—he jerked a thumb at his sister—"doesn't call you that. String Bean, I mean. She calls you Lindsay. I heard her."

Lindsay shrugged lightly. "I know. But that doesn't mean you have to. In fact, only two special people in the entire world call me Lindsay."

Special people? "What does Lewis call you?" he asked skeptically.

"Lindsay, of course. But we're good friends." She smiled inwardly at James's instant frown. "'Course, you could be a good friend, too… if you wanted." She kept her voice light and her eyes fixed straight ahead. The fog was beginning to thin and she thought she saw the outline of a large house up ahead.

James bit his lower lip, not liking the idea that Lewis was a "special" person and he wasn't. And this woman *had* clobbered Milo and hacked off his leg, which was, in James's estimation, better than his birthday and Christmas all rolled into one. "I um… well, I guess I could call you Lindsay, too. I mean, if that's what Lewis does."

Lindsay glanced down and gave him a brilliant smile, charming the small boy before Ginny's eyes. She understood completely how he felt, and only barely managed to clamp down on the impulse to stop the buggy and give Lindsay a big, sloppy kiss.

"Great!" Lindsay clasped James's knee. "You can't have too many friends." They were silent for a few moments while Ginny pulled the buggy around to the back of the house and into the open door of the stable. A lantern mounted to the door had been lit, awaiting her return.

"So Ginny is your special friend too, right?" he asked as he jumped down from his seat.

Lindsay blinked innocently at Ginny, who looked as though she'd swallowed her tongue. She let go of the redhead's hand and patted her back as Ginny choked, shaking the entire buggy. "James," Lindsay laughed, ignoring the sting it caused her sore throat. "That's exactly what she is."

Lewis had been waiting up for them in the parlor, and every bit of warmth and joy that James's reunion with Ginny had lacked was made up for by the welcome he got from Lewis. The two boys hugged and laughed and punched each other relentlessly, but gently, when the hugging grew too embarrassing.

Edith and Trudy had left water heating for a bath, reasoning that any boy who'd been living with Milo Porter would need one before toddling off to bed. After a long soak, James was too tired to fight Ginny when she dried him off and carried him to bed.

Ginny finally saw a genuine smile stretch across James's face and a little bit of her heart was put at ease by the sight. She tucked both boys into bed in one of the spare bedrooms provided by their hosts, and kissed them each on the cheek before saying goodnight. She was delighted when James allowed the gesture of affection and didn't miss Lewis's sleepy wink. She had a co-conspirator in that boy and she was certain he'd work on his broody brother. Ginny smiled to herself when she heard James whisper to Lewis about her new short hair and her odd clothes. She lifted the lamp from the dresser and used it to guide her down the long hallway.

She could see the outline of Lindsay's lanky profile in the shadows, leaning heavily against the wall at the end of the hall. Ginny smiled unconsciously at the sight. "You wouldn't believe how much I've missed you," she said when she drew even with the other woman.

"Sure I would," Lindsay whispered, her lips curling into an answering grin. Ginny lifted her hand and traced Lindsay's face. Dark circles surrounded her tired eyes and she imagined that she didn't look much better herself. Her fingers trailed down the silky skin of Lindsay's cheek, stopping at her chin when they traced over something rough. Thinking it was a smudge of mud; she tried to wipe it away with her thumb.

Lindsay sucked in a breath through clenched teeth. Jon Bergquist had given the wound three tiny stitches and the skin was still tender. "Oh, God. I'm sorry. I didn't mean to hurt—" Ginny lifted the lamp higher, finding a small but deep cut in the shape of a tiny 'C' on Lindsay's chin. Her eyes searched Lindsay's desperately. There was more there than physical pain. There was fear. "What's the matter?"

Lindsay looked away. "Nothing."

"Nuh uh, Lindsay. There's too much between us for you to do that now." She repeated her question, watching curiously as Lindsay struggled to express herself.

"This place is so fine," Lindsay finally muttered. "I don't feel right bein' here."

Ginny took in her surroundings, paying more attention than she had the first time she'd been in the old, but grand home. "It is nice here, I suppose. But that doesn't mean you don't belong."

Lindsay shot her a slightly irritated look as she suppressed a cough. "That's just what it means and you know it!"

Ginny sucked in a breath. "Lindsay—"

"This a bang-up place if I've ever seen one—big pictures on the wall and pretty, chiming clocks—and in the bedroom there's that tall bed with the fancy cloth that comes right out of the ceiling and hangs over it. I'll feel like I'm in one of those teepees Indians sleep in when I'm really just in bed!"

"You don't always sleep in boxcars."

"No, but even the best places, the ones I sleep in when I'm really lucky, are like Christian's orphanage—clean and simple. Places where I could cuss and do anything else I liked and nobody would bat an eye. But here—" She shook her head. "I think I should sleep with the horses." What she didn't tell Ginny was that every time she saw something nice, she wondered what price it would fetch on the street.

Ginny's expression grew impatient. "You'll do no such thing."

"But—"

"Do you think I've ever slept in a house so fine?"

Lindsay's eyes widened a little. Sometimes it was easy to forget the life that Ginny had been living before they met. "I guess not. But you don't feel… well… out of sorts. I can tell."

Ginny sighed, mortally tired. She lifted a hand then let it fall. "I guess I haven't given it much thought. I've been busy thinking of other things." Her voice softened. "Like worrying to death over you. Lindsay, right now we both belong wherever it is we need to be. And tonight, we need to be here. It's too late to find someplace else to stay and the thought of sleeping outside in the damp so we can all catch our deaths, doesn't appeal to me. I won't put the boys through that and I can't leave them here alone." She wasn't above begging. "Please, Lindsay."

Lindsay frowned, but nodded. Even if she felt painfully out of place here, her place was near Ginny. She would make do.

"What happened to you?" Ginny asked worriedly, her finger gently grazing Lindsay's tiny stitches. "Are you okay? Really?"

Lindsay's gaze warmed, and she threaded her hand in thick red hair and gently tugged Ginny's head forward, brushing her mouth against warm, inviting lips. "I am now," she breathed, pressing her forehead to Ginny's.

"Me too. When are you going to tell me? What—?" Ginny frowned and pulled away, replacing her forehead with her hand. "You have a fever," she accused in a voice laced with worry. "I was afraid of this." *And I love you to death and can't stand the idea of you being ill.*

"I think I'm catching a cold."

Ginny let out an unhappy breath. "Probably," she said, the words sounding curt because she was worried. She grasped Lindsay's chilled hand and threaded their fingers together, guiding the other woman toward the room that had been set aside for her. "Let's get you to bed then."

Lindsay smirked. "Shouldn't I get cleaned up first, too?"

Ginny stopped and turned to face her. She sniffed the air, her nose wrinkling in reaction. "I didn't want to say anything. But now that you mention it..."

"I stink like shit," Lindsay said flatly.

"You smell like a sweaty horse," Ginny corrected with a small smile. "And for the life of me I can't figure out why."

"I rode all the way from Talking Rock to Atlanta. I earned every bit of this atrocious stink."

"You what?" Ginny's jaw sagged. "But that's at least fifty miles!" They began walking. "And you're afraid of horses."

"You're telling me this?" Lindsay steered them back downstairs toward the washroom that held a large tub. She had no desire to fight with a tiny china washbasin and rag, even if it meant hauling her ass up and down the stairs once more. She was so stiff from riding, and then the manic trek to Troy by train, that she craved a soak in the worst way.

At the bottom of the stairs her steps faltered a bit.

"Lindsay!" Ginny grabbed her and held her as she got her balance. "Hey...careful."

"Uh oh." A wave of exhaustion crashed over her and it took far more effort than it should have to steady herself. "I think I'm running out of steam," she murmured, rubbing her burning eyes.

"Sweetheart, when was the last time you ate or slept?"—A beat—"And don't lie."

Lindsay sighed and opened her eyes. "I ate morning before last. But I threw it up."

Ginny closed her eyes. "Oh, Lindsay."

"The last time I slept was with you in the barn." Ginny opened her mouth, but Lindsay cut her off. "I *had* to find you. Have mercy on me, all right? I was a little busy getting here." Lindsay's eyes begged her partner to understand and, reluctantly, she did.

Ginny shook her head and wound her arm around Lindsay's, urging her toward the washroom again. This was going to be the quickest bath in the history of man. She hoped that Edith and Trudy wouldn't mind, but she was going to raid the icebox too. Desperate times called for desperate measures. She only hoped that someday she could repay their kindness.

They drained the tub and Ginny filled it with several more buckets of hot water that took far too long to heat. Knowing how much Lindsay enjoyed it, Ginny lathered her hands with a large cake of white soap and washed Lindsay's hair, while her friend leaned back and purred like a feline. They talked the entire time, trading kisses and stories until Lindsay had explained that it was Rat Face who'd kept her from making the train. And Ginny had told her of Christian's telegram that had paved the way for them.

"But there's still one thing I don't understand. How did you find me?"

Lindsay began to shiver and Ginny cursed herself for not remembering to bring anything for her to change into. Their nightshirts were still upstairs in their bag. She grabbed another linen towel, vowing to do a load of laundry for Edith and Trudy in the morning. Her eyebrows pulled together as Lindsay wrapped it around herself. Lindsay's ribs were more prominent than when they'd met; and she realized with a start that her request that Lindsay not steal was literally causing her to go hungry. Silently, she cursed her selfishness and wondered whether she should release Lindsay from her promise.

"As soon as I jumped off the freight train in Troy, I went to the best place in any town for information on just about any subject."

"Umm... you barged in on a gossipy sewing circle?" Ginny tossed

Lindsay's clothes in the sink for washing in the morning, and retrieved the oil lamp from a nearby table. Despite the house being quite grand, the elderly sisters hadn't bothered to have electricity installed. But Ginny didn't miss what she'd never had.

Quickly, they scurried out of the washroom and toward the stairs, Lindsay's bare feet chilling quickly on the cold, wooden floors.

The rail-rider's low chuckle made Ginny smile. "I never thought of a sewing circle. You're probably right, but I wouldn't know where to find one anyway. I headed for the saloon."

Ginny's mouth formed a small 'O'. She would have slapped herself in the forehead, but she was too busy holding the lantern in one hand and Lindsay's hand in the other. "The one near the depot, I take it?"

Lindsay nodded. Taking a deep breath she forced herself up the steps, though she was sorely tempted to curl up on the floor right where she was.

"Smokey's."

"I guess you heard about what happened this afternoon then."

"Seems a Yankee girl and gravedigger named Milo got into an argument over the boy Milo had gotten from an orphan train recently. Knowing you, I figured if I didn't hightail it over to the cemetery, I was likely to miss whatever unimaginable trouble you were getting yourself into." She couldn't stifle her smug grin. It was about time the shoe was on the other foot.

Ginny rolled her eyes and pointed to the first door at the top of the stairs; and she and Lindsay padded directly to the bed, not bothering to stop anywhere else. "You got all that information just by asking? It was like pulling teeth for me."

Lindsay slid under the soft quilt and clean sheets, not bothering to get dressed. Her eyes immediately drifted closed as her head sank into a down-filled pillow. "Oh, God, this is wonderful. And you shouldn't doubt me, I have a way with people, you know." She coughed weakly.

"Uh huh." Ginny stripped out of her clothes and looked longingly at the soft bed that held Lindsay. She worried her lower lip, then padded over to the bedroom door and threw the lock.

"What are you—Yeow!" Lindsay squealed; and her eyes popped wide open when two cold feet and a very naked, warm body scooted under the covers and pressed itself against her.

"Shh," Ginny whispered, snuggling as close as skin would allow.

"You'll wake up Edith and Trudy."

"And cause them both to have conniptions if they find us naked in bed together." But Lindsay closed her eyes at the feeling of warm satisfaction being this close to Ginny gave her. There was, she admitted to herself, nothing in the world like it. "You're so soft," she whispered absently, her original train of thought derailing.

"Mmm." Ginny smiled and placed a delicate kiss on Lindsay's collarbone.

"So are you." She rested her head against Lindsay's shoulder and threw her leg over lean hips, effectively pinning her to the bed. "So you wheedled the information out of someone at the bar?"

"Not exactly," Lindsay murmured sleepily, Ginny's naked skin warring with the Sandman for her attention.

Ginny yawned, the traveling and worrying about her brothers and Jane was catching up with her with a vengeance. "What does that mean?"

"I didn't have any money to bribe the bartender, and the big club he kept by the till discouraged me from trying to pound it out of him." She ran her fingers through Ginny's hair, delighting in its smooth texture. "So I bought the information the only way I could."

Lindsay sounded so unhappy about what she'd done that Ginny's stomach dropped. *Oh, my God.* She pushed herself up and stared down at Lindsay. "You mean—?"

"That's right." Lindsay nodded sadly, crushed.

Ginny's heart began to pound.

Lindsay's scratchy voice was filled with self-disgust, and she didn't dare open her eyes to see Ginny's reaction. "There's some stupid, bastard bartender walking around Troy, Alabama with Lewis's navy blue blanket."

Ten days later…

Lindsay had been right. By the day after she arrived in Troy there was no hiding the fact that she'd caught a nasty cold. Much to her annoyance, and Ginny's insistence, there would be no traveling until she was well.

But Lindsay was getting better quicker than Ginny had anticipated;

and, barring a relapse, they would be heading west on the following day's noon train.

For once, good fortune had smiled on them; Edith and Trudy had been more gracious than they could have hoped for. The two sisters had offered them use of their home for as long as they needed it. Lindsay, Ginny, and the boys were doted on like long-lost visiting grandchildren.

The women were sitting in the parlor talking, and the boys had just finished their daily, much-hated, mandatory bath and were both tucked into bed. It was only seven o'clock, but the sun had set.

"Now, Ginny," Edith chided gently, "just look at her. Take the poor thing to bed."

Ginny's cheeks began to heat.

Oblivious to the innuendo, Edith plowed ahead. "She's worn to the bone." The white-haired woman pointed at Lindsay, whose head was bobbing as she fought to stay awake. A tiny string of drool hung suspended from the corner of her mouth and her eyes were open just a crack.

Ginny's blush deepened and she fought the urge to fan her flaming cheeks. They hadn't gotten much sleep the night before. Lindsay had been feeling much better and they'd traded kisses and sensual touches well into the night. *Oh, my.* Ginny's belly twisted pleasantly just remembering. She shook her head. "I guess it's bedtime."

Lindsay's head shot up and eagerly she mumbled, "Bedtime?" She looked at Ginny hopefully.

"Time to sleep," Ginny corrected with a faintly elevated eyebrow and just a hint of a smirk.

"Oh." Lindsay scowled.

"Well, good night, girls," Trudy told them, pushing herself to her feet.

"Sleep tight, girls," Edith added as she followed her sister out of the room.

"Night," Lindsay and Ginny called in unison.

Ginny stood first and extended her hand to Lindsay. The davenport was so soft that it tended to swallow its occupants, and she groaned as Ginny pulled her to her feet.

"It was a good day today, don't you think?" Ginny asked as they headed for the stairs, their hands still entwined.

"I guess."

"The boys really like you."

"Uh huh." Lindsay yawned as they began climbing the tall staircase. "I like them, too."

"Lewis asked me if you were going to be staying with us… well, I mean…you know… permanently." The words tumbled out in a nervous rush. "Uff!"

Ginny yelped when her arm was nearly yanked from its socket. She'd kept walking, waiting for Lindsay's reaction, not knowing that Lindsay's feet had frozen mid-step. "You trying to kill me?"

Lindsay swallowed so loudly that Ginny heard it. "What did you tell him?" The expression Lindsay wore wasn't what Ginny expected, and it made her heart clench.

Ginny frowned as she lifted her hand and cupped Lindsay's cheek, feeling her friend lean in heavily to the touch. She hadn't meant to worry her. "Actually, I lied my pants off."

Lindsay's eyes widened. "Yo-you did?"

"Uh huh," she said solemnly. "I told Lewis that how long you stayed with us would depend on you." Blue eyes twinkled. "But we both know I have no intention of letting you go. So it looks like you're stuck with me until you can escape my clutches and wily ways, Broccoli Bunch." She wriggled her eyebrows, pleased to see a relaxed smile transform Lindsay's face. "Careful what you wish for. You might get it."

Lindsay's heart resumed beating, and for a second she was speechless.

"Lindsay?" Ginny said worriedly. "Hey, was that an answer you can live with?" She searched the other woman's face, hoping that Lindsay understood the deep emotion behind the blithely spoken words.

Lindsay nodded. "Yeah," she croaked softly. "And I happen to like your clutches." This time it was Lindsay who smirked. "And I love your wily ways."

A bubble of embarrassed laughter exploded from Ginny. "Oh, Lord."

They were so close to the same height that it seemed odd to Lindsay to be looking up at Ginny, who was standing two steps above her. She leaned forward and laid her head against Ginny's chest as two arms circled her. She sighed against the material of the soft gray dress, feeling the redhead kiss the top of her head.

They stayed that way for a long time till Ginny finally asked Lindsay if she was sure she was in good enough shape to travel the next day.

"I'll be fine. I've had more rest this past week than I have my entire life. I think I've gained ten pounds."

"Mmm. You and me both."

"We needed it."

Ginny nodded and kissed Lindsay's head again. "I guess we did."

They finished climbing the stairs and got all the way into their room with Ginny remaining silent, deep in thought.

"You'll find her, Ginny," Lindsay assured softly as she closed and locked their bedroom door. The lamp by the bedside wasn't lit and she left it that way, not needing to see to strip out of her clothes and wearily tug on her warm nightshirt. She heard Ginny's soft sigh and the rustle of clothing next to her as shoes and dress were slipped out of.

"What if we don't find her?"

They crawled into bed and pulled up the sheet, blanket, and quilt that Edith had added to their bed that afternoon. It was going to dip down close to freezing tonight and the elderly woman wasn't taking any chances with Lindsay's precarious health.

Lindsay rolled over on her side and propped her head up with her hand, admiring the barely visible, gentle sloping of Ginny's nose and the soft planes of her heart-shaped face. "You said that same thing about both your brothers, and they're right down the hall, safe and sound. Maybe luck doesn't have anything to do with this, Ginny. Maybe it's about hard work and not giving up."

Ginny mirrored Lindsay's posture, kissing the fingers that moved to delicately trace her lips. "Maybe." She rolled that over in her mind a bit before smiling sadly. "We both know that sometimes hard work isn't enough. I worked from dawn to candle-lighting until my fingers bled, plucking chickens in the Lower East Side for half the pay of the man standing next to me. And even with my wages and Alice's and Mama's and Arthur's, we were barely making it in a slum. If hard work was all it took for success, then we'd have been millionaires."

Lindsay didn't have an answer to that. "What makes you think you'll have worse luck with Jane than you did with the boys then? No reason your streak can't hold."

"Streaks never hold. That's why they're called streaks. I know just how lucky I am to have found the boys at all, much less have them here with me now. I keep telling myself that that might have to be enough."

She swallowed thickly. "That I'll have to be strong for them when all our luck runs out and try to be thankful for what we have."

"Bullshit."

Ginny blinked.

"Sometimes you think too much." The flash of white teeth removed the sting from what Lindsay had said.

Despite herself, Ginny grinned. "You have quite a way with words, Lindsay Killian. You know that?"

"Don't I though?" Her hand moved to the soft, warm skin of Ginny's slender throat. She longed to kiss it, but was afraid once she snuggled that close and closed her eyes she'd pass out from exhaustion before she could do anything else.

As if Ginny had read her mind, she lay back flat on the bed and lifted an arm. "C'mere."

"Nuh uh," Lindsay whispered. "You come here." Lindsay lay back and opened her arms in invitation. Ginny scooted forward, gladly melting into the comforting embrace.

Twin sighs of pure contentment sounded in the dark room as two sets of eyelids fluttered shut. "Ginny?"

"Mmm?"

"If your luck runs out, you will have to be strong. But just when you think you can't be strong anymore, I'll be there to make up the difference. Together we can be as strong as we need to be." Lindsay felt Ginny's ribs expand as she sucked in a breath. "Does that sound all right?"

The sweetest of kisses was her answer.

Their lips lingered there, neither woman wanting the moment to end. Then, because it seemed so natural that she never even considered doing anything else Ginny parted her lips and welcomed Lindsay's gently probing, hot tongue into her mouth.

They both moaned as their kisses turned hungry; and Lindsay carefully rolled atop Ginny, their naked legs tangling together. Blinking dazedly, she pulled away long enough to look at Ginny's eyes and hoarsely said, "I thought you said we were going to be to sleep?"

Ginny's face flushed with desire. Her nostrils flared, as the heat pouring off Lindsay's body dripped down on her and melted over her like hot wax, infusing every inch of her with delicious warmth. "I think I lied," she said unrepentantly, arching up and softly kissing Lindsay's tender throat. Then, ever so briefly and unseen by Lindsay, her brow furrowed in question as she considered that Lindsay might be too tired for them to continue. "Is that okay?"

Lindsay's voice dropped an octave lower than normal. "It's perfect." With butterflies stirring in her belly, Lindsay slowly drew a hand up Ginny's leg and let it rest on a warm, naked thigh. When Ginny smiled and welcomed the touch by shifting to give her better access, she gave the supple flesh a little squeeze; then used only her fingertips to trace around Ginny's navel.

Ginny sucked in a breath at the unexpectedly sensual touch.

The eroticism of their moment sang through Lindsay, making her feel slightly dizzy with anticipation and need. She thought of saying something more, of telling Ginny just how much she was feeling. How a dozen different emotions were bubbling up inside her; and how every single one seemed hell bent on bursting free at the exact same time. But the sensation of soft lips dancing lightly across her skin was making it hard to do much more than groan softly and pray this would never end.

With a soft kiss on her partner's throbbing jugular, Ginny left Lindsay's neck, and allowed her head sink back down onto the fluffy down-filled pillow. She reached up and stroked Lindsay's cheek with her knuckles. She was nervous and excited, but felt very loved and safe. And as she looked up into the eyes that were swimming with emotion, holding nothing back, she knew with a bone deep certainty that this was utterly right. That *they* were right together.

"I want to feel and see more of you," Lindsay murmured, tugging at the hem of Ginny's nightshirt; then glancing up into her eyes in question.

"Yes." Ginny swallowed and nodded. "I want that, too. And to see you." Nightshirts were eagerly tossed aside; and their bodies came together in an explosion of sweet sensation, and softly muttered words of encouragement. They kissed well into the night, losing track of time completely and not caring a bit. When Lindsay's ribs finally began to cry in protest; they shifted their bodies until they were lying side-by-side, facing each other, delighted to find their mouths free to roam and explore unhampered.

Emboldened by the throaty groan of pleasure that escaped Lindsay's lips and by her own desires, Ginny allowed her fingers to skim across an inner thigh and dangerously close to the apex of Lindsay's legs. She was about to go farther still when a hand reached down and long fingers wrapped around her wrist. Ginny's hand froze, and she quickly searched Lindsay's face, worried that she'd done something wrong or gone too far. But her heart resumed beating when a warm, sensual grin eased its way across Lindsay's lips; and her hand was gently urged forward by the subtlest of movements.

Ginny's eyes darkened further and she hesitantly allowed her fingers to rake through soft, drenched curls. "Does that feel good?" she whispered, a little taken aback by her own body's devastating response to what she was doing. There was a vague aching in her breasts, and a not so vague aching between her legs.

Lindsay could hardly speak. Of their own accord, her hips bucked forward, trying to force more contact. Her heart was threatening to pound out of her chest. "Very," she finally croaked.

They took their time, fumbling occasionally; but mostly smiling or moaning in gratification, as they teased and tasted their way toward learning new, wonderful things about each other and themselves.

When they finally came to rest, a fine layer of sweat covered cooling, softly panting bodies. Exhausted, Lindsay lay her head on Ginny's stomach, her pounding heart straining the confines of her chest. She wrapped her arm around the younger woman's slim waist as Ginny traced lazy patterns on the slick skin of her back.

Ginny's other arm was thrown over her eyes, her breathing still a little rough as her body blissfully floated down from a dizzying height. "Lindsay," she sighed when she could summon the strength to speak. "I—"

Lindsay's breathing hitched and a warm tear snaked its way onto Ginny's belly.

Red eyebrows drew together. "Hey," Ginny cooed gently, worry coloring her tone. "What's wrong, honey?"

Lindsay sat up a little and wordlessly shook her head too overwhelmed to answer Ginny's question.

Ginny scooted down in the bed, pushing aside damp sheets as she went; and not stopping until their faces were only a few inches apart. She swallowed thickly when she saw tears shining in Lindsay's dark eyes.

"Please tell me what's wrong." Ginny's stomach clenched at the idea that what they'd shared hadn't been the same satisfying, magical experience for Lindsay that it had been for her. Hot tears gathered in her own eyes as she repeated her question; expecting Lindsay to be embarrassed and turn away from her as she had on the other rare occasions she'd seen her friend cry. But this time was different.

Unashamed, Lindsay looked her squarely in the eye as she spoke, the intensity nearly taking Ginny's breath away. "I didn't think it would be like that," she whispered. She recalled Ginny saying those same words after their first kiss; and felt that same sense of awe and wonderment overtake her.

As gently as she could, Ginny used her lips to wipe Lindsay's cheeks.

"Neither did I," she admitted. "But I think—" For a moment she struggled with the right words herself. But when she found them, her voice was fervent. "I think it was *beautiful. You* are beautiful."

Without warning, Lindsay pulled Ginny into a crushing embrace so tight she wasn't sure where her skin stopped and Ginny's began. She let out a ragged breath, and buried her face in Ginny's hair. "You're more beautiful." Then she moved her lips to Ginny's ear, and gently whispered, "I love you so much it hurts."

Making love with Ginny had easily been the most intense experience of her life; and she felt as overwhelmed as she did sated. "You make me feel *everything*."

Ginny nodded. Understanding completely, she sniffed, not wanting to cry when she felt this wonderful. She turned her head and softly brushed her mouth against Lindsay's cheek, releasing a soft sigh. "You make me feel like that too. Like the feelings are so strong they're going to swallow me up. And that's a little scary. But at the same time, I feel so glorious I don't ever want it to stop."

Lindsay sniffed and closed her eyes. That was it exactly. "I've never been this happy," she murmured, hugging Ginny again. "I guess I don't know how to act." A smile tugged at Ginny's lips. "Well, neither do I. So I guess I won't be able to tell if you're doing it wrong, will I?"

A burst of laughter exploded from Lindsay, and any lingering anxiety she felt slid into perspective; then melted away in the face of the devotion being offered to her so freely. Life with Ginny was going to be so much fun. "I guess we'll figure things out as we go then."

"Mmm." Something suddenly occurred to Ginny, and the words were out before she realized she'd even said them. "I didn't expect you touching me to be so different from the times I've touch—" She stopped when she heard her own voice. "Oh, Lord." Despite what they'd just shared, her face began to heat wildly; and she knew Lindsay could feel it when the body plastered to hers began to shake with silent laughter.

"You don't have to be embarrassed about that. I don't believe you'll get hairy palms or go insane. Much."

"Very funny." But now Ginny was fighting to keep from laughing herself; and she knew her face was flaming.

Lindsay grinned recklessly, her normal confidence very much back in place. "And you're right. Tonight didn't feel like that the times I touched myself either. If touching myself felt like this, I—"

"Wouldn't need me?" Ginny interrupted playfully, her heart full to bursting. Lindsay pulled away enough to look Ginny in the eye; then, just because she could, she leaned forward and began nibbling at the corner of Ginny's mouth earning a soft groan as Ginny tasted herself on her partner's lips.

"I'd still need you," Lindsay answered after a long moment of exploration. "In fact, I'd need you to carry me around wherever we went. Because I wouldn't be able to walk"—A beat—"or lift my right arm."

Ginny burst out laughing, her skin coloring even more. "Lindsay!"

"Well, it's true!"

"Oh, I don't doubt that." Her expression suddenly went very serious. "I love you terribly, Lindsay." She gave the other woman a dreamy look. "You do know that, right?"

Lindsay swallowed hard and lovingly ran her fingers through Ginny's hair, the faint light streaming in the window casting her lover's face in mysterious shadows, and staining her pale eyes an enchanted violet. She couldn't help but smile. "It's the one thing I do know."

Leaving Troy, Alabama, was a bittersweet experience. Both Lindsay and Ginny found themselves liking the homey feel of the Southern town; despite the presence of Milo Porter, who, Trudy had discovered, was claiming the boy had run away from home and he was relieved to be rid of the lad. Folks seemed to know it was a lie, but they let Milo retain what was left of his dignity and didn't push the issue. And for whatever reason, the man decided to accept James's departure, and go about his own business.

Edith reminded Ginny of her own grandmother, who had passed away so many years ago. Her promise to keep in touch with the elderly sisters had been a genuine one; and she vowed to deposit letters indicating their progress in the towns they passed. When they were just about to board the train, Edith pressed a five-dollar gold piece in Ginny's hand, refusing to take no for an answer. She'd assured Ginny it was no financial hardship for her; and that it would help to ease her conscience for the small part she and Trudy had played in James's living in Troy in the first place.

Ginny knew it was a gift, plain and simple, because she and Edith had grown so close. Her thank you had gone on for several long seconds until both women were crying, as Trudy and Lindsay looked uncomfortably on.

While the two women shared a tearful goodbye, Trudy pulled Lindsay aside and gave her a five-dollar coin of her own, explaining in hushed tones that she knew the girl would need the money for her family. She gave Lindsay a knowing smile and rolled her eyes. She explained that Edith, her beloved but painfully unaware sister, still didn't understand why Trudy remained a spinster and insisted on spending all her free time with the lovely Widow Brown. In life, she explained drolly, allies were a precious thing, especially unexpected ones with healthy bank accounts.

Lindsay couldn't help but agree.

As repayment Trudy only asked that someday, when she was able, Lindsay would pass along a small kindness to another struggling young woman like her. And although Lindsay had a tough time believing there could be two people like her, she accepted Trudy's words, and gift, graciously. Lindsay laughed and gave her word, something that was starting to mean something on this new path she was happily wandering. She liked that.

Three days later…

James and Lewis stepped off the train in Opelousas, Louisiana. It was far too warm to wear their coats; and the boys had tied them around their waists as they moved through the depot with Lindsay and Ginny trailing behind them.

The foursome had spent a day traveling and then searching in Hattiesburg, Mississippi; only to find out that the baby girl, who had been adopted from the recent orphan train from New York City, was another child entirely. It had been a bitter disappointment and the first one of its kind that Ginny had faced with her brothers; their night in a small boarding house room wasn't a pleasant one.

To Lindsay's surprise, it was James who had been inconsolable. He was the last of the family to be with the chubby baby, and felt a crushing guilt about not being able to keep her with him. Though he swore he'd fought the Wards' employees tooth and nail when they tried to separate them. One look in the boy's stormy eyes, and there was no doubt that he was telling the God's truth.

As they stepped onto Bellevue Street, a man with an olive complexion and a head full of black curls stepped in front of the boys to stop their progress, but addressed Ginny and Lindsay. "Pardon." As an afterthought he yanked his hat from his head. "Is one of you ladies Virginia Chisholm?" His French accent was so thick that Lindsay couldn't understand a single word. Ginny, after spending months on Orchard Street where English-speaking, American-born citizens were a minority, had gotten fairly good at deciphering a variety of foreign lilts.

"I am. It's a pleasure to meet you." She smiled brightly at the man, surprising Lindsay, who was throwing him her most suspicious glare.

"Christian," she whispered to Lindsay without moving her lips. "Telegram."

"Oh. Gotcha," Lindsay whispered out of the corner of her mouth, visibly relaxing.

"Enchanté. My name is Emile Boucher." An enormous smile stretched his bearded cheeks. He was a huge man, easily six-and-a-half-feet tall and two hundred and seventy five pounds. "I have been checking the depot every afternoon for two weeks! And finally, you are here. Mr. Spence from New York sent a cable saying you might be here soon. I help place the children. Come." He ushered them all to his waiting wagon, and launched into an explanation of his and his wife Marie's involvement with the orphans; and how they found homes for Catholic boys and girls.

Sometime late that afternoon he pulled the wagon to a stop in front of Chenard's Bed & Breakfast. It was on a quiet residential street, well away from what little traffic there was in Opelousas, but still within walking distance of the depot. The man's face conveyed his true regret. "I'm sorry that is all I can tell you. We were able to find homes for a teenage girl and two little boys from the orphan train," he added sadly, not knowing what else to say.

Ginny was nearly beside herself, but she managed a polite goodbye. "You have my thanks, Emile. It would have taken us hours and hours to find out what you were able to tell us over lunch."

"Au revoir, Ginny." He turned and tipped his hat to Lindsay as she stepped down off the buckboard. "And good bye to you, green vegetable girl."

Lindsay grunted an acknowledgment as she offered Lewis, then Ginny a hand down. James jumped down on his own.

"Merci," Ginny said.

The big man nodded and grinned brightly. With a sharp whistle and a crack of the reins he started up his team.

They all watched for a moment as he drove away.

Then Lewis, James, and Lindsay all turned incredulous eyes on Ginny—and stared.

"What?" she asked, throwing her hands in the air. "Have I grown a horn on my forehead?"

Lindsay cocked her head to the side. "No. But since when do you speak French?" She herself knew curse words in several different languages, but that was about it. English was bad enough.

"Yeah," the boys echoed. "Where'd you learn that?" Lewis asked curiously.

Ginny rolled her eyes. "For Goodness sake, I don't *really* speak French." She pointed at her brothers. "You know that. All I can say is thank you. I bought our bread from Mrs. DuBois's bakery every single day. Did you think I never thanked her for it?" Her voice was rising, and she didn't try to stop it. "You know I don't speak French!"

Both boys took a step backward, their eyes wide. Then they glanced at Ginny again and back at each other, before taking another step backward. They could tell she was about to fall apart; and neither boy wanted to witness it. Ginny was always strong, and the thought of seeing her truly upset had them quaking inside.

"Where do you boys think you're going?" Ginny snapped, stomping her foot in the dirt, and letting their travel bag fall from her hand. "I'm still talking to you."

Lindsay's eyebrows shot straight up. *Oh, boy.* "Umm… Ginny?" She took a tentative step forward, a big part of her envying the boys the fact that they were getting ready to make a break for it.

Ginny's face began to crumble. "Mama always said we should say thank you." She promptly burst into tears, spinning around and presenting her brothers and Lindsay with her shaking back.

The boys both stood there helplessly, nervously shuffling their feet, their eyes darting from Ginny to Lindsay; and begging the rail-rider to do something. *Anything.*

Lindsay calmly handed James her five-dollar coin, and jerked her thumb toward the bed and breakfast door. "Go get us a room. We'll be inside in a minute."

The boys didn't have to be told twice. They tripped all over themselves running up the walk, but had the good grace to throw a worried glance back at their sister before disappearing.

"Don't lose the rest of that money or I'll kill you," Lindsay called after them. Gingerly, she approached Ginny and laid a hand on her shoulder. She barely had a chance to make contact before Ginny whirled around and pulled her into a desperate embrace.

"I'm sorry. I didn't mean to yell. I don't know wh-what's wrong with me."

"I do," Lindsay said very softly. "You're upset and worried." *Damn that Emile.* The news he'd given them about Jane was worse than not finding her at all. Emile had explained that the child appeared to have a severe case of the croup, and that no prospective parents would risk adoption with her so ill. Nobody wanted to bury a child they barely knew.

Ginny's cheeks were wet and her nose was running. "Sh-she's really sick." She sucked in an uneven breath. "He s-said so. Nobody would take her. What kind of people could turn away a sick child?"

Plenty of people. Most people. Lindsay sighed, her mind spinning as she considered what she could say or do that would make this better. She came up dry. "I know, honey." She tightened her hold on Ginny, feeling the soft cries turn to sobs as the redhead let go of some of the pent up frustration that had steadily been building. It wasn't the place Lindsay would have picked for it to happen, but she had accepted long ago that some things in life plowed full speed ahead whether the timing was convenient or not.

They'd all gotten their hopes up in Hattiesburg when the description of one of the children adopted out so closely matched Jane's. "Emile saw her weeks ago. She's probably fine by now."

"Or de-dead," Ginny stuttered between sobs. *Just like Mama and Alice and Helen and Arthur. Oh, God.*

Lindsay closed her eyes. *Damn.* "It's possible, Ginny. I won't lie and say it's not. Though I wish I could," she whispered into the ear near her lips.

Ginny's head was pounding, and her stomach was a solid knot of tension. "Lewis had it wh-when he was a baby and he… he nearly died."

"But it doesn't do any good for you to think like that."

Ginny barked out a watery laugh, still clinging to Lindsay. "Since when did you become all ch-cheerful and optimistic?"

"Since you started to cry."

Ginny's lips twitched into a reluctant smile. "It will be okay," she said softly, as much for herself as for Lindsay.

"It will." Lindsay did something she rarely did. She sent out a little prayer for Jane Robson and the people who loved her. As far as Lindsay was concerned, finding the toddler too late was not going to happen. She wouldn't let it.

"What shit hole are we in today?" Albert asked Bo as they walked the streets of Troy, Alabama.

"Who cares? They all look the same."

Albert had spent several days in a jail in Atlanta for disorderly conduct when he'd tried to pick a man's pocket. Unfortunately, the man thought that Albert was trying to grope him; he promptly had Rat Face arrested. Fortunately, he had been too embarrassed to testify that a man had squeezed his ass. So after three days of incarceration, Albert was set free and told get the hell out of town or risk being strung up for being a pervert.

Ignoring the warning, Albert and Bo had stayed in town another night; each winning a dollar and change when they happened across a friendly neighborhood cockfight.

Today, they arrived in Troy with one thing on their minds. A drink. The temperatures were moderate, but hours in a stuffy boxcar had left them feeling as though they'd been chewing on sawdust. Albert resolved to kill Lindsay after he had a beer. And Bo could hardly argue with a shift of priorities like that.

Albert's face had healed to something close to respectable, if you were a boxer, and it was with a pocket full of change that he and Bo stepped into Smokey's saloon. The place was nearly empty, except for a sour-looking man who sat near the piano in the back corner. He was restlessly rolling an empty shot glass in one shaky hand, and had an oddly short leg propped up on a chair.

Albert's gaze met the stranger's, and they both nodded slowly, warily. It was a case of like meeting like. Trouble meeting trouble. He smiled crookedly and jabbed his elbow into Bo's mid-section. "I think I've found someone to beat the hell out of at craps."

Bo looked at Milo and winced. It had been a long time since he'd seen someone seedier than Rat Face.

It was going to be a long night.

The next day…

The people of Texas were just as the boys had imagined they'd be: men in tall hats, wearing denim pants and vests; and some with six-shooters strapped to their legs. They spotted the occasional Indian, who much to the boys' disappointment, did not wear a full feather headdress, have their face covered in war paint, or carry a blood-dripping tomahawk.

Their time in Tyler, Texas, with its unexpected towering oaks and rolling pastures, was a complete bust. While it was on the list of towns where the train was meant to visit, apparently the stop had been cancelled due to lack of interest. They were in town all of ten minutes before they found this out, and were forced to stay the night to wait for the next outbound train.

The weather was mild, and in order to save money they decided to camp next to a pond at the edge of a ranch that lay on the outskirts of town.

At dusk, the boys discovered catfish swimming lazily in the clear pond water. They had nothing to rig a pole with; and after trying unsuccessfully to use their shirts as fishing nets—which earned them each a swat on the behind from Ginny—they realized they had absolutely no talent as fishermen.

"But we're hungry!" Lewis complained after Ginny warned him away from the water for the twentieth time.

"Mother hen." Lindsay snorted. "Cluck… cluuuuuuuuuck."

Ginny stuck her tongue out at Lindsay, smiling at the boy's squeals of delighted laughter. She was determined to enjoy this evening. To the boys tonight was a grand adventure.

James was coming around slowly but steadily, and she suspected that Lindsay easing her way into his heart had a lot to do with that. She wasn't about to spoil this night for them with dark thoughts and worries. There would be time enough for that tomorrow. Besides, today was her birthday; a fact she was surprised that both her brothers had remembered. And they were doing their best to make the evening special.

"No," she corrected with a grin. "I'm not a mother hen. I just happen to know that water is freezing cold, and that James and Lewis whine and holler like a tom cat getting an unexpected bath if you put them in cold water."

"Hey!" they cried.

"I do not," James insisted, but he was smiling at Ginny. Lewis was smiling too, and Lindsay suspected they were all sharing the same fond memory.

"And," Ginny continued after a moment, "I happen to know that none of us are going to catch one of those ugly fish." She gestured toward the pond dismissively, and sat down on the log next to Lindsay, whose gangly legs were stretched out comfortably in front of her. "The closest we've come to a live fish is the morning catch at fishmonger Pisciolio's stand."

"I'll bet Lindsay could do it," Lewis supplied helpfully.

James narrowed his eyes in thought, but was forced to agree. Lindsay did plenty of things he'd never seen a girl do before. Why should this be any different? "Yeah," he agreed resolutely. "She could catch a fish. She doesn't sound like she's from New York. So she's from the country," he reasoned.

Lindsay turned round eyes on James. "And since I'm not from New York City that automatically means I can fish?"

"I'd say so," Lewis piped up.

"Ahh… that's right." Ginny laughed. "You're from Pennsylvania. I'll bet you Quaker country girl types have lots of hidden talents." Haughtily, she began ticking off on her fingers. "Quilt making; oh, definitely canning; and butter churning; and—"

"Making pies?" James exclaimed hopefully, his mouth watering at the thought.

Lewis sniggered. "Don't we wish."

Lindsay's mouth worked several times, but nothing came out. Finally she blurted, "Country girl?" She pointed at her toes and then drew her index finger up the length of her body. "Do I look like a country girl?" She folded her arms across her chest, and tapped her foot as she waited

Her question was met with three innocent nods.

Ginny's eyes twinkled. She only managed to keep a straight face by biting her lower lip. *Gotcha, gorgeous.* "Let's see what you can do."

Lindsay's eyebrow jumped at the playful challenge in Ginny's voice. She loved seeing her this way, and would gladly make a fool of herself ten times over for a repeat of that sweet smile. "Fine," Lindsay shot back, lifting her chin and stalking over to the pond to peer down doubtfully. "Hey." She blinked a few times and pointed. "I can actually see one."

"Very good, Lindsay," Ginny said dryly, winking at the boys.

"Shut up, Yankee," Lindsay teased, using the taunt that she and Ginny had been subjected to everyday since they crossed the Mason-Dixon Line. Never mind that she was one too. Lindsay rubbed her hands together in anticipation. "I don't even need a pole. I can just reach in and grab one."

Ginny's eyebrows rose, but she remained respectfully silent as her friend tried time and time again. Once Lindsay actually managed to get hold of a fish, but the enormous, slimy beast flapped around in her hands, spraying her with water; and causing her to scream in disgust and terror and drop him back into the pond.

"Aww… Shit!"

Ginny fell backward off the log, holding her stomach as she exploded into laughter.

"I'm not sharing my fish with any of you. Not a single bite, so don't even think of asking."

Ginny's laughter finally died down enough so that she could speak. Lewis and James had gotten tired of standing alongside the dark-haired woman at the pond and had sprawled out on the bedrolls they'd purchased in Tyler. "Lindsay." Ginny chuckled, still lying flat on her back. "C'mon and sit down." She was actually feeling a little bad for teasing her so, but that didn't erase the silly grin on her face. "I have some food in our bag. We won't starve. Come relax."

"No," Lindsay answered stubbornly. "Leave me alone. I'm busy."

"Don't be silly."

"I am not—ooo… hello, beautiful." Lindsay spotted what she hoped was soon to be their dinner, and leaned way over, reaching out as far as she could.

Ginny propped herself up on her elbows, and shook her head knowingly. "You'd better be care—"

"I'm almost… there… just a little more… Yes!" Victorious, Lindsay yanked the fish out of the water and lost her balance. "Whoa!" The fish slipped through her hands, and to the background of the hooting, cheering boys and Ginny's nearly hysterical laughter, she ended up taking an unexpected swim.

Hours later, she found herself warm and comfortable in an old shirt she was using as her nightshirt, with her clothes drying near a crackling fire. Ginny was fitted snuggly against her under their shared blanket; and she greedily drank in the scent of wood smoke and grass as she gazed into a sky bright with twinkling stars. The boys' quiet snores filled the small campsite; and the women shared gentle kisses, tender murmured words and wishes, as shooting stars streaked above.

It was, Lindsay decided, damn near perfect. But there was one more Robson yet to find, and she knew without a doubt what Ginny's last, silent wish had been for.

"Thank you for tonight," Ginny whispered, dropping a kiss on Lindsay's throat, and closing her eyes. "It was a wonderful birthday. And a wonderful night."

A satisfied smile eased over Lindsay's face. "You're welcome." She wanted to thank Ginny for the same thing, and for tomorrow night too, and all the tomorrows after that. She was about to tell her that very thing when she heard Ginny's breathing even out and her soft snores joined her brothers'.

Lindsay realized that the moment had passed, but she knew she'd hold it close to her heart always. She let out a deep breath and thought of the possibilities her future now held. The ones the stars overhead hadn't bothered to divulge on the many nights she'd stared at them from a moving boxcar—alone. She grinned at the sky and whispered, "You've been holding out on me."

She closed her eyes, and let the peacefulness of the campsite sweep over her, and carry her into a deep, satisfying slumber.

Three days later…

Ft. Worth and Waco—two more stops; two more failures. Endless conversations, tears, and reassurances later and they still had nothing to show for their searching. In Waco, the dusty cow town they'd just come from, no one even remembered an orphan fitting Jane's description being among the children from the train. And Ginny was left to wonder if she'd missed Jane in one of the towns they'd already searched. Her darker thoughts hinted at something worse, but now it was just past sunrise, and the new day was ripe with possibilities.

There were several wagons waiting for the train's passengers as it rumbled across the wooden bridge that spanned the rushing San Marcos River. Lindsay and Ginny waited patiently until the train pulled away before leaving the platform, in case Christian had sent word ahead.

Lewis and James each took turns using the station's outhouse before slowly padding back to their sister. They hated sleeping on the train, but it was the best way to assure they'd have a full day to search in San Marcos.

There were only two more cities on the orphan train's route. None of them mentioned this fact, but it was never very far from Ginny and Lindsay's minds.

"I'm starving," James informed his sister. "Can we get something for breakfast?"

Ginny reached down and ruffled his brown hair. "Sure. It's a little too early to get much done. Let's see what we can find."

There were several horses tethered in front of a small restaurant, just down the road from the station. The smell of frying bacon sent the boys running ahead to locate its source.

Lewis anxiously peered through the clean glass window. "Can we?"

Lindsay and Ginny exchanged glances. "I dunno," Ginny said doubtfully. "It looks sort of expensive. How about we try something from the store?"

The children groaned, but were over the disappointment quickly and took off down the street, looking for the nearest store that was likely to sell food. Finding one quickly, they pressed their faces to the glass and stared inside. They saw the proprietress dusting off the shelves inside, and, despite the "closed" sign on the door, the woman waved the boys in. Lindsay started to follow.

Ginny stopped her with a hand on her arm. "Pick out something good," she said, yawning. "I'm gonna stretch my legs. I think all this sitting is doing something irreversible to my rump." She rubbed her bottom ruefully.

Lindsay looked at the body part in questioned and grinned roguishly. "Looks pretty good from where I'm standing."

Ginny's nose wrinkled as she smiled. "Go inside before the boys break something, and we have to stay and work off the debt." She made a shooing motion with both hands. "Hurry."

"Okay." Lindsay laughed, and disappeared into the store.

Ginny smiled when she heard a faint "Hey, don't touch that!" as the door closed. Blue eyes took in her surroundings. "Where to start?" she mumbled, walking a short way down the street. "Courthouse maybe? Church?"

Two men on horseback tipped their hats at her as they rode past, making her glad she'd changed into her dress on the train. It wasn't long until her stomach growled fiercely, reminding her it was time to head back to the store.

A few yards in front of her Lindsay emerged from the mercantile with an odd look on her face.

"What'd you find?" Ginny asked, hoping the boys hadn't actually broken anything. "Something good to eat? Biscuits maybe?" She grinned. "Seems like they eat those with every meal in this state."

Lindsay licked her lips and swallowed, walking out to meet Ginny. "Umm… Not exactly."

"Lindsay?" The blood drained from Ginny's face as she got a good look at Lindsay's expression. Something wasn't right. "What—?"

"We found Jane."

Chapter Fifteen

It took a few seconds for Lindsay's words to penetrate Ginny's brain. When they finally did, her jaw sagged.

Lindsay stepped forward and placed her index finger under Ginny's chin. A grin pulled at her lips as she lifted her finger, clicking shut Ginny's open mouth.

"Don't catch flies."

Irritated, Ginny pulled her face away from Lindsay. "Wh-what did you say? Say it again."

There was a look of guarded hopefulness in those light eyes that nearly made Lindsay forget where she was and pull Ginny into her arms and kiss away every doubt that still lingered there. "Ginny," she softened her voice, and gently grasped biceps so tense they felt like bands of steel. "We found your sister. She's inside the store… with the boys." Lindsay gave what she hoped was a reassuring smile. "Jane seems fine; she was laughing when I left."

"I… I can't…" Ginny blinked a few times. "I can't believe it," she whispered, looking away, her gaze a little unfocused. "She can't just be in the store." Ginny shook her head. "Not after all this time."

Lindsay couldn't believe Ginny was still standing there after what she'd just told her. *She's in shock, I guess.* "I know. It doesn't seem possible. But it's true."

Tear-filled, disbelieving eyes glistened in the morning sun as they swung up to meet Lindsay's. Ginny's voice dropped to the barest of broken whispers. "She's alive?"

"God, yes." Lindsay tenderly laid her palm against Ginny's cheek. "She's beautiful and looks just like you," she marveled, gently tucking a strand of wind-blown red hair behind Ginny's ear. "Only with blonde hair."

With a shaking hand, Ginny reached out and ran her fingers through the ends of Lindsay's hair. "When I was younger I had blonde ha—" Then, as though exploding out of mental fog, Ginny gasped and her eyes went round. "I have to go inside!" She pulled away from Lindsay, and bolted for the door, not bothering to look as she called out, "C'mon. What are you waiting for?"

Lindsay laughed, the action causing a sting of pain in ribs she was beginning to think would never heal, and hurried to catch up with the blur of motion in front of her. "Now that's more like it."

Ginny pushed open the door, the scent of tobacco and leather rolling over her. Her gaze frantically flicked around the store. This early, there were no other customers, and in the very back, by a rack of saddle supplies, she spotted James and Lewis on their knees, their backs to her.

Standing next to James was a smiling young couple. The man and woman looked to be in their late twenties, and were dressed in a store-bought, dark suit and dress. They were speaking animatedly to the children, their faces wreathed with broad grins.

Ginny took a step deeper into the store. "Boys?"

Two heads snapped around at the sound of Ginny's voice. Both boys were smiling wildly, and they jumped to their feet and dashed over to Ginny, flinging themselves at her in their exuberance.

James's hat fell off as he wrapped his arms around Ginny, forgetting that he was supposed to be mad at her. "We found her!"

Ginny smiled lovingly at his bright face, its unbridled joy making her heart swell. "That's just how happy I felt when I finally found you."

Her arm tightened around him, conveying the same warmth and affection she'd given him his entire life. "Really?" he asked, eyes wide as he studied Ginny's face intently.

Ginny's vision swam as she regarded the boy pressed tightly against her. "Really, honey."

Undone by the simple action and words, he buried his face in her dress and began to cry.

Bewildered, Lewis stared at his brother. *Why is he crying? This is happy, not sad. We found Jane!*

Ginny, however, understood completely. "Oh, James," she whispered brokenly, knowing that somehow she'd finally gotten through the anger that had clung to him like a leech ever since the fire, and wondering at his bizarre timing. Her other arm encircled him, and she pressed her cheek against the top of his head. "It's all going to be okay," she soothed, feeling his small body shake against hers. "I promise."

Through all this the couple stood quietly by, not completely sure what was happening, but somehow it didn't seem right to interrupt.

Lewis, however, showed no such restraint. "She's here!" He began excitedly pointing, growing impatient with his brother and Ginny's odd behavior. "Look, Ginny! Jane's not sick anymore. She got well!"

Ginny pressed her lips into James's hair before lifting her head and gazing across the room.

A small blonde head poked its way out from behind the woman's skirt, and Ginny's knees felt weak.

A warm hand, whose touch her body knew, came to rest in the center of Ginny's back, and for a second she leaned into the touch. "Lindsay?" She looked pleadingly at Lindsay, who immediately began helping her gently pry James from her body.

"C'mere," Lindsay encouraged softly, smiling when the boy wrapped himself around her, and continued to sob out weeks of angry frustration and disappointment. She used the other hand to corral an ecstatic Lewis; then held her breath as Ginny crossed the room. As an afterthought, she let go of Lewis just long enough to reach behind her and slide the heavy lock into place.

No interruptions.

Ginny glanced hesitantly at the man and woman standing quietly by, keeping a close eye on Jane. She assumed they were the adoptive parents.

The woman was tall and slim, her red hair was several shades darker than Ginny's and she had pale, lightly freckled skin. She wore a bright blue dress with a pale blue apron to cover it. In one hand the woman held a feather duster, with her other she gently stroked the back of Jane's head. *She must work here.* The idle thought crossed Ginny's mind.

The man was husky and about the same height as the woman, Ginny supposed was his wife. Clean-shaven, and wearing pressed trousers and a white linen shirt and tie, he managed to look comfortable yet dignified.

"I'm Laura Gable." The woman indicated the man standing to her left. "And this is my husband Calvin." She smiled. "I think you know everyone else here." Laura smiled cautiously. "You must be the sister those cute boys were carrying on about."

Lewis blushed, and James wiped at his wet cheeks with this sleeve, a sheepish look flitting across his face.

"I can't believe she has family." Laura glanced down at Jane, who was busily chewing her fingers, her big blue eyes fastened on her sister. "How perfectly wonderful for Jane." An unexpected scattering of tears fell when she blinked. "We thought she was alone in the world."

Calvin laid a hand on his wife's shoulder; and Ginny caught the gentle squeeze he gave it.

The lump in her throat was making it hard to breathe, and Ginny had to swallow several times before she could speak. She was pretty sure she was about to burst into tears, so she decided to save introductions to the Gables until later. She dropped down on the hardwood floor in front of the toddler, her eyes brimming with tears. "Jane, honey?" Another swallow. "It's me."

Jane's apprehensive expression made Ginny's stomach churn; and suddenly she was glad she hadn't had an opportunity to eat breakfast yet. She tried to coax her sister out with her voice. "It's me, sweetie. Ginny." Out of habit, she held her arms out, her heart pounding as the very real possibility of rejection slammed home with devastating force.

Jane stood her ground, carefully looking at Ginny, but not moving.

She can't have forgotten me already, Ginny's mind anguished. *It hasn't been that long, has it? Oh, God.*

Lindsay felt a little lightheaded after holding her breath for so long. It was like watching two trains on the same track, heading straight for one another. Soon all there would be was carnage. Her heart was in her throat, and with every passing second that Jane remained mostly hidden behind Laura Gable's skirt, the tension in the room ratcheted up another excruciating notch.

Ginny told herself this was silly. What could she expect? Jane was just a baby, she would surely grow used to her again as quickly as she'd apparently forgotten her—but it still felt like a knife had been buried in her chest and someone was twisting it. Slowly.

Devastated, she began to lower her arms; her breathing hitched, and her eyes began to burn. "Jane," she whispered. "You have to know me… Remember?" *I was there when you were born. I held you right then, before Arthur even.*

Jane's eyes suddenly lit with recognition, and a happy grin curled her pink, wet lips. "Gin-neee!" she warbled happily.

Lindsay's eyes closed, and she sucked in an enormous breath. "Thank you, God," she mumbled, feeling Lewis and James begin breathing again as well. Unceremoniously, she plunked down on her bottom, taking the boys right along with her as Ginny scooped the baby into her arms.

"Jane!" The redhead squeezed her sister as tightly as she dared. Her eyes were screwed shut, but that didn't stem the tide of hot tears streaming down her cheeks.

The little girl laughed and placed a sloppy kiss on Ginny's mouth.

"It's about time," James grumbled, his own eyes still red and teary.

Lindsay's attention was drawn unerringly back to her friend and the reunion Ginny had been dreaming of. James was right. "No shit," she finally answered, hearing the boys' muffled snorts at her choice of words. She sighed happily, an unconscious smile tweaking her lips when she saw Jane give Ginny another enormous, wet kiss. "No shit."

Lindsay and Ginny allowed their clasped hands to swing gently between them as they walked along the dirt road in the quiet neighborhood where the Gables' large home sat. Lindsay had been more than pleased when Ginny informed her that it was quite common and acceptable for female friends to hold hands in public; and she found herself reveling in this simple, loving gesture.

The warm wind and sun caressed their faces, and the fabric of Ginny's dress, and Lindsay's shirt. Jane was walking along in front of them, and they both gazed down at her as she explored while they talked. The early evening sun was hanging low in the sky, splashing the horizon and the tops of the juniper trees with shades of indigo and crimson.

It, by all accounts, had been a gorgeous day.

The Gables had offered them use of two rooms in their home until they could make plans for the future, and everyone seemed happier than Ginny could remember.

Their bellies were full, and they'd freshly scrubbed the day's worth of sweat and grime from their bodies. Even their clothes were clean, having been washed by Laura while they bathed, and then quickly dried in the warm breeze.

Lindsay took a deep breath and gathered her thoughts. "B-ba-bat. B—A—T."

"Yes!" Ginny crowed, letting go of their joined hands so she could slap her partner on the back. "You did it again."

Jane turned around to see what the shouting was about.

Ginny waggled her fingers at the toddler, who mirrored the gesture before quickly being distracted by a tall weed.

Lindsay's face lit up. "Really?"

Ginny beamed. *You're learning so quickly, Lindsay.* Ginny had been teaching Lindsay to read for weeks, using a single, many times folded sheet of newsprint they kept in their bag. But Lindsay had memorized the articles long ago, and so they were trying something else.

"Really," she confirmed. She cocked her head in question, the breeze blowing her hair back and away from her heart-shaped face. "Another?"

Lindsay stopped and licked her lips nervously. She rocked back on her heels, tempted to stop while she was on a roll. She'd never gotten three words in a row right before. "Okay," she said hesitantly. "One more, but that's it."

Ginny laughed. "All right. Last one for the day. Cat." Lindsay rolled her eyes. "I don't like cats."

"You don't have to like them. Besides, since when are you in love with hats, and bats, or the word fat?"

"Okay, okay. C-ca-cat. Ca-ca—" She paused. "K—A—T."

Ginny shook her head, wishing they'd stopped after the last one. "That was really close, but not quite right, sweetheart. It starts with a C not a K."

Lindsay's forehead wrinkled. "But the ca-sound is the sound a K makes, right?"

"It does. But a C also makes that sound. Sorry, love, they sound alike, but you picked the wrong one."

"If they sound the same, then why do we need them both?"

Uh oh. Ginny winced inwardly, knowing she was about to try and explain something that was just as baffling to her as it was going to be to Lindsay. "Well, they don't always sound the same. Umm… sometimes the C sounds like an S, and sometimes the K is silent."

Lindsay just stared.

"Like in the word 'knot' or 'knife,'" Ginny went on. "There is no K sound, but it still starts the words."

"Knife starts with the letter K?" She lifted a single eyebrow.

"Uh-huh."

"Bullshit."

"It does!"

Lindsay put her hands on her hips. "So let me get this straight. The K can sound exactly like a C, which can sound like an S, or the K can sounds like absolutely nothing at all?"

"Yes," Ginny said weakly, cringing. "But—"

Lindsay raised a hand to stop her, and made a mental note not to bother with the useless letter K ever again. "Never mind. I was just checking." But she was clearly a little dejected.

Ginny gazed at her fondly, fighting back the almost overwhelming urge to gather Lindsay in her arms and kiss her senseless. "Don't get discouraged. You're doing so wonderfully, Lindsay." She saw the beginnings of a smile, and let everything she felt inside show on her face. "I'm *really* proud of you."

Lindsay felt her cheeks heat. "I still can't read."

"Soon," Ginny promised. "Very soon."

Jane let out an unhappy squawk as she tripped over her own feet; and Lindsay and Ginny's attention was drawn downward. Ginny helped Jane to her feet, kissed her scrape gently, and dusted off her chubby knees.

Lindsay watched in amazement as the tears that had been threatening to fall disappeared as quickly as they came, and Jane began marching across the grass as though nothing at all had happened.

"She's fearless, isn't she?" Ginny noted absently, grateful for this time alone together. "She always has been. Right from the first."

Calvin Gable had insisted that they close the store as though it was a true holiday. After hearing the boys' delightful recounting of their night spent by the pond in Tyler, he had gamely stripped off his jacket and stylish vest and tie in favor of an old cotton shirt. He borrowed a fishing pole from the nearest neighbor. With Ginny's blessing, he and the boys, and a picnic basket, so heavy that Calvin was the only one who could carry it, set out for the river just after noon. Ginny had no doubt they would have a wonderful time.

Ginny gazed down at her sister as she toddled along, exploring every rock and stick she came across, with a curious, discerning eye. "Nuh uh." Ginny let go of Lindsay's hand, and scrambled to get to the girl. "Not in your mouth, honey," she scolded gently, holding out her hand so that Jane could spit out whatever she'd deposited into her mouth.

Lindsay grimaced.

"Jane," Ginny warned, a single eyebrow twitched. Jane shook her head defiantly.

"You love to make me do this, don't you?" Ginny muttered, but it was clear by the tone of her voice she really didn't mind. Kneeling, she probed the inside of Jane's mouth for a moment until she was able to scoop out the small stone from between her greedy lips.

Lindsay laughed when Ginny had to wipe her soaked fingers on the skirt of her dress.

"Just wait, Pea Pod," Ginny teased, allowing Lindsay to haul her to her feet. "You'll get your turn."

Imperiously, Jane crossed her arms over her little, somewhat portly chest and pouted fiercely, her lower lip protruding farther than Lindsay thought humanly possible. In response, Ginny stuck her own bottom lip out, then stuck out her tongue for good measure. It was obviously an old, well-loved game between them, because the little girl instantly mimicked the action; but was only able to hold the pose for a few seconds before she and Ginny dissolved into helpless giggles.

"Oh, Lindsay." Ginny shook her head as the last of her giggles died away and Jane began marching down the road again in search of new booty. "I can't believe how this day has turned out." Despite coming on the heels of laughter, the words held a hint of melancholy. "She loves them." Her gaze shifted sideways to her partner. "Did you hear what she called Laura?"

Lindsay nodded, suspecting this would be a sore spot with Ginny. "Mama."

"Mama," Ginny confirmed in a whisper, her eyes going a little unfocused. *How could she? How could she not?*

"They seem like good people," Lindsay offered noncommittally. *Of course,* she thought somewhat guiltily, *they don't exactly know why we're here.* When pressed, all Ginny would say was that they had been looking for Jane. She never mentioned the future. "Nice house. Good business. They closed the store today without a second thought. You couldn't do that in hard times," she pointed out.

"Mm," Ginny agreed. "Back home I worked every day but Sunday at the factory."

Jane veered onto the lush grass, chasing a pale yellow butterfly, and Ginny and Lindsay amiably altered their path to follow her. It didn't matter where they went, so long as they were together.

"Mama took in washing on Sundays," Ginny continued after a moment of thought. "So Alice and I watched the children so Mama could work. Before we moved to Orchard Street it was just the same." She shrugged a little. "Different factories or shops every day after school, then full time as I got older. It all sort of blends together now."

She sighed and felt the hand wrapped around hers squeeze gently.

Lindsay drew in a large lungful of crisp air. "Children shouldn't have to work, Ginny. They should look like that," she pointed at Jane, who was still trying valiantly to catch the butterfly in her chubby hands. "That's the way it should be." There was a wistful quality to her voice that caused Ginny to stare at her for a long moment.

Then Ginny's brows drew together, and she turned back to Jane to watch her sister play. The croup had quickly been vanquished under the Gables' care, and Jane looked healthier and happier than she had before the fire. "No, they shouldn't. I'll get three jobs if I have to, but none of the children will have to work, Lindsay. Not until they're grown or they want to."

Lindsay's very serious eyes met hers, and a silent promise passed between them, together they would make sure Ginny's words became a reality.

"Bad butterfly!" Giving on up the butterfly, Jane plopped down on her bottom, and grabbed a handful of soft grass. Yanking it from the ground, she threw it straight up in the air and giggled as it rained down on her head, forming a prickly green crown that contrasted nicely with her pale locks.

Ginny smiled fondly. "One Sunday afternoon last summer, Alice and I took her to the park." Her eyebrows pulled together as she remembered. "I don't recall why, but the boys and the baby, Helen, weren't with us that day. At first Jane was afraid of the grass. We took our shoes and stockings off and I spent most of the afternoon coaxing her to take a single step, while Alice laughed at us both." Ginny grinned. "But Jane finally did it," she stated proudly. "You should have seen the look on her face, Lindsay. I think it was the first time she'd even seen grass, much less felt it tickle her toes."

"So what are we waiting for?" Lindsay asked, her face taking on a playful, if slightly challenging, expression. Before Ginny could even answer, Lindsay was on the ground alongside Jane, kicking off her shoes.

Jane squealed in delight and tried to tug hers off as well. Sounding like a piglet rooting around for a tit, she grunted and huffed, grabbed her foot and began wrestling with her shoe, toppling over onto the grass as Lindsay's hand shot out and tickled her belly. That made the already difficult task of removing her own shoes impossible.

Charmed, Ginny eagerly joined them. Both women recaptured a tiny piece of their own, mostly lost childhoods in that soft grass that afternoon, as their mingling laughter floated away on the late afternoon breeze.

"Look!" Jabbering excitedly about the rushing river and the men they'd seen there, the boys came barreling through the kitchen door of the Gables' lovely Victorian home. The pale blue structure had a gabled roof, corner turret, and was surrounded by mature trees that shaded its large, wraparound porch. "We finally caught fish." Both boys suddenly looked at Lindsay, who was sitting at the kitchen table, worried they'd offended her.

She let them stew for a few painful seconds before smiling broadly and saying, "I knew you could do it."

The boys both let out the breaths they'd been holding, and gave her toothy smiles in response. "And later Calvin's gonna teach us to play baseball. He says if we practice like the dickens we might be good enough to play for the Brooklyn Bridegrooms someday!" Lewis enthused.

"Wouldn't that be something?" James asked Ginny, his eyes searching hers for confirmation that someone like him could ever achieve such a thing.

Ginny couldn't help but smile. "It sure would."

Calvin appeared in the doorway, his body silhouetted by the setting sun as he proudly lifted a string of plump catfish, so fresh the whiskers on the last two still twitched occasionally.

Laura laughed, and gave her husband an adoring look that brought unconscious smiles to Lindsay and Ginny's faces. "I can't believe you caught something. But don't come in the house with those until they're cleaned. I think I can manage to cook them, but I won't," she cringed, "you know."

"Yes, ma'am," Calvin responded dutifully as his inquiring gaze flicked around the room. "Where's Janie?"

"Nap time."

Calvin looked crestfallen. "Oh."

"She was tired, Calvin." Laura patted his shoulder in consolation. "I'll get her up for supper, and then you can play with her afterwards, all right?"

His face brightened with the news. "Great. I want to tell her about fishing. Next time I'll take her with me."

Laura chuckled and poked his chest with her index finger. "She's only a baby and a girl at that."

Calvin lifted his chin with fake huffiness. "What's your point? She's my daughter, and she can do anything she wants." He nodded to himself. "And that might just include fishing." He tipped his hat at Ginny and Lindsay, who wordlessly waved their greeting.

Laura threw her hands in the air in bemused exasperation, and headed to a set of stairs located just off the kitchen. The larder was in the cellar and she figured she'd need an apron full of potatoes to feed this crew.

"Come on, Lewis and James, I'll show you how to fillet the fish." He chuckled. "I hope." Calvin clearly wasn't bothered by his inexperience in this arena; and both Lindsay and Ginny found themselves liking the amiable man more and more.

Ginny's eyes followed him curiously as he departed the kitchen. Jane could be anything, he'd said, and the conviction in his words made Ginny believe it was true. Would that change if she took Jane? She leaned back in her chair and forced herself to do what she'd deemed too heartbreaking and dangerous before.

She began to wonder.

Four days later…

Ginny lay flat on her back, looking up at the ceiling of the guestroom the Gables had generously given her and Lindsay. The day had been unseasonably warm and the window was open just a crack, letting in the cool breeze, a sliver of moonlight, and the constant hum of insects.

Ginny heard the mournful wail of a train whistle in the distance and her eyes strayed across the room to Lindsay, who was slipping into her nightshirt and blowing out the lamp. *I wonder if she misses her freedom,* she thought idly as her eyes tracked Lindsay's every move. *I wonder if I'll ever know what that's like, to be responsible for no one but myself—to travel where the wind takes me.* A tiny frown appeared. *I'm not sure I want to.*

The burden and joy of caring for her siblings was something she would gladly bear. But that didn't mean she'd forgotten about her own dreams, and the nights where she and Alice would whisper about their futures to the backdrop of the sounds of the city that never slept. *Well, you wanted out of the smelly slums, Ginny. But more than that you wanted someone to love, who would love you back every bit as fiercely.*

Despite her somewhat gloomy mood, Ginny smiled inwardly as she watched her partner studiously brush her teeth over a basin on the bureau. *Wouldn't you be surprised where I found what we both dreamt of, Alice. You'd die from shock and say that I was crazy.* Her grin turned wistful. *But once I told you how wonderful it was, how she makes me feel and all the things I love about her… you'd still be shocked and say I was crazy, you rat. But you'd be happy for me too. I know it. I miss you, Al. When is it going to stop hurting so badly?* Resolutely, Ginny pulled herself away from that train of thought and focused on the happenings of the past four days.

She'd gotten to know the Gables, who were a gregarious, kind couple that welcomed her and her family with open arms. On several occasions Ginny had been ready to tell them that this wasn't just a visit. That she wanted more than to find Jane, she wanted to take her. But Calvin and Laura were so earnest in their offer of friendship, and it was so obvious that they adored the toddler, who was thriving under their care. Every time she began to tell them, the words died on her tongue. She cursed her cowardice, hating herself for it.

Ginny closed her eyes, listening as Lindsay moved around the mostly-dark room. At first she was worried that the boys would tell Calvin that she intended to take Jane. Now she selfishly wished that they'd spill the beans and do her dirty work for her. "Oh, God, Lindsay. What am I going to do?" she whispered. Ginny had held in her worry all day, trying to give Lindsay a break from dealing with her endless problems. But it was finally too much. She needed to talk.

Lindsay padded across the room and sat down in the bed next to Ginny. She lifted a hand and stroked Ginny's cheek with the pads of her fingers. "You've sure taken to blasphemy." She was smiling as she said the words.

Ginny chuckled, though it was clear her heart wasn't in it. "Once you start, the words rolls off your tongue from then on."

Lindsay grunted her agreement. "Now what are you going to do about what?" Ginny had been as quiet as a church mouse all day, and

Lindsay breathed a sigh of relief, hoping her friend would finally share what was bothering her so. The silence had more than stung. After all they'd shared, to have Ginny turn away rather than talk to her—it hurt. And as so easily happened, hurt had given way to anger. More than once today Lindsay had bitten back harsh words that Ginny didn't deserve.

"They're happy," Ginny said brokenly.

"Uhh..." Lindsay shook her head a little, confused. "Who's happy?"

"Laura, Calvin, Jane. They're happy together and I'm about to ruin their lives."

Lindsay's gaze softened. "You aren't hurting Jane or ruining her life by claiming her, Ginny. You love her."

"And the Gables?" Ginny asked, already knowing the answer.

Lindsay sighed. That wasn't so easy. "I'm sorry," she finally offered. "I'll help you anyway that I can." She gestured aimlessly. "That's all I can think to say."

Ginny sighed and pinched the bridge of her nose to ward off her impending headache. With her other hand, she squeezed Lindsay's. "I know."

Lindsay glanced out the window, eyes unseeing, as she considered the impossible position they were in. Had Ginny told her last week that dealing with Milo was easy compared to the people who had Jane, she wouldn't have believed her.

"I don't like hurting anyone, especially good people," Ginny murmured, guilt settling over her like a heavy blanket. "Laura invited us to stay here for as long as we'd like, Lindsay." She could feel the beginnings of tears pooling in her eyes and she fought them back. "She wants us to be part of her family and visit whenever we like. She actually said that. "Come visit Jane whenever you like. We want her to know her family"."

Lindsay sighed. "Calvin told me the same thing today. I think he's finally starting to get over the fact that I wear trousers." A wry grin touched her lips. "He doesn't know what to make of me and still thinks I'm a little crazy."

"You are a little crazy." They shared weak smiles.

Ginny laid her hand on Lindsay's bare thigh, feeling the warmth of her skin sink deeply into her palm. "Today Calvin got on the floor and played with Jane. I mean, *really* played. Arthur loved her, but I never saw him do that. Not once." She exhaled slowly, her face telegraphing her awe. "I didn't even know it was something fathers did. God, Lindsay, I feel like a murderer laying in wait for just the right moment to stab Calvin and Laura in the back."

Lindsay chewed on her lower lip as she thought. "Maybe we can work something out? Something like we did with Lewis?" But even as she said the words, she knew they weren't true. The Gables didn't want an apprentice or a part-time child to round out an already bursting family. They wanted a real daughter. And it was clear that Jane meant the world to them.

"Maybe," Ginny replied absently, her eyes tracing the beams of moonlight as they washed over Lindsay.

"We should just steal her," Lindsay said after a moment of intense thought. "Run away in the night and go so far from here they'd never find us."

Ginny was quiet for so long that Lindsay didn't think she was going to respond, and the low sound of her voice made her jump.

"I don't think you'd have the heart to do that, Lindsay," she speculated. "I saw you with James today when he scraped his knee and was trying not to cry." The picture was forever burned into Ginny's brain. Her brother and her best friend, dark heads tilted close to one another as they whispered. Lindsay ruffling his hair with open affection that made her melt just watching. The relief on his face when sturdy arms enveloped him in a hug, and he was allowed to wipe away the few tears that had managed to leak out, his dignity fully intact. "You're better with the boys than you know. I don't think I could have when we first met, but now I can picture you sort of looking out for new rail-riders. Especially the young ones."

Lindsay ducked her head. "Well, I… err…" She could feel her face heat. "I only did that once or twice when I saw someone so green it was going to get them killed."

"You can pretend you're not a good person." Ginny's voice was tinged with admiration and unyielding love. "But I know different. You're the most tender hearted person I've ever met."

Lindsay snorted then inclined her head and smiled sadly. "You're wrong, you know." *Though I wish you weren't.* "I would do things that would make you shudder… if I had to." She lifted her hand; then let it drop limply to the bed.

"I'm not sure what will make you happy anymore." Frustration leaked into Lindsay's voice. "I know you don't want to hurt the Gables. I also know you want Jane, but there's a part of you that thinks she would be better off here, in this nice house, with its white picket fence, and beautiful furniture." Lindsay rapped the solid oak bedpost with her knuckles. "She would have a doting father." *That she wouldn't have with us.*

Ginny's eyes sparked. "It's not just the father part, Lindsay. I know what you're thinking and it's not true. I just told you how wonderful you were with the boys!"

"But not a father."

"Like I am?" she said angrily, pushing up onto her elbows. "The fact that I want to make a life with a woman is my choice, Lindsay Killian. I'm not a fool. I know I could have a man if I wanted; I've had the chance before and didn't take it. So the fact that there'll be no father in this family is my doing not yours. Besides, their father is dead and can't just be exchanged for another like a worn out pair of shoes!" *Just like Arthur couldn't replace Daddy.*

The words were shocking in their intensity and for several seconds the only sound heard in the large guestroom was Ginny and Lindsay's panting breaths. Lindsay gently cleared her throat. "The boys' father is dead to them. And to you. But, Ginny, your sister would only know Calvin as her father. She wouldn't remember anyone else."

An incredulous look crept across Ginny's face and she sat up. "Are… are you trying to tell me I should leave her here?"

"No, sweetheart." Lindsay grasped Ginny's hand with surprising strength. "I'm trying to get you to talk about what I know you've been killing yourself over since we got here. Help me help you," she pleaded, her tone softening. "What will make you happy?"

Ginny closed her eyes, pain lancing through her. "I don't know," she whispered.

"This indecision is killing you." *And me.* "Face what needs to be done and let's do it. The boys could let Calvin and Laura know why we're here at any time. Then we'll be out on our asses and having to make all these same decisions. Now is the time."

"You make it sound easy. It's not that easy!"

"Doesn't matter," Lindsay informed her bluntly. "It still has to be done."

"But can I live with myself once it is done?" Anguish bled into Ginny's eyes and she looked away.

Lindsay cupped Ginny's chin and turned the younger woman's head toward her, inadvertently using a little more force than was necessary. "Don't say that," she hissed. "Don't make this sound selfish when I know damned well you'd die ten times over for any one of these children. This wasn't your fault." Brown eyes gone charcoal in the moonlight flashed and her voice rose several notches. "Stop the guilt! I know you feel bad. I feel it too. But someone is going to get hurt here. Stop fighting it. Accept it!"

"That's not the point, and you know it," Ginny snapped, jerking her chin from Lindsay's hands as her ire rose. She yanked her hand from her friend's as though she'd been burned. "You want me to talk? Fine! This *isn't* about it being someone's fault. What happened was nobody's fault but Jeremiah and Isabelle Ward's or maybe God's—if I was sure there was a God anymore."

Lindsay ground her teeth in frustration, feeling so deeply adrift she wasn't sure she'd ever find her way back. What did Ginny expect her to say? What more could she do or offer? "We'll work things out. We have so far, right? You need to keep believing." *So that I'll keep believing.*

"Why? Why do I have to believe that?" Ginny demanded. She could feel another irrational surge of anger brewing deep inside her, and was helpless to stop it as it rushed to the surface, then boiled over. "You're always saying that! That I need to keep believing. What I need is to know *how* we're going to make this work."

A resentment Ginny wasn't even aware she harbored flared to life so brightly it blinded her. "Just saying we'll work things out won't make it so! We are two women, alone, Lindsay. Between us we have no worldly possessions and not enough money to last the month. I can't marry you the way I would if one of us were a man. I can't give you children of your own. Instead, you'll be tied to children who aren't mine either, for as long as we're together. How long can I expect you to want to live like that?"

Lindsay blinked, stunned, unable to speak.

Ginny's cheeks flushed pink, the words pouring from her like water bursting free through a crack in a damn. "What this is about is what we're going to do now, and how a scared witless, unskilled chicken stripper and an illiterate, drifter pickpocket are going to support themselves, much less Jane and the boys!" The words were out before she could stop them and she drew in a quick breath, as though she could suck them back. But she couldn't. They hung there between them, floating, ugly, and stark until she saw Lindsay's eyes flutter closed.

The silence in the room thundered and Ginny felt sick at her stomach. *Oh, no. I did not just say that.*

Lindsay's body stayed stock-still, though she felt the words rain down on her like blows. But it was when she opened her eyes, giving Ginny a glimpse of an open, wounded look so painful it hurt to see, that the tears that had been threatening for the entire conversation went cascading down Ginny's cheeks.

What have I done? "Lindsay, I'm so sor—"

A cold expression dropped over Lindsay's face, something she hadn't seen even in their earliest days together. Startled, Ginny was forced to blink a few times and remind herself that this was, indeed, her best friend and lover, and not a stranger.

Awkwardly, Lindsay stood, Ginny's death grip on her hand the only thing keeping her from bolting from the room.

Ginny's heart began to pound. "Lindsay, please!" she begged, hearing the desperation in her voice and not caring. "God knows, I-I didn't mean that. I swear. I'm just worried and afraid and I—"

"Am just spending time with an illiterate, drifter pickpocket, who can't marry you or give you your own children," Lindsay finished for her, violently hurling the words back at Ginny.

An icy fist closed around Ginny's heart.

"I heard." Lindsay swallowed hard. Her chest felt achy and hollow, and the sensation threatened to send her crashing to her knees. "You should keep better company, Virginia." She tore her hand from Ginny's. And without another word, Lindsay snatched up her trousers, shoes, and coat and stalked out of the room, her steady step never faltering.

I need to get outside, Lindsay thought desperately. She flung the door open. The walls were closing in on her faster than she could move, and she began to run, ignoring the pain in her ribs.

After a long, stunned moment, Ginny scrambled off the bed, her knees viciously slamming against the shiny floorboards. She stumbled to her feet and ran to the door, finding what she knew she would, a shadowy, very empty hallway. "Lindsay," she moaned quietly, "I'm sorry." *Dammit!*

For a few seconds she balanced on a razor's edge, not knowing whether to hunt Lindsay down and force her to hear her apology, or let her go. Her head was telling her that they needed this time apart, that she'd hurt her friend badly and that she was the last person on earth Lindsay wanted to talk to. Her heart, however, was screaming something altogether different, and the indecision caused her guts to churn.

Ginny wanted to howl. She wanted to weep. Instead, she continued to stare down the empty hallway and listen to the sound of her own thundering pulse as regret washed over her. Finally, she moved back into the bedroom and, with trembling hands, shut the bedroom door. She pressed her back against the cool wooden surface and slid to the floor like a rag doll.

"I'm sorry. I'm sorry. I'm sorry," she chanted under her breath. Dropping her head in her hands, she closed her eyes, too numb to cry.

Lindsay sat on a hill about a block or so behind the Gables' home. She gazed down at the train tracks in the distance and could hear the faint sounds of the rushing river beyond that. There were no trees on the hill, just tall stalks of swaying grass. With the town at her back, she could see for miles around her, the vast openness seeping into her and calming her like a potent liquor. Her knees were hitched up, her feet flat on the ground as she idly twirled a stalk of grass between her long fingers.

It had been several hours since she'd left the house, but the moon still hung high in the sky, painting the grass with its golden glow. The night air was fragrant and crisp, and she was glad she'd brought her coat, though it wasn't so chilly that she needed to button it.

A freight train had passed a few moments ago, and she'd thought about how easy it would be to catch it and let it take her wherever it would. There would be new faces and different places and calmness that came with the familiarity of it all. She could slip back into her old life with nary a thought for all this craziness and these impossible choices. She could just forget, couldn't she?

Lindsay tossed the stalk of grass and sighed. No, she wouldn't forget. Ever. And so the train had passed and she'd stayed on the hill, watching it chug out of her life, knowing that though it still called to her it was no longer enough to sustain her. No, what she needed to sustain her were eyes, that when turned toward her, shone warmly with love. She needed laughter and sweet kisses and someone to share her dreams with, even when she wasn't quite sure what those dreams were yet. She needed Ginny, who thought of her as nothing more than a stupid thief. *Which is true, String Bean,* she admitted glumly. *I've said it to myself a thousand times, but when I said it, it never hurt this way.*

She laughed but there was no humor in the laughter. "I pushed her when she wasn't ready and damned if she didn't push back." Lindsay chastised herself for getting her feelings hurt so easily. *When did I become all sensitive and pathetic? That would be the moment she stole my heart,* she answered herself wryly. *Shit.*

Ginny peered out through the darkness, spotting a solitary figure sitting near the top of the hill. They had both come to this very spot several times since arriving in San Marcos. It was a perfect place to sit and think and be alone with the world closed in on you. "Please let that be her," she said quietly as she began climbing the hill, a thick woolen blanket slung over her shoulders. "Otherwise I'm going to scare the living daylights out of some poor soul, and then probably be murdered for my trouble." But as she got closer she recognized the unmistakable set of Lindsay's shoulders and the moonlit profile she knew as well as her own.

If Lindsay heard her approach she didn't show it.

Ginny dropped down onto the soft grass next to her friend; close, but not so close that they were touching. She kept her eyes trained straight ahead, and resisted the urge to hurl herself at Lindsay, and scream her apology into the night. Gathering her courage she drew in a deep breath of cool, clean air. "It's beautiful here." Her voice was barely loud enough to be heard above the breeze.

"It is," Lindsay confirmed gently, still gazing out at the tracks and the rolling fields beyond.

Ginny swallowed and looked down at her pants. She frowned and picked absently at a small tear that was developing around the cuff. "I heard the train as I was walking here." Her heart lurched at what she'd felt. "I thought you might be on it." She dared a glance at her companion, whose jaw was set.

Lindsay nodded and turned to face Ginny. Their eyes locked. "So did I."

Ginny's mouth suddenly went dry and the bottom fell out of her stomach. "Wh-what stopped you?"

Lindsay's mouth quirked into a tiny, somewhat melancholy smile.

"You, of course."

A relieved sob tore itself from Ginny's chest and tears pooled in her soft blue eyes. "I didn't mean what I said. It was horribly cruel and I would do anything to take it back. I'm so sorry." She reached out for Lindsay, half-expecting to have her hand knocked away. It wasn't. And she breathed an audible sigh of relief, letting it rest shakily on Lindsay's woolen-clad shoulder.

Ginny regarded Lindsay's open face with more than a hint of shame.

"Forgive me? Please," she added raggedly when there was no immediate answer. *Please.*

Lindsay looked away for several seconds, then back at Ginny. She sighed, long and hard before simply saying, "Okay."

Ginny blinked slowly, her mind scrambling to process the answer she'd least expected. "Wh-what?"

Lindsay shrugged lightly, but her eyes had warmed. "I said okay." She pointed wearily to the tracks. "That's not—I just—It's not my home anymore. That's with you now."

Ginny started to cry.

"I might as well forgive you now," Lindsay paused and wiped away Ginny's tears. "Since I know I'll just go and do it sooner or later anyway."

Ginny surged forward and hugged Lindsay with all her might. "I'm so stupid. When I get scared, I say stupid things," she mumbled against a cool cheek, feeling Lindsay squeeze her even harder. "You're so much more than what I said. You have to know that, Lindsay. I swear it's true."

Lindsay's mouth worked silently for several seconds as she absorbed the feeling of Ginny in her arms. She drank in the words greedily, needing to believe them. "Really?"

"God, Yes!" Ginny pulled away, and grasped Lindsay's face with both hands. She looked directly into her eyes and spoke from the heart. "Didn't you hear all of what I said before? No matter what I stupidly said just then, you're not just some bum, Lindsay. You're not!"

There was a ferocity in Ginny's voice, a fiery gleam in her eyes, and a sureness in the strong hands pressed to her face that captured Lindsay completely. She forgot how to breathe.

"I'd marry you, if I could. I'd spend my entire life loving you, if you'd let me."

Lindsay turned her head and kissed Ginny's palm. Her throat had closed and she knew she couldn't speak. After a few hitched breaths, she moved her lips a fraction of an inch, and brushed them over a small scar caused by the tenement fire. When she turned back she was smiling. "Marry, huh?" It was the most absurd, lovely thought she'd ever had. And though she couldn't quite wrap her mind around the concept, it made her giddy nonetheless. "I dunno. Do you have a dowry?" she teased.

Ginny laughed, feeling lightheaded in her relief as a big part of her world righted itself. "I don't and you know it. I come with only a big mouth, a bunch of sometimes-bratty, but mostly-loveable kids, and an extreme dislike of chickens."

Lindsay gave her a lopsided grin. "Lucky me."

Ginny couldn't find even a hint of sarcasm in Lindsay's words. Lovingly, she brushed some blowing hair from the other woman's face. Then she leaned forward and kissed her on the mouth, wanting to convey everything she felt in one perfect gesture.

Lindsay groaned throatily and deepened the kiss; hot wet tongues collided in a passionate display that stole her breath away. "God, I want to touch you all the time," Lindsay breathed hotly between kisses. "I have to stop myself a million times a day."

"Lindsay…" Ginny threaded her hands in dark hair and crushed Lindsay's mouth to hers. "Mmm. Don't stop now," she growled, the intensity and urgency of her voice shocking her.

Lindsay leaned forward pushing Ginny onto her back, and they fell deeper into the tall grass, their blanket forgotten in the wake of urgent hands, ardent caresses, and soft cries of sensual delight.

They claimed each other on the windswept hilltop under the endless Texas sky. It was an explosion of desire, raw emotion, and love so fierce that it took most of the night to quench the flames that ignited between them.

Much later, dozy and sated, they snuggled closely together, and sat to watch the sunrise splash color across the horizon and drape it over the land. Lindsay pressed her lips to Ginny's temple. "I love you." The gesture and words were lovingly mirrored and then they talked. About everything.

Lost in thought, the young women strolled back to the Gables' house at a leisurely pace. When they opened the gate in front of the house a harried-looking Calvin trotted down the steps; he had a dot of shaving soap still on his face and he was slipping into his suit coat. "Ladies," he greeted, giving them a curious once over as he tugged on his dark felt cowboy hat and adjusted it until it was to his liking. "Early for you, Lindsay, isn't it?" he teased, surprised to see them both up and walking past dawn.

He and Ginny shared smiles, acknowledging Lindsay's preference for sleeping in.

Lindsay rolled her eyes. "Disgustingly early."

"Well, I'm off to work," he said brightly, reaching out and pulling a piece of grass out of Ginny's hair. "Don't want to go walking around with this all day." His bushy eyebrows scrunched together. "Were you two wrestling in the grass or something?" He brushed a cluster of grass from Lindsay's sleeve.

Ginny had the good graces to blush. Lindsay just smiled and nodded, her slightly roguish, utterly satisfied look helping Ginny's cheeks shift from a rosy pink to bright red.

"Oh," Calvin said, confused at the odd behavior.

Ginny began inspecting herself for more grass. She willed her hands not to shake as she performed her task, and tried not to think about what she was about to do. "Where is everyone?"

"Laura's in the kitchen with Jane, cleaning up breakfast. They're coming by the store later. Lewis and James are still asleep. I think one of them had a nightmare. When I walked by their room I heard James crying about a fire and someone named Alice." His slightly boyish face took on a seldom-used, grim expression. "By the time I got in the room, he'd quieted again."

"You're a very good man," Ginny complimented sincerely, her voice warm and sweet. "Thank you, Calvin."

"You're welcome," he said easily, a blush erupting from beneath his starched white collar.

"Those poor little boys," Ginny murmured, suspecting that nightmares were going to be fixtures in their lives for sometime to come. She vowed to talk to each of them later, and once again do her best to soothe their fears. *They've been through so much. We all have. Jesus, I wish this was finally over.*

Anxiously, Ginny glanced sideways at Lindsay, who lifted her eyebrows in question. The redhead's fists clenched and unclenched and for a few seconds she held her breath, but finally nodded.

"Are you sure?" Lindsay asked in a low voice, ignoring Calvin for the time being.

"Go. I'll be okay." Ginny tried to smile but it didn't quite reach her eyes.

Lindsay hesitated. "Ginny—"

"Go." She felt a little sick but was determined to press on. "Like we discussed," she whispered.

Their eyes locked and held, neither one blinking as Lindsay studied Ginny's face.

"All right," Lindsay allowed after a moment. She didn't feel right about leaving, but apparently Ginny was sticking to her decision, and their plan to talk to the Gables separately. Lindsay gave herself a mental kick in the arse. *Dammit, Ginny. How did I ever let you talk me into this?* She stepped forward and glanced up at Calvin who had no earthly idea what was happening. "I'll walk with you to work."

"I was going to saddle—"

"No, you weren't."

His eyebrows jumped. "I wasn't?"

"Nuh uh." Lindsay shook her head. "You only think you were."

"But—Hey!"

Lindsay grabbed him by the arm and began dragging him toward the road, leaving the larger man no choice but to yield to her insistence. "We need to have a talk."

Helplessly, Calvin looked back over his shoulder at Ginny, who was standing in front of the house with her arms wrapped around herself in mute comfort.

Lindsay expertly lifted his pocket watch then held it out in front of her to check the time. "You're going to be late."

Calvin's eyes bulged and he reached for the watch, and Lindsay held it just out of his reach.

Ginny shook her head at Lindsay's antics, watching as the pair strode down the street and toward town. It took a little pep talk to get herself up the front steps and into the house. She breathed a sigh of relief when she closed the front door behind her. She was struck by the heady aroma of freshly brewed coffee and cinnamon rolls, but it was Laura's gentle voice that guided her to the kitchen.

When she reached the kitchen, she stopped in the doorway, unseen. A slow, charmed smile worked its way across her face at what she saw.

To Calvin's surprise, Lindsay didn't have much to say as they walked past the buildings and shops that comprised San Marcos' downtown district. They had talked about the weather and other things Lindsay couldn't care less about. Eventually, Calvin decided to play tour guide, giving Lindsay a run down of the stores they passed and the owners, all of whom Calvin knew. The streets were full of people, horses, and wagons, and he stepped aside to allow an old woman to pass in front of him. "Pardon me, ma'am," he said politely.

The old woman smiled approvingly at Calvin's good manners.

"Hold up, Mr. Gable!" A skinny Mexican boy of twelve, with feet that looked to be at least three sizes too big for his gangly body, raced up to Calvin and held out a piece of paper. His coal-black hair was slightly tousled from his run. Breathing heavily, he shifted from one foot to the other, exceedingly pleased that he'd caught Mr. Gable before he got further down the street. "*Telegrama*," he said needlessly, the rocks crunching beneath him as he moved.

Calvin grinned at his youthful energy and glanced down at the paper.

The boy whistled through his teeth. "Longest one I ever seen." He unapologetically stuck his hand out for a tip. "And I've seen many."

Calvin fished a nickel out of his vest pocket, and pressed it into the boy's palm. "Here you go, Enrique. Don't spend it all on candy this time and get sick."

The boy's face lit up at the sight of the shiny coin. "Gosh Almighty!"

Calvin turned to say something to Lindsay and his mouth dropped open. He spun around in a circle, his eyes flicking from place to place. "I'll be…" He pulled off his hat and scratched his head, still looking.

She was gone. Vanished without a sound or a trace in a street crowded with people.

Chapter Sixteen

"Shhh. Be very quiet, String Bean." Albert's moist lips were pressed against Lindsay's ear and his dirty beard scraped her skin. He fitted his body tightly against her back before she could even think to move. In deference to the rising temperature, she'd taken off her coat as she and Calvin walked downtown. It was slung over her arm, effectively hiding the razor-sharp knife jabbing her ribs. "Not a single damn word." His knuckles turned white as he gripped the knife's handle.

"Not one."

Her heart began to pound wildly and for a second she thought of screaming. *Shit! Why is he doing this? Why won't he just leave me alone?* From the corner of her eye she could see Calvin talking to a boy she didn't know, but her attention was drawn away from the scene by the stinging feeling of metal piercing her skin.

She hissed in pain, instantly stifling the automatic response when she heard his warning growl in her ear. A rivulet of warm blood trailed down her abdomen, making her squirm. In a blinding flash of clarity Lindsay realized exactly what was going to happen. *He wants to kill me?* Anger swept through her. *If I'm leaving this world today, bung hole, I'm taking you with me.*

"Move." Albert prodded urgently, his voice so low she barely heard him. Discreetly, he gave her shirt a firm tug to the left, directing her movements.

"That's it. Not a sound." His dark gaze flicked from person to person, scanning for any sign that someone had figured out what he was doing. But the citizens of San Marcos appeared to be minding their own business as they traversed the streets.

About time I had some good luck, Albert thought bitterly. He and Bo, who he'd sent to steal a wagon the moment they'd laid eyes on Lindsay, had been roaming the streets of San Marcos for the past two days. Albert was tired of the endless Mexicans, Germans, and cowboys who populated the town. He was sick of the green hills, lush pecan and oak trees, and the disgusting smell of fresh air. The big man craved the endless noise of the city and the smoke and rat pits he knew he could find any day or night. He wanted to go home.

But after looking for Lindsay for two days he wasn't about to wait for a safer time to nab her. *The bitch owes me for all this trouble*, he told himself. *Even if I do want to go back to New York City, I can't stop now. Not after I've come this far. I won't!* He knew what he was doing was ridiculously dangerous, but desperation and unspent rage had rendered him even more reckless than usual, and he cursed himself for taking this job in the first place. Only losers worked for a living. And hunting String Bean was far too much like work.

It only took a few steps for him to pull Lindsay into the narrow alleyway between the doctor's office and the blacksmith. The odor of horseflesh was overpowering and Lindsay's stomach roiled, both from nerves and the reminder of the animals she still feared—even after what seemed like an endless ride atop the gentle Diablo.

Albert pulled out a thin brown cloth sack he had tucked in his shirt and handed it to Lindsay. The bag was damp and reeked of sweat. "Put this on." He moved the knife against her ribs a little, making sure she wouldn't forget who was boss.

It didn't work.

"Go to hell, lard as—Uff!" A meaty hand clamped over her mouth and nose, yanking her head.

"Shut the fuck up!" he hissed, spraying saliva on her cheek.

The outline of the nearby building swam before her as the oxygen in her system began to dwindle.

"Put this sack on your head or I'll kill you now and save myself the trouble later." Gingerly, he removed his hand.

Lindsay gasped, pulling in a large lungful of air before wiping her face with her sleeve, half-hoping she'd go ahead and puke. The least she could do was make sure she heaved all over him before he stabbed her.

Nervously, Albert glanced at the opposite end of the alley. "Where are you?" he whispered.

"Expecting someone, Rat Face?" she choked, her mind scrambling for a means of escape. The knife digging into her flesh reminded her that she didn't have one.

"Put the bag on your head."

His voice was as flat as she'd ever heard it, and her worry grew exponentially. She should, she realized, be more afraid. After all, the man was part of the trio that had literally thrown her to the dogs. But this was still Rat Face—someone she'd come across off and on over the years when she rode the rails along the East Coast.

He was a pig and a crook and easily led by men who were his intellectual superior, which was just about everyone, but on his own she'd always believed she could manage him. Her gut, however, was telling her there was something very different about this time. She obeyed his command, and her world grew dank and dark, causing her to shiver and poke herself with the tip of the knife. More blood pooled at the waist of her denim pants.

"Very good, bitch."

A wagon pulled up to the entrance at the far end of the alley and stopped. Lindsay could feel Albert let out a relieved breath.

"Walk," he commanded. Just before the wagon, he stopped. "Where have you been?"

Bo looked at Albert's captive, and then back at Albert. "At a party."—A beat—"Where the hell do you think I've been?"

Lindsay's head snapped up at the sound of the voice, her mind reeling. *Bo? It can't be. You shit! You're working with Rat Face?*

"Dammit, keep your voice down. Help me into the wagon," Albert said impatiently.

Bo climbed jumped down, his shoes kicking up a cloud of dust when he hit the ground. "You cut her tongue out?" He tried not to let his anxiety show.

"No." Albert laughed and kneed Lindsay in the back, only thinking at the last minute to move the blade so he wouldn't skewer her.

The woman let loose a loud grunt and a string of invective and threats that caused Bo's eyebrows to crawl up into his hairline and stay there.

"You'd better hope she doesn't make good on any of that, Rat Face."

Albert sneered. "Dead women don't make good on anything."

Awkwardly, the men loaded Lindsay into the wagon. Bo crawled up to the driver's seat and Albert stayed in back with Lindsay. "Lay down and don't move."

Bo glanced over his shoulder, wondering what he and String Bean had gotten themselves into. He forced his voice not to quiver as he spoke. "Where to?"

Albert thought for a moment, one hand coming up to scratch at his beard. Then his face broke into a startling smile. "The river."

Naked and giggling happily, Jane sat in a washbasin next the sink getting her morning bath. The morning sun streamed through the windows giving the kitchen a cheery, bright quality that Ginny could never remember on Orchard Street. Steam rose gently from the water, and the chubby toddler's skin was flushed pink and covered unevenly with lavender scented soapsuds. Her blonde hair was piled haphazardly on her head in a great mass of bubbles. "Mama!" she squealed, laughing and splashing at Laura, whose smile stretched from ear to ear.

"Come on now. You know what to do," Laura instructed gently, sticking her hands in the water and tickling Jane's thigh.

Soapy water splashed onto the colorful rag rugs that covered the floor.

Jane grinned and began mashing the bubbles on her belly in a fair imitation of scrubbing herself clean.

"That's my girl," Laura praised proudly, the twinkle in her eyes evident from across the room.

The scene made Ginny's heart hurt, and the smile slid from her face.

The front of Laura's dress was wet, and when she pushed back a stand of hair with the back of her hand she deposited a dollop of bubbles on her forehead.

"Bubbles!" Jane crowed with delight, pointing at Laura's forehead.

Laura's eyes narrowed playfully. "Think that's funny, do you?" Giving up on trying to stay even somewhat dry, Laura bent and placed a sloppy kiss on Jane's face, allowing happy little hands to smear bubbles where they may.

Ginny swallowed thickly and closed her eyes. *Forgive me, Jane. Please.*

Gathering her courage, she stepped into the kitchen, startling Laura.

"Oh!" The woman instantly straightened, and tried to wipe the bubbles from her face and out of her rust-colored hair. An impish look settled on her face that made Ginny forget Laura was ten years her senior. At that moment, they seemed much more like friends.

"Gosh. Sorry," Ginny apologized, smiling at Jane when the little girl began saying her name over and over and splashing excitedly at the sight of her.

"Good mornin'. There's coffee." Laura gestured toward the pot on the stove with her chin as she reached for a soft towel.

"No thanks." Ginny went a little pale as she slumped into one of the chairs at the small breakfast table.

Laura noticed her pallor immediately. "What's the matter?"

Ginny stared at Jane for a long moment; then closed her eyes. When she opened them, she gazed directly at Laura. Her voice quivered but there was a determined set to her shoulders that caused the older woman to take notice.

"Laura," she paused and swallowed again, afraid the words wouldn't come.

"Yes?" Laura felt a surge of dread.

"We need to talk."

Even through the bag on her head Lindsay could hear the sound of the water. She remembered that Calvin had told her it had been the wettest winter folks could recall, and that the river was swollen and rushing. She shifted uncomfortably and her temper flared. Albert was resting his feet on her chest and had bound her hands together with his belt. Roughly, she knocked his feet away. Albert laughed. "Feisty to the end, String Bean. I gotta allow, I've always hated that about you."

"Fuck off," came the slightly muffled reply.

"Nope," Albert said amiably. "Your ugly puss don't do it for me."

"Maybe you'd prefer the driver then? He more your type? Ow!" A kick in the ribs shut her up. "God," she moaned, clutching at her side, her brown eyes squeezed tightly shut to hold in tears of agony.

Albert glanced around. They were still close to town, but it looked private enough. "Good enough." When Bo didn't stop he smacked him hard in the back of the head, earning a withering glare. "Stop the damn wagon already, harelip!"

"Fine. Whoa." Bo pulled back on the reins and the horses dutifully stopped. Lindsay could feel the wagon shift as both men jumped out. Then she was being forcibly dragged from the back. She landed on the ground with a loud thump, and the bag was torn from her head, taking a chunk of hair along with it. She blinked a few times as her eyes adjusted to the bright morning sun. The outline of a large body blocked her vision, and she was hauled to her feet by the belt wrapped around her hands.

"What are you going to do?"

For the first time since he and Bo had left New York, Albert looked unsure of himself. He'd only planned to catch her and had never really thought this far ahead. An image of himself holding her head in the river and making her suffer the way he had these past weeks had danced across his consciousness, compelling him to direct Bo to bring them here. But now that it came right down to it, he was losing his nerve. "I don't know," he barked, surprising Bo. "I need to think."

Lindsay laughed. "Good luck at that."

"Quiet!"

"Why don't we just take her back to town and say we caught her stealing this wagon?" Bo suggested. "That'll get her sent to jail for sure. Then we can go back to New York and collect the reward. Easy as pie."

He looks a little heavier maybe. And the horrible mustache is new. "There's a reward out for me?" she squeaked, suddenly realizing that Jacque or Jean must have died. She went a little pale. "They're dead?" she asked weakly, not sure she wanted to know, but curious nonetheless.

Albert made a face. "Who?"

"Jacque and Jean."

Albert chuckled grimly, he'd enjoyed hearing those assholes cry like little girls, and just knew it was Lindsay who had cut them down. "Those damn Frenchies ain't dead."

Lindsay expelled an explosive breath, her legs feeling like jelly. "Thank God." Then her brows furrowed. "Who would pay—?"

"Enough!" Albert's gaze bored into hers. "You aren't in any position to be asking questions. You're worth ten dollars to me, String Bean. That's all you need to know."

Her eyes went round as saucers. "Ten dollars!" *I'm lucky half the rail-riders in the country aren't after me!*

"You made the wrong person wrathy," Bo finally piped up. "A man in a nice coat came down the tracks and made it clear there was money in it if you never made it back to New York."

"And you agreed to help do me in?" Over the years she'd been in her share of trouble, but never, never had someone been so angry with her that they were willing, or even able, to pay that sort of money to get rid of her. *What's different about my life now? Ginny*, her mind screamed. *That's the difference. But—*

Then, like a lightning bolt striking from out of the blue, the answer hit hard, and burned her to the core. Her face took on an incredulous expression. "Jeremiah and Isabelle Ward? Jesus Christ." She screamed inwardly as her anger began to brew more violently.

"String Bean—" Bo began.

"Shut up." Her eyes flashed. "You make me sick," she spat, her words laced with venom.

Bo felt a sinking sensation deep in his chest. "It's not what you think, String Bean."

"Isn't it?" Lindsay looked at Bo for a long time. She felt like kicking his ass, and then hiding behind a tree and sitting down for a good cry.

He squirmed visibly under her stare, eventually pulling off his Derby and fiddling with it just to avoid having to look her in the eye.

Unable to stand the sight of Bo for another second, Lindsay refocused her attention on Albert. "You might as well take me to jail and see what happens over the wagon. I can swim like a fish," she lied easily. "I won't be drowning today, Rat Face." *I hope.* As discreetly as she could, she began working to loosen the belt that held her wrists together.

Albert threw his hands in the air, his frustration spilling over into his actions. There was *something* between Bo and Lindsay. He could feel it. He just knew that shit was going to try to double cross him before he could do the same thing back. "Argh! We can't take you back and turn you in. You'd just say that *we* stole the wagon, and there's no telling which one of us would end up with a stretched neck. I heard they hang horse thieves in this part of the country."

"Hang?" Bo gasped. "For stealing a horse?" He looked at the wagon and the *two* horses that were standing patiently in front of it.

Disgusted, Lindsay glanced back at Albert, and straightened her back, ignoring the shooting pain the movement caused her ribs. "They'll need a really strong gallows for you, Rat Face. I bet your head pops clean off when they hang you."

A dark shadow passed over Albert's face. "Shut up."

She cocked her head and said with a great deal more calmness than she felt, "Why?"

"Because I'm in charge here." Growing more irritated, the big man patted the knife that was now held in the waistband of his trousers.

Lindsay snorted and rolled her eyes. "You think that means something? You should have never taken that knife off me, Rat Face. I'm not taking orders from you anymore." The timbre of her voice deepened. "And you're going to be very, *very* sorry you kicked me."

Doubt flickered in his eyes.

"That's right, idiot. You fucked up *again.*" Before he could reach for the knife she distracted him by saying, "I've got news for you, Rat Face. You can roll shit in sugar, but it's still just shit." She sniffed the air and took a step backward, bringing her so close to the river that her heels hung over the edge of the bank. "And you stink."

That did it. With a roar, Albert lunged forward, not stopping until he collided with Lindsay and raised his fist to pummel her.

She twisted her upper body just as he hit her, sending them both plunging into the river. Lindsay heard Bo and Albert's strangled cries mingle just as river swallowed her.

Bo let out a second yell of frustration when both bodies disappeared beneath the surface and didn't reappear. "String Bean!" He began running along the riverbank, trying desperately to see where they might pop up. "For once in your life, couldn't you just wait? I had a plan, you know!"

Ginny's pronouncement was met with a slowly drawled 'all right' from Laura. She gave the younger woman a curious, but not worried, look. "Just let me rinse off Janie, won't you? I don't want her to catch a chill."

"Of course. Let me help." As Laura poured a pitcher of warmed water over the squealing toddler's head, Ginny rushed over to the stove and retrieved a large towel, which had been set on a cast-iron warmer.

Laura kissed Jane's wet cheek before passing her to Ginny. "Whoa." Ginny laughed softly as she wrapped Jane in the towel. "You're getting so big."

Enthusiastically, Jane nodded. "Big bubbles!"

"Yes, they were." Ginny hugged the girl to her.

Laura took two cups from the cupboard. "Please sit down. We haven't had much chance to talk, just the two of us. In fact, both Calvin and I have noticed that y'all avoid any discussion of what brought you here, other than to visit your sister."

Start with something easy, Ginny told herself. This was so much harder than the similar situation in Talking Rock. Calvin and Laura weren't just well meaning people who had taken in her sister. Despite herself, she'd come to think of the kind young couple as friends. "We all love it here in San Marcos."

Laura smiled warmly. "It is a nice place." Her cheeks tinted. "Of course, I'm not like you. I've lived here all my life and only traveled as far as Dallas."

Ginny sighed, thinking of the many times her family had picked up and moved house; and how with the exception of one building that had electricity, and their final apartment on Orchard Street, they all blended together in her mind. "There's nothing wrong with staying in one place where you're happy."

"Is this what you wanted to talk about?" Laura asked a trifle surprised. Ginny's voice had sounded so ominous before.

Ginny stroked the soft skin on her sister's arm. "Sort of. I… I mean, not really." She paused and drew in a deep breath.

Laura frowned. "Goodness. What's the matter? You looked peaked all of the sudden." When Ginny didn't answer right away Laura tried to steer the conversation in a more cheerful direction. "We've all enjoyed your visit so. Calvin and I were hoping you and the boys and your friend could stay at least through planting time." She blushed a little. "That's presumptuous of us, I know. You probably have someplace you need to get back to."

Both Laura and Calvin had been curious about how a family could adopt out a child, and then still afford to take a train trip to visit the baby. But every time they mentioned something about Jane's parents, or Ginny's current situation, the younger women closed down the conversation.

Ginny's voice was flat. "No." She looked directly at Laura. "No place."

The taller woman reached out and squeezed Ginny's arm. "Please tell me what's the matter. I'm confused."

Unable to meet Laura's gaze, Ginny moved away from her and took a seat at the long walnut table that sat in the center of the room. Jane was still in her arms. She had to swallow a few times before she could speak, but when she did, she was surprised at how calm her voice sounded considering the guilt pounding away at her. "This trip wasn't a visit, Laura."

Laura's brow furrowed. "What do you mean it wasn't a visit?" She gestured around the room. "You're staying with us and spending time with your sister. I figured that you wanted to meet the family that adopted Jane so that you'd know she was someplace nice where she was well cared for and loved." The cups forgotten, she took the chair opposite Ginny at the table.

Ginny felt as though a weight was pressing against her chest. Every breath was painful. "I didn't come for that." Her voice dropped to a whisper. *Forgive me, Jane.* "I came here to take her."

Albert grabbed desperately at her as the current carried them downstream. His fumbling grasp and the current flipped them upside down in the water, and water shot up her nose, burning her sinuses and causing her to gag. She could hear Albert's scream underwater and caught glimpses of his terrified face from close up as they moved. Her back crashed against rocks, which tore her shirt.

Then her feet hit a rock, and she twisted again, wrenching herself from Albert's grasp, and pushing toward the surface. Then something amazing happened.

She stood up.

The water only reached the tops of her shoulders. "For Christ's sake!" she sputtered, coughing up a little river water as she processed the unlikely news that she was actually alive. She rolled her eyes and her teeth began to chatter in reaction to the heady amount of adrenaline singing through her bloodstream. Shakily, she lifted her bound hands to her chest, acknowledging the pain that accompanied heartbeats so fast she couldn't distinguish one from the other. Happy to be alive, she let out a nearly hysterical whoop.

Lindsay began slowly plodding to shore, moving carefully so as not to be caught up in the current again and carried farther downstream. Albert was nowhere to be seen, but Bo was frantically running along the shoreline, and was nearly even with where she intended to climb out.

"I can't believe you did that!" he shouted, his face flushed with anger and worry. "I know you can't swim unless you learnt in the past five years."

Lindsay made a face, irked at herself, and the stupid decision she'd made. "I can't." Her knees were shaking, and she was afraid she was going to topple over. Bo offered his hand to haul her up, and the indecision in Lindsay's eyes broke his heart.

"Take it," he pleaded, his voice dropping to a whisper. "Please, String Bean."

Reluctantly, she allowed herself to be pulled onto the riverbank and into a fierce hug. Bo squeezed her gently but firmly, and a feeling of familiarity washed over her.

Lindsay had been thirteen and Bo fourteen when they met in a railroad yard in Baltimore. The dark-haired teen had beaten Bo at craps after he'd joined the game late and lied about knowing how to play. Then, worst of all, she found out he didn't have the money to pay his debt. Lindsay exacted payment in a rather unusual way—by making Bo her slave for a day. His thin, still-growing frame, harelip, and gentle mannerisms made him a frequent target of the older and sometimes cruel men who rode the rails. And the teen jumped at the chance to spend time with someone not only closer to his own age, but who actually laughed and smiled every once in a while, and didn't scare him to death.

Being Lindsay's slave, he had discovered, consisted of handing her things when she remembered that she was supposed to be bossing him around; otherwise they spent their time getting into trouble and acting like kids, something neither one could afford to do around the other riders. They ended up traveling together for three weeks that long hot summer, marking Bo as the first and only real friend Lindsay made on the rails.

Their parting was as haphazard as their meeting. At the time they were like leaves in the wind, following no particular path and resisting any attempt to be controlled. Bo had wanted to jump a train heading south and Lindsay north. So with a quick and awkward goodbye that was bereft of even a handshake, they exchanged crooked smiles, and Lindsay gave Bo a wink over her shoulder as they both set out walking in opposite directions. She never looked back.

Lindsay allowed thoughts of the past to recede to the small place in her mind where she stored memories worth keeping. She focused on the man before her, still not quite believing it was him. "Bo?"

Every ounce of color fled Laura's face. Her mouth went slack and Ginny could hear her swallow. "You wh-what?"

"Laura—"

"You *what?*" Laura repeated loudly, her voice thick with disbelief.

Jane turned round eyes on her mother, and at the sight of Laura's face, her lower lip began to quiver. "Shh," Ginny tightened her hold on her sister, bouncing her a little. "It's okay, honey." She refocused on the trembling woman before her, doing her best not to throw up. "Let me explain."

"Give me my daughter, Ginny," Laura demanded, opening her arms, her eyes suddenly wide with fear.

Jane saw the outstretched arms and instantly brightened. She squirmed in Ginny's hands as she stretched as far as she could as she reached for her mother.

"Mama!"

A spark of rebellion flared in Ginny's soul, and her refusal sat poised on the tip of her tongue for several intense seconds. But that wasn't the way she wanted to do things. Not after Laura and Calvin had been so kind. She passed the girl back to Laura, taking care to make sure the towel was wrapped snuggly around her. "Please, Laura—"

"What sort of crazy talk is this?" Laura held Jane close, her words ruffling drying blonde hair. "You can't just *take* my daughter away. We adopted her!"

"That wasn't legal," Ginny shot back, her own frustration getting the best of her.

"That's impossible! We sent letters. We signed papers. We did everything we were supposed to."

Laura was beginning to panic, but Ginny's emotions were raging just as fiercely and she was in no position comfort the other woman. "I don't care what papers you signed! She and the boys were stolen, and then taken out of New York."

"No. No." Laura shook her head wildly. "We asked about Jane's family. The man from The Foundling Placement Society said that Jane's mother had recently died from consumption and that she didn't have a father."

"Our mother did *not* die from consumption. Though that might have been a more merciful death. And Jane surely had a father," Ginny ground out, her anger and hatred for the Wards multiplying with every passing second. She ran trembling hands through her hair, and wished that Lindsay were there, if only for moral support.

Tears filled Ginny's eyes as she thought about that dreadful night. "It was cold and snowy that night. It was New Years Eve and while we were all asleep, a terrible fire broke out in our apartment building. Everything happened so fast! Too fast. Alice told me they'd all be right behind me. To take Jane and the boys and run."

Laura shivered at the hollow quality Ginny's normally bright voice had taken on.

"Mama, my stepfather, and two of my sisters were—" Ginny's mouth moved ineffectually for a few seconds as she recalled the acrid smoke that had stung her nostrils and throat. She covered her face with her hands that still bore the scars of that night, but flashes of light and shooting flames still danced before her mind's eye. She could hear again the deafening roar of burning wood mingled with the moans of the dying building weaving itself around with the piercing screams of its occupants.

Ginny removed her hands from her pale face and tucked them under her armpits. "Jane and the boys and I got out of the building," she said dully. "Everyone else died."

Laura sniffed and wiped at her eyes. "Oh, Ginny, I'm so, *so* sorry. So that's why you put her up for adoption. You realized you couldn't care for all those children all alone."

"I'm not alone," Ginny offered simply. Laura could draw her own conclusions about her relationship with Lindsay. "And I *never* put her up for adoption. I would never do that."

"But we asked about Jane's family," Laura insisted. "We—"

"The Foundling Placement Society lied! I was injured in the fire, and by the time I woke up in the hospital the kids were gone. The Wards tore apart my family as badly as the fire did! They took the children to adopt out." Her mouth twisted into a sneer. "Or sell."

Owl-eyed, Laura gasped. "We would never *buy* a child!" Unconsciously, she turned sideways slightly, protecting Jane from even Ginny's view and squeezing the toddler so tightly to her that she squawked in protest. "I'm sorry, sugar," she murmured, kissing Jane's cheek and relaxing her grip.

Ginny's anxious gaze flicked from Laura's face to Jane's; and when she was convinced the girl was all right she sat down at the table and wrapped her arms around herself in a vain attempt at comfort. She leaned forward a little as she spoke, thankful she hadn't accepted Laura's offer of coffee. If she had, it would be all over the floor right now. "I know you wouldn't buy a child. I know you are good people; that you love Jane." Rhythmically, she began to rock forward and backward in the chair. "I know *all* that. But I… we love Jane too. She's my *sister*."

Laura blinked stupidly and with slightly wobbly legs, took the seat opposite Ginny. "How could the adoption agency do something so cruel?"

"I've been asking myself that for weeks and weeks."

"I feel sorry for what happened to you and your family." Anguish colored every single word. "It's too horrible to even imagine, but you can't take my baby. We didn't do anything wrong." As it began to dawn on her that she truly might not have a legal or even moral claim on the daughter she'd come to cherish, the fight seemed to drain out of her. "You just can't take her." Her voice cracked. "Please."

Both women began to cry in earnest, and it took several minutes before Ginny was capable of explaining what she knew she had to do.

Lindsay could hardly believe it was him—*Bo.* Something about the smell of him and the feeling of his body drew her thoughts to Queens; and flashes of a man with broad but slender shoulders lifting her from the ground and carrying her for what seemed like forever. "Bo," she repeated, looking and finding the boy behind the man's face.

Uh oh. She roughly pushed him away and promptly fell to her knees where she emptied the meager contents of her stomach, which consisted mostly of river water, on the thick grass, her body still reacting to the shock of nearly drowning.

"Y-you," she choked out between heaves. A single brown eyeball rolled upwards. "You saved me?"

Bo nodded, knowing what she was referring to and wondering how she knew. He was sure she'd been unconscious the entire time. "I couldn't let you lay there and freeze to death, String Bean. Right place, right time is all." He studied his shoes, unwilling to reveal the crush he'd harbored since he laid eyes on the sometimes wild, always unpredictable, girl.

"So you saved m-me." She threw up again. "Ugh." Lindsay closed her eyes. "Just to help Rat Face kill me. Nice," she murmured sarcastically. "Very nice."

Bo winced as dry heaves racked her body once there was nothing left to throw up. He reached down to put a hand between her shoulder blades, seeing several shallow, bleeding cuts on her back and scars across her neck and shoulders that looked recent. With her hair wet and slicked back, he also caught sight of her ear, which looked as though a good portion had been torn away. A lump developed in his throat. *Jesus, String Bean.*

When she was finished, she sat back on her ankles, panting tiredly.

Bo gently cleared his throat and once again offered her his hand. This time necessity overruled her pride and she took it. "I'll bet you're wondering what I'm doing here with Rat Face?" He glanced back at the river. "Where is that fat—" Before he could finish his sentence Albert exploded from the water no less than two feet from Lindsay. Gasping for air, his arms flailing madly, he reached out and latched on to the back of Lindsay's pants. "Save me!" he screamed, in an octave usually associated with choirboys or eunuchs. "Can't s-swim!"

Bo and Lindsay screamed as well, and Lindsay began kicking at the man to detach him from her leg. Bo's strong hands grabbed Lindsay and she felt like a rope in a tug of war, with two men pulling her apart. "Hang on, String Bean!" Bo cried out. "I won't let him get you."

"Get..." She managed a sharp kick to Albert's cheekbone and heard the crunch of bone over his wailing. "Off..." Finally Bo dug in his heels and tugged as hard as he could. "Of me!"

Lindsay's eyes bugged out and she thought her arms would be pulled from their sockets. "Stop! Dammit, stop!"

Miraculously, Albert held on; and as she was tugged forward by Bo he was pulled from the river on his belly. When he was mostly on dry land he let go, sending Lindsay and Bo sprawling face first in the brush. Albert lay on the riverbank panting and moaning, and he decided then and there that he'd never try to drown someone again. Back home he could always just toss them off a tall bridge and be done with it. No fuss, no mess. Yes, he'd stick to that from now on.

Bo was back on his feet first. He picked up his hat, and stomped over to Albert, his face contorted in rage. He shoved his hat back on his head. "What is wrong with you?" he exploded, kicking at Albert's protruding belly, and noticing with relief that the knife was gone. He glanced over his shoulder and Lindsay's studied gaze told him she was seeing the same thing.

Albert's chest was rising and falling so rapidly he couldn't speak.

After a few tense seconds he rolled over and managed a "What?" His expression was a combination of dismay, gratitude, and stark terror.

Bo gave him another hard poke with the toe of his tattered shoe; then moved to help Lindsay up. It took several moments, but between them they were able to pry the wet leather belt off her wrists.

She rubbed the tender skin gingerly, certain she was going to have some bruises in addition to the cuts on her back to explain to Ginny. She stalked over to Albert, who was now lying on his side. "Give me your hands," she commanded darkly, her entire body shaking with pent-up anger. She let loose a vicious punch to his mouth just to get his attention, but even though his head sagged and he groaned in pain, he wouldn't offer up his hands. He was as stubborn and stupid as an old nag.

When Albert didn't respond she tried one last time. "Last chance before I throw you into the river and follow you downstream until I'm sure you're drowned," she warned him, meaning every single word. "I don't honestly know what's keeping me from it now. And I swear to God, I won't ask you again."

The timbre of her voice chilled him to the bone and his head snapped up. The eye above the cheek she'd kicked was already beginning to swell shut and his mouth was throbbing. He recognized her mounting anger; and without a word he held up his wrists and allowed her to tie them. He was beaten.

"That might be the first smart thing you've ever done," she told him, pulling the belt so tight he cried out in pain. "Shut up! You're the luckiest bastard in the world today, just because you're alive. Don't forget that."

Prudently, Albert remained silent, instead choosing to glare at Bo.

"Oh, not you too," Bo said, pointing angrily at Albert. "I have to be on *somebody's* side, you know." He smirked a little. "Just not yours."

"Traitor," Albert spat.

"Pretty much," Bo agreed, brushing several chunks of dirt from his pants. "Somebody had to make sure you didn't actually kill her when you found her. 'Course, after what I've seen here today, I seriously doubt you could have done it anyway."

Albert narrowed his eyes. "That wrong train you insisted we take out of Baltimore wasn't an accident, was it?" Comprehension began to dawn. "Shit! Shit! Shit!" For several heartbeats he couldn't think of anything else to say. Then words came pouring out in a fast, nearly incoherent stream. "You asshole! It was you! You! You're the one who was supposed to wake us up for the train we missed in West Virginia!"

One of Lindsay's eyebrows twitched. Not only couldn't she believe what Bo had done, now Albert was going to have an apoplexy before their very eyes.

"It's your fault we had that hangover our first day in Texas, and spent an extra day just laying around. You were buying the beer."

Bo grinned unrepentantly.

Albert's mind scrambled for every rotten detail of their trip. "The arrest in Atlanta!"

Lindsay's eyes formed twin moons.

Bo held up his hand to forestall him. "Now wait a minute. I didn't tell you to grab that man's ass."

Lindsay blinked then turned slowly to Albert—both eyebrows at their zenith.

"I didn't do that," he complained loudly. "I was picking his pocket. Not grabbing his ass."

"Says you," Bo quipped, "you buddin' sodomite."

"Snake!" Albert seethed, his mind awhirl with painful, hideous revenge scenarios. "I'm gonna—"

"You're gonna what?" Lindsay growled, bending over and grabbing Albert's ear. She twisted it until he squealed like a stuck pig. And then she twisted it some more.

"Nothing!" Albert squeaked, his face contorted. "I'm going to do nothing. I swear!"

Lindsay let go of his ear and, with a sour look, wiped her hand off on her tattered shirt. "That's what I thought you said." She turned to Bo and her gaze softened. She thought of everything Bo had been through on her behalf and felt a lump develop in her throat. She swallowed a few times; then let out a long breath, absorbing that fact that he hadn't sold her out for ten dollars after all. It felt wonderful. "Thanks. For everything"

Bo smiled at her words and saw his action mirrored in the form of a dazzling grin that wrinkled the skin at the corners of Lindsay's eyes and showed off her teeth. It was the most beautiful thing he'd ever seen.

He felt his cheeks going warm, and he looked away, his feelings for Lindsay written all over his face. "Umm… It wasn't anything. Really."

"Oh, for Christ's sake," Albert groaned as he rolled his eyes, and flopped over onto his back so he wouldn't have to watch the disgusting scene. "Fuck her and get it over—" He was interrupted by Lindsay staring curiously at his leg. Albert followed her gaze.

"What's that?" she asked.

Bo stepped over and peered down. "That's a fat piece of shit."

"Well, yeah," she agreed casually. "But I mean there." She pointed to Albert's ankle. "Something's moving under the pant leg."

"There's nothing there," Albert said irritably. He shook his leg for emphasis then his eyes popped wide open and his jaw dropped. His mouth worked for a few seconds, but no sound came out.

Bo and Lindsay looked at each other then back at Albert.

The bearded man began to scream bloody murder and shake his leg wildly, grabbing at his trouser cuff and twisting. "Ahhh! So-something is in there!" He was bordering on hysterical. "In my pants!"

Albert's screams abruptly stopped and his face turned bright red; he gasped then let out a gut-wrenching yell as the veins in his forehead popped out, his face twisting in pain. He held his leg very still as a slender olive-colored snake, about two-and-a-half feet long, slithered out of the bottom of his pants and back into the water.

Bo and Lindsay both shivered and took a large step backward. Albert began to howl.

"It bit me!" he sobbed, grasping frantically at his calf. A tremor took hold of him, and he began to shake helplessly.

Lindsay searched the area around her feet while Bo picked up a stick as a weapon.

"Do something," Albert yelled, his leg throbbing in time with his heartbeat; the area around the bite felt like it was on fire. He tried to stand but the world spun, and he crashed back to the ground, a sodden, pathetic heap.

They ignored him. "I hate snakes," Bo said, his eyes intently scanning the area around them.

"Me too," Lindsay agreed as she looked as well. They poked and prodded until they were fairly certain there were no more where they were standing. Then a thought struck her and she laughed. "Poor snake, getting a bite of Rat Face."

Bo joined her in a chuckle. "Bet it'll get a stomach ache."

"Or die outright."

Albert lifted his pant leg to reveal to two deep puncture marks. They weren't really bleeding, but the tissue around them was already puffy and very red.

"What do you think that was?" Bo wondered out loud. "A rattler?"

"Rattler?" Albert moaned. "I'm gonna die. Oh, God, I'm gonna die!" He began to cry.

"I don't think it was a rattler." Lindsay shrugged one shoulder. "I didn't see any rattle at least."

Her words seemed to calm Albert for a moment, but soon he began cry again and curse them both. Finally, tiring of his antics, she snatched the long stick out of Bo's hands and poked roughly at the bite. "Does that hurt?"

"Fuck yes!" Albert nodded, his beady eyes filled with fear. A cold sweat broke out across his forehead as he waited for her to continue.

She examined the area carefully, as though she knew what she was doing. Then scratched her chin thoughtfully. "Good."

Bo burst out laughing.

"So how did you find me, Bo?" Lindsay asked, bored with Albert's ugly face and bitten leg. She braced herself against a tree and tossed aside the stick, wishing she could lean back against the trunk, but mindful of her back. Her entire body ached.

Albert began to scream again but Bo talked right over him; and the pair effectively ignored him as Bo filled her in on the list of cities they'd used to find her, and how they'd been close behind her almost since she left New York City.

"Please help me," Albert sobbed, his stomach roiling. "I—" He stopped to vomit, and both Lindsay and Bo cringed.

"Ugh," Lindsay said.

"I think the big baby is making himself sick on purpose," Bo accused, shooting Albert an evil look.

"Or it could be the poison," Lindsay supplied helpfully, noting that the area around the bite marks had gone from red to dark purple. Albert's complexion was usually pasty white and sallow. At the moment, however, his skin was a dull gray and covered with a light sheen of sweat. But did he have to continue to cry like a baby? "Rat Face, I once heard that you'll just send the poison moving through your body quicker if you thrash around and pitch a fit." She pushed away from the tree. "So shut up and settle down, 'cause once it goes to your heart, that's the little black thing the size of a raisin and located in your chest," she reminded him blithely, "you're done for anyway."

"Die like a man, and not a mouse," Bo said flatly.

Lindsay cocked her head as she gazed at Albert. "Or rat, in this case."

Ginny gathered Jane up in her arms and hurried out of the kitchen. She could hear Laura crying behind her, and her heart clenched so painfully she thought her chest might split in two. *I did the right thing. This was the right thing,* she chanted mentally, tightening her grip on her sister as she bolted up the stairs, taking them as fast as her dress would allow.

The guestroom she shared with Lindsay was cool, and she shivered as she set Jane on the bed and moved to the fluttering drapes to close the window.

The girl was dressed but her blonde hair was still damp, and Ginny used the towel wrapped around the chubby toddler to dry it thoroughly. "There," she sniffed back her own tears, "all clean and dry."

Jane grabbed at the towel, exploring its slightly rough surface with curious, chubby fingers.

"You wanna go see Lindsay, sweetie?"

The blonde thought for a second before nodding decisively. "Yes."

"You're so smart. That's just what we both need, I think," Ginny commented as she shucked her dress, and began changing into what she'd come to think of as her traveling trousers. With a start, she realized what she was doing.

Her mother would have stepped into the closet so the toddler couldn't see her nakedness. Even Alice, whose bold behavior often inspired Ginny and infuriated her parents, would have, at the very least, turned her back on the girl and hidden her breasts with her dress. Yet here Ginny stood, completely comfortable in her nudity, shoulders squared, chest and chin lifted proudly. Despite what had just transpired, a small smile twitched at the corners of her mouth. She was proud of herself.

With gentle persistence and a heaping dose of love, her lover had convinced her that every curve she had was well appreciated and nothing to be ashamed of, making her feel at once treasured, sensual, and confident in her own skin. Ginny could wear men's pants, talk to strangers as though she was their equal, and find her way across this big country to achieve a goal she wouldn't be denied. And do it alone if she had to. Sometime between New Years and now Ginny Chisholm reckoned she'd actually grown up and become her own woman. *I'm sorry, Mama, I know you'd think so much of the way I feel about myself now is unseemly, but I just don't believe that. Not anymore.*

Ginny's musings came to an end when Jane untucked one of the bed's pillows, and began pounding it with her fists, making deep indentations into the mound of feathers. She laughed and Ginny couldn't help but laugh too. It looked like fun.

Jane turned to her sister. "Where's Mama?"

Ginny sucked in a breath, a little unsure of what to say or how to react. Just hearing the words hurt. "She's… she's busy, honey." She sat on the bed and tugged on her shoes. "Are you ready to go see Lindsay? We'll get the boys and we'll all go, okay?"

Jane's big blue eyes lit with glee. "We going fishin'?" She'd heard her brothers talk of little else over the past few days, and was beginning to associate the word with them.

Ginny smiled fondly at her. "Not this morning." She brushed several pale strands from Jane's face. "C'mon. We need to go." She reached out for Jane and the girl settled happily on her lap. Impulsively, Ginny threw her arms around her and gave her a good squeeze. Her throat closed and it was several seconds before she could speak. "You know I love you, don't you, Jane?"

Jane responded by placing an open mouth kiss on Ginny's cheek and laughing. "Yes. Love you."

Tears pricked tired eyes. "I don't think you're going to believe that tomorrow, sweetheart," she warned thickly. *Please let this have been right for her. Please.* "I'll remind you every day though that I love you, I promise. So will Lindsay and your brothers. We all love you." She released Jane from the hug and ran her fingertips across the baby-soft skin of one cheek. "We were so sad when we couldn't find you."

Jane scrunched up her face. She was tired of the heart to heart talk that went right over her head, and decided to end it as quickly as possible. She climbed down off Ginny's lap and headed for the door at a dead run. "Boyzzzz," she warbled loudly, causing Ginny to let out a weak laugh as she recognized the joint term she herself usually used for their brothers. "C'mooon."

Ginny stood and followed Jane as she headed down the hallway. She wondered if she shouldn't take their bag with her. The older woman didn't seem the spiteful sort. *But then, who could blame her,* Ginny thought. *I'd have kicked me out without even finishing the conversation!* At the stairway she paused, knowing that she should probably go down and see if Laura wanted to head to town with them—she'd be needing to get to the store. Ginny took a step, then stopped, admitting to herself that she couldn't face Laura Gable. Not now. She still had to face Calvin and just the thought of it was making her sick.

"I don't wa-wa-want to die!" Albert sobbed, rolling into the fetal position as his stomach cramps got worse. "Please! Please do something. Anything. Isn't there a doctor in that Mexican-filled town?"

Lindsay and Bo both shrugged. Bo chewed his mustache. "Them is the breaks, Rat Face."

Albert suddenly stopped moving and forced himself not to yell the words. "You could suck out the poison. I heard of that. Sucking it out."

Lindsay and Bo looked at him as though he was insane. "Yeah, right," Lindsay finally snorted. "Like I'd suck any part of you. Suck it yourself."

"Bet he's tried that before, but that gut got in the way."

"You're gonna make me puke again, Bo."

Bo tilted his hat back farther on his head. "That reminds of me the joke about a puppy and his—"

"I'm serious!" Albert cried, trembling. "I remember now. You cut an X over the bite and suck it out." His eyes begged them. "You can save me. Please! I'll do anything."

"Now you're talking." For the first time since Albert was bitten Lindsay looked truly interested. "Would you go home and leave me alone?"

"Yes!" Albert nodded furiously. "I promise."

"Can I believe him, Bo?"

"Nope."

Lindsay snorted softly. "That's what I thought. Sorry, Rat Face."

"Oh, Jesus, you can't just let me die. You can't!"

Lindsay crouched down next to Albert. "Oh, yes, I can," she said quietly, her gaze boring into his. "And you know you deserve it."

Albert gulped.

They stayed that way, their gazes locked, for a long time, until Lindsay sighed. She grabbed Albert's calf and roughly pushed up his pants leg, which had worked it's way down again with all his thrashing.

"Thank you. Thank you. I swear I'll leave you alone. I swear it."

"I know you will," Lindsay said evenly. "I'm going to make sure of that." She pulled her pocketknife out of her trousers and held it over the wound. "Just so you know, I'm leaving San Marcos tomorrow and I'm not coming back. I'm not coming back to New York again either. You'll never find me again, so give up on me and the damn ten dollars!"

"Yes. Yes." Albert said quickly. "I already gave up." And for once, the look on his face told Lindsay he was telling the truth. "You aren't worth the ten dollars."

Lindsay smirked. "I could have told you that." She pressed the blade to his flesh and cut a gash into his leg, warm blood spilling over the metal and dripping to the ground.

He hissed.

"One more," she warned him. She went slowly, wanting him to feel every second of this pain—to know it as a reminder.

Bo looked a little faint and turned his head.

"All done," she announced.

Albert waited. When she just sat there his heavy eyebrows pulled together. "Wh-what are you waiting for? Suck out the poison." Lindsay's gaze flicked to Bo in question.

"I am not sucking it. I'd rather he die."

Lindsay sighed. "Help me then." Together, with Lindsay pushing on Albert's leg and Bo pushing on Albert's shoulders, they folded the man enough to where he could suck on his own shin. Lindsay heard his pants rip and knew that his muscles were probably stretched to the point of agony, but she couldn't help believing that it served him right.

Albert sucked and spat. And sucked and spat. Until he was so lightheaded he couldn't continue and his lips were ringed with blood. Then he fell back onto the grass and waited to see if he would die. He looked up at the blue sky and felt tears burn his eyes. This time he cried quietly.

Lindsay and Bo stepped away, talking in low voices as they waited to see if Albert would recuperate. Their conversation lasted for a while and for a few minutes they reminisced, recalling their crazy adventures with the fondness only time and distance can provide.

Much to their surprise, eventually a hint of color had returned to Albert's cheeks and he stopped shaking.

"What's happened to you, String Bean?" Bo asked affectionately, forgetting about the scars and seeing so much more. Drenched and tattered she looked better than he'd remembered, the attractive fire in her that always lurked just beneath the surface, burnished by something deeper.

"Love happened."

His eyebrows jumped and he looked confused.

"Never mind," she laughed, realizing just how ridiculous that sounded. "I guess I just grew up."

He dug his shoe into the soft soil. "You grew up really nice too. I knew you would."

She smiled warmly at him. "So did you, Bo. I meant what I said before." Shocking him, she pulled Bo into a hug. "Thank you."

Unseen by Lindsay, the man beamed. He'd gotten the hug that had lived only in his childhood dreams. Life was good.

She released him, but this time there was no awkwardness when their eyes met.

"Are you sure I can't give you one of the horses so you can ride back to town?" He'd tried to convince her to come with him, but one look in her eyes told him it was a lost cause.

"Oh, I'm sure." She regarded him seriously. "But how about your shirt?"

He was unbuttoning it before she finished making her request. Bo turned his back while she stripped out of hers and slipped into his.

"Done."

When she held hers out to him he just shook his head. "It's a warm day. I have another in my bag," he lied.

"All right." She lowered her hand, letting the ruined garment fall to the ground. "Watch him, Bo," Lindsay said softly, her gaze drifting to Albert. "You know you can't trust him."

Bo shrugged. "I don't have to trust him. I'm gonna do just what you said. Load his stupid ass into the back of that wagon and drive to the next town. I'll dump the wagon, and then after tomorrow you'll be gone. He won't follow you anymore. I think he only came this far 'cause he was madder than a hornet's nest. By the looks of it, that snakebite will slow him down for quite a while. If he forgets his promise I'll let the sheriff know that he stole the wagon."

Lindsay nodded approvingly. She tucked in the too-large shirt and rolled the sleeves up to the middle of her forearms. The cotton was a deep forest green and the sun-warmed cloth felt good against her skin. They shared crooked smiles and Lindsay winked at her old friend. After a moment's hesitation, they began to walk in opposite directions, just as they had five years before.

Bo's feet ground to a halt and he sighed, unable to stop himself from turning and watching her go. He admired her steady gait and the way the wind tossed her dark hair. She exuded confidence in every step, and if he listened hard enough he could almost hear what he thought was a whistle as she rambled back to town.

Their tracks would never cross again, but they'd never forget each other either. And sometimes that was as good as life got.

Ginny pushed open the door to the Gables' general store with one hand. She was holding Jane with her other, and Lewis and James came barreling in behind her.

Calvin smiled his greeting and began wrapping up a stack of purchases on his countertop.

The boys ran in the back of the store to examine a display case that held pocketknives.

Ginny smiled warmly as she watched them go. She turned when she heard Calvin's voice.

"Mrs. Lichtman, will you excuse me for just one moment?"

The woman nodded politely, though she was anxious to get back home with her purchases.

Calvin trotted over to Ginny and pressed a piece of paper in her hand; deciding not to comment on her queer choice of clothing, he was only thankful his Laura wasn't a slave to the oddities of what he assumed was big city fashion.

"This came for you this morning. I haven't had a chance to read it."

Ginny looked around for Lindsay, but was distracted by the sound of her sister's voice.

"Daddy!" Jane exclaimed, an enormous smile creasing her chubby cheeks. She extended her arms to Calvin, who scooped her up without question.

"C'mon, Janie, I'll teach you to wrap things." His enthusiasm was infectious and Jane clapped her hands happily as they walked back to the counter. Over his shoulder he said to Ginny, "There's a bench outside; enjoy the beautiful morning and read your telegram. The kids and I will be fine. Lindsay's around here somewhere."

Ginny worried her lower lip. She wanted to talk to Calvin before Laura did, but her cursory inspection of the telegram told her it was from Christian Spence, and her curiosity quickly got the best of her. Setting aside her reservations, she waved at Jane, who waved back. Then she called out to the boys. "Be good and mind Calvin." Trying not to look as upset as she was. "I'll be back in a bit."

Both boys rolled their eyes but dutifully responded, "Yes, Ginny," in drone-like voices that made it very clear they didn't believe she needed to remind them of that any longer.

Ginny pursed her lips and shook her head. "You're lucky I love you both even though you're rotten."

Lewis and James laughed, but never took their eyes from the display case.

At the end of the bench stood a brightly painted cigar store Indian, who stoically gazed at each passersby. "Mmm, you don't look too happy," she mumbled glumly to the wooden statue. "I know just how you feel. Of course, it could be those." She wrinkled her face at the box of cigars clutched in the chief's hand.

Her gaze dropped to her own hand. "Maybe this will be good news." *I could use some good news.* When they found Jane, Ginny had splurged, and sent a short telegram back to Queens to let Christian know of her success and to thank him for all he'd done. She never expected a reply.

The sun was shining and the temperature had risen into the upper sixties, making Ginny glad the boys had talked her into allowing them to leave their coats. Feeling shaky, she sat down and people-watched for a moment, taking the rare opportunity to sit all alone—save for her Indian companion—and gather her thoughts in peace.

She let the wind ruffle her red hair and smiled a little as a couple walked by her arm in arm. San Marcos, she decided, was very nice place. Quiet but vibrant, it was far smaller than what she was used to. Which was a good thing. There were no congested tenements, no streets clogged with people, horses, dilapidated carts, and packs of homeless children who wandered aimlessly, stealing and barely scraping by as the twilight of their youth came years too early. The streets here were wide and clean and the sound of the wind, bugs, and birds wasn't lost amidst the traffic noise.

Ginny sat there long enough to relax. By the time she opened the telegram, she didn't feel as out of control as when she'd left the Gables' house earlier that morning.

She was shocked by the telegram's length and was tempted to count the words, but breathed a sigh of relief when she saw the "Reduced Rates" sticker that was used for charitable organizations and churches.

> G&SB Success!
> God was with you
> Reported in Times J&I Ward local entrepreneurs and child welfare advocates indicted for fraud
> Foundling Placement Society closed pending investigation
> Three cheers! (from C not Times)

Ginny struggled a little with the word 'entrepreneurs' but was able to glean most of its meaning from the words around it. Then she looked up from the telegram. "I can't believe it," she whispered, every ounce of the awe she felt showing in her voice. She shook her head. "You inspire me, Christian Spence. If God is with anyone, he's with you." She looked back at the paper.

"Lindsay." She clutched the paper to her chest. "Oh, Lindsay!" Ginny jumped to her feet, the desire to show her partner the telegram so strong she suddenly remembered she hadn't seen her inside the store.

She had the door halfway open when she spied a lone figure walking at the very end of the street. Ginny froze and for a few seconds watched, grinning when she saw Lindsay fussing with her hair the way she always did when she forgot her hat.

She didn't remember the dead run she made down the long dusty road. Didn't remember people's curious stares as she wove between the riders and wagons, or how she tucked the telegram into her pocket and pumped her arms harder, feeling the cool breeze against her face as she got closer and closer to her goal.

It wasn't until she threw herself into Lindsay's arms that she started thinking at all. And even then she couldn't do more than start to cry and hang on for dear life.

"Whoa!" Lindsay wrapped her arms around Ginny, determined not to make a sound even when her tender ribs were squeezed tightly and strong arms wrapped around her back, pressing against her newly acquired cuts. "Take it easy." Lindsay stroked Ginny's back. "It's okay," she soothed, realizing that the morning must have been hell on her partner. Not that hers had been much better. "You did it then?" Lindsay asked.

Ginny nodded and sniffed as the emotion she'd been holding in since she spoke with Laura came pouring out and threatened to swamp her. The telegram forgotten for the time being, she buried her face in Lindsay's neck, greedily soaking in the comfort that was so easily given and desperately needed at this very moment. "I-I," she stuttered; then started over. "Yes."

Lindsay closed her eyes in empathetic pain. "Aww, Ginny," she said softly. *Damn.* The redhead began to cry harder; and, glancing around, Lindsay decided that there was probably a better place to do this than the middle of the road, even if they were well past the last downtown building. "Here." She led Ginny to a grassy spot about twenty yards away and near a grove of black cherry trees. It couldn't be seen from the road and was as private as they were likely to find.

Once they had both dropped onto the grass, Lindsay opened her arms and Ginny found her place again.

Ginny collected herself as best she could and plucked at Lindsay's shirt, a puzzled expression on her face. "Are you going to tell me why you're in someone else's shirt?" Her eyes lifted, then narrowed. "And why your hair is damp?"

Lindsay traced Ginny's cheek with her knuckles, doing her best to gently remove the tears. "I think my story will be a lot longer than yours. And it can wait." She gazed sympathetically at Ginny. "Talk to me. Tell me what happened."

Ginny swallowed a few times, torn between wanting to forget and needing to get it off her chest. "I spoke with Laura."

Lindsay nodded encouragingly.

"And I told her why we really came here." She cringed, remembering the look on Laura's face.

"She wasn't happy, I take it?"

"That's an understatement." Ginny rubbed her eyes with the back of her hand. Lindsay let out a low whistle. She liked Laura and part of her was selfishly glad she hadn't been there to witness that.

Ginny licked her lips, feeling Lindsay's hand stroking her arm in silent comfort. "And then…" She swallowed thickly and raised her eyes to meet Lindsay's. She tried again, but the words wouldn't come. *God, how can I be doing this when I can't even say it?* "I-I"—A deep breath—"I…"

"And then you told her that you weren't going to try to take Jane," Lindsay finished, her own eyes filling. "That you thought she'd be happiest with them."

Ginny nodded miserably as a fresh wave of tears splashed onto her cheeks. "I did," she whispered, feeling as though the air was being squeezed from her chest.

"I-I-I've never… I've never heard someone cry so hard in pure relief as when I said I wasn't going to try to ta-take Jane. I thought the woman was going to fracture in two."

Lindsay had an overwhelming urge to hug Ginny until there were no more tears left to cry. But she had more to say first. She cupped Ginny's chin with her palm.

Ginny leaned into the touch and closed her eyes.

"Was it the right thing to do, Ginny? 'Cause if you're not sure, I'll go snatch that child myself and we'll disappear."

Ginny was quiet for so long that Lindsay had begun to think her companion had made a horrible mistake. Her breathing quickened and her body stiffened as she prepared to stand and do just what she'd said she'd do.

"Lindsay." Ginny stopped her with a hand on her arm—a gentle tug of her sleeve. "Calm down."

Lindsay blinked. "You're the one who's been crying her eyes out, and you want me to calm down? You're a fine one to talk."

Ginny laughed through her tears and the simple sound made her feel a little better. "I'm telling you that because even though I'm crying, you're the one who is getting ready to do something crazy, right?"

A guilty expression shot across Lindsay's face. She scowled. "No."

Ginny reached out and affectionately smoothed the skin on Lindsay's forehead. "Uh huh. Sure you weren't."

The rail-rider couldn't resist any longer, and she pulled Ginny into another embrace, sucking in a deep lungful of morning air and the scent of her partner's skin and hair. She murmured her approval as Ginny wholeheartedly returned the embrace.

Ginny sighed, feeling frayed nerves begin to calm. "I just wanted to take a few minutes before I answered, because I wanted to think. Again. I don't want to have to ask myself that question every day for the rest of my life."

"Though you probably will," Lindsay said knowingly, kissing Ginny's cheek and tasting salty skin.

The corner of Ginny's mouth quirked, and she lifted one hand and ran her fingers through Lindsay's thick hair, enjoying its coarse texture. "Though I probably will." She drew in a deep breath. "The answer is yes. I've known that from almost the start." Her voice grew quiet. "Laura said we could stay with her and Calvin until we get on our feet. After everything, she still wants to be our friend and have us be a part of Jane's life and family."

"She's a kind person," Lindsay said wonderingly. She hadn't even known such people existed until she met Ginny and Christian Spence.

"She is. And so is Calvin. But it just—I dunno. What I did… It still hurts, Lindsay. She's still my sister and I can't help but think like I let her down."

Lindsay pulled back enough to place a tender kiss on Ginny's forehead. "I know it does. But you're wrong. You're not letting her down. You're being strong enough to let her go. There's a big difference. I know what it's like to be abandoned by your own flesh and blood." She took her hand and squeezed it. "This isn't it, Ginny. I swear it's not."

Ginny idly watched as a cricket crawled across her leg, and then jumped down into the grass and disappeared. "A promise to the dead…" She paused and thought of her beloved Alice, "*can't* be more important than what I owe the living. I loved all my sisters. But Alice is gone now. Jane and what's best for her had to come first." She looked at Lindsay with a painfully open expression. "Right?" Her voice cracked a little and sent a shooting pain through Lindsay's soul.

"Right," Lindsay breathed. What else was there to say? Lindsay believed that Ginny was right, that the Gables would be loving and good parents and that Jane would have the kind of childhood she deserved with them. They were already a family, really. And it had hurt Ginny to see, and then later to admit, that. She also believed that Ginny could be a wonderful mother to the toddler herself, but would be strained to the limit providing for the boys.

Ginny finally broke the silence. “It was an impossible choice… that had to be made. I do believe it was the right one.” She gave Lindsay a sad look. “You just might have to remind me—a lot. I-I don’t think I could have made it without you.”

Lindsay let her heart show a little when she said, “You don’t ever have to be without me, Ginny.” She smiled and cupped Ginny’s cheeks, stroking the puffy, wet skin below her friend’s eyes with her thumbs. “You are the bravest person I’ve ever met.”

“Funny,” Ginny sighed, falling in love all over again. “I was just thinking the same thing about you.”

Suddenly, Ginny remembered the telegram in her pocket. She pulled it out and showed Lindsay. “This is something that’s going to make you smile.”

Lindsay gave her a questioning look from behind dark lashes. “Yeah?”

“Oh, yeah.”

Later that night…

The sun had set and it was that magical time when stars began popping out of the purple sky. Rain had come to San Marcos on the heels on a strong southerly breeze that carried with it the rich scent of wet soil and bruised grass. But the showers had blown over quickly, leaving shallow puddles on the dirt streets. Lindsay and Ginny sat on top of the same grassy hill that Lindsay had fled to on the night of their argument. The children had long since been put to bed, and with a strong desire to stretch their legs, they’d headed to a spot that would forever hold a special place in both their hearts.

In the distance they could see a solitary train track and the winding river cutting a path through the terrain.

“Are you cold?” Ginny turned to face her partner and await her answer. Lindsay laughed, an affectionate smile transforming her face into a thing of pure beauty.

Unconsciously, Ginny smiled back, feeling the vibration sing through her as her heartstrings were plucked one at a time.

"How could I be cold when you're nearly plastered to me?" Teasingly, Lindsay poked her index finger at the warm body fitted tightly next to hers.

Ginny stuck out her tongue.

Lindsay suddenly wondered, "Are you cold?" Without waiting for a reply, she wrapped a long arm around Ginny's shoulders and managed to do the impossible—snuggle a bit a closer.

An impish grin curled Ginny's lips, prompting the appearance of her dimples. "I am if that's what it gets me."

Lindsay chuckled; and feeling more relaxed than she could remember, she turned her eyes back out to the open fields and the lonely train track. An owl hooted in the distance, his call mostly lost to the sound of the rustling grass and the night's breeze.

Then, out of the darkness a train appeared and snaked its way across the scene before them at a snail's pace, its forlorn whistle silent for the time being. Lindsay's low voice broke their trance. "What are you thinking?"

Ginny answered with complete honestly. "I'm hoping you're going to be happy tethered to the ground instead of going wherever the tracks takes you." But she didn't sound particularly worried. "I'm already devising a lifetime of ways to make you smile and keep you happy in my clutches."

"Keep me?" Lindsay snorted softly, amazed that Ginny didn't seem to notice the way she trailed after the redhead like lovesick puppy. "You don't have to worry about keeping me, Ginny. You're my best friend. You couldn't shake me if you tried." She took a deep breath and gave Ginny's words the consideration she believed they were due. "I suppose I'm not the sort to be tethered to the ground."

Ginny's heart skipped a beat and she opened her mouth to speak, but was stopped by two fingers pressing gently against her lips.

"*But* I'm *exactly* the sort who'd love to be tethered to *you*." She lifted a single dark eyebrow for emphasis. "Permanently."

Lindsay's words were so full of love and devotion that Ginny was hard pressed not to swoon. "So," she paused and turned her head to blink back happy tears when her vision went fuzzy. "What are we going to do now? Somehow we did it. We found them. We're together in the best way that we can be." She turned back to Lindsay and their eyes met and held. "We're a family no matter what." She nodded a little, silently reaffirming that fact. "What's next?"

"Mmm… I've been thinking."

"Me too."

"What about staying—"

"We should stay—" They started in unison, then abruptly stopped and broke into gentle laughter.

"Well," Ginny said, "I guess that answers that question."

Even in the moonlight, Lindsay could see the sparkle in her lover's eyes. She nodded solemnly. "I guess it does."

"It won't be easy. We'll have to find a place of our own to live," Ginny reminded her. "And find real jobs to pay for it."

"And I'll likely need your help with that," Lindsay reminded her right back, her gaze softening with every word. "But I'll give it everything I have. I promise."

"We can really make it happen, Lindsay." There was a touch of wonder in Ginny's voice as she considered the rocky road behind them and the long road that stretched out endlessly before them—one that they would travel together. "We can do *anything*."

And at that moment Lindsay had never believed anything so much. "I know we can." A cool gust of wind blew against her face, but it couldn't cool the warm glow she felt inside. Ginny was wrong. She wasn't tethered to the ground when they were together. With her, Lindsay could do anything. Could *be* anything. She'd never been freer.

Of course, Lindsay thought wryly, that sentiment was far too sappy for any self-respecting human being to actually say out loud. Instead she opted for a tender, but straight from the heart "I love you," which was just as lovingly returned.

Lindsay leaned backward onto the chilly grass, and crossed her legs at the ankles. She tugged Ginny down with her until they were looking up into a sky bright with twinkling stars, a full moon, and heavy with possibilities.

A star streaked across the sky. "Make a wish, Sweet Pea," Ginny said lazily. She heard the smile in Lindsay's voice as she spoke.

"Nah. I'll save the star for whoever's on that outbound train." Lindsay gestured aimlessly toward the tracks and train that was nearly out of sight. "They're the one who needs it. My wish already came true."

Publications from Spinsters Ink

P.O. Box 242
Midway, Florida 32343
Phone: 800-301-6860
www.spinstersink.com

ACROSS TIME by Linda Kay Silva. If you believe in soul mates, if you know you've had a past life, then join Jessie in the first of a series of adventures that takes her Across Time. ISBN 978-1883523-91-6$1495

SELECTIVE MEMORY by Jennifer L. Jordan. A Kristin Ashe Mystery. A classical pianist, who is experiencing profound memory loss after a near-fatal accident, hires private investigator Kristin Ashe to reconstruct her life in the months leading up to the crash.
ISBN 978-1-883523-88-6 $14.95

HARD TIMES by Blayne Cooper. Together, Kellie and Lorna navigate through an oppressive, hidden world where lines between right and wrong blur, sexual passion is forbidden but explosive, and love is the biggest risk of all. ISBN 978-1-883523-90-9 $14.95

THE KIND OF GIRL I AM by Julia Watts. Spanning decades, The Kind of Girl I Am humorously depicts an extraordinary woman's experiences of triumph, heartbreak, friendship and forbidden love.
ISBN 978-1-883523-89-3 $14.95

PIPER'S SOMEDAY by Ruth Perkinson. It seemed as though life couldn't get any worse for feisty, young Piper Leigh Cliff and her three-legged dog, Someday. ISBN 978-1-883523-87-9 $14.95